SINISTER THOUGHTS KILL

by

Jeanne L Drouillard

Argus Enterprises International, Inc
North Carolina***New Jersey

Sinister Thoughts Kill © 2010
All Rights Reserved by Jeanne L. Drouillard

A-Argus Better Book Publishers, LLC

For information:
A-Argus Better Book Publishers, LLC
Post Office Box 914
Kernersville, North Carolina 27285
www.a-argusbooks.com

ISBN: 0-9845142-8-7
ISBN: 978-0-9845142-8-1

Book Cover designed by Dubya

Printed in the United States of America

Other Sammi Evans Mysteries
by
Jeanne L. Drouillard

Thinking Out Loud
Your Thoughts Can Trap You
Thoughts Can Be Murder
Thoughts Can Be Deadly

Dedication

This work is dedicated to those who know we have the power of choice over our thoughts and realize this privilege and control is what makes us individuals

Special Thanks

. Vicki Wettach – your continued editing help does enhance each story. Thanks.

. Maxine McCormack and Vicki Wettach – our discussions always help me to strengthen my thoughts….. and I think Biggby's Coffee Shop now considers us regulars.

Follow Sammi Evans on Facebook, Twitter or on her website at www.sammievansmysteries.com.

CHAPTER ONE

Sammi Evans Patterson couldn't believe it wasn't snowing yet. It was the middle of December and although the weather was cold and messy, it hadn't yet provided any snow that was necessary for the holiday season to be in full bloom. She felt a little disappointed as she looked out the front window hoping to see a blanket of snow covering their front lawn. *Snow was needed*, she thought, *when would it come?*

Her husband Dave had wandered into the room quietly and noticed her looking out the window. As she turned and noticed him, she knew he was in tune with her.

"You want some snow, right?"

"Absolutely. This is so unusual. It's already the tenth of December and no snow yet. What's going on in Pennsylvania this year?"

"I'm sure we'll get some. It's certainly cold enough. God, yesterday that cold wind went right through my coat and got me chilled to the bone."

"Good thing we're finally going on vacation. What day do we leave?"

He smiled as he thought that although they were close to a year into their marriage, they hadn't yet been on a honeymoon. However, the trip was now planned and getting closer.

"We leave on the twenty-seventh and fly directly to Aruba to spend at least seven days in the sun. I can hardly wait."

"I want to look refreshed and relaxed when I get home," she added eagerly.

"But before then we've got to get our tree up and decorated, as well as the house. This weekend is my deadline. I want everything done by then."

"What type of tree do you want?"

"I want a ..."

The telephone rang. Dave immediately looked up at the clock. It was nine thirty on Friday night. He couldn't imagine.

"Yeah, Tom, what's up?"

Tom Harrington was one of his police buddies and important in his inner circle. Sammi noticed that he listened intently for more than five minutes; he didn't utter one word. That was unusual. When he did speak, he seemed somber yet focused. Later, as he put the phone down, he turned to her and took one particularly deep breath in an effort to clear his head.

His expression told her volumes, but she waited until he spoke. "God, Sammi, this one's tough." He stopped again before he could continue. Then he began in earnest.

"I don't think you know Randy Baker, do you?"

"No, I don't think so."

"He and Tom have been friends for years. They went to high school together and their lives have intermingled frequently since then. Anyway, his wife's been found dead in their home. She was shot through the back of the head and the police think it was Randy's gun that did it."

Sammi sat up to attention. This would be an emotional situation under any circumstances, but having the husband accused, well ... she waited for Dave to continue.

"Tom doesn't buy it for a minute. He's beside himself right now. But he's asking to be involved in this case and wants us there, too."

"Of course. What does he want us to do?"

"Nothing right now. It's out of our jurisdiction. The murder happened over in Kingston so we'll have to get permission to help out. That'll be up to the sarge."

"Wow. Do they have any clues?"

"Tom doesn't know. He got a courtesy call from a mutual friend so the information is rather sketchy right now. It seems they have one child, a ten-year-old. Don't know if it's a boy or girl, but the child has already gone to foster care. Tom and Jill have made a request to social services that the child be allowed to stay with them. Honestly, Sammi, Tom sounded in tears."

"With Jill being a teacher, she could get that child into her school and be around when needed. Gees, that kid must be so devastated."

"I'm going to meet Tom at the station tomorrow. He wants to talk with Jim, the sarge and me alone and go over some of the evidence against his friend. He didn't see them all the time, but they did keep in touch and Tom says he was happy with his family; he'd never have done this."

Sammi sat quietly. Anyone could snap under stress and she knew Dave realized it, too, but they had to wait and see the evidence. The fact that she had been shot with Randy's gun didn't help the situation.

Dave came over and sat down beside her. He put his arm around her and relaxed his body. She felt he knew that he wouldn't be getting too much relaxation in the near future.

He said, "I know that Tom's positive Randy didn't do this. Yet friendship can cloud your judgment. I want you to listen in when we question him. I'm sure Tom will want you there as well. You can listen to his thoughts and then we can all be on the same page."

"Of course I will. I wish with all my heart that he didn't do this," she said.

"So do I, for everyone's sake. So do I."

There was a considerable pause before Dave spoke again.

"The thing is that he hasn't been arrested yet. It might be too soon for that, but it seems that no one knows where he's at. That's the bad part. It appears that he took off."

That was the last word spoken. It always looked bad when someone ran off, especially since he left his ten-year-old child. They both sat in their own bewildered thoughts, miffed at the turn of events. They'd have to wait and see the evidence. The evidence is what told the story.

* * *

The next morning Dave was quiet as he ate breakfast and prepared to meet Tom. He had tossed and turned some during the night, but caught enough sleep to set his mind in gear early on. It was one of those times when a person didn't know what to say, but the policeman in him would take over and talk would center on the evidence like in any other case. Someone had to be objective and Dave knew that Tom would have a hard time doing it himself. Also, the sarge had to be on board with this one.

The phone rang. It was Jim Mucci, their other partner.

"Hi, Jim, did Tom call you?"

"He's beside himself. I guess they haven't located Randy yet. That wasn't a good move on his part. What could have possessed him to take off like that?"

"Don't know. Probably wasn't thinking straight under the circumstances."

"True, but he left his kid, I hear. Why would he do that?"

"Can't imagine. I wonder where he went and better yet, I wonder if he plans to get back here today. That would certainly help."

"It sure would. I'll be down at the station about one o'clock. See ya then."

Dave paced the kitchen without saying another word. Sammi knew that he was thinking in many directions right now. This case already seemed strange and it would be dreadfully emotional, more so than usual.

"This sure puts a damper on the holiday season," he said.

"I know but remember that you won't be alone working this. And part of your job will be to keep Tom rational. From what you said, he was a basket case."

"I haven't heard him that upset in a long time, but I

can understand it. His friend's wife is found murdered and right now, all the evidence points to the husband. That alone is tough. I'll have to wait until I talk to Tom and try not to form any conclusions myself yet. I think I met Randy once about a year ago, so I don't even know him, not really."

"Like you always tell me, follow the evidence. See what the clues say."

"And if he turns up soon, which I hope, I want you in on the questioning. It'll go a long way to know where his mind is at. I'm sure that's why Tom wants us on this case."

"I'll call Jill later today and see how she's doing."

"Good idea. Call you later."

He gave her a quick kiss and then he was gone. After he left Sammi took a few minutes and an extra cup of coffee to think over the situation. Whenever children were involved, it heightened the emotional side and the situation automatically became increasingly delicate. How could a little child handle this? And who had found the body? That wasn't even clear right now. She hoped it wasn't the child coming home from school and finding his mother shot and lying dead on the floor. That would be hard for an adult to handle, but devastating for a little child. She'd have to wait to find out the details. She'd call Jill later, but in the meantime she decided to go pick out a Christmas tree for them. She was sure Dave wouldn't have much time for a while and she wanted to get her mind on other things. There was an entire world out there with its own private business going on. This city was full of powerful stories, some incredibly touching, some unbelievably bizarre.

Sammi thought about how she could help in this case. She had a special talent – she could hear other people's thoughts and the few that knew about her gift would make sure she was in strategic positions for optimum benefit. Yet this was different from being excited about catching criminals at their own game. That gave her pleasure. She didn't think there would be much about this case that would give her peace of mind.

* * *

She found a delightful White Pine tree about six feet tall with a wonderful shape and personality. It called out to her about the effects of the Christmas spirit on a household and shamelessly neglected any sadness around her. This tree had its own life and Sammi decided it was meant for them. She was able to get it set up in their living room, but wanted Dave to help her decorate it. She waited for a while and as the dinner hour came and went, she decided to call Jill and see what was happening at their house.

"Sammi, this is so devastating. I knew Beth quite well. She was as delightful as you could imagine; such a tragedy."

"I understand you've volunteered to care for the child."

"Yes, they have a little boy named Denver. He's ten years old and quite bright I understand. We're waiting for social services to make up their mind, and it does seem they're leaning in our direction. After all, we know him a little and we're friends with his parents. Better us than complete strangers, I would think. Also, we have a history of taking in children occasionally so our record stands on its own."

"I think you'd be a great choice. Has Randy shown up yet?"

"I don't know. Honestly, I haven't heard from Tom since he left this morning. I'm sure the three referees are sifting through everything they have right now. And, of course, they have to wait and see what Sergeant Brady decides to do. God, this is so awful."

Despite the devastating situation, Sammi found one note of amusement. Dave, Tom and Jim referred to themselves as the three referees and now their wives and friends thought of them that way as well.

"Yeah, I wonder what happened."

"Well, one thing's for sure," said Jill. "Randy didn't do this. He loved his wife and kid. He was a real family man. So to me, this seems like a major frame up. That's the only explanation I can think of."

Sammi was quiet. She couldn't imagine being in Jill's shoes.

"I'm glad you'll be around. You can help them sort out the answers and put things in perspective. At times like this, your talent is awesome."

"I'll be glad to help any way I can. Do you want me to come over for a while?"

"No, thanks, I'm okay. These guys should be getting home soon. I hope they have good news."

"Later," said Sammi as she hung up.

The waiting was the worst part of it. Her mind was going in every conceivable direction. What possible explanation could there be for this killing? And if Randy didn't do it, then who? And why? This was not a random shooting. This had been purposely carried out. Why would anyone want Beth dead? And then the frightening thought crossed her mind; who, except her husband?

* * *

When Dave arrived at the station around 1:00 P.M., the group was already there. Sergeant Brady had arrived to discuss having his three referees available for the Kingston police. He knew the sergeant over there, a friend of his for years, but it would be Kingston's call. Did they want these extra police officers involved?

When the sarge put down the telephone after talking to Detective Statton, he nodded his head. They were aware of Tom's friendship with Randy Baker and felt that could give them another perspective on this case. The extra help would be welcomed.

"Great," said Tom. "I'm not sure how I would have handled sitting on the sidelines."

"Well, okay then, luckily Kingston is close enough that you can be available for both places, but I'll allow you priority on this case, for a while at least."

"Tyrone and LeBron are both up to speed here and we've got Amilio, too, so we feel that we can give Kingston some help without creating a shortage. Besides, we'll be around if you need us," said Tom.

"Good enough," replied the sarge, "what do we know so far?"

"Very little," said Tom. "Randy hasn't surfaced yet. That's so strange that he would take off like that. It's not like him. So we're not sure who found his wife; we hope it wasn't the child. I've talked to Detective Statton of the Kingston office. He's to be the lead detective I hear, and that's a lucky break. He's a twenty year veteran and has tons of experience. I know him and he's good. He told me within a few days they'll know a lot more."

"But what do they know right now?" asked Dave.

"Let's see, she was found in the living room, shot through the head from behind. It looks like Randy's gun was used in the murder, but ballistics aren't back yet. But there was a lot of disturbance all over the house ... drawers were all opened and dumped, furniture was overturned and it was obvious that someone was looking for something."

Everyone looked at each other in confusion.

"What on earth...?" said Jim, but found it difficult to finish his thought.

Tom simply shook his head. He didn't have any answers.

Jim said, "That definitely points away from Randy. He wouldn't ransack his own home."

Tom said, "Unless he was trying to make it look like a robbery. You know someone's going to use that line."

"Let's meet with these guys early next week, Monday or Tuesday and see what they've got. This looks very strange to me," said Jim.

They sat quietly for a few minutes realizing that it was hard to discuss anything. There weren't many facts or clues or evidence to discuss. Finally, Dave asked for some background information.

"Tom, tell us what you know about Randy and his wife. We should know something about them before we dive into this thing."

"Okay, well, Randy's a great guy. I went to high school with him and we played football together for four years. We've always kept in touch. He met his wife Beth in college. Randy is some type of account executive for ASAC Globe Ventures, Inc."

Jim whistled. "You mean that big company that has a lot of international dealings and offices all over the country? What's their main product anyway?"

"They have their fingers in a lot of things, but I understand computers both here and abroad and advance technology as well as numerous international dealings. I'm not sure what all they do, honestly."

"Okay, we'll have to check out this company. Go on," said Dave.

"Anyway, that's what he does, but his wife Beth is ... was a real brain. She ended up becoming a teacher and then getting a Master's Degree and teaching math and philosophy at the college level. But she also studied a lot of philosophy on her own and seems to have been a sought after independent thinker and speaker. I know she's received plaques for different presentations; don't remember the specifics, but Randy was quite proud of her. And their son Denver is quite bright. He could have gone to a gifted school, but they decided to keep him mainstreamed. But then, with his parents around he had all of the expertise near him that was needed."

"Quite a family," said Jim.

"That's right. I'm telling you guys that Tom adored the ground Beth walked on. He loved his kid and he loved his wife. He didn't do this."

"Would seem that way," said Dave, more to offer Tom support than anything else.

"They married right out of college; Jill and I went to their wedding, and I've never heard that they had any problems. The last time we got together with them was probably six months ago. They seemed as happy as ever. Really guys, this has all the markings of a set up to me."

"But why would he run?"

"He must have had a real good reason," said Tom. "I'm sure he'll be back. He'd never leave that kid."

"Do you know where the kid was found?" asked the sarge.

"No, I don't."

"Okay, well I don't think we can do anymore today. This is too new and we don't know anything. We'll start in next week. I expect you three will be spending most of your time in Kingston."

"No doubt we'll be going back and forth," offered Dave. "We'll have to play it by ear."

"Just keep in touch. I need to know what's going on. And Dave, I'm sure you'll bring Sammi in on this one."

"For sure."

"Yeah," said Tom. "We're certainly gonna need her."

* * *

When Dave walked through the door, Sammi was eagerly awaiting him. She was anxious for any new information. But Dave spotted their Christmas tree and turned to Sammi.

"So you went out and got one by yourself?"

"I thought you'd be too busy for a while, and when you do get time we can decorate it together."

"That was thoughtful. Thanks."

She smiled and waited.

"You go sit in the living room and I'll get us some coffee. Then I want to hear everything ... bring me up-to-date."

Dave welcomed sitting on the large brown sofa that they both loved. It was comfortable and beckoning when his body was tired and weary. It even seemed to understand when he was confused and gloomy and adapted to his form in a special way. He took a deep breath and waited. Sammi was back in a moment. He told her everything he'd heard thus far.

"That certainly isn't very much, is it?"

"No, there aren't many details yet, but we did get permission to join the case down in Kingston. All three of us will be working both stations for a while."

"So they don't know who found the body, or they're not saying?"

"Actually, we haven't talked to anyone yet. We'll most likely all head down there on Monday morning for a meeting. We have to get up to speed on this one fast."

"What about Randy? Anyone hear from him yet?"

Dave slowly shook his head as an expression of disgust crossed his face. "Nope, no one's heard from him. That makes him look so bad. God, I wish he'd turn up. Where could he have gone?"

They sat quietly on the couch thinking of possible scenarios as to why Randy would run. It didn't make sense. He was a levelheaded guy, and although this was a desperate situation, he knew what running would look like. Why would he run?

Sammi spoke first. "If all is as it seems and they were a loving couple and Randy is innocent, he must have had a darn good reason for taking off like that. Maybe he thinks he can solve this himself and couldn't do it from a jail cell."

"But they'll find him soon enough and then what? His reputation is tarnished for running and he's not going to solve this in a day or two, that's for sure. No, there's got to be another reason."

Sammi asked. "So he works for ASAC Globe Ventures, Inc. What's that all about?"

"We don't know. We've got some people researching that already. I think Julie might be in on that part of it. We know they deal with a lot of international stuff, but I don't think Randy had much to do with that part, at least Tom said he hardly ever traveled."

"What was his job at this company?"

"No one knows for sure. Tom thinks his degree was

in corporate business and he has an executive-type position there, but we're all guessing right now. I've had about all I can take of this right now. Tonight and tomorrow will probably be the last completely peaceful days for a while. What would you like to do?"

"I'd like to decorate the tree tonight and tomorrow we can go Christmas shopping together and get everything we need. Then that'll be one thing off our minds."

"I thought you were finished. You're always ahead of the game."

"I'm finished, but if I know you, you haven't even started, right?"

He nodded. "But I'm lucky because you do most of the shopping for us and I only have to shop for you. Now, how can I do that if we're together?"

"I plan to make myself scarce for a while, and I do have a few last minute things. Let's try to finish up everything tomorrow. You don't need anything distracting you starting Monday."

"Good idea."

With that they both got out their boxes of decorations. This was their first Christmas together in their home since they got married and both had their own special decorations. Sammi was quite sentimental about some of the special ornaments she had gathered as a child and Dave was equally pleased with some of his. The tree wouldn't hold all of them so they placed some of them in different areas around the house making every room a gala event.

"This looks great," said Dave. "It puts me in a festive mood."

"Right and I got a Christmas card today from my brother Raymond. It's nice that we connect around the holidays at least."

"It's the same way with my brother Karl. The rest of the year, he doesn't seem to exist. What about your other brother Neal?"

"Well, he disappeared from our lives over twenty

years ago. I think that's what he wanted to do even before that," said Sammi without feeling. Emotions had disappeared years ago.

Dave nodded. Many families grew distant and disappeared from each other. Sometimes that was best.

By Sunday night, their shopping was finished. They'd had a grand day, stopping for dinner at their favorite restaurant and returning home in time for a restful, uneventful evening of relaxation and togetherness. They both knew this would be the last one for a while.

* * *

Tom hadn't been able to settle down. He was considerably agitated and paced the floor of his living room unable to get in control of his emotions. This had been going on for a few days now, in truth since he'd heard about his friend Randy's situation. *What could have possessed him to run off like that*, he thought. *Now he's in worse trouble than before. Running always signals guilt to a lot of people. But I know that he must have had a darn good reason. He's a smart guy and I know that he'd never run away and leave his kid–he's doing something that he thinks needs to be done. God, I need to know.*

"Honey, you've got to settle down," said Jill. "Have a glass of wine; that should help you relax."

He nodded; his wife was right. He had to get in control. What was happening to him? He had to keep his wits about him or he wouldn't be of any help to anybody. He was so glad to be on the case. And with Dave and Sammi, Jim and Julie, he felt he had a powerful team of workers with him.

Jill brought him his glass of wine and in about ten minutes, his body did start to relax. He stretched out on the couch as his mind was still mulling over the facts that he knew. And they were scarce at best. Then he thought, *I've got to stop doing this. I have to wait until I learn more. There isn't anything more I can do tonight.* Then he took a deep breath, slowly let it out and forced his body into relaxation.

Jill came and sat down beside him. "I'm thinking of Denver right now. He's with Social Services, right? I hope he isn't too scared."

Tom nodded. "Poor little guy. His entire world has been torn apart. Can't imagine how he's been handling it?"

Just then, the phone rang. It was Social Services. They had decided to let Tom and Jill care for Denver for the foreseeable future. She could get him into school right away and be there for him. That turned out to be a plus. Also, because Tom was a good friend of his father they felt he would feel comfortable with them. They hoped to turn him over to them by the early part of the week. He'd need more clothes which they would provide as the crime scene wouldn't be opened up to them for a while yet.

"I'm so glad. Now, we can clearly be a part of the process that helps Randy and Beth's situation. I feel relieved."

Tom was quiet until he said. "For some reason, this does help me to relax some. Taking care of Denver will go a long way to help us solve the case."

"And I can get time off whenever I need it," said Jill. "I've saved so many vacation and sick days in the last two years that I know this situation will work out. I wonder how he's doing."

"That's a hard one to guess," said Tom. "He's one of those intelligent little guys. Randy used to say that he kept a lot of things to himself, he was a real thinker, so I imagine that will be true even more right now."

"I hope we can get him to talk a little, for his own sake. But then we've got Sammi and she could tell us what's on his mind."

"That's another reason I wanted to get him. He might have some valuable information, whether he knows it or not. And I sure wouldn't want him repeating it to anyone else."

"Things are working out. We'll have to wait and see what happens."

The phone rang again. It was almost ten o'clock on Sunday night.

"Tom, this is Randy."

"My God, where are you?"

"Look, I've only got a few minutes, so please, just listen. There's so much going on that won't be brought out for a while that I had to take control of a few things so evidence wouldn't get lost."

"But you left Denver."

"No, I didn't. I took him over to one of the neighbors. They're good friends of ours and Denver is comfortable with them. They said they'd keep him until the police took over."

Tom let out a big sigh of relief. "Okay."

"You didn't think I'd leave my son in a vulnerable position; my God, Tom."

"I know ... but everything happened so fast."

"And you didn't ask me, Tom."

"Ask you what?"

"If I did it. You didn't ask me if I killed Beth."

"Randy, I don't have to ask. I know you didn't do this. But what the hell is going on?"

"I wish I had time to tell you, but I'm still on the move, at least until tomorrow; that's when I'll be turning myself in. Then I don't think I'll have any freedom for a while. But I had to run at this time, remember that. I wanted to make sure I could get in touch with you. I'm going to need your help."

"Hell, Randy, I've got myself and two of my best buddies assigned to this case."

"But it's in Kingston."

"I requested to be on it and they've already accepted us."

"Thank God. But my biggest concern is Denver. Could you guys possibly take care of him?"

"We put in the request as soon as we heard and got a call from Social Services about an hour ago. They'll bring him to us possibly Tuesday or Wednesday."

It was obvious even over the phone that Randy was crying a little.

Tom said, "I'll be there with you all the way, buddy. You're not alone."

"God bless you both. Beth was caught up in something and actually so was I ... I'm not sure if they meant to get her or me. Either way, they wanted to eliminate me. And I think Denver may know a few things, but he'd stopped talking so I think he'll clam up for a while. Be gentle with him. Gees, he's just a little boy. I've got to run. Bless you both."

And the line went dead. Tom stood there looking at the phone realizing that Jill heard most of the conversation. He filled her in on the rest.

"I knew it, Tom. Randy's a good person. But what in the world did they get caught up in?"

He shrugged his shoulders and shook his head. "After tomorrow we'll be able to see him and I hope to get more of the story. I've got a feeling that he won't tell all of it immediately and when he does it will almost certainly be exclusively to our group."

Jill nodded, knowing Randy had to be cautious.

"I can't even imagine what this is all about," said Tom, trying to understand an impossible situation.

* * *

Tom put in a conference call to Dave and Jim.

"Thank God," said Dave. "At least he'll turn himself in before he gets caught. That'll help a little."

"But he didn't say what this was all about?" asked Jim.

"No, simply what I've told you. He seemed very edgy like he was looking around and being careful not to be trapped by someone. He wasn't ready to get caught yet."

"I think we've got a real bad situation on our hands here. Can we get to him tomorrow after he turns himself in? He didn't say where or what time?" asked Dave.

"No, he didn't. He seemed so rushed and wanted to

get a few things settled; but he told me that he didn't do it." He paused for a moment. "But I knew that already. I know that you guys don't know him ..."

"But you do," Dave said. "And that's good enough for me."

Tom added. "Don't forget that we'll have Sammi in on some questioning and that should convince the rest of you. It's easier for me; I know him personally. But I'll be glad when Sammi can let you guys know what she hears."

"Okay," said Dave. "I think we should meet in Scranton tomorrow morning. We need to put in a call to Kingston right away. As soon as they know or hear anything, I want them to contact us. They need to know that we're first string on this one."

"I'm sure Detective Statton will be our main contact and we're lucky there. We'll all be working like one team." Tom added, "I think this one is going to need all of the talent and luck that we've got."

* * *

Sammi was happy when she heard the news. Once Randy turned himself in and cooperated, it would go a long way in getting him in good standing with the law.

"Is there any chance that they won't arrest him? Could they keep him as a person of interest and warn him not to leave town, or something like that?"

"It's always possible. With him running, though, it doesn't help, but if there's no real hard evidence against him they may keep him under surveillance for now."

"And he'll have to get himself a lawyer right away. Then maybe he can post bail."

"He'll need to get a good, experienced one. From what I've heard so far, this case will have a lot of sneaky turns and surprises. Randy hinted at that."

"I know you've talked about his gun being used, but that isn't proven yet. Let's say that it was his gun that killed Beth and his fingerprints are on the gun. That still doesn't prove that he was the one who pulled the trigger. You'd expect his fingerprints to be on the gun if he owned it."

Dave smiled. He knew that she was trying to put the best possible scenario on the circumstances.

"Some have been arrested on far less than that, but it'll depend on a lot of details that we don't even know right now. Kingston police will have to tread lightly. If there's no history of any problems between them, that should help. And since it happened sometime in the afternoon, possibly a neighbor or someone saw or heard something."

Sammi had to think about that one for a minute. She sat in deep thought before she ventured to say, "You know, committing this murder in daylight, in the middle of the day seems so brazen to me. That doesn't make much sense."

"That's a tough one. Under the cover of night is usually more common, but of course it depends what these killers wanted to accomplish. They no doubt had to have watched this area for a while and knew the pattern of behavior of the Baker family. Why Beth? Why did they kill her? How could she have been a threat to anyone?"

"I agree. It seems to me," she said, "that Randy would have been the more logical target."

"Unless they needed to get both of them out of the way and decided to kill Beth and frame Randy for the killing. Now whatever he says for his defense will be under heavy scrutiny and probably less believable. But who's behind this? That's going to be a hard thing to prove?"

Sammi said, "It sounded like Randy had a pretty good idea who was behind it. It sounds like proving it will be somewhat difficult."

"And except for our group, will anyone else believe him?"

CHAPTER TWO

At the station on Monday morning, Dave found himself tending to his usual routine. Nothing had come through yet and there was no sense wasting time. He was in the middle of his paperwork when Amilio Hernandez, approached him.

"Hey, amigo, you've got yourself caught up in the middle of another one, I hear. You and the entire group have been tapped, how come?"

"Tom's a long-time friend of Randy Baker."

"He's the guy whose wife was killed?"

"Yeah, that's the one."

"I've heard it doesn't look too good for him. He ran, they say."

Dave nodded. Amilio was another cop that was close to this group. They had a history together that was secret and complicated, but had caused them to form a trusting and loyal relationship.

"We'll have to wait and see, but there are strange circumstances already. We know almost nothing right now and we hope to meet with Kingston later today or tomorrow. Then the real work will begin."

"I'll be available if I can help in any way. Your face tells me that you don't think he did it."

"Right now, it doesn't make any sense at all. It's so damn confusing."

Anyone could see how frustrated Dave had become already. Yet that could work in his favor.

"But you do your best work when your back is up. And then you've got Sammi." Amilio winked at Dave. "In time between the both of you, you'll figure it out."

"Well, I'm glad to know you'll be available if we need you. What are you working on right now?"

"I'm sure it's second to your case, but mine's pretty

annoying, too. A girl was killed, a prostitute. It happened a while back and nothing's been done. It was put on the back burner, but for some reason they've brought it forward again. Don't know why. Someone was no doubt complaining. So they gave it to me."

"I'm glad, Amilio. I know you'll give it proper attention whether she was a prostitute or not."

"Of course, she deserves every consideration as far as I'm concerned. I know you realize, amigo, that some people just hate prostitutes and want them dead or gone. But the usual feelings aren't there for me. No, no, something is different about this one."

"I didn't hear much about it; when did it happen?"

"Maybe six months ago or even more, I think. There weren't any leads so no one did anything. They only gave it to me last week because it seemed to hit a dead end. I'll see what I can find out. Not much to go on though, I can tell you that."

Dave took a moment to look over at Amilio. He was one sharp police officer and had worked as a double agent a few of times. He was talented playing both sides of the fence. Slight in his build and looking like a perpetual teenager, his dark hair and piercing black eyes from his Mexican heritage belied one of the most investigative and penetrating minds Dave had ever run across.

"Tell me what you have. I've got a little time right now."

"Okay, amigo. Her name is Tina O'Leary. She was beat up pretty bad and dumped in a vacant lot near a bar called the Castaways. It's a private club which caters to rich businessmen and that's where she spent the last moments of her life. I've recently started studying the file which had the names of most of the clients on hand that night, but they were never sure how many names were missing from the list. Plus the important fact was that the party that night lasted until 4:00 AM and everyone stayed late. Tina took off early because of a personal issue that she needed to take care of. It wasn't likely that any of those men who stayed on could have assaulted her."

Dave listened intently to Amilio who had gotten himself hooked up in a case that obviously intrigued him. He couldn't hide it.

He continued. "Pictures showed that she had been partially redressed in a hurry, but one red high-heeled shoe has never been found, and her car keys were missing as well. Yet her car had never been claimed and simply left in the parking lot. She had been wearing a sexy black lace top, you know, the kind you can almost see through and it was torn on the left side of the front. Let's see, what else? Oh yeah, her short red mini-skirt was imitation leather and she wore no bra, or it was missing. She had put up quite a struggle. She had lots of cuts and bruises on her body. She finally lost her fight for survival by strangulation, as the finger marks on her neck show."

"Why take the car keys and not steal the car?"

"Could be he was smart enough to realize it would be too sharp of a trail," said Amilio. "Anyway it doesn't look like a hate crime."

"Right, I've seen a few of those in my time," said Dave. "They usually either mutilate the body or write some type of hate note. None on this one, right?"

Amilio shook his head. "And it doesn't show any marks of a body being dragged. The pictures of the crime scene didn't show it, but I understand it had rained that night so that could have ruined any traces of that."

Dave said, "He'd have to have some strength to carry her out here. And his footprints should have been heavier in the dirt if he was carrying a one hundred and twenty pound female."

Amilio thought about that and said, "But remember the rain."

Dave nodded. "Was there any DNA? The rain probably didn't help there either."

"There was enough, amigo and we've got it on file. So I'll have to run that through our database."

"I'm still wondering about that shoe."

"Maybe it was lost when he was carrying her," said Amilio.

"But then it should have showed up somewhere in that field. You might have to retrace your steps and study it out again."

Amilio agreed. "Good idea, amigo, good idea. See ya later."

Dave went back to his paperwork. He had to admit that all murders deserved attention. No one deserved to die in the painful and shameless way of these two gals.

* * *

By Monday afternoon, the phone call came through that Randy Baker had turned himself in to the Kingston police, but Detective Statton informed them that they wouldn't be able to talk to him until possibly the next day or later. They would be holding him at least for now, but he was not officially under arrest. He'd asked for an attorney, but hadn't chosen one yet. He was asking to see Tom Harrington.

"You're not going to be allowed to see him until tomorrow, at the earliest. All the preliminary stuff is taking place right now," said Sergeant Brady.

"We can't get to him at all today? ... I mean he's asked for me," said Tom.

"Doesn't matter. He's been offered his one phone call and wanted to save it for now. So our hands are tied at this time."

"What's he thinking?" said Dave.

"Can't imagine," said the sarge. "They've tried to question him, but he refuses to answer anything until his attorney is present and for some reason he's holding off on that; doesn't make much sense to me. Probably if he got a lawyer and answered some questions, they'd let him go."

"How come we can see him tomorrow?"

"When they get all of the preliminary paperwork and protocol in order and they check with the chief in charge, they'll let him have some selected visitors." The sarge had to remind him. "In a way, right now, you're all going to be considered visitors. Later on, that should change."

They all understood. At first, every precaution was taken to follow exact procedure. And right now, no one was sure that Randy would even be charged.

"I hate this waiting," said Tom. "I need to get to him and talk face to face. Then we can start figuring out what this is all about and figure out a plan."

"But we have to follow procedure," said Dave. "You know that. You don't want to screw everything up by being overly anxious right now. Catch up on your paperwork here, if you can concentrate at all. You won't have much of a chance to do it later."

Dave's phone rang. It was Sammi.

"Anything yet?"

"Well, Randy did turn himself in ... that's the good news, but we can't get to him until at least tomorrow. And he's hesitating on his choice of attorneys. This is confusing as hell. All we can do is wait for now."

"Wow. You'd think he'd grab an attorney right away."

"Maybe he doesn't really know a good criminal attorney."

"I'd imagine his place of employment would offer one. It's a big corporation, right?

"That's true."

Then Dave was interrupted. "Got to go. See ya tonight."

They all marched into Sergeant Brady's office together. There was a new development. Detective Don Statton from Kingston was asking for all three of them to meet with him. And he wanted it this afternoon.

* * *

When they walked into the Kingston Police Station, they were directed to a large conference room, off to the right side of the main area where they could meet in privacy. Coffee was available and they talked about anything that made sense until Detective Don Statton came through the door.

"Hi, Tom ... good to see you."

He was introduced to the rest of the group. Don Statton was in his late forties, a meticulous dresser for his husky build, a habit that carried over into other areas of his life. He was particular and methodical about his casework, too.

"Okay, guys, I'm sure Tom's told you we've worked together before. And he speaks highly of both of you, so I think we'll have a tight group to work with. I don't know that much right now, don't even know if Randy will be charged at this time, but I want to share with you what I do know and one rather strange occurrence that happened earlier today. I'm big about sharing information and keeping us all up to date. I think we'll have the best chance that way."

It was clear that the referees already liked his open method of working. As a team, they hoped to solve this heinous crime and they wanted to do it quickly. It was important for moral reasons, but also to keep the community from panicking.

"First of all, ballistics isn't back so we're not sure about the gun. But it's known that Randy did have a registered gun in his home which was not in the gun case. We're assuming that the weapon used was his gun and, yes, it was left behind. Now that's strange on its own. Someone wanted us to know it was his gun that was used."

"Randy's not that stupid. He wouldn't have used his own gun and then left it there, my God," said Tom, in an emotional tone.

"Does seem like a rather dumb thing to do," said Jim.

"Okay, okay," said Don. "I know that we're going to study this case from the point of view that Randy didn't do it, but we still have to look at all of the possibilities."

They were all in agreement there.

"Okay, well the strange thing that happened earlier today is about the attorney bit. He hasn't made that call for an attorney; I mean most detained suspects are screaming for their phone call to a lawyer right away. It seems like he doesn't know who to call. But, an attorney was here within the hour of him turning himself in. He was from ASAC Globe Ventures where he worked. Now that would have seemed to me to be a done deal since this lawyer even said that the company would be covering the costs, but Randy didn't want to talk to him. Hell, he didn't even want to see him. And, of course, he didn't have to."

"But how did he know so quickly that Randy had turned himself in?" asked Tom.

"Good question. We don't know and he wouldn't say. But our questioning him about it made him squirm a little."

"What's his name?" asked Dave.

"I've got his card. Let's see, Michael Bronton, attorney for ASAC."

"Why wouldn't he at least want to talk to him?" asked Jim.

Dave said, "Something doesn't figure right on that one. I'm assuming that he earns a decent salary, but attorneys can get pretty expensive real fast. There must be a story there somewhere."

"Okay, well, let's move on. We're still not sure where the little boy was throughout all of this. He gets home from school about 3:15 PM, sometimes a little later and Randy said that he was home by 4:00 PM. That would mean that the little one must have found his mother before Randy came home. But the police took him to Social Services right away and as expected he was severely traumatized so I'm guessing he must have found Beth first and waited for his dad."

"God, how awful," said Tom. "That kid has a lot to get over. And he's not talking much?"

"Actually," said Don. "I don't think he's talking at all

right now. But I heard he did ask for his dad."

"See, see," said Tom. "If Denver had the slightest inkling that his dad had killed his mother, he would be afraid of his dad. But he's asking for him so that says a lot."

They all agreed.

"Now I don't know how, but I've heard that the crime scene was contaminated. Maybe they think the boy did it, or Randy, but certain things around the body weren't right. Somebody did something."

Tom said, "Could be it was done by the murderer."

"They didn't think so. It was done after the blood had settled slightly. There was no doubt that something was changed at least a half hour after she bled out."

"Wow, this thing gets crazier all the time," said Jim.

"And we heard that the entire house was ransacked, right? Somebody was desperate to find something," said Dave.

"Oh yeah," replied Don. "Sometimes things are turned over and messed up a little to make it look like a robbery, but in this case, every room had been searched in a quick and messy way. And a lot of time was taken, especially in the bedrooms to search behind things and under drawers. Someone was quite frantic to find something. Of course, we don't know if they found it or not."

Silence covered the group for a few minutes. Who could make sense of all this? Every time that they thought about a logical explanation, something else came up that defied all reason.

"We should be getting some kind of report by late tomorrow or Wednesday. It won't be complete, but it will have a decent amount of facts."

"Can we see the crime scene?" asked Tom.

"Not today. It's still closed off. By tomorrow I want to get over there myself. If you guys want to come with me, that'll be fine," said Don.

"Sure, we do. How about you give us a call when things fall together? We're not that far away."

"Okay, well, tomorrow then. Let's plan for later in the day and then, I'll be sure we'll have a go signal."

With that, Don left the room. The three got up and headed for home. There wasn't anything else they could do right now. Tom hated to be so close to Randy and not allowed to see him, but rules were rules. Okay, by tomorrow they should be allowed to see the crime scene and hopefully get a meeting with Randy.

* * *

About 11:30 AM on Tuesday, Sammi walked into the police station to meet Julie for lunch. She walked over and talked to Dave for a few minutes as Julie indicated that she needed to finish something.

"Hi Dave, what's happening?"

"We're going back to Kingston about three o'clock. Don said we'd be allowed to see the crime scene and probably have a little bit of time with Randy."

"So they're still holding him right now?"

"At this point he's not officially arrested, but detained as they call it. I think that if they do arrest him in the next few days and that seems likely, he'll be able to post bond. Tom wants him to stay with them and then he can be near his son, too."

"That should work better for both of them."

"So you and Julie are having lunch?"

"We're going to try to do it more often. I don't get to see her much anymore."

About this time, Amilio walked over.

"How're you doing?"

"Okay. I see you're all settled in."

"Yeah, I am. And I wanted to tell you both that Marlina and I've set a date for the wedding and we want the two of you to stand up for us. Okay?"

They both smiled.

"Of course, we'd be honored," said Dave. "When's the big day?"

"Probably in June. She's doing most of the details."

"You're finally going to do it, Amilio. I'm glad for

you," he said.

"And I'm adding a middle name of Terrence, too."
He winked at Sammi. "That's important to me as well."

"Nice touch," she said.

"Sammi, you got a minute; you, too, Dave? I'd like
to show you both the pictures of the crime scene. Did
Dave tell you that I'm working on a prostitute's death?"

"Yes, he did. That's sad, isn't it?"

"Amiga, it was a nasty death for her. Okay, here we
are ... pictures of the crime scene. Any thoughts would be
appreciated. This is an older case and I'm trying to catch
up here."

He showed them several pictures of a woman in the
middle of a vacant lot that was badly battered and bruised.
It was hard to look at, but they needed to look from the
point of view of detached agents.

After a few moments Sammi said, "Killer's no doubt
right-handed."

She caught both of them off guard.

"Why do you think he's right-handed?" asked Amilio.

Sammi answered casually as was her habit. "First,
look at the placement of the body; it's on its right side.
For a right-handed person to place a body on its left side
would be a little awkward. And then her black lace top, it
was torn on the left side. That had to be someone facing
her and using his right hand."

"He could have torn it from behind," said Dave.

"That's possible, but think about this. If he tore her
shirt from behind with his right hand, it's more likely than
not that his arm had to cross her body and the tear would
have started on the left side and torn left to right, but that
isn't the case. If he were left-handed, the tear would still
have an angle. But it was torn from the top in a straight
downward motion; most likely from someone facing her
who was right-handed because if the person facing her
was left-handed the tear would still be angled."

Amilio was impressed. "You sure do notice things."

"What about the contents of her purse?" she asked."

"It was empty except for lipstick and powder. There was a place to store your keys, but they were missing. Her purse was one of those real small things with a long chain that you wear over one shoulder. It had barely enough room to have anything in it."

"Wow, this guy didn't want to leave any trails, did he?" said Dave, staring closer at the pictures. "Too bad about the rain, footprints could really have helped."

"Sure, a good footprint would have been appreciated."

"How much did she fight? Were her fingernails broken or did she have any skin under her nails?" Sammi asked.

"The report isn't very thorough. Dave and I thought that since she was a prostitute nobody took much time on this one."

"Wait a minute. What's that in her right hand?" asked Sammi.

Amilio took the picture from her. "I thought that was a shadow of some kind."

Dave said, "Let me see that." He looked again at the picture, wrinkled his nose and simply shook his head. He had nothing to say.

"Do you have a magnifying glass?" she asked.

Dave provided one.

"No, that's something in her hand. Can we have these pictures blown up? I'd like to see what that is."

"Yeah, for sure. Fighting like she did I would have thought her fingers and hands would be totally empty, but it does seem strange."

Dave said, "She could have grabbed onto something and held it."

"Or someone could have purposely placed something in her hand after she died," said Sammi.

Either possibility seemed valid. They'd have to take a closer look.

Sammi asked. "Did she have any family or friends

that were interviewed? That could always help."

"She had one friend at that bar where she worked, but I don't think anyone paid much attention to her. I'm sure they were thinking, another prostitute, how much could we believe her? But I'm going back to talk to her. She might know something."

"We've got to follow any lead we've got," said Dave.

"I have one other thought about those keys," said Sammi.

They both looked at her.

"Well, it's popular nowadays, for women especially, to have a picture of their kids or boyfriend attached to their key chain. It's possible the killer wanted that picture more than the keys. Just an idea, but since the car wasn't taken ..." she didn't finish.

"That's certainly a thought. Hey would you two like to come with me when I talk to that friend of hers? I was thinking another woman and not a policeman might help in the interview."

Dave nodded as well as Sammi.

"Sure, not tomorrow though, I'm going to be on call for Kingston. Try to set something up for later in the week." He turned to Sammi, "Could you make it?"

"Sure I'd like to talk with her."

"I've got to say, Sammi, that you certainly have a good eye for detail. Your gal is quite observant, Dave." He smiled as they left.

Dave went back to his desk and Sammi went to meet with Julie who was now ready for lunch.

* * *

Julie and Sammi were pleased to have found the time for lunch. With their busy schedules it wasn't often they found occasion to get together; there always seemed to be other people around and they couldn't get the closeness and memories up front as they liked. They did have a long history together.

"I still think of our days back in high school," said Julie. "It seems long ago on the one hand, but sometimes it seems like yesterday. We shared so much."

"I know. And I tend to get nostalgic at times. I love to think of the good old past, because to me it was."

"Me, too. And here we are now, both happily married and still lucky enough to be close to each other." Sammi laughed. Then she got serious. "So I hear they've got you working on ASAC Globe Ventures, Inc. What have you found out? I'm so curious about this entire situation."

"That death was such a tragedy, but I think when we discover the reason, it's going to be a mind-blower. I believe there's a lot behind this whole thing. Anyway, I wonder if this company is mostly legit or not, because it's been up on charges several times and beat them all. Perhaps they're real good at hiding things."

Sammi's interest thickened. "What type of charges? In fact, what do they do?"

"They're into computers, but also computer programs and microchip enrichment and all type of advanced technology. But they also deal in some rather delicate areas of government stuff, like radiation plants, nuclear testing, and submarine information. Honestly Sammi, there's a whole list of things, but mainly they've got to do with new technology in any field. They were accused of selling some American technology secrets to other countries, but it was never proven. I understand they've been under close scrutiny for several years now."

"Wow, possibly they thought Randy or his wife found out something."

"That's always possible, but the referee group wants me to concentrate on anything subversive I might find. It doesn't have to be gigantic, simply a little side-step, but that's the type of thing that Dave thinks might give us a clue as to what's going on. And if we suspect something like that, well, I'm sure Ben Collier will be involved again."

Sammi sat there listening to the beginning of another unbelievable venture. Julie was one of those gifted people, extremely bright, particularly on computer technology and therefore especially valuable in these areas. Sometimes when Sammi listened to her explanations, she was a bit overwhelmed.

"I'll be interested in what you find out this time. Another conspiracy, hopefully not targeted at Pennsylvania, but even bigger than that. We're lucky we've got you on our side."

Julie laughed. "And what about you? God, girl, you have such a unique talent. It's amazing to me. You can hear what other people are thinking. I think you'll be quite valuable on this one."

"What does ASAC stand for anyway?"

"It's the name of the owners. A was Benjamin Ascott, founder and original CEO; he died about ten years ago. S is for Smiley Sturges, an excellent inventor, I hear. I believe he's still around, but in a smaller capacity. The second A was for Ascott's son who bombed out after a few years, but they kept his initial in the title anyway. The only one left of the original group now is Matthew Carnigan. He's about fifty-two and has brains that he doesn't always use. I'm not sure of his capabilities, but he's more of a ladies' man and it's gotten him in legal trouble a few times. He almost succumbed to an arranged marriage to a wealthy gal a while back, but then backed out. Can't imagine that would have worked out with his roving eye, but then that type of marriage falls into a different category. But, I've barely touched the top of this study, so I have to say ... to be continued."

"So far it's intriguing."

"The wealthy do live by a different set of rules. They feel they're entitled; that's the best and easiest way to say it. Their attitude is unbelievable, not all of them of course, but some."

"I guess if you've been raised that way ..."

"You'd never think you had something to overcome. But the important thing is to find out if they're in any way connected to this murder. That's our main goal. These types of personalities that we have to deal with can be difficult."

* * *

Sammi beat Dave home that night. She wasn't sure when he'd get back from Kingston. She decided to eat, take an early bath and possibly start wrapping presents for the holidays. It was already December 15th and time was getting close. She couldn't help but muse about this latest murder. She wondered if Denver had made it to the Harrington home yet. She wondered if Randy Baker would be let out of jail soon. And most of all, she wondered who had killed Beth Baker and why. They seemed like an ordinary couple at first sight. Randy had a good job, but he had worked hard for it. He didn't start out as an executive, but had worked his way up the line learning a lot about the bottom rungs of the ladder. His wife had earned a good reputation as a college professor in math and philosophy and also as an influential speaker. *Wow,* she thought, *she certainly must have had a good head on her shoulders. And they had a gifted son.* Intelligence wise they were above average, but economically speaking they were upper middle class at best. She'd heard their home was modest and unpretentious and they were a model family. How could this happen? Why?

She heard Dave's car pull into the garage at the exact moment she desperately needed someone to talk to. She was there to greet him at the door.

"You look tired; want a cup of coffee or a glass of wine?"

"I'll take the wine," he said.

"Any new developments today?"

"No, not really. We went over details that we already knew about, but we did get to see the crime scene. And it was ghastly."

Sammi reacted a bit.

"Well, there was blood all over the place. Their family room is rather large and she was killed in the middle of it, yet the blood managed to reach the wall and sofa at the far end. And the house was messy. Someone or maybe more than one searched thoroughly for something."

"And who knows if they got it or not."

"That's true. We don't know that. Jim thought that if they had found what they were looking for, possibly one or more rooms would have been left intact, but they may have found it in the last room. Honestly, Sammi, I've seen a search mess before, but nothing like this. Everything was turned over or inside out. They sure tried to be thorough. Even their bookcase had books thrown all over the place. It was a sight."

"I'm wondering what they were looking for? What could these two people have that they were so desperate for?"

"I don't know. And who were they? We don't have a clue yet. But I'm sure Randy will have some ideas when we can get to him."

"No doubt. He must know what this is all about and that's probably why he needed some time to do ... whatever."

"Tom got a call from Jill just before we left for home. Denver was brought over this afternoon. She said he isn't talking at all, but he smiled a little when she said they were friends with his dad. Still he didn't talk."

After he ate dinner, Dave came to sit on the couch with Sammi. He took a couple of involuntary sighs and a large sip of wine as he tried to relax and make sense out of all this chaos.

He shook his head. "What does it all mean? I'm so blank on this one."

"I think everyone is, except for Randy. Let's wait and see. And you've got to relax now."

"Okay. By the way, you were good today. I think you impressed Amilio totally with your assessment of the pictures of that murder scene. Hell, I was impressed, too."

"Oh yeah, I impressed you, did I?" she said obviously pleased.

"Okay, I know you hear thoughts and that's remarkable, but that wasn't the case today. You have such an eye for detail; I don't think I realized it before, that's all."

She smiled.

"And now Amilio is trying to lasso us into helping him out. That's not fair, really. I'm available; we all are to help out on this one, too when we can. This was a real stumper and recently dumped on him. He'll need some help. But now, Amilio wants to use you, too."

"I think it's more than that."

Dave turned to look at her. "What do you mean?"

"It's bugging him that he can't figure out how I get information. He told me he was amazed that I was the one who realized he was the mole and said someday he'd figure me out."

Dave laughed aloud.

"But today, I think I confused him. What I talked about was right there in plain sight and he knew it. It wasn't anything mysterious. Now he thinks I've got an eye for detail."

"That's right. It was available for anyone paying attention."

"But he still thinks there's more to me than that."

"Does that make you nervous?"

"No, I'm rather used to it by now. Ben is still trying to figure me out and so is Jill's brother and now Amilio. Some day something might slip and one of them will find out what I can do. So be it. I'm sure any one of them would keep my secret and work with me. But I'm enjoying watching them try to figure me out. The journey is half the fun."

"Well, I'm still trying to figure you out, too," he said teasingly.

"And I hope it takes you the rest of your life."

CHAPTER THREE

By Wednesday, word was given that the referees would be allowed to meet with Randy. They were still holding him, but it was looking doubtful whether he would be arrested or not. Yet, he was still being referred to as a detained suspect. When he'd get out of jail was being kept under raps for now. He still hadn't chosen an attorney and wasn't talking so everyone was guessing about his fate.

By the time they got to the jail it was after lunch. Detective Statton was out on another matter, so they would be on their own. They were led to a conference room where they waited for him to be brought in.

"God, I'm getting nervous," said Tom. "These last several days have been tough."

"You settle down, Tom," said Dave. "We're all here working with you. This will be like any other case as far as looking at the evidence objectively. You can't afford to lose your perspective."

"I know, I know, but it's hard," he said as he put his head down.

Just then, the door opened and in walked Randy in handcuffs, but they were removed immediately. Tom went up to him straight away, and gave him a man's hug, and told him that they were all with him and would work their butts off to prove his innocence.

"Thanks. How's Denver?" asked Randy. "He's my first priority."

"We got him yesterday and so far he's not talking much at all, but he's eating and not crying anymore. I was told he had cried a lot at the other place. But he seems settled in with us and more comfortable since I told him you and I are friends."

"Tell him you saw me today, okay? And tell him I sent him this message, 'keep your thoughts strong.' That was sort of a secret message between Beth and him, so he'll know. That should help."

Randy had tears in his eyes. He looked embarrassed. Tom introduced him to Dave and Jim. "Tom's often mentioned you guys; I guess I should feel lucky that you're all together on this."

Again, Randy let out some tears. "Sorry," he said.

"We understand," said Jim.

"But there's a time for tears and this is not one of them. Give me a minute."

They all sat there for a few minutes allowing Randy time to get his emotions under control. Then, as if he turned a switch, he became calm and rational.

"So tell us your story," said Dave. "Tell us what you know."

"Okay, that day I came home about four o'clock and walked into ... have you guys seen the crime scene yet?"

They nodded.

"That's what I walked into, but more important, Denver was inside the closet. He must have seen everything. I asked him why he was in the closet and he said his mom had told him to get in the corner of the closet, kneel down and not make a sound. He knew."

"God, that's awful. I'm surprised he's holding up as well as he is," said Tom.

"He's a bright kid and ruled a lot by logic ... our whole family was like that. I mean we showed emotion and love ..." Randy needed another moment. "Look guys, I know my behavior has confused everyone, but it was necessary. When I saw what they did to the house, I knew immediately what they wanted ... and they didn't get it. I immediately got my camera and took pictures of the crime scene. I believed someone would try to contaminate it to make me look guilty. They got our gun away from Beth, and she knew how to use it, too."

Randy stopped again. So Tom asked, "Why didn't

you take your company's attorney?"

"I believe the company's behind this. There's corporate fraud and international secrets being compromised by them and they knew I was aware of some of it. I heard something accidentally because of my job, but they weren't taking any chances. I believe they killed Beth, who didn't know anything much at all, instead of me because now they can blame me and I'll look bad no matter what I say."

"That's why you didn't want their attorney?"

"Absolutely. As soon as I heard who it was I knew what they were doing. He'd have made me guilty for sure and most likely accomplished subversive goals through it. And I don't know what other attorneys they might have in their pocket. I can't take a chance and tell them what I know. I think even Denver would be in danger then."

"So what were they after?" asked Dave.

"Okay, a few months back I was in a meeting with some of the top guys. I've always had a lot of suspicions; hell, half the people working there know something's going on. But it was all kept well hidden away. Out of nowhere this man bursts into our meeting room and starts yelling and screaming all kind of threats to the CEO and upper managers. He said he had proof and they were going down on selling international secrets to China or Russia, one of them, that compromised the integrity of the United States. He said this time he would make sure that the charges would hold. When he was removed everyone looked considerably nervous, and there was a tête-à-tête and I wasn't included. When they finally remembered I was there, well, you can imagine the stiffness that I got from everyone. I knew I was in big trouble."

"God, they really are crooks," said Jim. "I know this company has beaten the odds many times in court on these same types of charges."

"Well, they've been lucky so far, but evidence is piling up."

Dave asked, "Whatever happened to that man?"

"He turned up dead about a week later. They said it was suicide and that he'd had a breakdown and had been exhibiting delusional behavior. The verdict was accepted and his meltdown that day didn't help. Nothing was even investigated."

"Holy Cow," said Tom. "You must have known you were in danger. Why didn't you call us?"

"Honestly, I thought it would be more like being fired, or that they would try to prove that I was the one who had leaked information. That's why I made copies of pertinent data. I know they didn't catch me doing it, but they've always been suspicious of me even before. But I never thought they'd resort to murder."

"And that information was in your house?"

"I had copied it on computer, on paper and on microchip and had an extra copy in our bank vault. I knew Beth was dead; I checked her out, so they'll have evidence of me next to her body. But I was careful not to disturb anything else. And I did take a lot of pictures of every room in the house, just in case. I've hidden everything in separate locations. That's why I needed those few days."

"That should be helpful," said Tom.

"I need to find an attorney I can trust. They're so spread out that I don't think that will be easy."

"We'll have to think about that one," said Dave.

"Okay, then," said Tom. "Denver is the one who found the body, right?"

Randy had a bunch of involuntary tears coming down his face. "Well, she was alive when he got home from school. I guess the men, and Denver said there were three of them, drove up and started walking slowly toward the front door. Beth apparently recognized one of them and immediately went for the gun and told Denver to stay in the closet. You see, she'd given several presentations at ASAC in the past few years so she knew some people there. And that was another problem. The top guy, Matthew Carnigan had the hots for her. She finally refused to go there at all anymore and this guy was infuriated. He was always after her and when she wouldn't put up with it anymore; he took it personal. She was good at her work and he planned to use her to make an inroad into the European market for them. So you see they hated both of us for different reasons."

"Gees," said Dave. "That kid must have seen the whole thing."

"He at least heard it. He didn't even come out when I first got home. He was too scared. But when he heard the flashes of my camera, he peeked out and then saw it was me."

Randy couldn't go on. He was too emotional and sat there, embarrassed yet unable to stop the tears. After all, he was still mourning the death of his wife, whom he loved deeply.

"Take it easy, Randy," said Tom. "That's enough for now, unless there's anything else of major importance that you want us to know."

"Those are the major things, but there are tons of details as you can imagine. I've got to make sure Denver is okay. When I get out I need to see him right away."

"Of course," said Tom. "I want you to stay with us."

"Oh no, that's not a good idea. I think they might still be after me. I'll put everyone in danger."

"Why?" said Dave. "I would think they'd want your story to play out in court and then they can challenge everything you say. That would play right into their hands."

"Sure," said Jim, "they want you alive right now. It's in their best interest."

Randy hadn't thought about it that way. That could be true. And it would help Denver if he was around. God, he didn't know what to do.

"Have they given you any clue as to arresting you or not?" asked Tom.

"No, they haven't, but I overheard a couple of guards talking this morning and they hinted that they might have to let me go soon."

"Okay, then," said Tom. "The first thing you do is call me and I'll come and get you."

"Gees, Tom, are you sure?"

The referees seemed to agree on this one. Randy was worth more to ASAC alive than dead.

* * *

They met outside and talked at length before they dispersed.

"Damn, this is going to be one complicated mess," said Jim. "As we get more details from Randy I think this corporate crap is going to be big. Julie will be a good one on this case."

"No doubt," said Dave. "We'll have to let the sarge know right away. If there's anything concerning fraud or national safety involved, I think he might call Ben Collier. Also, I was thinking that lawyer we had, Ken Richardson might be good. Or what if we asked Ben to recommend one? What do you think?"

"That's an idea," said Tom. "He's got to get a lawyer, that's for sure, but one we can trust."

"Okay then, let's get back right now and meet with the sarge. We've got to get this ball rolling the right way."

So it was back to the Scranton office to meet with a very surprised sergeant who couldn't believe this latest twist.

"Holy shit. What on earth do we have here? Murder, espionage, crimes against national security? But what about proof? What do we have?"

"Randy does have some proof, but how much or if it's enough, I don't know. But that proof is what Beth was killed for. That's what they were looking for."

"And he's worried about the right lawyer. I can't blame him there. Who knows who else this company's got on the take. We have enough indications here that I'm going to call Ben Collier and let him decide. No surprise, right? He needs to get in on the ground floor. And he might have some good ideas for us, too. We'll meet again, probably tomorrow as soon as I talk to him."

* * *

"My God. What's that company all about anyway? It sounds like a front for something else," asked Sammi.

"Good point. No one is sure right now. Julie's looking into it."

"Yeah, we talked a little at lunch, but she said that nothing was ever proven against this ASAC group, although they did get charged with a lot of things."

"That's what happens when you've got a lot of high priced lawyers. And that's why Randy wants to be real careful what lawyer he gets."

"I can understand that; so now what?"

"Sergeant Brady is going to connect with our old friend Ben Collier and see what ideas he has. If this turns out to have anything to do with the safety of the United States, the feds will be all over this. And, of course, he might have an idea for an attorney."

"Right. So as of now, it's another waiting game."

"It looks that way. But I'd guess that he'll call the sarge back right away when he hears what it's about."

"I'd think so."

"So for tonight that's about it. Sad about that little guy, though. When his dad gets released and moves in, I'd think that would help him a lot."

"That'll make a big difference."

After a few minutes of silence, the atmosphere seemed to relax a little. It prompted Dave to ask, "Has everything been pretty quiet around the bank lately?"

"Seems that way; we haven't had any problems. There hasn't been that much in the last couple of years. But then the president usually uses me as a lookout anyway. I'm to try to find a problem before it happens. So I've been able to ward off a few potential complications."

Dave nodded. "That's good, especially right now. I think we're going to need you for a while again."

"The president understands my role. And if the FBI is in this again, they'll get the okay for me. Approval's hardly needed anymore anyway."

Dave started his ten o'clock yawning routine. With so many long days and multiple problems on his mind his body started shutting down about this hour.

Sammi teased, "I think it's your bedtime. You need to get more rest to keep up with all this stuff going on."

"Right, I'm so beat these days, but I've been getting sleep."

"Not enough honey. Six hours is nothing for all the stress you're under. Try to get eight hours tonight, okay? You need it."

"And keep your schedule open for Thursday. I think Amilio is trying to get an appointment with that prostitute."

"Okay. That's a big interest to me. It's another murder and even though she turned out to be a prostitute ... well, I'd like to know her story before I make any judgments about her."

"She deserves every consideration as far as I'm concerned." Dave's jaw took on a stern position. "This is another murder that shouldn't have happened."

* * *

The phone rang and startled them both. Ten o'clock phone calls usually spelled trouble, but it was Jill.

"Hi, Sammi, sorry to call so late. Tom and I were talking and thought it would be so helpful if you could stop by for a few minutes tomorrow, if possible. This kid isn't talking at all. He's eating and seems calm enough, but he won't say one word. We've gotten a smile out of him and he doesn't seem afraid, but ..."

"Of course, when do you want me?"

"Maybe tomorrow or Thursday, whatever's best for you. I'd like to get the beginning of a conversation with him and you'd know what's on his mind. We do know what's on his mind in a way, but I know you could figure out how to get him to talk a little."

"I'd be glad to try."

"I'd invite you and Dave over for dinner, but that's not the atmosphere I want. I wanted something casual, that won't scare him and, gee, I don't know."

"Look you're doing all you can right now. Take it easy. I'll stop by tomorrow after work, okay?"

"That'd be great, Sammi. Thanks."

"Sure. See ya then."

She looked over at Dave as she put down the phone. He'd heard the conversation; she didn't have to say anything.

Dave said, "It must be rough trying to get through to that kid. And imagine what he has bottled up inside of him. He hasn't been able to talk to his dad, the only parent he has left."

"Do they have any relatives around?" asked Sammi.

"I was thinking about that on the way home. Not that I've ever heard of. I think Tom said Randy mentioned a brother on a missionary venture in some other country, but I don't remember where. I'm not sure about Beth. And their parents ...." He didn't finish.

"Denver would know that."

"Yes, we'll have to ask him, if needed. I wonder if someone else should be notified. But I would think Randy would have said something."

She nodded. "I'll stop by tomorrow and see what I can find out, although I hear that Denver's rather smart. He may be the one who'll catch on to what I do. I'll have to be careful."

In spite of the situation, Dave had to smile. "Yeah, a little kid would be the one to find out about you. How funny."

Even Sammi had to laugh at that thought.

* * *

The next day Dave had barely enough time to walk into his office, unlock his desk and check his phone for messages before Sergeant Brady called them into a meeting. He'd spoken to Ben Collier who was quite excited about the latest events.

"It seems Ben is very familiar with ASAC Globe Ventures, Inc. They've had them under surveillance for a few years and they've been close to nabbing them at times, but they always seem to squirrel their way out of trouble at the last minute. The last time was the closest they came to convicting them but they did plea out to some much lesser infractions and ended up paying some fines, but that's all. This sounds like bigger stakes to him."

"So he's interested in helping out?"

"Oh yes, in fact as of right now the FBI is involved, and they might use Amilio again, if it's feasible. After all, he still technically works for them. Don't know the details yet; he said he'd get back to me on that."

"Okay, what about a lawyer for Randy? Did he have any ideas?" asked Tom.

"What about Ken Richardson?" asked Jim. "He was terrific."

"But he's a prosecuting attorney," said the sarge. "What Randy needs is a defense lawyer. I mentioned it to Ben and he'll get back to me on that within a day."

Silence covered the group for a few minutes.

"Listen guys, this lit a fire under Ben. He's going to talk to his superiors right away. Not sure if they'll send another agent here, like he said, we've got Amilio and he's one of their best. But regardless he'll get back with me by tomorrow and give us at least some of the details."

"In the meantime, Randy's still in jail."

"Looks that way for now."

"It's already the 16th of December. I was hoping he'd make it out before Christmas. It would mean a lot to his kid," said Tom.

"We'll all know a lot more tomorrow. I just hit Ben with this a few minutes ago. He knows we need to know what stance the FBI will take and he'll get back to us as soon as he can. But until then, we better stay on hold. Concentrate on your other stuff. That's all."

And they were dismissed.

* * *

They gathered at Dave's desk, which was the usual pattern for them. For a few minutes, they sat looking at each other trying to get a handle on the situation. They were again in a waiting mode.

"God, I wonder when we'll finally start working on this case. Everything tells us to stop and wait. We can't seem to move forward," said Tom. "In the meantime, Randy's still in jail, can't see his son and doesn't have a lawyer. It's been almost four days since he turned himself in."

"Following the law sucks at times," said Jim. "I imagine Ben will get the ball rolling fast. In the meantime, let's get our Scranton stuff out of the way. I'm sure we won't have much time later on."

"Good idea," Dave said. "Luckily I'm pretty caught up right now. Any of you guys need my help?"

They both shook their heads. They were all in a waiting position right now. And Ben was holding the ball. A few routine calls came in, which was almost welcomed and kept their minds off the task ahead. This crime would take all the talent they had and Sammi was a big part of that.

* * *

Sammi walked into Jill's home a little after five o'clock. Denver was sitting in the far corner of the family room and barely lifted his head as she entered. Jill brought her over to him. He still managed, even in his unimaginable frame of mind, to have some hint of manners about him. He gave Sammi a slight smile before he looked down again and went off into his private world. Jill found reason to leave the room and give Sammi an opportunity to work with him.

She situated herself on a chair nearby and waited. Denver's mind was filled with shock and disbelief even now, so that most of his thoughts were beneath the surface and rather deep in his subconscious. When that happened, she couldn't hear anything. It reminded her of the time when Dave had been shot and was in a coma for five days. Much of that time she couldn't hear anything as his feelings and ideas were too deeply buried, but slowly they began to rise up as he gradually came out of his unconscious state.

So Sammi sat patiently waiting, but decided to offer a few comments to bring him back to the surface a little.

"I understand you're ten years old, Denver. You've been through a lot for a young boy." She said this as softly as she could, barely above a whisper.

His eyes didn't move, but his thoughts came closer to the surface and told her that he liked the sound of her voice. It was caring and smooth and not harsh at all. Sammi took notice. She was aware that we all had our own private representational system. Some people had to see things to understand, others had to hear things and others had to feel things. Although it was true that everyone used all three systems and other sub-ones, they usually reacted strongest to their main system. And Sammi knew immediately that Denver's main system was hearing. So she talked to him with that in mind.

"Tell me, Denver, it's so quiet in this room. Would you like to hear some music?"

His eyes reacted slightly, but then seemed to go back to their old disenchanted glare. He was thinking -- *they'd never play what I like. I like classical, like Liszt and Chopin. I know not many people like that.*

Sammi took note. It wasn't something she could manufacture out of thin air, but if Jill picked up a few albums, it could put Denver at ease. But she took a chance anyway.

"My favorite is Lieberstraum. Do you like it?"

Denver looked over at her and held eye contact for a moment. Surprisingly he said, "That was my mom's favorite." But with that came tears, which were welcomed by Sammi. He was showing some emotion, at least.

"What else did she like?"

He gazed in her direction and it was obvious he wanted to say something. Finally he commented, "She liked the piano concertos." He pursed his lips in remembrance and then put his head down again.

Then Sammi started a serious conversation being careful to hold that tone of voice that had started everything.

"How are you doing, Denver? Can you tell me?"

He shook his head and then said, "I want to see my dad."

"I know you do. And we're trying to help him. He did send a message for you."

Denver's eyes got real big and he shifted in his chair placing his body in anxious expectancy. "What? What did my dad say?"

"He said to tell you what your mom always said, "Keep your thoughts strong."

It seemed that calmness came over his entire body. It was as if his total being took a deep breath and inhaled the instructions that he'd forgotten. After a few more deep breaths, which he took while in his own world, he turned to look at Sammi.

"My mom had a special connection to the universe, you know. She taught me a lot of things."

The intelligence of this young lad was quite apparent in his sentence syntax and in his pronunciation of words. During this time, Sammi could hear Denver trying to remember the sound of his mom's voice. The thought flashed through his young mind when his mom told him, "Get in the closet, kneel down, stay quiet and don't move."

Sammi took another chance. "And your mom kept you safe right until the end, didn't she?"

He nodded.

"She must have loved you very much."

He nodded again.

"I'm sorry for what happened to your mom."

Then Denver started crying and Sammi went over and sat by him. She put her arms around him and let him cry as he grabbed on to her. Jill came back into the room and together they sat and talked with him.

He looked up at Jill and said, "I'm not mad at you,

but sometimes I don't feel like talking."

"I understand," she said.

Then Sammi added, "But sometimes it does help to talk a little."

He took a deep breath and agreed.

Sammi got up to leave. She had served her purpose by opening the door to communication with Denver, however slight. His thoughts were of trust and feeling safe in this household, but he desperately wanted to see his dad. His heart was aching to see the one parent he had left. And he didn't understand what had happened. He had gruesome memories on his mind, which occasionally flashed up into his consciousness. She could tell he was trying to deal with them, but couldn't and pushed them back down where he didn't have to think about their horrifying reality. Also there was another thought, which concerned Sammi; Denver had a secret. She caught the colors around it. It wouldn't be something that he would think about logically for a long time, but he had a secret and he kept it guarded with all he had.

CHAPTER FOUR

After lunch on Thursday Sammi met Dave at the police station. Amilio had made the appointment for two o'clock with the manager at the Castaways bar to determine the best way to contact Charmaine Bolder.

"I've read the transcripts of the earlier interview," said Dave. "There wasn't much there. I'll bet that they didn't even spend twenty minutes with her."

"Shame," answered Sammi, "she might have known a lot."

Dave frowned. It didn't seem right. Nobody seemed to care about this prostitute because of her profession. Yet she was a human being who deserved as much respect as anyone else. Society seemed to have its benchmarks.

"I agree. That's not right. Hopefully with Amilio's help we can give this person the proper attention."

It was obvious that Dave was irked at the lack of attention on this case. He looked further into the file, hoping that someone had put in an extra note or explained an extra detail, but there was nothing there.

His last comment was "This is shameful."

At this moment, Amilio came in.

"Hey amigo, you look so serious."

"Yeah, well, it bugs me that no one did anything on this. We don't usually work this way. Who had this case?"

"I think it was Officer Donner, but to his credit, he had four other things going on at the same time; that's what he told me. I think someone else gave him his priorities."

Dave went back to reading the file.

"And you amiga, how're you doing today?"

"I'm ready for this interview. But I need to ask how do you feel about this case? You always have a rather casual take on everything, but I'm curious about your feelings on this one."

Sammi already knew how he felt and it was close to Dave's attitude. But she was curious as to what he'd say out loud. Although Amilio was always trying to figure out how Sammi worked, she had some questions about him.

"You know, back home in Mexico, we had a lot of prostitutes. It was the only way some of them could support themselves and help their families. I know it's not the best profession, but I think you have to look at the person and why they're doing it. That could tell you a lot."

Dave said, "Nobody's all good or bad. I'm curious about this one."

"In Mexico a lot of people think prostitution is okay. It's just another way to make a living. Here in America, people think differently."

As the clock passed the one thirty mark, they decided it was time to leave and see what this case was all about.

* * *

As it turned out Charmaine Bolder no longer worked at the Castaways. She had moved on shortly after Tina's death and her last known address provided no help. But the manager was helpful with some information about both of his former employees. And he thought that Charmaine liked a certain area of town and gave them a clue as to where to ask around about her. It took an entire day, but they found her. She was working a new club in the suggested district called The Bounty.

Knowing the evening hours were the best time to catch Charmaine, they arrived early on Friday night and were noticed by almost everyone in the place as they entered. The bouncer came up immediately and asked them to sit at a nearby table saying he would get the owner.

"Hello, I'm Rich Sanfield. I own this place. What do you want with Charmaine?"

"We need to ask her some questions regarding the death of Tina O'Leary several months back."

"I remember that. It happened when she was working at the Castaways. Too bad, I heard she wasn't a bad broad."

"Can we talk to Charmaine? Is she here?" asked Amilio.

"Yeah," then he turned and yelled loudly at the bouncer. "Get Charmaine out here." Turning back to the group he said in a softer tone of voice, "You can sit here and interview her right at this table. It's less obvious that way. Okay with you?"

Dave and Amilio nodded.

Within a few moments a rather attractive girl, about thirty years old, with a lot of makeup, flashy jewelry and skimpy clothes approached their table.. She plopped herself down in the empty chair and seemed confused about the visit.

"I thought her case was closed a while back. No one ever found out anything so I thought she ended up in one of those cold case files I hear about."

Sammi noticed immediately that she talked quite intelligently and had knowledge of the English language. She didn't slur her words or swear, or use improper slang. She was educated and could hold her own.

"You knew Tina, right?"

She nodded.

"What can you tell us about her?"

"Probably anything you want to know," she said and then took a moment to look back in time. She seemed comfortable and at ease even as she stared at two policemen and another woman waiting to interrogate her.

Then she continued. "Let's see, she was proper, even for this profession. And she handled herself with dignity and class. She was one of the more refined people I've known. And she wasn't dumb. Many people think all of us are illiterate, but we're not. And Tina was certainly one of the brighter ones."

"You're not dumb either, Charmaine. What college did you go to?" asked Sammi.

Both of the guys reacted. They felt Charmaine was not as bad as some they had met, but how could Sammi know that she had gone to college?

Sammi was quite sure from the beginning that this gal was well educated. Partly, it was her use of certain words, but mostly her pronunciation and phrasing. In fact, she believed if she closed her eyes, she could picture herself talking to Charmaine in any educational setting she knew. And Charmaine's thoughts maintained a strong level of knowing.

Charmaine smiled back at her. "You're pretty sharp; I don't think these guys realized. But I did graduate from a local college back in my home town."

"What did you study?"

"I was studying to be a teacher."

"Specializing in what?"

Charmaine paused for a moment and said, "Sammi, I'd imagine you'd have a good guess, right? Go ahead."

"I'd guess English. You have a good command of the language."

"And you'd be correct." She turned to the guys. "You'd better pay attention to this gal, she notices things."

Dave showed some pride. He knew that Sammi was building up a rapport with Charmaine which could be valuable. Again, Amilio was impressed watching Sammi work first-hand.

When she was ready, she turned her attention back to Sammi. "Okay, sweetie, what questions do you want to ask me?"

And that's how the interview started, with a definite decision by Charmaine that she would deal mainly with Sammi, whom she liked immediately.

"We're trying to find out as much as we can about Tina. Was she educated like you?" Sammi wanted to stay on the same theme as a way to keep Charmaine in a good frame of mind, but also she had heard some thoughts on her mind and realized that learning was one of the reasons these two girls had built up a friendship. And Charmaine knew things. Of this Sammi was certain.

"She didn't graduate, but she did go to college. And she read everything she could get her hands on. She was quite bright, like I said, smarter than me. She read stuff like Emerson and Thoreau; can you believe it? I'll bet you guys are shocked. But I'm telling you, she was clever."

"Why do you think she was working here? Did she ever have another job that you knew of?"

"Yeah, she did some accounting stuff a while back. She was good with math, but she wanted to be hidden away. She had good reason."

Sammi waited and simply looked at Charmaine who was trying to decide what more she should say. So she egged her on some.

"I heard she left the Castaways early that night because she had an appointment. Do you know anything about that?"

The look on her face said it all. They waited. The guys let Sammi take the lead. She had built up an instant rapport and was doing quite well. She also knew when to give this woman a little more time and not rush her. Trying to push her could possibly get her to clam up and then she wouldn't say anything. But Sammi found her thoughts revealing.

About this time, a waitress came around to take an order. Coffee was offered and they all accepted.

"No one paid much attention to me the first time they came around. I knew things and nobody would listen to me."

"I'm listening," said Sammi. "We all are."

She looked over at the two guys, felt satisfied with their interested expressions and pressed on. "I had to keep some information to myself because nobody cared much; after all they thought of her as only a prostitute, but she was much more than that. I'll tell you her story as I know it. I don't know for sure if Tina was married or not, but she hooked up with this guy a while back. I think she was an accountant back then. Anyway, she got pregnant and had a little boy. Soon after, this guy started roughing her up. I think he started when she was still pregnant because she told me she was afraid it would hurt the baby. Anyway, by the time the baby was several months old, she took off. He had slapped her around a bit and that was bad enough, but when he slapped the baby, she was horrified. She was afraid for her baby in that environment. She went into hiding in another state for a while--I think this happened in California, but I'm not positive about that. He found her again and again because she found work as a secretary, accountant and jobs like that."

When she took a breather, it gave Dave a moment to look over at Sammi. He was amazed by her lately, more so than usual. Sammi looked over and when she caught his glance, she looked away quickly. They were both happy when Charmaine continued with a little encouragement from Sammi.

"I can appreciate the fact that this is difficult for you. I get the impression that you two became very close."

"We did. People out there forget that we're human. Everyone has a different story as to why they ended up in this line of work, but usually it's out of some sort of desperation. At any rate, Tina needed to survive and take care of her son. Her ex threatened her many times and said he would take away the boy. That really scared her so she moved here and took a profession where he'd never find her."

"What happened to the boy?" asked Amilio.

"Well, that's a story I don't know too well. I know she didn't have much family and once told me that even if she did, she'd never leave the boy with them. He'd most likely find him, claim fatherhood, and be able to take him. But she'd found a place somewhere and I don't know where that is; honestly, if I did know, I probably wouldn't tell you. However, I do know the last couple of weeks she'd gotten real nervous. She told me she thought her ex was closing in. Don't know why or how, but she was scared."

"What was her reason to leave early that night?"

"I'm not entirely sure, but it did have something to do with finding a way to make sure this ex of hers couldn't find her. And, most of the money she made went for the care of this child. Now that's not a sleazy person."

"I do agree, Charmaine. She was something special," said Sammi.

The guys had remained silent, but were in agreement. This put Charmaine at ease. Sammi knew that she realized someone was finally interested in Tina's murder.

"Do you know this ex's name or where we could find him?"

"That I don't," she said with some hesitancy. "I think she had the baby in California, maybe around Los Angeles, at least she talked about LA occasionally, so I'm guessing he was from there. But a few weeks before she died she said, "If anything happens to me they should look to Bobby. He's wanted me dead for a long time."

Sammi caught a few other thoughts on her mind. She knew more, much more, but she wasn't ready yet to share. She'd give her more time. But she had to get that information out of her, which was kept quite hidden at this time.

This ended the interview. Nevertheless, Sammi gave her a card and said if she remembered anything else to call her anytime. She also told her how much she appreciated the information she'd given them. There was no doubt about the pride that crossed Charmaine's face and stature as she rose from the table. Some of her lost pride was invigorated and her self-importance reconfirmed.

* * *

Amilio was the first one to speak as they left. "How the hell could you tell she'd been to college?"

"Her command of the English language was excellent. She wasn't using unnecessary nasty language as a cover up or improper slang and she didn't talk sloppy in any way. Her pronunciation of certain words was a dead giveaway to me; she knew how to pronounce words with ease."

"Yeah," said Amilio, "I did notice that she talked better than most, but I don't think I would have jumped in with that college bit. What if you were wrong?"

"It still would have been a compliment to her. But I wasn't wrong."

Sammi had heard the thought about college on Charmaine's mind and she knew Dave was aware. But Amilio's interest was stimulated.

"Well, I'm impressed with you. As soon as you acknowledged that, she instantly became your friend. We got a lot of information out of her."

"I think she was ready to talk to anyone she thought would listen," said Sammi in an unassuming manner. "She's been keeping a lot inside for quite a while."

Dave had been holding back and enjoyed hearing them banter back and forth.

"A lot of this trail is cold, but if we can backtrack some info to California, we may find some lead," said Amilio. "California's a big state, but we know the child was born around Los Angeles about five years ago, at least that's what Charmaine thinks. And her ex's first name is Bobby. We know Tina's real last name, too, so we have somewhere to start. It's worth a shot."

"In the meantime, I'm going to invite Charmaine out for lunch in the next few weeks. I think she might have more to tell me."

The guys looked over at her and couldn't disagree. No doubt two gals alone would help her open up. But Sammi had another reason. Many times she could hear more thoughts from people if they were in a calmer atmosphere. She had already heard a few noteworthy suggestions from Charmaine. It wasn't anything she was ready to talk about, but ideas and quiet innuendos seemed to come her way better in certain settings.

* * *

Later that night Dave was amused and shared. "You really had Amilio going today. He thinks you're a mystery."

Sammi smiled. "But I didn't hear too many thoughts from her today. She stayed quite guarded and when people do that, their thoughts get down to that lower level that I can't always hear."

"So you didn't hear her thinking that she had been to college?"

"It crossed her mind quickly, but I wasn't sure from her thoughts whether she attended or simply wanted to. It was mostly from outward observation and I decided to take a chance and ask. Didn't think there was much to lose."

Now even Dave seemed impressed, but he was also thoughtful.

"Okay, what's on your mind?"

He laughed. "Well, if you must know, I think it's a shame that no one bothered about this case. Most of the trail is cold by now and something could have possibly led somewhere back then. I mean, it's another murder around here that should have had an honest attempt at being solved."

"That's true, but Amilio said that there was a lot going on at that time. What else was going on, do you know?"

"No, I'd have to look that up, but I'd like to know more. And who decided on the priorities at that time? Sergeant Brady wouldn't tell anyone to put a murder like this on the backburner for any reason."

"That might be something good to know. What were you working on? ... When was it? ... I'm guessing about seven months ago?"

"I'm going to get the file out on this one again. I don't even know for sure when that murder happened.

And what were Tom, Jim and I doing at that time? In fact, I was wondering if you and I were even back from Philly. Something doesn't add up. I know I heard about this one, but certainly, no one was talking much about it. And now, I wonder why."

"Did they finish with those pictures yet? I had asked Amilio to get a blowup of her right hand. She was holding something and neither one of us could make it out."

"That's right and that seemed strange. When a person fights for her life, as she apparently did, how could she have something in her hand? Seems to me it must have been planted by someone after she died. Maybe we've got a clue here. You know Amilio is right. You do notice things."

"Just my normal curiosity. All the pieces have to fit for me, so if anything's out of place it bugs me."

Dave smiled, but he had a renewed interest in this case. And he liked working with both Amilio and Sammi. They were both experts in a different way and a thought-provoking team to be around.

* * *

The next day, being the 20th of December, Dave was happy to call Sammi at the bank and give her some news.

"What's up?"

"They're letting Randy out of jail today. They figured they couldn't hold him any longer without charging him and they don't seem ready to do that. Tom is picking him up this afternoon."

"That's great."

"But we can't get too excited; we're all suspicious about this one. They could yank him back at any time under any pretext, and he's been warned to stay close by. So Jim and I are meeting with him and Tom tonight. We've got to get all the facts while we can. Honestly, Sammi, I've got a feeling they're going to arrest him within a few days."

"That seems crazy."

"I know, but there's a law about holding someone

too long without charging them. I don't remember the length of time exactly; it's a legal question. But I think they're letting him go for a while to circumvent the law and then they'll bring him in again.

"Like a crazy cat and mouse thing."

"Right. Tom wants you there tonight. We've got to take advantage of this time with him while we can."

"Whatever happened with the lawyer thing? Have you heard from Ben?"

"No, I think he'd call Sergeant Brady. They keep postponing us on everything, but now I hope things can move forward. Look, honey, I have to go. Stay open for tonight, okay?"

"Right."

Sammi couldn't help feeling a little encouraged by the latest developments. At least Denver would get to see his dad for a little while, and if he did have to go back to jail, he'd be sure in his mind that Tom and Jill and his dad were all good friends and that should help him tremendously. It seemed that Denver had opened up a little with Jill after Sammi met with him. And she did buy some classical music which put him in the same frame of mind that he'd experienced at home. It jogged his mind and memory.

* * *

When Sammi and Dave arrived at Tom's home that night, the atmosphere was thick with both excitement and worry. Randy was in a frenzy, but trying to keep himself stable for his son, who'd noticeably improved when his dad walked through the door. Their reunion brought happy tears and it took a few minutes before anyone could settle down. Denver needed the proper affection from his dad, the only one who could give it to him. And, as expected, the rapport of father and son helped smooth the situation and calm the entire group.

"You've been a brave boy, Denver. I'm proud of you."

Denver barely nodded, but had a hard time taking

at a distant college and she said she found a greeting card on her podium from this Matthew Carnigan. It said, "Don't forget me because I'll never forget you." It was always something and we were living a nightmare."

"All this was happening because he wanted her to give lectures in other countries? Isn't that rather extreme?"

"Well, that was part of it. These lectures were to promote their activities in other countries and if it hurt the U.S., they didn't care. Their end goal was making as much money as they could, and getting as much control and power as possible. Remember Beth was good at influencing people. Of course, Beth would have no part of it. But now, she knew what they were doing and they let her know that no one could get out of their group."

"She must have been scared," said Dave.

"After that, she was, but we kept holding on. We were stupid. I know we both thought that if we played it straight they might move on to someone else. But I especially should have known that they don't work that way."

"You mentioned subversive, in what way?"

"For one thing, they were ready to trade government secrets which they had privy to with other countries for special equipment deals which would gain them almost a monopoly in certain areas for their firm. It's usually about money or power for these guys. It's hard to make ordinary people realize the egos of these power people. They feel they're entitled to anything they want and won't stop until they get it. We should have sought help a long time ago."

Randy had tears again. He felt he should have known and was therefore responsible.

"What about a lawyer? Did you get one yet?" asked Tom.

"That's going to be the hardest part. I don't know who I can trust and I can't let this information get into the wrong hands. I don't know what to do."

"Give us a few more days. My sergeant may have an

idea there."

"In the meantime, I'm going to spend all my time with Denver. I don't think they'll leave me out here free for any length of time. They probably think I'll high tail it to where I've got the evidence stashed, but there are three places involved and each place does contain a complete set of the evidence. I was playing the odds. But with Beth gone, a lot of this doesn't seem worth it."

"But you've got Denver," said Jill. "And he's definitely worth it."

"That he is," said Randy and showed the first sign of a smile on his face all night.

Randy was exhausted and this ended everything for the evening. He needed the best lawyer that was available and they would need all the help they could get. The details of this case were unbelievably mystifying and never seemed to end. A good lawyer would also need a strong team of special investigators on this one.

* * *

Sammi was quiet on the way home. At first, Dave thought it was because of the emotions involved in this case. It was hard to settle down. Young Denver seemed to be the most logical in this entire group. Yet whether that was good or bad was yet to be determined. Finally, Dave couldn't stand it and had to ask.

"What's on your mind?"

She turned to him knowing he always sensed when she was troubled. "This situation has all my emotions in turmoil. First, that little kid witnessing the murder of his mother. I don't care how smart he is, he's having an unbelievably rough time. Then Randy finding his wife like that, and of course, Tom was right; he wasn't involved in any way. His story is exactly as he told it. And he really loved his wife. He's the one I'm worried about right now. He's ready to break. Tom should get him to his doctor for something to help him cope, at least for a while."

"This isn't a fun time, is it? I've almost forgotten we're so close to Christmas. Hard to turn it on and off, isn't it?"

Sammi said, "True, and we've got the death of that prostitute, too. We must remember that she had a five-year-old, too, so that's another kid without a mother or father to raise him."

They were both quiet after that. Their line of work could be depressing at times. And the holidays didn't make it any better. *Oh well,* thought Sammi, *it won't be long before we take off for a week in Aruba. We sure need that vacation this year.*

CHAPTER FIVE

It took a couple of days for Ben Collier to get in touch with them. His superiors were enthusiastic at the possibility that this time they might have a good chance to get something on this company and damage them for a long time. They were playing for big stakes and the reputation of America could be in the balance.

"Okay," said the sarge to his group, "we've got an attorney for Randy. He's good; he's very, very good and he's retained by the FBI. This is going down as a gamble for the security of this county so whatever Randy knows will be effectively logged in that way."

They all nodded, but weren't sure how this would play out.

"He'll be here probably tomorrow, to start some of the preliminaries; I understand he's one of their best. I know they want all the information they can get on this group and since Randy hasn't been arrested yet, that's what they'll concentrate on. I think he'll have others with him and together they want to target this ASAC group."

"And this way," said Dave, "we'll be able to get a better idea of what this ASAC group is planning against Randy. We should be privy to some of the inside information, right?"

"I'd think so. We'll be in their confidence as much as they'll allow us, because they'll need our help, too. But at least it'll mean that Randy will get some decent representation."

"Yeah," Tom said, "and if they do arrest him, we've got someone that can help immediately. That's great; I feel better about this already."

"Okay, that's all for now. I wanted to let you guys

know about the attorney."

* * *

The group was in a better frame of mind when they gathered at Dave's desk.

"I wonder how many attorneys the FBI will put on this case," Tom said.

"Good question. They'll be even more in the background than we'll get to see. But that's good. It's hard to fight these big companies." Jim was quite serious about that.

"I'm sure the FBI will use investigators from their own division," Dave added, "but we're right here and we know these people and this area. I'm glad that we'll be in the middle of it."

"I'd think they'll consult with us," said Jim.

"Oh, I'm sure they will," said Dave. "We'll have to wait and see how this one plays out. I know they'll be running this game their own way."

Then Dave's phone rang and the group split up. Dave listened for a few minutes and shook his head in disbelief as he put down the phone. *God*, he thought, but couldn't help an involuntary smirk. *Another speeder caught on Highway 6, near Blakeley. He was drunk, had no driver's license, no insurance, but insisted that he should be let go because he was a nice guy and an upstanding citizen.* Officer Humphrey couldn't help but share this one with Dave.

"Hey Dave, you and Sammi want to come over tonight?" asked Tom. He came over as soon as he saw him get off the phone. "I mean you don't have to, but if you're not doing anything it might help if we could get Sammi to figure out where little Denver is at this time."

"How's he doing?"

"Well, he seems better the last few days with his dad there. But even Randy thinks there's something not right. Like I said, if you have a little spare time, we'd appreciate it."

"I'll check with Sammi. We can find a few minutes,

I'm sure."

"That's great. It's so close to Christmas, but of course, not a happy occasion for Randy and Denver."

"I can imagine. We'll hang in there, buddy. We'll stop by sometime tonight for a few minutes."

When Tom walked away, Dave thought that this was not an easy position for them either. Dealing with the little boy in such a precarious state of mind was difficult alone, but then Randy had lost his wife and would no doubt be arrested for a crime that he hadn't committed. And he had an entire corporation to fight for his reputation and possibly right some of the wrong this group had done. It seemed impossible and unachievable. He thought about his father and wondered, w*hat would he say right now?* He smiled for a moment as he realized that he had told Sammi repeatedly about his father's philosophy. *Follow the clues, one at a time, and they'll lead you to the truth.*

* * *

At dinner Dave knew he was dumping his burden on Sammi, but couldn't help it. He needed to discuss things.

"I can't help but wonder if Randy has a chance in this game. Those companies play for keeps and even though the FBI has good lawyers, I would guess that they have many experts as well."

"I'm sure they do. They didn't get away free and clear in those other trials without the best representation they could find. This will be quite a battle as it plays out."

Dave puckered his lips and shook his head. "God, it's one thing after another. It never ends."

"Hey, you knew that when you got into this profession. You're getting overwhelmed right now. You can't afford to do that. We've got a long way to go on this one. And it's not entirely on your shoulders, remember that."

He smiled. She was right. He was taking everything so personal. In fact, it was possible that his ego was getting too big. Not everything depended on him alone; he was only a small part of it.

"I always need you to keep my perspective in

check."

"I get that way now and then. It's normal, but we'll do the best we can and let the universe take over. All we can do is plant the ideas out there and believe in them."

"It's so simple for you, isn't it? I'm envious."

"Dave, it's not simple at all. Anyone who thinks that believing in something you want to happen is easy just doesn't get it. You have to keep a knowing about yourself and in yourself and you have to believe in something before it happens and not be deterred by any contradictory evidence. That's not easy. And what's more, you're smart if you keep it to yourself while you keep working on it. You have to be your own best confidante. Believe me, that's not easy."

Dave looked at her with confusion on his face. He smiled as he said, "You know, of course, that you lost me after the first 'believing' explanation. But this time you didn't throw in those colors and that other stuff you sometimes do. I'm not making fun, but I don't totally understand what you do."

"That's okay. Even I don't always understand how it works, but I know it works when I do it right."

"Let's back down from the universe and go over to see our friends. They've got their problems right here on earth."

He noticed her smile. She knew that the problems might be here on earth but the answers and solutions were above them and in the atmosphere around them.

"This gift I've got keeps me constantly dealing with the universe. I'm not dumb enough to think that I'm the one doing this hearing of other people's thoughts. It comes from somewhere else. I don't know why, but it makes me continually aware that the world is bigger than what we see, think or feel."

"I can understand that. That's why you're so sensitive to things and notice all those little details."

And she was right, thought Dave. It definitely was one reason why she noticed things. She was always aware of something bigger around her and everyone else, and from there she got suggestions.

* * *

"It's good to see you again," said Sammi as she caught Denver's friendly gaze. "I'll bet you're glad to have your dad here with you."

That got a big smile from him and he looked at his dad with childlike adoration in his eyes.

Dave, Tom and Randy got into a huddle for a few minutes and that gave Sammi time to have a few words with Denver.

"I hear that you're going to join some Christmas activities at the school during the holidays," she said.

He nodded his head and some delight crossed his face. After all, he was still a kid and Christmas was important to him.

"But I don't know any of the kids there."

"Well, Jill knows all of the kids and she'll make sure you're introduced to every one of them."

"Sometimes I like to stand in the corner and look around. I don't mind that."

"You'd rather do that than play?" asked Sammi.

He nodded. "My mom used to worry about that, but I don't always have a lot in common with them. They don't like to hear what I talk about. But when I stand back and listen to them, they accept me and I like what they do."

Sammi realized that Denver had mostly mature thoughts. He knew that these kids were playing what usual ten year olds played, but he enjoyed the older kids most of the time. Yet the older kids didn't always accept him, so that made him feel that he didn't have a real place to be.

"Mom said that it used to happen to her, too. She was super smart as a child."

"Really, I didn't know that."

"Yep, she was and she taught me a lot."

"Like what?"

"Well, she taught me to listen behind the words of what people say. The motive was the most important thing. She said to hang on to strong thoughts because they could always get you through."

About this time, the men returned and you could tell by the look on Dave and Tom's faces that they were surprised at what this child was saying. Dave was thinking, *how old is this kid, anyway?* Tom simply shook his head. Gifted children were amazing to them.

Randy offered, "The conversations between Beth and Denver put me out in left field at times, but I was glad of who they were."

Sammi realized that Denver was feeling relaxed in this setting with his dad around. His feelings, although still quite excitable when he thought about his mom, were settling down some. He had a lot of mourning to do and they both had a difficult funeral to face in the future, but the initial shock was moving on and the reality of the situation was upon them.

In order to keep things on a light note, Sammi asked, "What grade are you in, Denver?"

He looked at his dad and smiled. "Well, I've been put in Grade 6, but I do 8th Grade math and science. However, they were about to give me some high school math to give me more of a challenge. And, of course, I was studying Philosophy with my mom, which was one of my favorite subjects."

The adults were amazed and yet not, realizing the intelligence of the parents. Although Randy was the lesser of the two in I.Q., he was also way above average and prone to logical thinking. This family had a lot to offer the world.

Then the telephone rang. It was ten o'clock on December 23rd. Tom listened for a few minutes but his facial expression was in shock. He put down the phone and turned to the group with nervousness and anger.

"It's not good news, Randy. Ballistics came back and only Beth's fingerprints and yours are on the gun. And your foot print was found in the blood near the body. They're on their way over here right now to arrest you."

Denver started to cry. Randy simply said, "On December 23? Couldn't they wait a few days? I'm not going anywhere."

"They're not waiting."

"Okay," he said and went off to have as private and as long a talk with his son as he could muster. He hugged him, and held him, and told him that everything would be okay. This was the best way to prove he was innocent.

"I know you're innocent, dad."

"But we have to prove it to the rest of the world. And we will. But I want you to stay with Tom and Jill. They're our friends and they'll take good care of you. I know you'll be good and make me proud."

Randy had tears coming down. Within a few moments there was a knock on the door. The time had come. They agreed not to put the handcuffs on him in front of his boy. But as he was going out the door Denver said, "Ms. Sammi knows things just like mom, dad. I can talk to her."

"That's great, son. I love you."

"I love you, too, dad."

Tom and Dave walked outside assuring Randy not to worry. Denver would be fine and Sammi would be around for him whenever he needed her.

* * *

They were both quiet on the way home. Neither could muster up the energy to talk about what had happened tonight. They were both exhausted.

When they arrived home, Dave wanted to know if Sammi had picked up anything helpful from Denver.

"I did. He is starting to cope better, but then that's because his dad was there. Now he has another adjustment to make."

"Yeah, I hope he doesn't go backwards too much."

"But he's such a thinking child and tonight his thoughts were on the surface a little. He has a secret,

Dave. And I've no clue what it is, but he thinks this secret is solely for him and hasn't even shared it with his dad."

Dave looked over a little worried. "Do you think it's got anything to do with his mom's murder or possibly something else that could help Randy?"

"It's kind of muddled right now, but I've got the feeling it has something to do with the murder scene, but that's simply a guess. I can't quite make it out yet."

"Gees, if it's something that could help, I hope you can figure it out."

"In time, I'm sure. He's coping better than most kids right now, but it's still too soon for him. And this secret of his is quite guarded, like a last thing from his mom."

"Well, I was hoping that they'd wait until after Christmas to arrest Randy, but it's almost like they get pleasure doing it now."

"Come on, Dave. If you weren't involved with this case at this end, you'd feel differently."

He paused for a moment and then said, "You're right. This sure makes you see the other side of the coin."

Sammi nodded. Everyone had a different point of view.

"Okay, well all the gifts are wrapped and tomorrow night we're going to Jim and Julie's house. They've invited a few others from the station and that should help change our mood a little."

Dave was pensive; there was no doubt. She wasn't even sure if he'd heard her.

"Do you think that Tom and Jill will come and bring Denver? There will be a few other kids there. Maybe it would help."

"But I don't feel like celebrating that much myself, so I guess the others feel about the same."

Sammi had another thought and needed to settle it in her mind. "Remember in a few days we'll be going on vacation. That will be welcomed relaxation and put us in a better frame of mind when we return."

Dave had a strange reaction, but it was what she expected.

"That's right. We leave on the 27th. It'll be tough to be gone at this time, but ..." he didn't finish.

"Getting away will be good for us. We'll come back with a fresh perspective."

"Yeah, right," he said, but his heart wasn't in it.

* * *

The buzz around the station the next day was unbelievable. Sergeant Brady had gotten a call from Ben Collier to say that the attorneys wouldn't be arriving until the 26th since Randy Baker was presently being held on no bond. A hearing would be held on the day after Christmas to see if any agreement could be reached. The no bond was partly because of the gruesome and appalling crime scene plus the fact that Randy had been on the run for three days before he turned himself in. That along with the fact that he left his son alone, who had no doubt witnessed this horrific crime, was the cincher.

"This is total crap," said Tom. "I'll bet ASAC is happy about this one. It makes Randy look bad from the beginning."

"Settle down, Tom," said Dave. "There's going to be a lot of this going on. Don't be surprised at anything. Just be glad that you and Jill got the boy. That's the best thing that could happen."

"And he's got a real feeling about Sammi, too. That should help."

The meeting with Sergeant Brady didn't bring anything to perk up their mood. The ballistic report showed only Randy and Beth's fingerprints on the murder weapon so Tom reread the report twice to make sure no other comments were made as a suggestion. Nothing else was stated; that was the final decision. And Randy had told them that he checked on Beth to make sure she was dead, and, of course, that made a clear footprint in the blood around her body. Things looked as bad as they possibly could.

"There's one strange thing, though," said Tom.

"What's that?"

"Well, Denver doesn't usually get home from school until about 3:45 PM or even later, but that day they got let out early for some teachers' meeting. That's probably what saved his life. They weren't looking for a little kid because they thought he wasn't home yet."

"I think we better get Jill and Denver some security. When they find out there might possibly be a witness, they could be in danger," said Dave.

"That's a thought, but they did arrest Randy so don't you think they're relaxing right now?" asked Jim.

"Still, it might be a good idea not to take a chance. We could get a female officer to stay with them and they'd think she was simply Jill's friend. She wouldn't be in police garb."

"You may have a point. Not worth taking a chance; let's wait and see."

"What are you guys doing for Christmas? You two have the toughest job right now," said Dave.

"Well, we thought we'd take Denver to church tonight. That's always a way to get a little peace into your system. Then later we'll stop at Jim's for a little while. Tomorrow we plan to stay around home."

"Sammi and I are going to church tonight, too. I like the Christmas Eve services and then we'll pop over to Jim's place, too. I hope we can a get a little time to revive our system. It's going to be hard on Denver. Will you take him to see Randy?"

"Not yet. Randy says no. But we got him a present from his dad. In time, he'll let him come, but he thinks the jail scene will be too traumatic for him. And he's been through so much already."

"I'm sure it'll depend. If he can't get bond, not seeing his dad could be much worse."

"We've discussed it and Randy says we'll see what happens later."

* * *

They were both quiet that night preparing for

church. It wasn't the festive mood it had been in the past, but they tried to see the bigger picture. After all, it was Christmas Eve.

"I was thinking," said Sammi, "other years we've been in a great mood because life was better, but there were other people having a tough time somewhere. There's always good and bad happening around us."

"I know and you're right, but I can't shake my mood. And I'm sorry to put a damper on all of this."

"You're not, honey. I'm right there with you. But I was thinking that we have to look at the total picture. Somewhere in the world, someone just had a wonderful wish come true. To get the best results you want about anything, you have to stay on the positive side with the universe. You get the most amazing outcomes that way."

Dave looked over and smiled. "You're right, I know." He knew what she was doing and she was succeeding. There was plenty to rejoice about tonight. There had been a horrendous murder and worse because of their association with the victims. But he had to remember that during this year some big-time felons were finally caught and put away for a while. And he had to remember that little Denver had been spared. Most of all, he had realized his love for Sammi and was happier than he'd been in years. Those were a small part of his blessings, and he would concentrate on them in church and in the future. His father always told him to concentrate on the successes, and that would make everything else easier. He knew that his dad would have loved Sammi.

* * *

The church was decorated magnificently and the lights and aromas coming in from all sides passed through his body causing warmth and a certain glow making him feel part of something much bigger. This was centering for him, and as he held Sammi's hand he knew it was the same for her. He looked over at her and their eyes connected. So many unspoken thoughts crossed his mind quickly. Yes, there was so much to be thankful for in spite of the evil in the world, and a big part of it was sitting next to him in the church pew.

The sermon on Christmas Eve centered on acknowledging your blessings, which was a suitable and appropriate topic. Also the pastor touched on forgiveness which was a little tougher for Dave. When he thought of forgiving killers and assassins, he couldn't quite hold the thought. Then he remembered something he had heard as a child and was hearing once more right now. You could hate the deed, but try to forgive the one who committed it. Yes, that might be a little easier, and when the preacher mentioned that their lives might have caused them to stray in that direction, that was something he could connect with. Looking into the lives of some of these killers and hired assassins showed many reasons why they turned out the way they did. And if you looked into the life of their parents ... the circle went on and on. Yes, that helped him understand a little and gave him more reason to be thankful for his own blessings.

* * *

Jim and Julie had a modest and attractive ranch-type home, yet there was plenty of room for his two girls from a previous marriage, when they came to stay. They had a beautiful holiday tree and many decorations around the house, mostly created by his two daughters. They had outdone themselves this year. They loved their new stepmother and were happy that their dad was finally settled in again, as they put it.

"Hey you gals, this is beautiful," said Sammi and watched them relish in the compliment of a beautiful decorating job. They realized everyone had already arrived as they went around and wished the entire group holiday greetings and happiness.

Sammi immediately noticed that Denver was sitting off by himself in the corner. Jill was up next to her immediately.

"We can't get him to move or enjoy anything. I guess that would be expecting too much. But it's Christmas, so I hope he's enjoying good memories, at least that."

"Any word yet from his dad?"

"Not today, we're hoping to get a call through to him tomorrow. The officer in the holding cell told us we could and that should help. When you talk to this kid, he seems to understand what's going on and accepts it. That's the scariest part. How do you talk to a kid like that?"

"I'll give it a try," said Sammi as she went over and sat by him.

She didn't say a word for a few minutes, but tried to match his mood by creating the same type of body language that he was exhibiting. Somehow, that had a way of connecting with someone and Sammi knew by his thoughts that tonight would be more difficult than it had been in the past.

After a time she knew he was ready so she said, "I'm glad you're here tonight, Denver. I would have missed you."

He acknowledged her comments, but looked down. He was thinking mostly of his mom. She liked the fun of the holidays and she was always singing around the house.

Sammi connected. "I'll bet your home was a lot of fun at Christmas, with singing and music."

He nodded. "My mom loved to sing all of the holiday songs. And she had a nice voice."

Then he shook his head and for the first time made a telling comment. "I don't know why anyone would want to kill her, you know. It doesn't make sense to me. They tell me I'm a smart kid, but I can't figure that one out."

This created a few tears, which he tried casually to wipe away. His thoughts said that he wanted to keep the mood happy. That's what both his parents would have wanted. But he felt like discussing a few things and he knew Sammi would understand. Of this he was aware.

"You're a lot like my mom. I have a feeling that you recognize hidden things. My mom did, too. She could tell you things that would happen tomorrow and next week and most of the time she was right. Not all the time, of course, but a lot of times she was right. My dad would shake his head and laugh. We were happy; my dad loved us both a lot."

"I know he did, Denver. He's very lost without your mom. He's lucky to still have you around."

"But I can't see him right now. I wanted to see him on Christmas, but they won't let me. Why not?"

"Well, I know your dad doesn't want you to see him in jail. That's not an impression that he wants on your mind. You can understand that, right?"

"But I know he's innocent, so it doesn't matter. It helped a lot when he was around for those few days. It made everything so much easier."

"I'm sorry he's not around now."

Then Denver turned to her and said, "But you know things, too, don't you? You don't have to tell me how, but I know you're a lot like my mom."

"Sometimes I know things, but not all the time. And every one of us knows things at different times, don't we?"

Denver almost gasped. "That's exactly what my mom used to say. That's why I can talk to you."

Then Dave and Tom came over to join them. Tom told him stories about his dad when they played football together in high school. And Denver was caught up in these tales. Tom almost got some laughs from Denver when he told him how, although his father was a good player, he fumbled the ball a few times, but recovered in time to make a goal.

"My dad told me about a few things, but it's good hearing it from someone else. I think I appreciate these stories of my dad more than anything."

Then it was time to eat and there was a lavish display of food and refreshments. It was a fun evening, despite the dire circumstances. And Denver did make a strong attempt to fit in and managed to mingle somewhat with the other kids. His mind was always jumping back and forth from the past to the painful present, but he made a focused concentration to keep his thoughts strong on a positive future. That's what his mother would have wanted and that's what he was determined to do.

* * *

Dave and Sammi slept in the next day. They decided they would spend the day alone, maybe go outside and enjoy the outdoors and relish in the positive atmosphere that they wanted to create around themselves. This was their first Christmas together as a married couple and it was special. Although they had received some invitations for parties and other events, they declined. This year, more than ever, they needed to renew their strength and this was done best by themselves.

They watched 'It's A Wonderful Life' on TV and Dave remarked, "I can't believe that I don't get tired of that movie. There's something about it."

"I agree. I watch it every year. It has such a nice message. Everybody is important and everybody needs friends. I guess we all need to hear it now and then."

"We've been so lucky you and I," Dave said. He laughed as he saw the look on her face, "Yes, I do get sentimental on Christmas and during the holidays. I miss my dad, because he was a great guy and taught me well. My mom and dad had a good life together and I know they cared about each other. I had a happy household to live in as I was growing up. So many kids don't have that."

Sammi was quiet. Then Dave remembered and said, "Oh, I'm sorry, Sammi. I forgot."

"Oh no, that's fine. I'm glad you had a good young life. I knew that both of my parents loved me, but they argued all the time. Actually, my mom was the one who argued with everyone about everything and my brothers always took the bait. I used to retreat and talk to my dad. He was such a peaceful person. He gave everyone the benefit of the doubt. But our household was always in turmoil and that's why I retreated and spent so much time with my grandparents. And luckily Grandpa Ryan and I had a lot in common."

"You were lucky about that. It must have been hard growing up hearing unpleasant thoughts in your own household, and if you hadn't had your grandpa ..." he didn't finish.

"I would have almost certainly thought I was going crazy. I did have those problems for a while until I realized that grandpa could hear other people's thoughts, too ... he had the same gift. And he helped me a lot to get this talent under control and use it responsibly. I miss him and the conversations we had to this day."

Dave nodded. Then they sat for a while, relaxing, taking it easy and enjoying the rare down time they had, but Sammi could tell that Dave had a problem on his mind that he couldn't seem to bring to the surface. She decided to push the issue.

"Okay, I know you've got something on your mind. It was there yesterday, it's still there today and it's not going away until you talk to me about it. What is it?"

"You're right, as usual," he said trying to lighten up a little. "I can't seem to decide the right thing to do. And it's the holidays and I don't want to upset you, but ..."

She waited. He was starting to talk and he would continue when he found the right words.

"Okay," he said finally, "it's about our vacation. We've been looking forward to it for so long. It's supposed to be our honeymoon, which we never had. And going to a great hot spot in the middle of our winter here is perfect, but ..."

"But, what?"

"I hate to leave right now. I know there's never a perfect time to get away from my work. But right now, with Tom's friend being arrested for the murder of his wife and knowing that between the two of us we could help, well, I hate to leave. I'm trying to be totally honest with you; I don't like the idea of being that far away for that long."

Sammi was quiet. She didn't say a word. She knew he'd continue.

"Anyway, I know it's too late to change anything and it wouldn't be fair to you. I know you've counted on this trip for so long. I hope I don't ruin everything."

All of a sudden, Sammi jumped up from the couch and ran to get something that seemed to be stuck in the back of the Christmas tree. It was a medium-sized gold box with a red bow. Dave looked surprised.

"I almost forgot to give this to you. It's your last present."

"But you got me so much already. I can't imagine what this could be."

"That's right, honey. I don't think you could imagine this one."

Dave looked at her strangely and slowly opened the envelope. It consisted of what he thought were the plane tickets to Aruba. He looked puzzled.

"Turn them over. Look on the other side."

He did and he saw the huge lettering of "CAN-CELLED" sprawled in red across the reservations. His jaw dropped and he turned to look at Sammi with new affection.

"And I didn't read your thoughts, either. I didn't have to. Honey, it was obvious that your heart and thoughts would be here. I feel the same way. I cancelled them yesterday. We'll go some other time ... maybe when this case is over."

"I don't know what to say. You always seem to know. I'd be so much happier going some other time."

"Me, too. And we'd probably both enjoy it more later on."

He gave her an affectionate hug and a tender kiss and then held her again for a while. "Christmas is such a blessed time -- and you're my greatest blessing."

Dave went into the kitchen and came back with two glasses of Piesporter wine. They sat next to each other on the sofa, quiet, yet happy in their ability to be there for each other. It was approaching midnight and Dave leaned over and took one more chance to say, "Merry Christmas,

Sammi. I love you."

She smiled and said, "And I love you, Dave Patterson, Merry Christmas."

CHAPTER SIX

The day after Christmas was a busy shopping day for some. Many presents would be returned and special bargains were to be had at many of the local popular stores. And children were on holiday vacations which could entail anything from trips to grandparents and relatives to going skiing somewhere in Colorado or other well-known ski resorts. Families all over America would be enjoying themselves in the happy seasonal fun that so many waited for all year long.

For others prosperity wasn't always on their side. Yet, even though their vacations wouldn't be as lavish or expensive, they, too, would be enjoying time off from work and school in some other way. This could be as much fun as anything else and the holiday attitude seemed to extend around the country. People were nicer to each other and more tolerant of irritating circumstances at this time of the year. Patience seemed to be in excess for a greater part of the population.

Back in Scranton, the seriousness of the Randy Baker predicament weighed on many of them. Luckily, Denver had been able to talk to his father on Christmas day and was waiting anxiously to find out if his dad would remain in jail or not. He knew it depended on lawyers, judges and many people who didn't know his father at all. They didn't know what a good guy he was and how much he loved his family, yet they would be deciding his fate. That didn't seem fair to Denver. Yet, he tried to remain positive about everything. That's what his mother would have wanted.

"Mr. Tom, if you see my dad today, tell him I love him and miss him. Will you do that for me please?"

"Of course I will, Denver. I'll see him in court today.

I hope to get a few minutes to talk to him, but you never know."

"I understand, but if you do get a chance to talk to him, tell him, okay? That's all I ask. "

"I promise that's the first thing I'll tell him, even before I say hi."

Denver had to smile at that. Jill and Tom both noticed that he smiled a little easier and quicker now. They were so worried about him, but he was holding on quite well.

When Tom left for the station, he was hoping that today would have a happy ending. There had been enough problems and unlucky circumstances for this family; today was the day to begin seeing some light in the distance.

* * *

The lawyers planned for an early meeting at the station with the three referees and Sergeant Brady. Ben Collier thought it was a good idea for them to know the ones who would be doing a lot of the background work and making their acquaintance early on to get the preliminaries out of the way. It would make for a more comfortable association. Later, there wouldn't be much time for anything but the trial work.

They were seated in the conference room as the lawyers arrived. Introductions were made and it was obvious that each group were eyeing each other and trying to size up each other's abilities.

Sergeant Brady began by introducing his group and then the lead lawyer took over.

"I'd like to introduce myself and my group so you'll know a little about us. I'm Ronald Donovan. I was in private practice for almost fifteen years and then the FBI recruited me and I've been with them for ten years. I've always been on the defense side of the table."

"And this here is Stephen Harrison," he said pointing to his colleague. "Don't let his baby face fool you." Stephen was particular young looking and had fooled others into thinking he was inexperienced. His light blonde hair with blue eyes made it that much more difficult for him to be taken seriously at times. "He's been with the FBI for ten years and had ten years experience before that. He's one of our best."

"And this other fellow is Paul Ryan. He's had his own practice for ten years and has been with us for five years."

"Now we're all quite experienced on the defense side. I've brought with me the people I think will do the best job here. We're quite interested in several aspects of this case. But today we have to talk about Randy Baker. This is our only interest at this time and we'll see where that leads us. We've read his file and are totally familiar with everything the police have at this time. Our goal today, is to get Randy out of jail. What I'm going to present is the fact that he's a devoted husband and father, and has a son that needs him, so I don't believe he's a flight risk. His record is clean and he has exhibited exemplary behavior all of his life, no convictions, no arrests, nothing that could be construed as questionable behavior. We don't want to bring up the fact of his association with ASAC at this time. That would probably be detrimental and although the prosecution knows where he works, they have no idea of the ramifications of that company in connection with this murder. We want to keep it that way until the bail is set."

Sergeant Brady asked, "If they know he works at ASAC, wouldn't the rest of it be apparent? That would seem obvious to me."

"And it is, but usually at a bail hearing the biggest reason for failure to make bail would be a flight risk. Now I don't believe at this time that the prosecution could be aware of a connection with this company in that sense. They would know that they've been brought up on charges in the past, but they beat every one of them. Besides, it's our best shot, right now. We can only hope they don't play that card at this time; hopefully they aren't fully aware of it yet."

Tom asked, "So you don't think they know there might be a connection?"

Mr. Donovan replied. "Let's hope not. They could refuse bail on that alone. I hear the lead prosecution is James McLean and he's good. Then he has Gary Duncan, he's been around for a while, too. And a newer one has been added named Wayne Berman. I don't know much about him, but we'll find out."

After discussing a few more details of the situation, they adjourned. The attorneys had pressing details to study before the one o'clock court time.

"Are any of you planning on coming to court today?"

"We all are," answered the three referees almost simultaneously.

"Okay," said Ron, "we'll see you all in court and hope for the best."

* * *

There were three worried looking faces sitting around in that conference room. Sergeant Brady had already left, but the referees remained trying to get their position in balance.

"Okay, there's nothing more we can do right now," said Tom. "It's in the hands of the professionals and we have to let them do their jobs. But it's going to be hard."

Dave said, "Don't forget they're going to need our help and I'm sure they'll keep in close contact with us. They know you're a personal friend, Tom, so you'll always have information they'll need."

"That's true; that's true," said Tom.

"These guys have a great reputation. I think your friend's in good hands," said Jim.

"I know, I know. But I can't help but worry."

"That's what friends do," said Dave.

"And we have other work to do also. Let's get that done while we have some down time."

As they were walking out of the room, Tom looked

over at Dave and said, "When are you and Sammi leaving on your trip?"

"We decided to postpone it," he said as he shifted in his tracks. "Hell, Tom, our minds and thoughts would be here on this case anyway. We'll go after this is over with." Anyone could see that Tom was touched. He looked stunned as he glanced at Jim. He heard him say, "That's what friends do, right?"

And they all answered in unison, "Right."

Now it was off to other duties while attempting to put this in the back of their minds, if they could, until the next chapter arrived.

* * *

At one o'clock, they were all in court. There were three anxious referees and other friends sitting in the available seats. When Randy was brought in everyone crowded around him until the judge got very excited and exerted his power. "Order in the courtroom, order in the courtroom. I insist on keeping order in my courtroom. Everyone not involved directly in this case, take a proper seat."

They all sat down, like they knew they should have done in the first place.

"Now, Mr. Randy Baker, you are accused of the murder of your wife Beth Lynn Baker. I see you do have representation. How do you plead?"

"Not Guilty, sir."

Mr. Donovan immediately stood up and gave his argument. "Mr. Baker is an outstanding citizen, good husband and father. He has no blemish at all on his record and there's no reason to believe that he would be a flight risk."

"Just a moment," said Mr. McLean. "He's accused of murdering his wife in cold blood and that doesn't sound like a good husband to me."

"That's right," said Mr. Donovan. "He's accused, not convicted. And what about our law that says innocent until proven guilty?"

Mr. McLean continued with, "And what about the fact that he took off after the crime and didn't turn himself in for three days."

"But he did turn himself in of his own free will," said Mr. Donovan.

"Because he knew he was about to get caught, and we have reason to believe that he has absconded with secrets from his employer, ASAC which we will prove during trial. If he makes bail now, he could leave with these secrets and never come back."

It was obvious that Mr. Donovan was shocked and caught off guard. He didn't think they knew about this fact yet, but he countered with, "There's no proof of this innuendo at this time and all other facts make him to be an outstanding citizen."

"By the time we present proof, Your Honor, during the trial he could be long gone," said Mr. McLean.

"Okay, okay, you two, hush up for a moment." Then the judge said, "There seems to be a hint of possibility that Mr. Baker could run. I must admit it is weak and possibly quite exaggerated, but I have to consider it. There will be no bail for Mr. Baker at this time. He's to remain in custody, but the possibility of bail may be addressed again in the future."

And then the gavel came down.

The disappointment on Randy's face was evident as was the weight on his body as his shoulders drooped considerably. But he took a deep breath and tried to put on a strong face. He gave a half smile as he saw the three referees and felt when the facts came out, he'd have a good chance.

* * *

"How the hell did they know this quickly?" said Paul Ryan. "That doesn't seem possible."

"They no doubt had more information than we could have guessed. But it was quite a surprise," said the lead attorney. "Still we have to go with what we've got, but we need to be careful. And we've got to start studying everything and make sure they don't know more than we do."

"Gees," said Tom, "I was hoping he'd get out on bail."

"We all were," said Ron, "but you never know how a judge will rule. Even without that secrets stuff he's accused of taking, there was a decent chance he wouldn't make bail because of the circumstances of the murder. I mean she was shot with his gun; his footprint is in the blood next to her body and he took off for three days before turning himself in. And what's done is done, for now at least. You have to play the hand you're dealt."

Tom puckered his lips and looked at Jim and Dave. They were all disappointed, but realized that their hands were tied.

Ron Donovan said, "Hey don't let this get you down; there will be a lot of disappointments. We've only begun. I'm sure we'll talk to you soon."

"Right, keep in touch," said Tom.

As they walked away Tom added, "It's going to be hard to tell Denver. I know he was hoping his dad would come home today."

"That's the rough part. The kid knows his dad didn't do it, but he sees him in jail right now."

There was a cloud of frustration on these police officers as they walked out of the courtroom, but life didn't always turn out the way you wanted. And this entire case would be played out one step at a time. They had to learn to shrug off the irritation of the moment and move on by keeping a positive view of the future.

* * *

That night Sammi had questions of her own. "Wow! This didn't turn out the way we'd hoped for, but then, you never know about the legal system. Was it because the prosecution brought up about Randy stealing secrets?"

"I don't know. Ron Donovan said that he might have been denied bail anyway, but that certainly didn't help."

"What do you think was the main reason he was denied bail?"

"I'm not sure. The crime scene was gruesome and then he disappeared for almost three days and left his kid. We know now that he made sure Denver was okay, but that was a hard sell to the judge. And running is usually a sign of guilt. I always felt that would go against him."

"Now what? He sits in jail. That certainly doesn't help Denver. How did they know about the secrets?"

"That confused all of us and irked Donovan to no end," said Dave. "He was hoping they hadn't figured that out yet."

"But if these killers didn't find anything in the house, and Randy disappears for a few days ... well, it does seem obvious."

"True, but they don't know for sure. And to bring it up at a bail hearing is kind of stretching it, I think."

They were both quiet for a time. Something didn't make sense to Sammi. Her mind was working overtime.

"How did they know Randy had anything in the first place? He was quite sure no one had seen him. And these guys came over to his house, in the middle of the day yet, to demand some secret stuff ... No. I think there's something else involved here."

Dave was thoughtful as well, "You've got a point. When you put it that way, it seems like a pretty stupid thing for them to do."

"And why did they have to kill her? That doesn't make sense to me either. If they didn't get what they wanted, they could have threatened her and left."

Dave disagreed. "No, not likely. She knew who they were. After something like that, Randy and Beth could have gone to the police. They were already scared."

"But what proof did they have? That company could have said that no one was sent out there. That would have been real hard to prove."

"True. I don't know. A lot of this doesn't make sense to me yet."

She didn't like what she didn't understand. And so much was unknown; it would help having something concrete to discuss, but right now wasn't the time.

Dave wondered how Tom was holding up. He worried about this case during the day and would visit Randy when he could and when he was needed. But Tom also had Denver at home during the evening trying to help him cope. Dave felt that Tom would need someone to share the burden or he wouldn't make it through. And that's why Jim, Tom and Dave were the three referees.

* * *

Amilio came over to Dave's desk the next morning. "Hey, amigo, I see you're still here. Aren't you supposed to be on the way to Aruba with Sammi?"

"Couldn't leave right now."

"I know," he said as he patted him on the shoulder. "Hard to leave amigos in trouble."

"So what's up with you?"

"I've been thinking about a few things. A lot doesn't make sense about this prostitute, Tina."

Dave took an interested pose. There wasn't much any of them could do at this time about Randy, except to be on call when needed. So he had time and Amilio's case had caught his attention, too.

"Well, she was educated and smart. She had class we've heard from a few people that knew her. Her keys were taken, but they left the car. Crazy, huh?"

"Remember Sammi thought there could be something on that key chain they wanted."

"I've been thinking about that. But why take the time to drag her out to a vacant field? Why not leave her where you killed her?"

Dave thought about that and couldn't think of an answer.

"There's no evidence that she was killed in that field, none at all. There would have been a messed up area with lots of footsteps shuffling around as they fought, and there's nothing. No, she was killed somewhere else and then carried to this exact spot. Why? Why not dump her at the beginning of the field? Why take the time to carry her way out in the middle? That doesn't make any sense. There's more chance to get caught that way."

"You've put a lot of thought into this, haven't you? But maybe the killer didn't want her associated with the murder scene. So they moved her away from there."

Amilio could agree with that. "Well, I did talk to Officer Dolan. Remember I told you he had the case for a while back then. He had made a few notes on his own, not much really, but at least it was something. He was out in the field where the body was found and his notes say that except for the man's footprints, there weren't any others. No footprints of high heels or even one high heel and a woman's foot; that wasn't there. So she definitely was killed somewhere else and carried there. That's the stupidest thing I could imagine, don't you think?"

"I don't have any answer for you."

"Think of it, Dave. Who kills someone somewhere else and takes the time to carry them out in the middle of a field to dump them?"

"Again, the murder scene could have been telling and they didn't want the body to be found right away?"

"So that's why they left it in an open field that's not far from a residential area? People pass by every day and kids play there. No, he knew the body would be found. So there's another reason and figuring that out could be a clue."

"Looks like you have your work cut out for you. Could be you should look in another direction for a while. Something might turn up elsewhere that you can tie together."

"I know, but usually it's easy to prove why a killer did something. It's hard to find out who did it and get enough evidence to prove it, but usually why they did certain things makes sense. This one doesn't."

"Give it time, Amilio. Did you get a blowup of that picture yet? Sammi's anxious to see what was in her hand."

"I think I get them this afternoon. I told them to especially enhance her right hand, so we'll see."

Then Amilio was called away and was gone in a second. Dave knew that Amilio was giving this case his all. He was a good one to do that.

* * *

Dave spent some time thinking about Beth Baker's murder scene. It was as gruesome as he'd ever seen with blood flying in every direction. But these guys were definitely looking for something and had put in a lot of effort in their search. ASAC must have suspected that Randy had copies of some secrets and they must have been extremely worried about their operation to risk so much on a suspicion. That idea brought him back to Sammi's idea. There must have been something else involved here. Beth was not killed on the idea that her husband might have some information hidden around his house. To be logical, most people didn't hide stuff like that around their house. It would be in a safety deposit box or a P. O. Box somewhere. And Randy had done that as well. Dave kept running his fingers through his hair, but nothing was coming through for him.

He was almost glad when his phone rang. He didn't want to speculate anymore.

"Did those pictures come through yet?" asked Sammi.

"Amilio says possibly sometime this afternoon."

"Okay, that hand of Tina's keeps bugging me. Can't imagine what she was holding?"

"You're getting a lot like me, Sammi. Your mind is always whirling around about unknown facts."

"There's too much unknown about this one. The fact that it's an older case doesn't help. To have to backtrack now is difficult."

"If I know Amilio, he'll come up with something. He plans to look into her background."

"Well I plan to call Charmaine right after New Years

and get together with her. I know she's holding in more information. That might help him move in a good direction."

"That will make Amilio happy. This is another case that needs a lot of help."

"What did you want to do on New Years?"

"I don't know. It depends. Do you have a preference?"

"Jill asked us to stop over for an early dinner. Then we could come back here and have some quiet time. That's enough for me this year."

"Sounds good. Have to run. Later, okay?"

* * *

Dave was called to Sergeant Brady's office on a routine matter, an old case that he'd been privy to. It took but a few minutes and when he came out, Amilio was immediately at his desk.

"Here are those pictures of Tina's hand and now it's getting even more bizarre. You look at this, Dave. What does that look like to you?"

Despite the fact that the picture was enlarged quite a bit, Dave still got out his magnifying glass. He couldn't believe what he was seeing. He turned to look at Amilio who had an equally questioning look on his face.

"Okay, amigo, what does it look like to you?"

"A flower. For God's sake, it looks like a flower."

"That's what I thought, but then I figured I must be going crazy. The flower isn't even messed up. She fights for her life and ends up with a perfect little flower of some kind in her hand?"

"You know," said Dave. "Both of these murders seem to be so bizarre. Maybe that's the way murders will be from now on. But these two seem to be particularly confusing."

"Well, yeah. It wouldn't be possible for her to keep this flower perfect like that while she was fighting for her life. That means that the murderer killed her and then put this flower in her hand. Why? Must be kind of a message or something, right?"

"Must be. Really weird, though, I must say. Sammi just called and asked if you'd gotten these pictures yet. Do you have an extra? I'd like to show them to her tonight."

"These three pictures of the right hand are extras for her. After all, she's the one who saw something anyway. I thought it was more like a shadow."

They both stared at the pictures for a while longer. Then they were put away.

"Sammi plans to have lunch with Charmaine sometime next week if she can. She hopes to get more information out of her."

"I know if anyone can do it, Sammi's our girl. And anything at all would help on this case because so far, I'm nowhere." Amilio's frustrated look said it all as he walked away shaking his head, but Dave knew that his mind was working overtime.

* * *

New Year's Eve at the station was quiet considering the time of year, but Dave was only there until about three o'clock and headed for home. He was in a relatively good mood considering everything that was happening. He was starting to take things more in stride. Both of these cases had a long way to go, but he felt confident in the end they would be successful.

When he walked in the door, Sammi was hustling to get ready to make it to Jill and Tom's place by four o'clock. And they were out the door and on their way by 3:40 P.M.

"You sure can move when you have to," Dave teased. "What time did you leave work?"

"I was there until two thirty. Mr. Marconey is worried about some leaks coming from the Carbondale office. I may be out there in a couple of weeks. The rumblings aren't good."

"What's going on?"

"He doesn't know exactly, but they've been receiving some phony bills again, mostly the high numbered one, like $100, but I guess they've had a few $20's also. Not sure what it's about. He was wondering if it was people from out of town coming here just to move fake bills. Still he might want me to be out there for a while to see if I can find out anything."

"I don't remember hearing anything about that."

"I didn't know about it either and there may be no one on the inside involved. Still, he likes me to check it out."

"At least it's close by."

She nodded.

* * *

Denver had a happy look on his face when Sammi walked through the door. It was obvious that he liked to talk to her. Their minds were in sync and he felt close to his mom when she was around.

"I miss my dad of course, but I miss my mom, too. But we have to accept things that occur; that's what my mom used to say."

You certainly are very mature in your thinking," Sammi said.

"Well, I do hurt inside, but it won't change things if I complain about it. And I know mom would want me to go on, be happy and remember all the good stuff she taught me. Besides, it's not that I believe she's totally gone. I feel she's still around me." He turned to Sammi. "I think you know what I mean. She used to talk about the fact that she felt her parents were around her, too. This is a total universe with a lot of different ways of living and things don't disappear, but are still around in some different form, right?"

Sammi smiled. This boy said exactly what was on his mind.

"I do know what you mean, Denver."

"And besides, we're coming into a new year now. Catching my mom's killer and getting my dad out of jail will be a priority, and I know that will happen in time."

Sammi decided to take a chance and said, "Did you

remember anything else about that day that you'd want to talk about."

Sammi looked over at Denver's half-smile. He realized that she knew something, but he wasn't ready to say anything yet. And she wanted him to know that he could talk to her, when he felt like it. But his secret had almost reached the surface and Sammi was getting an inkling of what it was about. She also felt there was no need to talk about it right now. By the time it was important in the weeks to come, it might be easier for him.

"So you'll be starting school next week. How do you feel about that?"

"I'm not sure yet. Ms. Jill said that we're going to have a meeting with the principal to evaluate me. I sure hope they put me in the 6th Grade at least. I was quite bored in the 5th Grade and that's something I don't need right now. I need something to stimulate my mind."

Sammi had to smile. It certainly was different talking to someone like Denver. It almost seemed that there was a young adult stuffed inside that little body.

"Make sure they know your preferences. I'm sure they wouldn't want you to be bored either."

"That's what I'm hoping. That could help me keep my mind occupied during the day. It's not likely they'll let me out of school when my dad's on trial, but that won't be for a long time anyway."

Sammi simply nodded.

"But they might want me to testify and that would be different. Then they'd have to let me go to court."

"You're right."

After dinner they all talked together and had some laughs going as the children played games. But Denver eyed Sammi quite often at times, even Dave noticed. She knew he was trying to evaluate her and he compared her to his mom in some ways, like in the use of mind power. These were simply feelings to him, yet he knew with certainty that they both had special talents. And now, especially, that was precious to him.

CHAPTER SEVEN

Sammi had the same evaluation of the object in Tina O'Leary's hand. When she saw the photos that Amilio provided she thought the flower was definitely a message or a statement that the killer wanted to send. And their job was to figure out what the message was.

"Isn't it weird, though?" said Dave. "A killer would take the time to bring this flower with him and put it in her hand after he had placed the body the way he wanted. This is totally bizarre."

"It does seem that something powerful is going on here."

"Amilio is trying to backtrack through her family history and also see if she had other friends around that could be helpful, but from what Charmaine said, that seems unlikely. She stayed mostly to herself."

"I made a dinner date with Charmaine for Friday night. I want to give us time to talk a little and see if she feels comfortable enough to tell me what else is on her mind. I know I should be able to pick up more of her thoughts, but if I could discuss it with her, it would help even more."

"I got the feeling that you liked her," said Dave.

"She does have spunk. She doesn't feel sorry for herself and we don't know what got her into that profession. She does have a college degree and she's relatively intelligent, so what gives with her?"

Dave just stared back at Sammi. She had a good point.

"I hope that Friday clears up a few more things in my mind. I'd hope she'd have the guts to get herself out of that line of work. She had many thoughts on her mind, but nothing precise. So I'll be curious what pops up on

Friday."

They were both silent for a few moments and then Dave changed the subject. "Tom said they put Denver in the 6th Grade, but will reevaluate his math and science skills as noted in his file. They'll give him a week in those classes but it seems probable that they'll move him forward a little. I hope they find the right spot for him; he doesn't need to be bored or dissatisfied right now."

"Yeah, having the right mix for him at school should help him a lot."

"But Tom says that he did have a positive attitude toward the school and all."

"I would expect that from him."

* * *

"Sergeant Brady got a call from Ben Collier today. He said that Ron Donovan was completely pissed off when the prosecution brought up the possibility of Randy stealing secrets. Somehow he thought that should have been concealed right now. He didn't know how they could have gotten that information already."

"But the company knows -- at least Randy thinks they're the ones behind all this for that exact reason."

Dave continued. "But the prosecuting attorneys are interested in trying him for first degree murder, not for stealing secrets. They were hired by the state to prosecute a murder; they aren't hired by ASAC, so he didn't think that they'd had any dealings with ASAC at this time. He was sure they would as the trial progressed, but not yet. He thought there was something fishy there."

Sammi wondered about that one. It did seem soon for ASAC to have their hands in this case. It seems that they would want to stay out of it right now.

"I see what you mean. With all of their problems in the past you'd think they'd want to be ignored, except for the fact that this was one of their employees, so that'll make headlines anyway. I wonder why that happened."

"It seems to me," he said, "that they want to run the show on this one and they'll try to manipulate things behind the scenes."

"Do you think they could get away with that?"

Dave said, "Not if Ron Donovan has anything to say about it. He'll bring them all out in the open and they wouldn't like that at all."

"This'll be one interesting case," said Sammi. "And Tina O'Leary will be another one."

"True," said Dave, "that's another strange one. The fact that no one did anything about it surprises me. Usually that type of case everyone jumps on. But it was so hushed up and kept in the background. That's starting to get my curiosity up."

Sammi hoped that talking to Charmaine would give her some answers or clues that seemed to be escaping everyone at the moment.

* * *

Charmaine Bolder smiled at herself in the mirror, as she got ready to meet Sammi for dinner. No one would guess her profession right now. She had on a classy beige blouse and dark brown skirt with little make up and jewelry that showed good taste and refinement. She looked like she was going to work in an office. And she liked this image. It represented more precisely who she really was, inside where it counted. But she had chosen her profession for reasons few would guess.

She and her younger brother Phil had been placed in an orphanage when she was ten. Both of her parents had died in a devastating car accident and the only known relatives refused to take responsibility for them. She lived under the rule of catholic nuns for the next several years. She remembered thinking of all the little penguins that had been her teachers and how they walked around that classroom like God himself. But there were a few nuns she liked and would never forget. Some actually showed sympathetic feelings, mixed with kindness, and treated her as if she was a human being. Yet, she got out of there as soon as she could. She was on her own with no relatives, no friends and no one who cared one way or another about her. Her brother had won a scholarship to a local college so she worked as a cook in a restaurant and was able to attend the same school. She had dreams and she had goals back then, but they seemed so distant now. Her cat, Maybe, was letting her know that she was still around making her usual satisfying sounds.

"Well, there you are looking at me funny, right?" she said. She usually talked to her cat as if she was another person, because to her, she was her best confidante. "I do look different, don't I? But it's me, the real me, going out to meet a friend for dinner."

Her cat came over, rubbed against her leg, and meowed again.

"No, I won't be out too late, and I've left you food. So you should be happy right now."

But her cat was still agitated a little. Something was bothering her.

"And you're supposed to be so independent, but you're not. You sure are a different kind of cat."

She picked her up for a few moments until she heard her purr in contentment. *She just needed attention. Sure, that was it, she needed attention, like we all do.*

Her reminiscing continued as she thought about her younger brother who had shared an apartment with her for a while. They were beginning to make an inroad to carving out a life for themselves. Then, he got killed in a freak accident while a passenger on a motorcycle and once more she was totally alone. She drank heavily for a while, driving her deeper into depression and loneliness. She lost every job she was able to acquire, and finally had to hit the streets. It was Tina O'Leary who found her hungry, sick and scared with nowhere to go. She took her in and got her a job at the Castaways. At first, she was a bartender's aide of sorts, but then, she knew where the money was and that attracted her. It was in prostitution, and with her face and figure, she did quite well. She got her own apartment and some clothes and always knew where her next meal was coming from. It wasn't anything she ever thought she'd do, and it was miles apart from the convent school where she was raised, but this was who she was now.

Glancing at the clock jarred her back to the present. Charmaine wasn't totally fooling herself about Sammi. She knew that she was after information about her friend Tina, but that was okay. She wanted Tina's murder to be solved and was hoping that, once in a while, she could have lunch with someone like Sammi. Not many regular people wanted to associate with her, once they knew her profession.

As she turned to walk out the door, Maybe was there looking at her and meowing again. She turned to her and said, "I know you still miss Tina, so do I. After all, you were her cat. And she named you because she thought maybe we could turn our lives around someday. And maybe I will, maybe I will."

* * *

Sammi noticed immediately that Charmaine was dressed tastefully as she approached the table. This was one girl who knew how to dress for any occasion. And Sammi knew that she saw approval on her face.

"Good to see you again," she said as Sammi asked her if the table was okay.

She had chosen one near the back part of the restaurant, which would give them freedom to converse quietly without interruption and also without any chance of being overheard.

"No, this is a good spot." she said with a tone of approval. "I was glad you called. I was hoping to see you again."

Sammi felt an instant rapport and a feeling of ease as she saw her slide into the chair on the other side of the table. No one would ever guess where this woman worked, or her usual life style. She carried herself with grace, style and a look of pride that conveyed itself outward to the world.

"I'm glad, too. I wanted to get to know you better."

After drinks were ordered, Charmaine started out bluntly and honestly.

"I know you must be wondering how I got myself into this profession."

Sammi admitted, "It had crossed my mind because you're a bright gal ... I could tell that as soon as you began to speak. I knew you were an educated person."

"I don't think the guys would have picked that up. But honestly, a lot of other gals I know wouldn't pick it up either. You're someone who pays attention; I could tell that right away."

"Then you must pay attention as well," said Sammi.

Charmaine smiled, and the waitress brought their wine and they ordered dinner.

"I don't often get a chance to get out and talk to someone outside of my business. I'd like to do it more often but ... anyway I'm glad you wanted to meet with me."

Sammi knew this was the time that she had to be totally honest. "And I'm sure you've guessed I have some ulterior motives, too. I have to be honest with you."

"I figured that because I pick up things, too, but I'm glad you mentioned it."

She was quiet for a few moments which prompted Sammi to ask, "May I ask how old you are?"

"Oh sure, I'm twenty-nine as of last week. Never thought this would be my life, but I'm doing okay."

"But with your intelligence I feel you could be doing so much better."

Sammi noticed a caring smile sent in her direction. "That's nice of you to say."

"But I mean it. I can't help but feel, with your intelligence, you could be carving out a better life for yourself. You could work out a good profession and create a better and possibly safer life."

She thought for a moment and said, "A while back I thought that way, but now, if anyone hears about me, they don't want me around."

"Why not?"

"Well, you know ..." she said in an edgy tone to her voice as her eyes looked down.

"Charmaine, there isn't one of us that has a perfect past. My God, you could turn your life around any time you want. But then, that has to be your decision. Either way, I'm impressed by you."

"Really, you're impressed by me?"

For a gal who seemed to have it all together inside where it counted, Sammi could tell she was genuinely surprised at that statement. Yet this gal knew what life and the world was about. She wasn't sure yet why she chose this life, but she knew sometimes a decision was out of your hands, at least for a while.

"Yes, I'm impressed and surprised by you. Why aren't you using your intelligence in another direction? But then ..."

"Right. I guess it would be hard for you to understand."

Then the food came and they ate. Conversation was skimpy but friendly expressions and warm looks continued. When time permitted, Sammi wanted to get to the story of Tina O'Leary, at least from Charmaine's point of view.

"Tell me if I'm wrong, but I had the impression that you knew a little more than you told the three of us when we talked to you."

"You weren't wrong. I only warmed up to you because those other guys who came around when it first happened didn't put much importance on anything I said. There was another one with them, he was a little older and he was almost dismissive of me. Now I wanted to help out Tina, but I felt they didn't really care; after all, to them she was just a prostitute."

Listening to her attitude about the last group of investigators, Sammi was surprised that she had told them as much as she did.

"Now your boyfriend and his friend were a little

more congenial."

"My boyfriend?"

"Yeah, the good looking one; I felt something between the two of you. He is your boyfriend, right?"

Sammi had to smile. She felt they had acted so professional, but Charmaine was intuitive and she had guessed correctly. It made Sammi wonder about her even more.

"Well, he was my boyfriend, but we married last year."

Charmaine smiled. She knew she was right. "Anyway, I did hold a lot back because when you don't get respect, it doesn't make you want to cooperate. But I can go a little further with you."

Sammi was focusing in on her. She wanted to pick up everything she'd tell her in words and if for some reason she started to back off, she needed to pick up more from her thoughts, and luckily her thoughts were coming through allowing her to compare her words and her ideas. They seemed to be in tune with each other, but Charmaine was a fast thinker and sometimes her thoughts changed subjects rather quickly.

"I can tell you more about Tina. You already know the basics that she was a good person and she certainly helped me out, and I'll take her secrets to my grave if I think it's the right thing to do. But I need to tell you that her ex- did come around one time. I figured out real fast who he was."

"So you could identify him?"

"Yep, and I know his name. It's Bobby Armore. He's about six feet, has dark hair and piercing dark eyes and has a tattoo of an eagle on his right upper arm."

"When did he come by?"

"It was about two months before she died. She was in a total panic after that. We had already confided in each other quite a bit by that time, but she told me a lot more after that. She figured he'd get her sooner or later."

"What did you think about him? Do you think he

killed her?"

She nodded and Sammi picked up the thoughts on her mind and she felt he was the one. She was thinking that the other guys that came around the bar would have helped Tina out any time she asked. She was popular with all the guys, even the bouncers.

"Another thing, when he showed up, I went outside and got the license plate off his car."

Sammi knew her surprised expression gave her away, but this was a good piece of news. Charmaine could identify the ex-husband and she had gotten his license plate number.

"Well, Tina almost had a heart attack when he walked in that door and I knew immediately who he was, so I thought it would be a good idea to do that. But that was several months ago, he might have changed cars by now."

"What state was he from?"

"California and he was driving a newer black Buick that was quite impressive and reeked money, if you know what I mean? Still it seemed strange."

"Why strange?"

"Because he was dressed in an expensive suit, and he walked around with an air of ... I don't know ... like people who have everything they want and feel real important. Yet, something seemed to be out of character, but I'm not sure what."

"Do you have that license plate number any more?"

"Oh yeah, I brought it with me cause I figured you'd want it. But just one thing; you didn't get it from me, okay? If anything ever comes up, you didn't get it from me. You've got to promise?"

Sammi sat back in her chair and wondered what, if anything, the police would have done about this information, had they had it a while back. She hated the thought that they might have done nothing, but there was a good chance of that.

"I promise, Charmaine. I didn't get this from you. Is

there anything else? You and Tina were very close and I imagine before the end you two shared most things about each other."

Charmaine stared at her for a few minutes. Then she sat forward in her chair and put her elbows on the table. This was perhaps the most serious time of the entire evening.

"Yes, we did. But first, I need to tell you about me."

She spent the next few moments telling her about living in a catholic orphanage and how Tina took her in from off the streets when she was sick and homeless. She made it obvious that she would only do what she thought was best for Tina.

She paused and almost showed tears for a few moments. It prompted Sammi to realize that some kids had unbelievable challenges to surmount. She probably could have done much better had she even one person in her corner.

"We both wanted to get out of this business for our own reasons. We were going to help each other make it past this life. I was going to help her finish her college degree and then we'd be able to take off and start fresh somewhere else." She stopped at this point and laughed somewhat. "Two prostitutes with a college degree and a good education with hopes of becoming a success in the world, right? But then we planned to move away and change our lives and Tina was going to get her boy back."

Sammi reacted to that statement which prompted Charmaine to say, "She didn't give him up for adoption. She couldn't do that. She had to keep the dream alive that someday she could get him back. But her ex- was always tracking her and she wanted the kid safe. And he is safe, but I won't tell you where he's at."

Sammi didn't want Charmaine to realize that she'd picked up some of her thoughts and she knew where the child was being raised. And she thought that Tina must have been wise indeed to think of such a clever place.

"I don't think that's necessary. You've given me

some good information here. I think we're going to start looking for this ex- of hers, but that's between you and me, okay?"

Her face lit up. She was being taken into Sammi's confidence. It made her feel like a real person. Sammi heard her hoping about a possible friendship with her and she knew without a doubt that Charmaine wanted to have a friend on the right side of life.

"I'd like to keep in touch and I know I'll want to talk to you again. And I'll keep you up-to-date on all of the progress that I can."

"Thank you so much. I'd appreciate that."

"I do have one more question though," she said while eyeing her reaction to more probing on her part.

"Can you tell me anything else about this Bobby Armore? Anything at all that you think might help."

"Well, Tina was always afraid of him. She felt he had a lot of contacts in the world and had spies looking for her."

"What type of contacts, did she say?"

"No, she didn't. But one time she did tell me that Bobby was smart and had been to a good college. And she said that he got a job with a company that had a lot of offices all over the United States. I can't remember the name, but it had a lot of letters in it."

"You mean it was a long name?"

"Well, the name did have a few words in it, but it started out with a lot of letters."

Sammi tried hard not to react, but wasn't sure she succeeded.

"Would you know the name if you heard it again?"

"I might. I've got a good memory."

What about MCI Corporation or LLC Documents, Inc. or ARNP Distributors."

But Charmaine shook her head at each name. Then Sammi threw it at her.

"What about ASAC Globe Ventures?"

"That's it; that's it; I'm pretty sure. I remember because I was thinking it must be a worldwide-type company."

"So you're pretty sure it was ASAC Globe Venture."

"I'm pretty sure that's what it was. But I don't know what he did or anything else."

"That's okay. You've been quite helpful. I appreciate your time tonight and I hope we can do this again sometime."

Charmaine's face lit up. She was happy and Sammi could tell how important it was for her to have her friendship. And although this murder case was of utmost importance and getting information from Charmaine was essential, her mind begged her to realize that this gal was a vital person, too, and one who needed and deserved a good deal of encouragement.

"Oh, one last thing I wanted to ask you. Did she carry a picture of her little boy on her keychain?"

Charmaine's face light up. "Yes, she did, but how would you know that?"

"It was just a guess because her keys were missing, yet her car was never taken. I was thinking if it was her ex- that he might have wanted that picture more than anything else."

"Yeah, Bobby would do something like that I'm sure."

They agreed on that point.

Sammi added. "I do get busy sometimes, but I always try to take time to meet with old and new friends."

There was no doubt that Charmaine's eyes were getting cloudy. She turned around to try and hide it, but Sammi had seen it. It never ceased to amaze her that sometimes when you extended yourself for a fellow human, it was quite rewarding. She knew that Charmaine was happy about the comment, but she sincerely meant it. And she did plan to meet with her again and not simply for business. She couldn't explain to another living soul how happy this made her feel.

* * *

As usual Dave was totally impressed with the information Sammi had retrieved. But even she had to admit that she felt she'd struck gold. If this Bobby was associated with the ASAC group, it was at least possible that the two murders had some type of connection.

"I know that seems far fetched, but ..." said Sammi.

"I don't know; I'm beginning to believe like Jim. All these crooks are connected in some way or another."

"But remember, the license plate number, Charmaine was very adamant about the fact that she didn't want anyone to know it came from her. Giving it to me made her nervous but her thoughts told me it was something she felt she had to do. Yet she was uneasy about it."

"We'll make sure of that. We'll keep that between you and me. We don't have to tell anyone where we got this information. I'm sure it will give Amilio some helpful clues to work with."

"What's the latest on Beth Barker? Is anything being released?"

"One neighbor did see three men walk up to their front door. But that's about all. There doesn't seem to be any other proof of another gunmen or even anyone who entered the house. There were no footprints, no fingerprints, nothing."

"This means," Sammi said, "that they wore gloves and no doubt covered their shoes so that even with all the ransacking they did, there's no evidence of who did it. That sounds premeditated to me. Guess I was hoping something else would show up."

"We all did. That's why the investigation at the house took so long. They spent two extra days going over everything that was touched and it produced nothing. There aren't any leads."

"So what does that mean for Randy?"

"He stays in jail, at least for now. And that's another thing. Ron Donovan wanted to keep it a secret that nothing had been found. He wanted to push the envelope and let them think we had something. But in court the other day during a go around for something or other, the prosecution knew they didn't have anything."

"Were they bluffing?" said Sammi.

"No, no. It was apparent that they knew we were drawing a blank at this end. Something's funny here."

"How can they know what's going on?"

"That's what Ron's trying to find out and he's getting increasingly suspicious of the happenings around here."

They were both silent and then Sammi offered, "Could there be a plant somewhere?"

"We all thought about that, but it seems unlikely. The police are solid and so are the FBI lawyers."

"Still, something's happening."

"I guess we'll have to wait and see."

* * *

A few days later Dave got called into Sergeant Brady's office. His face was stern and serious.

"I got a call from Ben Collier. I guess that Ron Donovan has been in touch informing him that he's got a problem here somewhere. Ron's been concentrating on it, but can't figure out what the hell's going on and that's not good. They've been blindsided every time they turn a corner on this case, especially in court, and he's got to find out what's happening. He's asked Ben to send out a few more agents to help."

Dave nodded his head and listened. He didn't yet realize what this had to do with him.

The sarge continued. "Ben said that before he did that he wanted to try something else. He could find a few extra men if it came to that, but asked Ron if he realized about you and Sammi. He didn't go into any specifics, but said that Sammi always seemed to be able to find out things when others failed. I guess Ron didn't know about you two and would like your help. To keep things open and fair, I guess Ben wants Ron to call you immediately. Are you and Sammi going to be home tonight? He wants to talk to you both, in privacy."

"I can make sure we are."

"Okay, I told him I'd call him back and let him know. Ron seems to think that the answer is nearby, but covert enough that none of his group is catching on and they've all been trying, himself, Gary and Paul. No one has any clues."

"Okay, we'll talk to Ron tonight. I'll let you know."

"Keep me informed. Do we have anything new yet to report?"

"Not really but we did find one thing that was too much of a coincidence to ignore. Sammi and I were talking about it. Amilio is working on the death of that prostitute. Clues do show a trail back to her husband who had tons of hate for his ex-wife for disappearing with their son. Anyway, this guy apparently works for that ASAC group. We don't think it's in this state, but he did show up here a few months before her death. Now that info is confidential right now."

He saw Sergeant Brady look up with shock and surprise.

Dave continued. "That's the same place that Randy Baker works. Could be there's a connection; I've let Amilio know and he's digging a little further. Now we just found out the other night and we haven't told the police yet because information is getting out. And damn it, I don't want this out right now. Okay? We're going to have to start trusting our group alone for now."

The sergeant nodded and arched his eyebrows. "I can't disagree with that. This looks like one of those cat and mouse games again. I'll bet Ben will be in the center of this mix real soon, probably throwing out phony information."

"And that means Julie will be working with us, too. The three referees will be at it again."

"And hopefully getting results. Damn it, Dave, this one is hurting us. What the hell's going on here?"

"I don't know, Sarge, but we need to know now so that we can beat them at their own game. This is nasty business."

"Right. Let me know what you and Ben and Ron decide, that is, if it's not secret."

Dave smiled. "I'll let you know all I can."

* * *

Dave called Sammi to make sure she'd be home tonight.

"Right, I'll be home."

"We need a break, and we need it now. I'm not blaming you because if you'd been around you would have heard something."

"If I'm around the right people. I think the tough part is going to be finding out who the traitors are."

"You've got a point. Many times it turns out to be someone you least expect."

Then Sammi changed the subject.

"Marlina called me today. She'd like us to have dinner with her and Amilio this weekend."

"Great. Saturday's best for me."

"Okay, I'll call her back. It's nice to hear her sounding so happy these days."

"Later, okay?"

Dave worked on for almost a half hour with no phone calls and no interruptions. He caught up on a few reports he needed to finish and thought he'd be done early enough to end up in the gym for a while. He'd been lax lately and his tense body was telling him how much his workouts helped keep his stress level down. As he cleared up his desk, locked it and gathered his equipment, Amilio picked this moment to stop by.

"Hey amigo, you going for a workout? Good idea. I should do it more often."

"Why don't you?"

"Don't know. My body gets lazy and my mind won't cooperate either."

Dave smiled. "I understand, good buddy, but you need it as much as I. Why don't you join me right now?"

Amilio smiled, almost said something, but realized it was a good idea.

"Okay, amigo, I'll get my stuff and meet you. Did you know Marlina wants us to get together this weekend?"

"Sammi just called me. Saturday's best for me; how about you?"

"That's good for me, too. I'm looking forward to it. It's been a while for the four of us."

"Okay, then get your stuff and meet me in the gym. You need a work-out, too."

"Okay, big brother. I'll be right behind you."

Dave laughed as he walked out toward the gym. Yeah, he still considered Amilio his little brother in some ways, but in other ways Amilio was way ahead of him.

* * *

That night Dave and Sammi sat waiting for Ron's call. They knew they'd again be pulled into situations that would take both their expertise to evaluate. Sammi seemed to be looking forward to more involvement, while Dave was more apprehensive.

"But we're not playing with amateurs here. And these guys will be playing for keeps. We'll both have to be careful to keep our cover perfect. No screw ups or a lot of people could lose."

"It would be better sometimes for me to go it alone," said Sammi.

"Not a chance. I could never concentrate on anything else if I knew you were in the line of fire alone."

"I'm never going to be alone."

"That's true, because I'm always going to be around," said Dave.

Sammi decided to stop this conversation because it wasn't going anywhere. Dave worried so much about her and she could understand it, but what she did was well hidden and no one ever suspected her, not during the investigation nor after. That had been well proven in the past. Yet, Dave couldn't relax with her going it solo. So she gave in – at least for now. But there might come a time when their pattern would change.

The phone rang. Dave answered.

"Hi, Ron, just a minute ... Sammi get on the extension." He paused. "Okay, Ron, we're ready."

"Ben Collier has spoken to me about the two of you. He's spoken highly and said that he is sometimes in awe of especially you, Sammi. Well, I sure need a miracle right now. Someone is finding out what we do at each step of the game."

"Do you have any suspicions at all?" asked Dave.

"None. I tell you, None. And I've given it my total attention particularly in the last few weeks. In fact, I had Sam Brady send over some guys to my rooms and other areas to make sure they're not bugged. And they weren't. I don't have any idea where to start looking. But I've got to do something."

"So what exactly is going on from your end?" asked Dave.

"My private information is getting out. What I mean is some of my strategy for the case and some of the few clues we've found are being leaked. And believe me this case is tough. The clues all point to Ron's guilt, but my gut feeling tells me he's innocent."

"I'm glad to hear you say that."

"Well, remember I'm his defense attorney and I'd defend him with everything I've got no matter what I believed. But this guy isn't stupid. He wouldn't leave his gun at the murder scene, and a perfectly clear footprint, and oh, well, a lot of other things, too. But now I'm afraid to turn my back on anything or anyone. And believe me, that's a hard way to work."

"What do you want us to do?"

"Exactly, I don't even know. But I need someone to help me find out what the hell's going on here."

"Okay," said Dave.

"Honestly, Ben told me that when Sammi's around things just seem to happen. If you could help at all, I'd be grateful. I've got to give this Randy a fair shake and right now it's tough."

"When's the next time you go to court?" asked

Sammi.

"Next Tuesday. And we'll be in front of the judge for a little while. We're again going to ask for bail to be set. I don't think we'll get it yet, but I plan to keep asking. It'll look so much better for him if he's out on bail when the trial starts."

"Any idea when that'll be?" Dave asked.

"No, I don't know. It's a little ways off. But I've got to start putting together a good defense and that seems impossible right now.

Sammi said, "Well, I'd like to come to court and watch the proceedings. Any problem with that, Ron?"

"No, not at all," he said, but sounded surprised.

"Okay, then."

"I'm surprised, I guess; that's all."

"Dave and I need to get a better feel for all these characters involved in this case. I think the best place to do that would be in court."

"All I ask is that if you find out anything ... well, I'd rather not have anyone see us meeting together. I think phone calls would be better."

"We'll let you know by phone or we could use Sergeant Brady."

"That's a good idea. He should be in on this, too. Well, thanks again."

"We'll be in touch."

CHAPTER EIGHT

Saturday night proved to be total enjoyment and relaxation was on the menu for all. Amilio and his fiancé Marlina had wanted to see a movie and then they went for a late dinner at Dave's favorite restaurant; the one with the private little rooms where you could talk and not be overheard.

"This was fun and it's nice to have Amilio around and not always in the middle of danger," said Marlina.

"Danger is always around every day. That's life," he answered.

"Well, I just feel better right now, that's all," she said and he gave her a nice hug.

"I know. You need to have me around."

She laughed and took his teasing lightly. They had known each other since they were little kids, both orphans and living in the same large foster home in a small Mexican village. They always remained devoted to each other and their loyalty grew as they matured. Even though Marlina didn't like all the chances he took as a policeman or double agent, she accepted what he needed to do with his life. And now they were planning their wedding for June.

"How big of a wedding are you planning?" Sammi asked.

"Just four of us," laughed Amilio. "I was hoping to elope with you two as our witnesses."

But Marlina held her decision. "It'll be small, but we've both made good friends over the years and a few from our Mexican village will come if they can. And we'll be married in St. Paul's Catholic Church because we were both raised catholic."

That did cause Amilio's eyes to head toward the ceiling and Marlina let him have his moment.

"He teases a lot, but you believe in God, right?"

"Oh sure I do. But not like I did when we were forced into those routines as kids. My God, that'd turn anyone away from religion."

Dave laughed. "I can't picture you going to mass every morning before school."

"I did. And I learned not to talk in church or I'd get hit in the side of the head by a nun or a priest, whoever was around."

Marlina shook her head. "You said you liked to go to church back then."

"I did, because then I wasn't in school."

"You're such a tease. You were good in school and you loved it."

Amilio got serious for a moment. "Yes, I must admit I did like school. It taught me a lot of things I needed to know. And I didn't mind church all that much. I really believed in miracles back then. I sort of still do. But back then, I kept thinking that someone would come along and adopt me and Marlina and my other friend, but it didn't happen. And slowly, I stopped believing in these so-called miracles that the bible said could happen and I started to believe in me. I then decided I was my own miracle and now that's what I think it's all about."

Everyone was silent and Amilio realized that he had thrown a serious covering on this part of the evening.

"Sorry, sometimes when I think back, I'm still not sure how I feel about everything. People tried to take care of us and teach us what we needed to know, right, Marlina?"

She nodded, but felt touched as well.

"But so much was missing from our lives and we knew it. Others in school lived in nice homes and went on fun vacations. I know cause I got to stay overnight with some of them a few times."

Then Amilio stopped and he got quiet.

Sammi began. "Amilio, I think that's why now, here in this profession you can understand people so well. You've seen all sides and have more understanding than most. And we all know how good you are in dealing with people."

Amilio looked over and smiled. And Sammi heard him thinking, *but I never thought it was fair and I cried a lot and felt ashamed. Now it doesn't seem to matter so much.*

Sammi knew she had to be careful with Amilio, then added, "My little friend Lena lived in an orphanage in Russia, but she had a mother who didn't want her. And it made her angry with the world most of her life. She made some very bad choices because of that. But you made some good choices and are doing great things."

"I think we have choices to make every day. How we end up is our own decision. Oh, I'm sure there's a little bit of luck involved, but we make our own luck. What do you think Dave?"

Dave had been particularly quiet simply listening and realizing that everyone had a different story to tell. And every story had some good sides and some bad sides.

"I do think a lot depends on your attitude and how much effort you put into what you want to accomplish."

"See, big brother. I was sure we'd agree on that."

"Well, of course. Some people only whine about things, and never get out there and put in the effort. I know you've got to have dreams, but you have to put your own effort in making those dreams come true. That I can totally agree with."

And everyone seemed to feel the same. This conversation gave Dave some serious thoughts. In all the years he'd known Amilio he seldom talked about his past. It was barely a few years ago that he found out he was an orphan and didn't have any family to talk about. And getting him to break that code of silence he'd developed was somewhat unusual. Tonight, with his fiancé and good friends around, his cloak was slipping somewhat as they began reminiscing and Dave was finally getting an insight into how Amilio felt about things. These moments seldom happened. Amilio always played the nonchalant, easy-going personality that got him into valuable situations as a double agent. His guard was always up and letting it down as he was doing tonight was not his usual behavior.

* * *

"So, Sammi," said Amilio, "anything new with our prostitute case?"

"No, not yet. But I'm trying to find out what kind of flower that was in Tina's hand."

"Why would that matter?"

She looked over at Amilio and smiled. "Because not knowing makes it one of those little details that irritates me. I need to know what kind of flower."

Dave smiled, too. *Yes*, he thought, *she always had to get all of the details.*

Amilio nodded. "Okay, but I can't see what that would have to do with anything. I think the fact that a flower was left means something, not what kind of flower it is."

"And you could be right. But I need to know."

"That's right," he said as he turned to Marlina. "Sammi here always needs to know all of the details, sort of like connecting all of the dots."

"It's the way I am."

"I've heard you've had good success in the past, so it must work for you." Then Amilio had to explain that one further. "Sammi, you're great. And maybe I should start paying more attention to details."

"You do just fine," she said smiling. "Your record is quite impressive."

"Hey, big brother, you're another one who impresses me. You always seem to be at the right place at the right time."

Dave simply shook his head. "This is quite a group we have. I know Sammi thinks the type of flower might be some kind of clue, and I don't think that's too far-fetched."

Then Amilio turned to Sammi directly as he said, "I'm teasing with you. I've told Marlina how clever you are and I'm still trying to figure you out. I'll have to keep trying."

She laughed. "Understood, but in the meantime I wondered if you found out about that license plate?"

"Oh yeah, amiga, and it's assigned to Robert Armore from Los Angeles, California. I've still got people working on this, but he does work for that ASAC group. I still haven't been able to find out what he does there. Dave, this ASAC thing has offices all around the country. They're very large and I think Julie is trying to find out exactly what they do."

"Good," said Sammi. "I'm curious about the activities in the past that brought them up on fraud and conspiracy charges. That might tell us one area that they deal in."

"Right, we've got a lot of work on this one."

"But first," said Sammi, "we have to find out how Randy figures in all this. I would think our first priority is to find out who really killed his wife."

All of a sudden quietness fell on the group. Sammi's statement made them all think deeply for a few moments and reflect where they were heading.

"I have a feeling when we find Beth Baker's killer, the other pieces of the puzzle will fall into place. I think a lot of hidden activities are going to be coming to light," she said.

"I'm sure that's true, amiga. But in the meantime, I hear the defense attorneys are having a rough time with information leaking out. That makes it rough."

"We've got to get that under control and fast. Can't imagine where the leak is coming from."

"This puzzle keeps getting deeper and deeper," said Amilio. "It seems that everything we look at has a double meaning. So I guess Sammi is right after all. It might make a difference what kind of flower was found on the body. It may really mean something."

Sammi smiled. She knew that Amilio was throwing her an olive branch and she accepted it, knowing he would keep trying to figure her out.

* * *

At home that evening they both laughed at Amilio's fishing expedition. It bugged him about Sammi and he didn't mind showing it.

"You've certainly got him wondering. It tickles me," said Dave. "That guy has certainly got his smarts and real expertise in a lot of areas, but he can't figure you out."

Sammi smiled. "And if he can't figure me out, as clever as he is, I'm safer out there than you think I am."

"Don't go there with me, honey. Sometimes these guys might not figure out what you do, but just get suspicious that you do something and it'll be enough for them. You'd still be in danger."

She put her hands on her hips and puckered her mouth slightly. "You won't relax about this, will you?"

"Of course not; I love you, Sammi. You're the world to me and if you think I'm going to willingly let you out there taking unnecessary chances by yourself ... well, I'm not. These guys are playing for keeps."

She had to agree. "I know and I appreciate your concern, but I've got to be able to do my job."

"And you can, but with some protection around you, and usually it'll be me. Look, I don't like to think about this, but what if something did happen and you couldn't do what you do any longer. We'd all be in a mess. So many people depend on you now. Most don't know how you do what you do, but they know that you can get results and they count on it. Hell, I do all the time. So let's not argue about this anymore, okay?"

"I thought this was a friendly, lively discussion," she smirked, and let it go. Dave worried too much about her out in the field on this case. She knew that he'd seen a lot of nasty situations over the years that had made a permanent memory in his mind. She decided to leave the subject alone.

* * *

On Monday, at the bank, Sammi went in to talk to Mr. Marconey. She needed information and wondered if he was in a position to help her.

"Now, I don't mean to put you on the spot, but I'm trying to find out about this ASAC Globe Ventures, Inc. They've got their hands in a lot of things and I'm wondering if they've ever had dealings with our bank."

Mr. Marconey mulled over his answer. He rubbed his chin with his hand and commenced carefully. "That's a touchy situation for me. I have to maintain the privacy of our customers and I could never give out any details for you at this time. But I can tell you that they have a few loans with us. But that's all I'm going to say. That's all I can say. I wish I could tell you more, but I feel that would be out of line."

"I understand." But Sammi had already heard that there were some unusual circumstances with the loans that dealt with Mr. Matthew Carnigan. Mr. Marconey thought he was a strange man, secretive and guarded and felt comfortable mostly with his associate, Mr. Smiley Sturges. He was the one who had all the smarts anyway. This Matthew guy was more interested in eyeing the women around the area. Although he realized that Matthew was at the head of this company, he imagined he was more of a figurehead, because in his opinion he didn't have it in him to run a big company.

"I wish I could tell you more, Sammi. But even in confidence, I wouldn't feel right about it."

"No, no, that's okay. Just one last question if you can. Was everything above board about the loan or did you have any concerns. I don't care to know what they were, just if you had some."

He sat still again and finally said, "Our bank does follow certain policies no matter who the people are. If they didn't meet the criteria they wouldn't have gotten the loan."

Sammi nodded. She almost felt bad about using Mr. Marconey. They'd been friends over the years and he knew how valuable she was. She had stopped a few fraudulent activities ahead of time for him personally. But she was reading his thoughts, which is why she was having this conversation with him in the first place.

"I guess that's all I need to know. Thanks for your time."

"If anything should occur in the future where the police or the FBI is involved in some way, then I'd like you to be involved and I could tell you anything you needed to know."

"Understood, and I do appreciate your position."

When she left his office, she took a few minutes to sit by herself on a lounge sofa in the outer area of the offices. She made a few notes and relaxed for a moment. She realized without a doubt that Mr. Marconey had real problems with Mr. Carnigan's behavior. It was lucky that Smiley Sturges was the main signer of the loan or there would have been questions as to whether he would have approved it. He needed a serious-minded businessman to deal with, not one whose every other thought went out to the nearest woman around and whether she would be a willing target or not. In fact, a few times Mr. Marconey thought that this Matthew Carnigan had a personality problem, a behavior disorder or was just someone they kept on a short leash and brought out when his presence was needed to sign some papers. Reflecting back on other comments she had heard about him, Sammi thought that she had discovered a lot about the head of the ASAC group.

* * *

Dave joined Tom to visit Randy at the jail. It was already well past the middle of January and the process was moving slowly. Randy was still being held with no bond and the future prospect was increasingly shaky. He didn't want his son to see him in jail and he was still mourning the death of his wife and blaming himself for the entire messy situation. There was no doubt he was falling into depression and no one seemed to be able to help him.

"You've got to hang on for Denver. That kid's doing pretty good, considering and he gets brighter every time he gets a message from his dad. He knows you're innocent and wants you to be brave. He sent you a message today, "Keep your thoughts strong."

Randy had to smile despite everything. He said, "How does that go? ... And the little ones shall lead us."

Dave said, "Hey, this isn't easy. Everything's against you, but we're not. You've got to hang in there. We're here today to get you to start thinking again. Keep your thoughts in that arena of finding out what the hell was going on at ASAC. Why would they want to kill Beth?"

"Okay, okay," he said. "We've got two main scenarios. I've told the lawyers, but they're having a hard time believing it."

"What?" said Tom. "Who has a hard time believing what?"

"Let me start at the beginning. Okay, scenario number one: They were out to kill Beth and blame me for it. Then I'd look like a liar no matter what and nothing I said would matter. Scenario number two: I was the only target and they simply meant to scare Beth but something went terribly wrong. When she recognized that one guy they could have felt they couldn't let her live, or not ... I don't know."

He stopped and put his head in his hands. He held that position of desperation for a few moments and then something happened; his demeanor totally changed. It was like he got strength from somewhere and his attitude and posture took on power.

He took a deep breath and started to speak. "Both of these situations make sense to me, but when I told the lawyers, well, especially that Paul Ryan, he thought that idea was stupid. He was positive that Beth was not any kind of target at all."

"Really, why not?" asked Dave.

"When I asked him he wasn't too clear. Something about I had to be the intended one because the company was sure I had taken secrets. And he was quite adamant that Beth was not involved."

Both felt that possibly that's what this lawyer honestly believed.

"But when I reminded him that Beth was the one who was killed, he looked embarrassed and just shut up. Somehow, I don't like that guy. The others seem okay, but that Paul guy is kind of weird to me."

What did Ron say?"

"He thought both scenarios were quite plausible and came up with an interesting third one. He thought that it was possible that they didn't think that Beth would be home yet, and actually that would have been true, but she had the day off. Could be they wanted to check the house and see if the stolen information was there. But when she opened the door with a gun, well, they felt they had no choice."

"That's another possibility. What did your Paul Ryan think about that?"

"He doesn't seem to cross Ron. He's pretty much of a yes man. I understand Ron feeds him information and gets him to do more research than anything else."

"But why did they wait so late in the day? It seems if they wanted to find the house empty, they would have come earlier," said Dave.

"That would seem more likely," added Tom.

"Don't know," said Randy. "Hell, I don't know why they did this at all. Everything I was able to get is available to a lot of other people working there. Now I was not a solitary person in my suspicions, in fact, I know a few guys around who were damn nervous about things and went out of their way to stay on the good side of the owners."

"Really?" said Tom.

"Have you mentioned this to your lawyers yet?"

"No, I just now thought about it because we were rambling on about everything."

"Good and don't say anything until we tell you."
Dave looked over at Tom suspiciously.

"Why? What's going on?"

"Nobody knows at this time, but we think someone isn't who they seem to be. So until we get back with you, keep this to yourself. Later, I'm going to want the names of these other people and probably talk to them, too. But as of right now, keep this to yourself. Got it?" said Dave.

"Yeah, I got it."

"More twists and turns. This is getting more interesting every day," said Tom.

"This is something I should have told them at first, right?" Randy asked.

"Actually," said Tom. "We're glad you didn't. We can't tell you everything right now; it would take too long, but I want you to keep remembering things like that. I'm sure you know more, but you take it for granted. It's something we all do. But while you're sitting here, I want you to look back over every detail you can think of, the stuff that you and Beth talked about that made you and her nervous. Anything at all, but don't tell anyone but us. We'll explain later."

"Okay. So I'll just work with the lawyers with things they already know and I won't give them anything additional. It's like I'm working with two sets of people."

"In a way, I think you are," said Dave.

It was obvious that Randy was slightly confused about the situation. He was stuck in jail and didn't get access to much information anyway. He was at the mercy of what his lawyers told him and what his friends passed on to him when they came to visit. And he felt that you couldn't always believe what you heard on TV. But it did seem that he was getting a little shrewd in his observation of his police friends. Something else was going on and he had to be careful. The police were working on his behalf. He trusted Tom completely, and of course, Dave was on his team.

Tom said, "I wanted to tell you that they've moved

Denver to the 7th Grade. He was getting bored and they wanted to keep his mind active and focused. But he still does 8th Grade math and science. He amazes this school. They even thought of putting him totally in the 8th Grade, but the kids are a lot older and this seemed like the best alternative fit for him."

"Beth and I always talked about that. The emotional and social side of a child is important, too. That's why we've kept him mainstreamed in regular school. He needed to have time for that part of his life to catch up."

Tom laughed. "Yes, I know. He told his teachers that he felt Grade 7 would be the best match for him to educate his total personality."

Randy smiled. "That sounds like Denver. We were sure if we pushed it he could have been in much higher grades, but then look what he would miss? And even the jokes and laughs and shenanigans that kids go through were important for him to experience in his age group."

"Having a gifted kid like that can be a challenge," Dave said, "but he's a nice little boy."

Randy nodded.

"We'll keep in touch and update you as much as we can. But keep to our program and think of everything you can remember that was suspicious at ASAC."

"Okay, but I'll only tell you guys."

"Right. That's what we want."

* * *

Denver Baker sat in his seventh grade history class, looking around at the other kids. This was his second week since he'd been moved to this class and he liked it, felt comfortable and seemed to be accepted. After all, he was ten years old and most kids in this grade were twelve and thirteen. Still he was as tall as some and that helped. What else helped was the fact that during the first week, the teacher called on him several times and he knew all the answers. That gave him a solid position and a few were already getting friendly with him because they knew he could help them. And that always happened to him.

It was a little rougher in math and science where he joined 8th Graders. Some resented him, that was obvious, but no one was mean or nasty. They just ignored him. Still he had his own little group that accepted him and that was all he needed.

Today, for some reason, he felt sad. He tried to fight it. His mom had taught him how. You had to switch your thoughts from negative ones to happy or at least to more constructive ones. His mom believed that everything happened in your thought world first and then manifested outward. He couldn't argue with that.

"Hey Denver, are you ready for this history test?"

"Sure, I'm ready."

That was his little friend Jonathon who was always so nervous before a test. He had spent ten minutes with him before they entered the classroom going over his notes.

"Don't you get nervous?" asked Jonathon. "Oh no, there's no reason for you to get nervous; you already know this stuff."

"I have to study, too. But give it your best shot, Jonathon. You'll do okay."

At one point during the test, Denver looked over at his friend. *He's writing a lot*, he thought, *must be doing okay.*

Before the test was finished, his teacher informed him to report to the principal's office after he was finished.

* * *

Mr. Finley's office was large with a formal atmosphere and gave him the impression that something had to be wrong in order to be summoned here. But he smiled as he was invited in and asked to sit down. Denver had no idea what he was doing here. He knew he hadn't done anything wrong; he never did as following the rules was part of his upbringing. So he waited, somewhat impatiently.

Mr. Finley began. "I wanted to talk with you for a few minutes and see how you're doing? You're an excellent student and behave very well and we're pleased to have you in this school. Of course we realize you're gifted, so we consider you an asset."

Denver sat and waited. He thought, *is this going to be one of those pep talks? You're so lucky to be smart. Mom used to think that was a waste of time. Everyone was gifted in some way. That's how he liked to think of his fellow students and spent his time trying to figure out in which area they were gifted.*

"I wanted to discuss the possibility of getting you with other intelligent students that we have at this school. We have a special group that is of a certain intellectual capacity and they seem to enjoy each other."

Denver's suspicions were immediately on alert. He had met a few other kids considered bright and they lorded it over the others. And they thought they were superior to everyone, at least most of them thought that way. He didn't want any part of that. It didn't fit in with his philosophy.

"You mean like Richard Benson and Don Watson."

"Yes, those are two of them and we have three others. You're all close to the same age and thought you could be of benefit to each other."

Denver slowly shifted in his chair. Suddenly he felt uncomfortable and ill at ease. He didn't want to be associated with some intellectual group. That's what he wanted to stay away from and that's the real reason his parents didn't put him in a gifted school. *How can I get out of this? I don't want to alienate anyone and upset their goals, but I like these other kids better. I don't want to sit around with the intellectuals and talk about how much smarter we are, cause I know that's what they do. Mom says that you never know when someone is going to bloom and pass you up in some area, so be friends with everyone. No, I've got to get out of this.*

"At this time, Mr. Finley, I think I'm more comfortable with the friends I've got. I'm not sure how I'll feel in the future; I might be interested in a group like that, but at this time I have a lot of other things on my mind. I'd prefer to leave everything as it is. Is that okay with you?"

He hoped he hadn't overdone it, but he didn't want to seem like he was unappreciative. He was, but this was not for him. He liked to observe the kids in his class. Like Jonathon, he did have trouble in history and he had helped him, but that kid could take apart an entire engine of a car and put it back together again, and he was showing him some of his mechanical feats. And little Willie in his class was considered a tough student to teach because it took him a long time to catch on. Yet once he had learned something, he never lost it. And Willie was one of the best pitchers this school's baseball team had ever had. You had to look at the entire person, his mom had said. Everyone has a gift she used to say and he was finding out that was true. Looking for the gifts in other people was a real amusing pastime for him.

"Of course, it's entirely up to you, Denver. We'd like you to know that you'd be invited to join this club if you wanted. If you have other interests at this time, that's good. But it will always be open to you."

"I appreciate that, Mr. Finley, possibly sometime in the future."

With that comment he was excused while thinking that he couldn't imagine any time in the future when that would happen. But he was on borrowed time right now anyhow. When his dad was exonerated, they'd be moving back to Kingston and he'd be going back to his regular school. It's just that he didn't know when that would be.

* * *

Riding home from school with Ms. Jill that day, he realized that she knew about the invitation to join the special club.

"It's your decision, Denver. It's entirely up to you. We wanted you to know that it was available for you, that's all."

"I know, but I like the normal kids better," said Denver, then he stopped abruptly. "I don't think that sounded right."

Jill laughed. "I know what you mean."

"I've got more to learn from them than I can learn from the others. Like my mom told me once, you already know how to be smart and get through classes with ease. Others don't, so they have other challenges. It might be good to get to know them. They can teach you a lot."

"Your mom was a very wise woman."

"She was. She was so smart. She studied a lot of philosophy, and she used to lecture on all types of theories. And she told me about some of them. But I think she watered them down a little for me."

Jill smiled. "I don't think she would have had to do that very much."

"I know this will sound crazy, but I know I'm smart. I love to read and I love to study. I'll always keep learning because there's so much that I'm interested in. But I'm still a kid and I have to learn all of the normal kid things. That's important to my growth, too. Mom made me aware of that."

They both thought over that statement the rest of the way home.

CHAPTER NINE

Dave and Sammi met for lunch on Tuesday before they headed over to the courtroom. Both were excited to begin a new angle at discovering anything they could in this most confusing case.

They walked into the courtroom with a few minutes to spare and sat down in the back row. They saw only the defense attorneys at the table; the other table was empty. That seemed odd to them. It was less than a moment later when Ron Donovan called them over to his table.

"It looks like there won't be any proceedings today. The prosecution called for a delay because of some schedule conflict. I guess we'll proceed another day and I'll let you know. But let me introduce Sammi to my assistants."

He introduced both Stephen Harrison and Paul Ryan to Sammi. Dave had met them both before.

"Well, this is a tough case we're on this time, and it's been slow going," said Paul Ryan. "Any help you can provide will be appreciated." He said this as he put out his hand to Sammi.

Sammi immediately wondered why he thought they were there to help. Why did he assume that? They could have been there to observe. She smiled and turned to Steve who was equally congenial.

"We were hoping to move along further on the possibility of bail today, but the prosecution got a continuance until Thursday."

"Hopefully, Thursday will turn out better," she said.

And they were all in agreement with that statement.

The two assistants didn't stay around long, but Ron waited to talk to them both alone. He showed them some of the significant paperwork he wanted them to be aware of as well as familiarize them with some of the proceedings that would be occurring in the next few days. He walked them through what would happen in court on Thursday.

"I want you two to be able to concentrate on what is necessary to help us; you don't need to be surprised at anything. All this will be some of the fluff that happens in a courtroom. Believe me, a lot of this is political."

"Yeah," said Dave. "There are politics in everything."

They all agreed.

"Any questions?" asked Ron.

"Not at this time," said Sammi.

"Good, let's keep a clean slate between us until we get this leak cleared up. And of course as we talked about, we'll keep it between the three of us."

"That's a good idea," said Sammi.

* * *

Walking out to the car, Dave wasn't sure but he was intrigued by Sammi's last comment. She didn't usually throw out such a leading statement.

"Look, I know it's much too soon for you to have picked up anything, but you were trying to tell Ron something. I mean nothing went on today, but you threw him out a hidden warning; I know you."

Teasingly Sammi said, "What did I say?"

Dave took it good-naturedly and played her game. "You told him it was a good idea to keep things between us and I caught your double meaning."

Sammi smiled. "You know me too well."

"Right," he said. "Now give. Don't tell me you picked up something already?"

"Oh yes I did, and it's not good news. Paul Ryan is a problem. He works for ASAC and has for years. He's a plant on the defense team. He's the one passing on information."

Dave had deliberately not told Sammi what Randy had hinted during their talk at the jail yesterday. Randy got bad vibes from Paul whom he felt frustrated his every attempt at reasonable explanations for the murder. Only Ron could get him to back off and Paul really catered to his boss. Dave was immediately suspicious, but didn't clue in Sammi. He wanted to know if she'd pick up something on her own.

"When we were introduced he was concerned about me, but he did blow me off, which is good. However, he wondered why we were in court today. Ron set his mind at ease when he told him it was just to get us familiar with court proceedings. That seemed to make sense to him. But do you know what he thought at that time?"

Dave smiled. "Of course I don't know. Are you going to keep me guessing?"

"Oh no, that's merely a figure of speech. He was thinking that he'd mention this turn of events to Matthew Carnigan; he felt he'd want to know. If we turned out to be nothing threatening, that was good for them. But he felt he had to let him know."

"Oh, my God, so he's the one leaking information."

"It would seem that way."

"God, I don't know how Ron is going to get around this. Paul is part of his main team and does a lot of research, right? So how do we let Ron know? He'll tell ASAC everything so they'll be informed ahead of time of anything they've got planned. We can't let this go on much longer."

Then Dave let Sammi know how Randy had given them additional clues but would not tell anyone right now. And if he remembered anything further, he would work with the three referees until this mess was straightened up.

"Why don't we wait until Thursday? Just a feeling, but I'll hear more at that time. And then we'll have to figure out a way to talk to Ron that won't have everyone wondering what's going on. We'll need a fairly long meeting to figure all this out."

"Okay, we'll wait until Thursday. Then I think we need to get to Ben Collier and let him figure out how to play this one."

Sammi looked over at Dave and smiled. "That's perfect. This game belongs to the FBI anyway."

"But, one other thing," said Dave thinking ahead. "It's going to look suspicious if we end up in court again on Thursday. We don't want anything to get Paul suspecting us. Any ideas?"

Sammi thought for a moment and said, "I've got it. Why don't we get Jill to bring down a few children from the school; not Denver, though. It could look like they're coming to court as part of a classroom project and I'll go along as a chaperone. But you'd have to stay away. Now, Paul might get suspicious, but I think he'd accept it. Anyway, I'll know what he's thinking."

"You'd be okay. And those types of field trips are common for kids. That's a good idea. Could you get it done that quickly?"

"I think so. I'll call Jill tonight. We don't need more than four or five kids, preferably seniors and I think that would seem plausible."

"Okay, I'll be anxious to find out what you hear."

* * *

In the meantime, Amilio had been trying to backtrack on the life of one Bobby Armore and he was getting an earful. The younger to middle years of this guy were one run-in with the law after another from petty theft to assault and battery and graduating to several assault charges that landed him in jail for several years. Then in his middle thirties, he seemed to settle down. He came from an upper middle class family, and had been able to manage graduating from college. His family seemed straight and neither one of his parents had any kind of criminal record or no known run-in with the law. This guy went that route alone. His record showed he was intelligent enough in his brain, but not in his outward experiences. He had a definite chip on his shoulder that had never gone away. Amilio hadn't been able to make the connection where this would have begun.

He approached Dave for discussion. "This guy's got

quite a temper and it's gotten him into trouble many times."

"But how did he end up working for that ASAC group, with his record? I hear they're quite particular."

"That's interesting and I'm still working on it. But it seems that he met a guy named Jonas Nester when he got out of prison the last time. I don't know all of the details yet that I need, but this guy works at ASAC, too. I'd like to see both of their employment records or at least find out who sponsored them, but I'd need a subpoena for that. Not a good idea right now."

"That's for sure. Everything you're doing right now has to remain covert. If there's any connection to the other case we can't tip our hand. We haven't yet figured out where the leak is coming from; not exactly."

"Oh, you've got some ideas?"

Dave smiled. "Possibly the beginning of an idea."

Amilio poked Dave's arm. "Sammi, right? She's starting to know what's going on."

"We'll let you know when we know."

"You've got one smart gal there. But if these cases are connected, everything has to be hush-hush. We can't let them know we're aware of anything. It could hurt the trial, but it could also be dangerous for a lot of people involved."

Dave agreed.

Just then Jim Mucci came over with a message for Amilio. "Hey buddy, I only this minute heard that your inquiry on those guys at ASAC will be coming early tomorrow, secretly. They're not supposed to give out that private information, but why am I not surprised that they'll let you have it?"

They all laughed. Amilio said, "I guess they like me."

"That must be it," said Jim. "You're such a lovable guy."

After Amilio walked away, Jim said. "I'm so glad he's back, but I have to admit that at times I feel that things are so strange. I mean, Amilio, well, okay but he doesn't even look like he used to and he definitely doesn't sound like that other guy. He's amazing, isn't he?"

"He is that," said Dave. "I remember some movie I saw years ago; I think it was called 'The Great Pretender'. It was the real life story of some guy who successfully played many different parts in his life like a doctor, for God's sake, a lawyer and several other intriguing parts that needed expertise. He went on for quite a few years before he was caught, and he wasn't officially qualified for any of them. I imagine he had to have quite a good brain in that head of his to pull it off, but..."

"Kind of think that Amilio could get away with it too, right?"

"He probably could. But, Amilio is our new friend and we can't forget that."

"For sure," said Jim as he walked away.

* * *

That night Dave cautioned Sammi to be careful at court the next day. True, they had picked up a good cover plan, but she was to stay in the background and do her work that way. They could stay in the back rows so that when the attorneys saw the kids, they would realize the main reason they were there. Although everything seemed to be carefully thought out, it made Dave nervous.

"I like it better when I'm there."

"I know you do, Dave, but that would look way too suspicious. We were there together on Tuesday and to-morrow in this setup, I'll look like a chaperone. That's what I want, but I can also listen in on all I have to. Now, if I remember this correctly, they're going to be arguing again about the fact of whether or not they should be allowed to come back to court and argue about Ron's bail, right?"

Dave nodded.

"Doesn't that seem like an oxymoron to you? It does to me. They're going to argue about whether they should be allowed to argue? Do I understand this correctly?"

Despite the seriousness of the situation, Dave had to

laugh. "Yeah, I know, but the law is strange. He's already been denied bail. They can't just come back and argue for it. They have to plead and connive to be able to be allowed to come back to argue again for Randy's right to bail. It's like an appeal hearing to see if someone can get a new trial."

"Well, I don't get it. But there are a lot of things about trials I don't understand. One was always the way they select the jurors and another is certainly this fighting to be able to fight for a bail hearing."

"The law can be complicated," he said.

"Regardless, tomorrow should be interesting about the bail hearing, but I also hope to hear something that we can use."

Dave told Sammi what Amilio was working on. He seemed to have some leads to look into.

"That's good. It seems like we're moving forward a little right now. God both of these cases have been painfully slow."

"Right. Luckily, Denver seems settled with Tom and Jill and he seems to understand more than they do about the aspects of the law and trials."

Sammi smiled. "I'm sure he does. But underneath all that intelligence and strong armor lies the heart and feelings of a young child who lost his mother and has a father in jail charged with her murder. He can be logical and rational to a point, but he keeps things hidden. He's having a tough time inside."

"I imagine he is. But time should help and when we get his father out of jail and the real murderer is in prison that should go a long way in the healing process. But this type of pain will always be with him."

Sammi didn't say anymore. She didn't want to discuss something she suspected because she didn't know anything concrete yet. But she knew Denver had a secret. She hadn't been able to hear it yet, because with all of the incredible feelings he had this secret was too deep. But, in time, she would.

* * *

Walking into the courtroom on Thursday, Sammi thought she was fairly well prepared, but had no idea what she was up against. The children they brought from Jill's school consisted of two girls and three boys, all eighth graders, who were opting for this courtroom experience as part of their class in Social Science. These were extremely dedicated seniors who kept a serious and reflective demeanor and planned to take notes during the procedures. There were other spectators as well which put an entirely plausible face on the audience.

She made a mental note as to what she wanted to do. At the defense side of the table were Ron Donovan, Stephen Harrison and, of course, Paul Ryan, the one whom Sammi figured was a plant from ASAC. She knew he'd be the main one she'd be focusing on today. But as a reminder she had to refresh her memory about the prosecution side, which consisted of James McLean as the lead prosecutor, and his assistants were Gary Duncan and Wayne Berman. She didn't feel they would get much of her attention today.

As the proceedings opened up the children were in full cooperation as their total focus was the courtroom drama, and they would have a paper to write later on. Jill suspected Sammi had a mission and positioned herself so she wouldn't be disturbed. As the opening arguments got started, Paul Ryan's thoughts were clamoring for attention and nervousness plus open anxiety was filling his mind.

We've got to keep this bail hearing under control. There must be no bail, thought Paul. *Matthew said that if it looked like we might succeed that I should ask for a continuance. Ron will have a fit, but if any of us requests one, it's usually given. I've decided that I could plead to Ron that I felt we needed more time to be sure we'd get a favorable outcome. I think I could get away with that.*

Sammi was amazed that Paul's mind was so overshadowed with worrisome thoughts about how Matthew would handle the outcome. He was quite concerned about having his approval at all times. She felt there was an even deeper reason for this. Then a solid hint came forward. Paul thought that if he could manage to confuse this case enough, he would be in solid to become one of the 'Gentlemen', whatever that meant. That strange thought crossed his mind several times. It was definitely his goal.

"Ms. Sammi, is that prosecutor going to win or not?" asked one of the students.

"Not sure yet, we'll have to wait and see."

"He seems to be winning a lot of points right now."

Sammi agreed, which brought her attention to that side of the table for a few minutes. And then she heard it. It was all she could do to remain calm and indifferent. Dave and Ben knew they had a problem with this Paul Ryan, and how to get Ron aware of him. But now there was more in the name of Wayne Berman, the third attorney on the prosecution side. Sammi heard Paul mention Wayne in his thoughts several times, but at first she thought it was friendly rivalry. But his thoughts took a different turn. He wanted to know how he was going to get the information to him.

Sammi was shocked. Why did Paul want to get information to Wayne Berman? A little concentration of Wayne gave her the answer. Wayne also worked for ASAC. This company was not taking any chances. They had plants on both sides of the aisle. And there was one more item she caught in their thoughts. These two attorneys would be arguing for jurors. *My God,* she thought, *they'll get all their own jurors in place and Randy won't have a chance.* She'd have to get this information first to Dave and then to Ben Collier as soon as possible.

Sammi wasn't sure how Dave was going to handle this one. She was hoping that the referees would be in on this, but didn't know if that was the best idea or not. She'd have to leave that up to Dave. And what about Sergeant Brady? He needed to be involved. To her it seemed logical, but should he? She was in turmoil inside caused by the position she was in at this moment. She was the single outsider who knew what was going on, and that unnerved her.

As luck would have it, the arguments were taking so long that the judge would not make the decision today. He checked his schedule and decided that his decision would have to take place later on Friday. This gave them all time to consider their closing petition and gave Sammi reason for a deep sigh of relief. She had time to let everyone know what was going on.

* * *

At home she anxiously awaited Dave, who'd worked a little later that night. She should have gone for a workout herself; she needed one.

When Dave walked through the door and saw her sitting there with a glass of wine, he knew something was unnerving her. He came right over and sat down next to her, put his arm around her and said, "Okay, you want to talk first or not?"

"Give me a few minutes. I need to unwind a little."

"Okay, but do I have to give you a lecture again about taking everything on your own shoulders? You get information, pass it on and then keep yourself on even keel so you can do it again later."

"I know and I will. But I need a few more minutes."

"Okay."

They sat relaxing as best they could Dave with his arm around Sammi and she with her body leaning in his direction for support and comfort.

"It helps to share the burden."

He nodded.

"Okay, I'm ready to tell you."

And she told him what she'd picked up today in court.

"Holy Shit. They have two plants ... one on each side of the aisle. Well, that should determine the outcome, right? Boy, they play hard ball, don't they?"

"This must be of utmost importance to them, like

life or death."

"Sure would seem that way. Well, okay."

"Who'll you tell first?" she asked.

"It's got to be Ben. I'd like all of us to be on this one, but it's his call. He'll even have to decide about Sergeant Brady. We're sort of working for him right now. This is mostly an FBI case, although around here they think we're just holding a murder trial."

"Okay, so Ben will decide?"

"Sure, after all these are his attorneys. I'm sure the FBI will be real happy to know about Paul Ryan. And they'll handle that Wayne Berman in their own way."

Dave put in a call to Ben Collier and told him the latest. He decided he wouldn't use the same language as Ben when he related his reaction back to Sammi. As serious as they were discovering this to be, Ben suggested they had to meet and discuss everything face to face where they couldn't be seen or heard. He'd get back with them after he'd talked to Ron Donovan. And although no specifics would be given to Ron, he'd have to know that Sammi had her own way of finding out information and all he needed to know was that it could be depended on.

It wasn't more than a half hour later that the phone rang. Ben had picked a restaurant in Allentown. It would be Dave, Sammi, Ron and Ben who'd meet later tonight. Luckily, the trial itself was still a few months away and they had time to put a plan in action. Sammi couldn't imagine what that plan would be, but that wasn't her decision.

* * *

On the way to the restaurant Sammi remained thoughtful. She was trying to remember everything she'd heard in the courtroom and was already forgetting some details. She was worried about that. Although the main thoughts were quite clear some of the lesser ones could be of some importance.

"You're not nervous, are you?" asked Dave.

"I'm hoping I can remember enough of the main

thoughts I heard. I know I've already forgotten some."

"You're making people aware of things that they'd never know about. Don't worry about it. Besides, didn't Ben say that this company had been up on charges in the past; it's just that they were never proven. These guys are already aware of some of this company's illegal trail anyway."

"That's true."

"So anything at all you can tell them will provide more clues than they've got right now."

"You're probably right. But the way they were setting everything up, Randy wouldn't have a chance."

Dave nodded. "But I think it's bigger than that. They're trying to cover up something bigger. If they had one of their people kill Beth, there'd have to be a good reason. And that's what they're trying to hide."

Sammi looked out the window and wondered where these clues would lead them. Dave knew that the wheels were turning around in her head. She worried so much and yet she could give out indications that no one else could. And this gave everyone advance notice.

"I hear this restaurant has a specialty on shrimp."

He waited for her reaction. She smiled. "And I haven't had a good shrimp dinner for a while."

"Look Sammi, the good part about tonight is that Ron will find out that you know things and we'll have time to set up some form of communication system that will remain secret between the four of us. I think later on it's going to be quite important."

* * *

When they arrived at the restaurant Ben and Ron were already there. And in keeping with their discretion, they picked a table in the rear of the restaurant with no close access to any other. It was private, secluded and would allow a tight conversation to occur with comfort.

"Well," said Ben, "I'm glad that we can have this meeting tonight. I've clued Ron into some of the things you've told me, but we need to discuss it further."

Ron said, "Something here is quite detrimental to our case. If ASAC has one of their attorneys planted on each side, we won't have a chance to make any progress. They'll know everything ahead of time. But I need to be sure ..."

At this point Ben took over. He looked over at Dave and Sammi and smiled. Then he began. "I have to lay the groundwork for you, Ron, and this is very important. I haven't had a chance to talk to you so now has to be the time. I've worked with Dave and Sammi in the past. Now Sammi here," he said looking over at her with respect, "has ways and means of acquiring information that I haven't figured out in over two years. We've tried to hire her several times, but it's not what she wants. But I know for a fact that when she's ready to give out information, her details are correct. But her methods are not something she talks about. I need to make that clear. Her methods are her own and that's okay with me. I care about results and I've given up trying to figure her out."

He then turned to Sammi, smiled and said in jest, "Well, sometimes I still wonder, but I don't spend too much time on it anymore."

Sammi smiled. Dave added, "You and many others have wondered, but she has her reasons."

"And that's good enough."

At this point Ron piped up and said, "Well, okay. If Ben is happy with you, I certainly have no problem. Ben and I've known each other for over ten years and I trust his judgment totally."

Ben couldn't help adding, "But she's a slick one, and you'll end up wondering how she finds out things before we're finished. I can guarantee that."

With that said, drinks and dinners were ordered and more serious conversation began.

"What can you tell us?" asked Ben. "Dave told me stuff over the phone and I repeated it to Ron, but I'd like to hear it first hand."

Sammi nodded.

"Of course," said Dave. He turned to Sammi as he said, "Sammi was a little worried that she might have forgotten some of the smaller details, but she'll tell you all she knows."

With that Sammi began. "Paul Ryan will be giving information on your private and secret discussions to Wayne Berman, who also works for ASAC. These two are supposed to keep the trial going in the direction that the ASAC Group has in mind and they are given orders as to what methods to use, mainly by Matthew Carnigan. I have information that they are the two who are supposed to interview and argue on the selection of jurors."

At this point Ron had to sit up and take notice. "How could you know that? We only decided late last week."

"That may be true, but if you think back, didn't Paul give you a diplomatic speech as to why he should be the one who would be put in that spot?"

Ron thought for a moment and realized it was true. He looked over at Ben and said, "Amazing."

"We've barely begun," said Ben. "You'll be amazed by Sammi all the way through this."

After a few more moments, Ben said, "We have to find a way to get Sammi here involved enough in these trials so she'll be around to pick up information."

Dave sat up in his chair and mentioned that this type of connection was making him nervous.

"Now look, Dave," said Ben. "We'd never put Sammi in a precarious position. If it ever gets to that I'll pull her, but I might even have Amilio in the vicinity undercover because he picks up a lot of stuff, too."

Sammi said, "Dave, I know Ben won't put me in a vulnerable situation. There should be ways that I could be around without arousing suspicion."

Dave looked over at Sammi first and then asked Ron, "What did you have in mind?"

"Don't know yet," said Ron. "Hell, I don't even know how we're going to handle this situation. We can't pull them both off the case ... that would be too obvious ... but I'm hoping to find a plausible reason to get Paul Ryan the hell out of there. After all, he might work undercover for ASAC but his job is with the FBI and if they needed him somewhere else suddenly, he'd have to go and get replaced. Now we might have to take that road, right, Ben?"

"We need to get one of them out of there and I think Paul is the logical one. You've got to have a team you can work with and trust. Wayne is fed information so if no one is there to give it to him, well, he might become dead weight, I hope."

Then Ben sat back and smiled. "And with Sammi around, at least once in a while, we can know about Wayne, right?"

"I could try and find out what I can," she said.

"Okay, this might take a few days. Ron, I'd like you to get to Philadelphia for a day or two. We've got to meet with our superiors and figure out how to do this and what to do about Paul Ryan. He'll have to be watched wherever he's at. Later, we can seize him, but not until this trial is over. ASAC can't be aware that we're on to him."

Ron looked over at Sammi. He didn't say anything verbally, but his expression was one of deep interest as if he was trying to figure her out.

Ben interrupted his thoughts. "Okay, then we'll meet with our uppers and clue you in to what's going to happen. I think they'll want to use Sammi further in some way. But I'll let them know your concern. We don't want anything obvious at our end either, but we need to keep abreast of what's going on."

Dave said, "We'll talk again when we hear your plan."

"Okay, that's fair enough."

Then Ron went over some of the details of Randy Baker's case. They didn't seem to have much information, but he was still hoping to get him out on bail. That decision would be made after the final argument had concluded on Friday.

Then Sammi remembered. "Oh, one more thing I need to mention. If it looks like you're winning and will get bail for Randy, Paul plans to ask for more time to confuse the issues. He believes that if any of your attorneys asks for more time that you'll get it. And, he knows you'll be mad, but believes that he can get it by you by saying that he thought it didn't look good enough to win bail."

Ron's shoulders said it all. He couldn't believe an assistant lawyer would pull such a charade and said, "That might be a plausible reason for getting him replaced. In fact that would be a very good reason, because no assistant of mine would ever go over my head. Let's see what happens Friday. And that might get him out of that seat without a big problem. And I could overrule him and get the bail anyway."

Dave said, "Obviously they want to keep Randy in jail."

"Sure," said Ron. "Someone who can't even make bail always looks half guilty already."

"Okay," said Ben, "but I still want us to meet in Philadelphia as soon as you can. We need to have a future plan in place."

"Oh, right. I'll check my schedule and call you. This cat and mouse game they play that has been going on for years might have met its match with Sammi here. I think it'll be a pleasure working with you."

"Thanks and I believe I'll learn a lot from you."

"I'm serious, Sammi. They've been so hard to catch on anything. And they've muddled this murder case so that no one is giving us anything we need. It's been hard, but if we can get clues from you as to what they're thinking of doing ... well, we might have a chance this time."

"And Randy is innocent," she said. "We know that so we have to find out who really committed this murder."

"And what else it's related to. They're in deep on this one and that's why they're trying to pull the strings."

Everyone nodded, knowing there was a lot of work ahead.

* * *

On the way home Sammi felt satisfied that she had given them usable information.

"You're always so hard on yourself," said Dave. "Anything at all that you give them is more than what they had in the first place."

"I know, but ..." and she trailed off.

"Let's have it. What's bugging you?" he asked.

"There's some things about what I can do that are hard to describe. I've mentioned before that I try not to get too technical when I explain things, but with you, we've discussed thoughts in more depth. So, as you say, what bugs me is this. Thoughts take in everything on any given subject, not just what comes out in words. And so I have a lot of fluffy information that comes to me and I have to make a quick selection of what points to remember. It's almost like a dream; you remember a lot when you first wake up, but then it quickly fades and sometimes, hard as you try, you can't bring it back. That's what happens to me. And I hope that I pick the right things to remember."

Dave didn't know what to respond to that one, but he answered her this way. "You've got to relax, honey, and do the best you can. No one could remember everything, but you give them enough, Sammi, you surely do. Look how we've worked together over the years. Everything falls into place in time. Every time you're around this Wayne Berman you'll pick up more and more. Then those missing blanks will get filled in. You expect so much of yourself."

"I want to do the best I can. Randy Baker's life is at stake here."

"That's true, but other people are working on this, too. The burden of responsibility is not entirely yours. I hope they do get Amilio on this one because he picks up a lot of stuff, too."

"That he does."

"And I'd be more comfortable with him around. For right now, you did great. Ron was amazed as people usually are when they first begin to work with you. But you're a perfectionist and you've got to learn to relax. Randy's life is our first priority, of course, but there's a lot more to this case than just Beth's murder."

Sammi nodded. She did have to agree with that.

CHAPTER TEN

Paul Ryan seemed relatively sure of himself as he planned his strategy for Friday afternoon in court. He felt he could ask for a continuance quickly and catch Ron Donovan completely off guard. Although he respected him as a sharp attorney, he did believe the judge would rule instantly and Ron would be left wondering what had happened. And he wasn't that worried about Ron. He had built up an excellent rapport with him, had learned to stroke his ego just enough to enable himself to garner a spot in his inner circle. He felt he was one of his favorites and had him fooled totally. Ron was an unsuspecting lamb, he thought, and he looked upon him as a conquered opponent.

His phone rang and shook him out of his self-congratulatory thoughts.

"Everything under control at your end?" asked Matthew Carnigan. "We can't take any chances."

"We're fine here. I want you to relax. I'll handle Ron."

"But he'll be furious if you cross him. Do you think they've got enough to get Randy out of jail or not? If not, you won't have to play that card. "

"I think it'll be a close call which will play right into my hand. I told you, Matt, I'll ask for a continuance and simply tell Ron I wanted to be sure."

"He's not stupid. Are you sure he'll buy it?"

"I wouldn't do it if I wasn't sure."

"Well," said Matt. "It'll be a lot tougher if Randy gets out of jail. He's got some connections, I'm sure. That guy was playing it smart and that wife of his was even smarter."

"But you don't have to worry about them anymore. I

mean, she's dead and he'll look bad now anyway."

"You don't get it, do you, Paul?" said Matthew irritated at Paul's complacency. "That's the way it looks today. Tomorrow everything could change. Even the press could be on his side and that would cause more problems." Matthew wasn't joking as Paul could tell by his tone of voice. This had happened before.

"You seem more wired up than usual. What's up?"

"I got a call today from Smiley. He might be a subordinate partner these days, but he's been getting suspicious of things. I wish I could have gotten rid of him a long time ago, but his contract is solid, and he has to remain with the firm as long as he chooses. He's interested in moving us forward, but he wouldn't like the methods we're using. Everything has to be straight with him. He might get close to the edge at times, but he'd never go over it. If he even suspected what we do, we'd have an even bigger problem that I'm not sure we'd surmount. He's got to be kept in the dark on everything."

"I thought you were sending him back to Russia for a while. Isn't he the one who's had so much luck bringing them around?

"True and everything was legal. Yeah, yeah, he's going back next week for at least two months and it can't be soon enough for me. He's been making me real nervous."

"Well, tomorrow should give us more time."

"Okay, then," and Matthew hung up.

Paul hated it when Matthew let his nerves get the best of him. He had heard that the firm was much more solid when the senior Ascott was in charge. He was one of the brains of this outfit as was Smiley Sturges, but John Ascott had died and Smiley was put in a subordinate position, per Matthew's suggestion. It was common knowledge that Smiley didn't seem to mind at all. It was obvious that he didn't like Matthew's way of doing business and didn't want to be in the front row on anything. So he was sent to different countries to keep him conveniently out of the way and he seemed to relish it. Paul thought it was too bad that they didn't have stronger leaders like they used to because this company could have been top notch instead of a wannabe.

* * *

Matthew Carnigan relaxed a little when he put down the phone. He knew that Paul was arrogant and a climber, but he usually had his position under control. He hoped he was right this time, because a lot was riding on Randy Baker staying in jail. Matthew was intrigued that Paul saw this company as a place to rise higher and higher, but he wasn't in the inner circle like he imagined himself to be. There were a few areas that Matthew allowed only five people to enter and Paul wasn't one of them. And Matthew wasn't sure he would ever be. His inner circle had to think a certain way about life, success, opportunities, women, prestige and entitlement and he didn't think Paul was there or ever would be. He might make it up the ladder to a certain rung, but he doubted he'd ever get to the top. Still, he could be useful, especially if he believed he had a chance at one of the top spots.

He buzzed for his secretary, Miriam. He liked the way she ran in, nervous and anxious to do anything he wanted. She needed this job desperately and that's why he could trust her. You had to have an edge against women; otherwise, they were not to be trusted.

"It's 10:01 AM and you didn't remind me of my staff meeting." He loved to one up her any chance he got. It made her sweat. He didn't think he'd ever fire her; she knew her submissive place and of the four secretaries he'd had in the last year, she was by far the best. However, that wasn't anything he'd want her to know.

"I reminded you last night that it had been moved to 10:30 AM for today."

He sat up in his chair irritated. She was right; now he remembered. But he couldn't let her feel superior.

"You should have reminded me this morning; that's your job. See that you do it next time."

"Right, sir, sorry. Next time I'll remind you in the morning."

"Alright then; that's all" he said gruffly. He hated it when she was right. But then he was the boss and that made him superior.

He thought back a little on his life. He did this occasionally to realize why he was above everyone else. He knew that he had made the top slot in the company solely because of his stepfather, John Ascott. That was the biggest reason, and he knew it. Melinda Ascott wanted her husband to take care of her son from a previous marriage; that's one of the reasons she married him and he vowed to do it. John never broke his vow to his beloved. So Matthew took advantage of special favors all of his life. He hadn't worked to earn the right to be where he was, and this irritated his step-father constantly. But his mother always made excuses for him and begged her husband to help him along. But it never did any good. He knew he was entitled to be where he was and he felt he should be allowed a lot more than the regular population. He felt only certain people were chosen for prestigious roles in life and he was one of them. He was privileged, distinctive and looked down on everyone, but a select few. He accepted his superior status and never questioned why, but felt in his bones that he was special. Although the five in his inner circle were not as special as he and could never be, they satisfied a certain longing in him in that they understood this little group was entitled to be on top of the world.

It was true that occasionally Matthew had some detrimental feelings about himself. That made him nervous. A crawly thought of not being good enough infrequently crossed his mind or comments from some of his mother's earlier boyfriends teasing him about being a wimp and not worth it never quite let go. He'd never forgotten those times. Sometimes he laughed, thinking it was probably a memory from an old movie, but other times it did worry him a little. But he usually shrugged it off quickly. After all, he was Matthew Carnigan and he was great. As a child he'd been to psychologists and such who always told him to remember who he was and not pay attention to those segregated thoughts that came his way. And he overcame them most of the time, but when worrisome business dealings started to surface, as they were now, some of those old ideas couldn't be excused so easily. He never did understand what they were all about anyway.

The phone interrupted his perplexing memories.

"Yes, Jonathon, it's good to hear from you."

Jonathon Morley was one of his inner circle and one of the few who had an equally ferocious passion for women. It had gotten him into trouble in the past, but was taken care of covertly so that he could maintain his status.

"I wanted to talk to you about the latest inconsistency with the microchip deal with China. I understand they want the entire system or it's no deal. Did you know that?"

Jonathon's voice was at a high vocal tone and his concern could be heard without mistake.

"Yes, yes, I've heard they're pushing real hard. But, we aren't going to budge on that unless they provide us with documentation as to how they'll cave in our competition on the sideline computers here in this country. Negotiations have been ongoing for a couple of weeks. How did you get involved?"

"I got a call from Phillip. He sounded confident but sometimes doesn't understand everything. Are we okay on this one? It's big and we need to keep this top secret."

"Of course, Jose's on this one, too; I wouldn't trust Phillip solo. He's not ready for that yet."

"Okay, I feel better about that." Then Jonathon fell silent.

"I feel you're more comfortable now. That's good. I suppose you've heard that I've cancelled our group activities for a while. Too much going on; we'll have to amuse ourselves in other ways for now." He laughed. Many would have thought he had a weird sense of humor.

"I guess any new conquests will have to wait. We'll have to lay low on that. But when this is over, we can resume our activities, right?" asked Jonathon.

"Absolutely, and get stronger than ever."

"Any news about the murder trial? I'll be glad when that one's over. Damn, Matt, he worked for our company. We'll never look good on this one no matter what happens."

"By the time we're done with Randy, they'll feel sorry for our company that he was such a traitor. Don't worry. I talked to Paul a minute ago and he says he's got it under control and he'll keep Randy in jail."

"Sure hope so. We've got enough other problems right now." Jonathon didn't feel as comfortable as Matt with all of the problems facing them.

"Everything's hitting the fan at the same time. Damn, I can't wait until it all dies down and we can resume our fun activities."

Jonathon laughed. "It doesn't get much better than that. Do you have anyone special in mind?"

"I always have someone in mind and they're always special," he quipped, "but it'll have to wait."

"Okay, later."

And that was it. Matthew puffed on his Behike cigar. He'd take one puff, hold it in slightly for a moment, then watched the smoke as it filled the space around him. Then he'd look at his cigar with pride knowing it was one of the best in the world, and, of course, he was entitled.

Being in a rather philosophical mood, his mind trailed back to when he was little. His father had died before he was six; he barely remembered him anymore. But he had a good feeling when he thought of him. Then he left and he could never understand it. It hurt him a lot and his mother immediately took up with a lot of other men. That made him mad. He didn't know why she didn't wait for his father to return. He remembered one incident.

"Are you going out again, Mama?" he asked.

"Yes, my sweetie. Mom's going out to find you another father," she said with a giggle in her voice. And she always pinched his cheek when she said that. He didn't like it.

But he would never again ask her why she didn't wait for his father to come back. Once when he said that, she actually slapped him. She'd never done that before, but she had been acting strange at that time. He couldn't understand it. He missed his father terribly and he was now somewhat afraid of his mother at times.

He snapped himself back to attention. He had to snap out of this reminiscing mood; it usually upset him. He didn't believe his mother ever really loved him after that and so he didn't like to think about those days.

* * *

The staff meeting that Friday consisted of his inner circle. They had to discuss their private activities with China and Russia and only his solid members could be privy to that information. These members were the trusted ones, but then, he had something on every one of them and that helped. Trusting people other than himself had always been hard for him. He learned early on that people weren't dependable; his father died and left him, his mother never had much time for him after that and, even as a grown man, he was cast aside by both his mother and step-father. That made him angry with her and hateful of him. In his early years he spent a lot of time crying about it, but now, he just got even.

As they walked in, he assessed them one by one as he usually did. First, was Jonathon Morley, his longest associate. He shared his appetite for women and in unspoken language, they understood each other. He'd been with the firm for over ten years and was now his chief of staff. Next was Henry Benson, who went by his nickname Barnie. Most people didn't even know his real name, but they knew he was shrewd and never thought of crossing him. He'd been with the firm for fifteen years and was invaluable in several areas.

George Addison was his most favorite in a way. If he had learned to trust anyone in his adult years, it would have been George, who had an uncanny resemblance to a picture of his late father. Finally there was Andrew Mincetti, the real brains of the outfit, at least as far as China was concerned. Smiley Sturges was handling Russia and these two countries were their target customers at this time. Even though they were trading favors with their main allies, the negotiations were difficult, as no one trusted each other and hard rules had to be followed on both sides. Here, Matthew felt quite comfortable as he was used to surviving in a no-trust world.

"Okay," he said opening the meeting, "I need to know where we're at with the latest China deal. I'll talk about Smiley's deal first, but you know why I don't invite him to these meetings."

"Really, Matt," said Jonathon rather confidently, "don't you think that he'd go along with this by now?"

"God, no. And I wouldn't take the chance. He's been straight-laced all the years I've known him. I know this time we're not going out on the limb as much as we usually do, but we can't trust him. We just beat that latest rap with the FBI and we have to be careful for a while. The feds will be watching everything we do. Smiley has been upset enough so I don't want any waves from him."

"Okay, okay," said Jonathon, "I thought that it would make everything easier. Hell, we always have to watch what we say in front of him. That's getting harder and harder."

"Well," screamed Matthew, "you sure as hell better watch what you say." He turned to all of them as he said, "We don't need that kind of trouble at this time."

He waited a moment to let that sink in. "Now, let's get to business. Andrew, you go first, what's the latest with China?"

"We're solid right now. They can deliver havoc for the Mayten Company, our main competitor. They have placed several of their people in top positions. When all is a go, their reputation will suffer a great loss, I'm told, and we'll have the main territory there."

"And what are we giving them in return?"

Andrew looked at him suspiciously. He knew what we were giving them, didn't he? Was this a test?

"You know, don't you?" he asked, just to be sure.

"Refresh my memory, okay?" Matt seemed irritated at the comment and everyone knew he wasn't up-to-date on the finer points. He always forgot details.

"Well, they want the formula on the Adner project. They know we can't give it all to them, but whatever we can get to them, they'll accept unless it's way too little. But we have over half of the details, so that should satisfy them."

"Ah, yes, the Adner project, a future space endeavor. And no one is suspecting us, right? We can't take a chance on this one." He smiled as he puffed on his Be-hike cigar and felt somewhat smug. He felt they were ahead of this game. After all, this was a future project, more than five years away and no one had been paying close attention to the specifics yet. This had been prime material.

"No, we're good on this one," said Andrew.

"Okay, now everyone knows why I don't like Smiley at these meetings. We need to be able to talk freely, so who can update me on Russia?"

George Addison spoke up on this one. "I talked to Smiley yesterday and he told me that we're within weeks of finalizing everything. And he's heading there in a few weeks. He feels that by the time he gets back everything will be under control. And remember, his dealings are all on the level."

"Right, that's right. That's the good part, you guys. If anyone comes sniffing around about China, they'll look into other things, too. And when they see that Russia is totally legit they'll back off some or at least think that they might have made a mistake about China. That should work to our advantage."

Everyone seemed to sit back in their large oversized chairs in unison, like it had been planned. It was a moment of relief for everyone. The plan was moving along as they wanted. And their goal was to make ASAC the biggest monopoly in United States in several areas. In other countries, they would be happy holding their own for now, but they needed most of the market in the U.S. to further their plan.

As the meeting broke up and others left, Matthew called George back for a few more words.

"So you're satisfied with what Smiley's done in Russia?"

"Right now it looks good and when he comes back from his trip, all should be in place. I'm sure he'll update us as he goes along. And this is a big deal -- all legit like we said, a great buffer and profitable as well. This is a win-win situation all around."

"Okay, we're simply exchanging technology with them," added Matthew, "and that's okay. It's still helpful, but doing business that way is so slow. But this gives us a validity that we desperately need right now so we have to play it up as much as we can. And Smiley's so good at that."

George laughed. "He doesn't even realize how much he plays into our hands."

"I know," said Matthew. He again puffed on his beloved Behike, "if he knew he'd probably pull the plug on us all and I don't think he'd hesitate for a moment."

"Good thing he wasn't in on the German deal. God, when the government started investigating, I thought we were done. However, our lawyers hid everything quite well. Of course, now they're watching us. We can't afford to slip up." That being said, George quieted down and relaxed. And Matthew offered him a Behike, a favor he only extended to a select few.

"This makes everything worthwhile," said George as he took his first puff, relaxed way back in his chair with a contented look on his face. He blew the smoke up toward the ceiling and watched it for a moment like a little kid playing a game. He was well into his fifties and had lost a good deal of his hair, but had an air of confidence as well as arrogance about him. His every word was spoken with command and authority and he liked his position as Matthew's confidant.

"We've come a long way, haven't we?" said Matthew. "So many others were left behind, but we knew how to get to this position."

"Yeah, and we know how to keep it, right?"

He laughed as he knew that Matthew was in a mood for a little ego patting. And he knew exactly how to stroke him.

"We do. But it's too bad we have to put our favorite game on the back burner."

Matthew reacted with enthusiasm. "Yeah, damn it. I've been missing that. But we have to keep an eye out for prime targets for the next time, right?"

"I've got my eye on a few lookers in the mail room, right now."

They both laughed. Women and their conquests were extremely important to them. In reality, it was their top priority and all this ASAC stuff was just keeping them in a position to play their most intriguing game, because if anyone ever caught a hint of what they were doing, then everything would be finished. But they'd been careful and hadn't been caught yet. They looked at each other with satisfaction as they continued puffing on their Behikes.

* * *

The courtroom was packed with more spectators than usual. Paul looked around in a slightly nervous fashion wondering what could possibly be intriguing this entire group. Ron kept calling his attention to more details and he hadn't had time to look over at the prosecution's table. He wanted to catch Wayne's eye to see what his expression would be right now. Did they feel confident or not? Would he have to play his ace card or take a chance on the judge ruling in the prosecution's favor?

This was a crucial ruling for him and his reputation with Matthew Carnigan was on the line. He'd advanced so far that he didn't want anything to ruin it now.

"Gees, Paul, what the hell's the matter with you? You seem all over the place. You need to pay attention here."

He stomped to attention at once. He had let his mind wander and he couldn't chance Ron angry with him or suspecting him in any way. He had to take control of himself.

"I was trying to see the expression on their faces over there. They don't look overly confident to me."

"Let me worry about that. I need you to be ready with the second section of this report. Don't be playing games right now."

He could tell that Ron was nervous. He didn't usually talk like that. Even Steve had passed him a cautious look. Ron was riled up already; that was for sure. He had a lot riding on today's decision.

"Okay, this second section deals with ..."

A bailiff entered the courtroom and asked for everyone's attention. There had been a cause for delay and the bail hearing for Randy Baker was moved back to 3:30 PM.

Everyone looked at each other surprised, but knew this was a common occurrence. Wayne from the prosecution's table looked over but turned away quickly when he spotted Ron noticing his glance to Paul. They all gathered up their books and papers and prepared to wait for a couple more hours.

Ron was thinking that he had caught a glance between these two guys and although that was not totally uncommon, usually talk and information stayed within their own table. Now was not the time to confer with the other side. Ron passed it off as if nothing had occurred, but was happy that Sammi had made him aware.

* * *

Paul knew that Ron was uneasy about the delay.

They all were. He mentioned that they would all meet in an available room and confer on their notes and strategy one more time. He definitely wanted to take advantage of the extra benefit of time allotted them.

Paul said, "Okay, I'll be right there. I've got to make a few phone calls. It'll just take a few minutes."

Ron figured he knew what that was about, but didn't waver. He'd handle the situation when the time came.

Paul called Wayne first. "What's going on here?"

"Nothing I know of," said Wayne. "Seems like a legit delay. We didn't instigate anything from our side."

"Okay, I'll have to call Matthew and he won't be happy about this."

"For God sakes it was a delay. He'll accept it."

"Do you want to call and tell him?" asked Paul.

"Hell no, that's your job."

"Right," said Paul. "That's what I figured."

And so he placed the dreaded call. And Matthew's reaction was expected. Anger and some very colorful words, but then he took deep breath and listened.

"Look, Mr. Carnigan, it was some legit delay; they didn't say what, but it will resume at 3:30 PM today."

"Well, I sure hope so. We need to get this to be over. If Randy's out of jail they'll have more investigations going on and that's trouble for us. They're doing enough background work with him in jail."

"But I've heard that even if he's let out he'd be tethered and confined to his home."

"We don't want to have to worry about who he sees and talks to without us knowing. In jail, we know. We know who visits, when and for how long. But once he's out, that could be a secret and that's not good. Anyway you assured me he wouldn't win this bail hearing."

"That's right. I told you what I plan to do."

"It'd better work, Paul. I'm counting on you, so don't let me down."

"Ron doesn't suspect anything, so he'll be caught off guard."

"Okay, I hope you're right."

That line made Paul nervous. Everything he'd been working on so far had come down to this one bail hearing. Years of work to get into Mr. Carnigan's good graces was suddenly pivoting on this one point. Paul had to admit that his hands were beginning to sweat.

* * *

He had no sooner walked into the meeting room than another message came down that the bail hearing was postponed until tomorrow morning at ten o'clock when a rather rare court agenda would fit them in. Everyone experienced disappointment, but Ron saw the beaded sweat beginning to appear on Paul's forehead. Now the obvious signs were apparent to him because he was looking for them.

"Damn, damn," said Paul. "What the hell are they doing?"

Ron looked over with quiet satisfaction as he said, "Tomorrow's fine. It'll give us that much more time."

"Well, we're prepared aren't we? What good will overnight do except cloud the issues again."

"Hey, settle down," said Ron. "Why do you care so much what day -- another day, so what? Happens all the time, you know that."

With that statement Ron kept eye contact with Paul and as he waited for a reply.

Paul tried to recover from what his demeanor was stating. "Well, I guess it doesn't matter that much. I wanted to get this over with."

Ron said, "Probably not as much as Randy Baker, but relax. Tomorrow will be the day."

And Paul once again had to make the dreaded phone call. This time Matthew didn't even talk, he simply listened and then hung up. But, in reality, Paul felt the delay could help his strategy. And he had to win this point, against all odds.

* * *

Ron put in a courtesy call to Dave and Sammi to let

them know. And he also clued them into Paul's obvious behavior.

"God, to me now, it's written all over his face. I never noticed it before."

Sammi said, "You weren't looking for it. You were busy working on an important strategy."

"But I was being undermined every step of the way. Anyway, right now I think it looks good for Randy. Nothing's ever positive because we never know how a judge will rule, but I think we're looking good."

"I understand Randy won't be allowed to wander around much, even if he does make it, right?" asked Dave.

"No, I think there will be conditions on his bail, but I could never guess right now what they would be. It could be anything from a tether to being watched or just trusted. I'm hoping for that and with a little son around, that could be a deal breaker."

"We're all hoping for the best and we'll know tomorrow."

"I'll call you. And thanks again Sammi."

After the call Dave turned to Sammi and said, "I couldn't make out how secure he feels. How about you?"

"I think he's so used to using lawyer jargon that he does it all the time. But in truth, he was right. You never know how a judge will rule."

Dave continued to stare at her.

"No, Dave. I didn't pick up anything else."

Dave returned to his own thoughts. Then he added, "It'll be a long night. God, I hope he makes it."

Sammi didn't answer. Dave's statement said it all.

* * *

A few hours later, the phone rang again. This time it was Amilio and he sounded excited.

"Hey Dave, get Sammi on so I only have to say this once."

"Okay," she said, "I'm here."

"I got an anonymous phone call that said, "Look into the death of Tammy Sinclair. I had but a moment to ask what it was about and the answer was ASAC. Then the person hung up."

"No kidding. Another murder connected to ASAC?" said Dave.

"Looks that way or at least someone thinks so."

Sammi said, "So if Beth's murder is connected to ASAC and the possibility of Tina O'Leary and now another one, at least maybe, I'd have to guess that they might be hiding a lot more than we thought. We need to change our thinking on this one."

Amilio said, "We don't know that yet, but this was a strange call. The voice was loud but muffled, and didn't say too many words and hung up fast."

"Man or woman," asked Dave.

"Not sure. Voice was disguised."

"Sounds like someone was pretty scared and taking a chance to make that call," said Dave.

"I'm gonna have to start looking through files, because I don't remember that name, do you Dave?"

"Nope. I can't say that I've ever heard it. Possibly it wasn't in our precinct and we don't know how long ago it happened."

"That's true, too."

Dave told Amilio that Randy's bail hearing was postponed until the next morning.

"God, what are they doing over there?"

"It seems that it was a legit postponement from the court's side. So we have to wait another day."

"Okay, well, I sure hope he makes it out of there. His little one could use him at home. How's he doing anyway?"

"Holding strong I hear," said Sammi. "He's a smart little guy, but his emotions are kept hidden. It should help a lot if his dad gets out of prison."

"He has a lot to deal with. He's how old?"

"He's ten," said Sammi. "A bright little guy, but still

quite young."

"Let's hope for the best."

When the call ended Dave turned to Sammi and said, "This is getting to be incredibly confusing. It could be the work of a serial killer, except for Beth. But if they're all connected, we've got a company that kills people off for various reasons and tries to cover them up."

"But for what reason? I don't think I buy the serial killer thing, at least not yet. Tina's ex-husband was probably involved remember? We'll have to wait and see about this other girl. You never heard of that killing?"

"Nope," said Dave. "Can't say I remember anything about it."

"It'll be interesting to find out what Amilio learns. Wonder if there will be any similarities."

"That's the thing we have to watch out for. If these crimes are connected in any way, I'm not sure what we've got on our hands here."

Sammi asked. "Do you think Randy could be aware of any of this?"

"Don't know about that. But it might be an interesting conversation to have with him when we find out more about these murders."

Sammi nodded. There were too many unknown factors right now. They were all guessing and possibly jumping to the wrong conclusions. They'd have to wait for more information, and the waiting was getting increasingly difficult.

CHAPTER ELEVEN

"Bail will be set at $500,000 and Mr. Baker will be tethered. And since I've heard all of the arguments, it is so ordered."

It seemed as though Paul Ryan was going to faint. He'd wasted all of his argument on one point, asking for a continuance and it didn't work. When he stood up and mentioned the word, he was immediately cut off by Ron who apologized to the court. He said, "Please excuse us, Your Honor, my subordinate colleague doesn't realize protocol yet. He'll have to learn. I'm ready to accept your judgment in this case. I believe we've presented our side of the case with honesty and common sense and will now respectfully await your ruling."

Paul finally realized that a master had outmaneuvered him. He had misjudged Ron's ability and shrewdness as he used Paul's own outburst to strengthen his position for bail. And he'd won. Paul knew he had lost a lot. Matthew would no doubt demote him to a considerably more subordinate position, if he didn't outright fire him. He didn't think Mr. Donovan would have any use for him either. How could this happen to him? He'd worked so hard and his entire life came crashing down on him because of one ruling, on which he had worked hard and spent hours researching. Nevertheless, he had lost and that's all Matthew Carnigan would care about. His head was spinning although he tried to remain focused.

"What the hell was that about?" asked Ron. "You don't pull that kind of crap on me. What were you thinking?"

"I didn't think we would make bail and I wanted to give us more time."

"On your own? Without consulting with me? I'm running this side of the aisle in case you didn't know. Well, you're gone. I can't trust someone like you."

"Oh, come on, Mr. Donovan. I made a mistake. I

meant well and I honestly didn't think we'd get bail."

"And that was your second mistake. The first one was trying to undermine me. I'm not sure what was really behind it, but I'm having you replaced."

"Oh, please, Mr. Donovan. I've worked so hard to get here and I wanted to work with you so much." He felt some ego stroking might help his case at this moment.

"You don't have the type of legal loyalty that I must have around me. Someone else will possibly put up with your antics, but not me."

And with that Ron turned around and started gathering up his paperwork and placing them in his briefcase. It was a subtle hint that the discussion was totally over.

* * *

Paul Ryan sat on a bench outside the courthouse trying to gather his thoughts. He had a dreaded phone call to make and he didn't for the life of him know what words he was going to use. To say that Matthew was going to be angry was a huge understatement. He did realize that he probably wouldn't be fired; he knew too much about the inner workings of the company and about the Gentlemen's Club. That was one club that he probably wouldn't ever get an invitation to join, especially now. But he tried to turn his thoughts around. How could he make this out to be a plus? If anything, Matthew was quite vulnerable at times, especially when he was desperate. Maybe he could ... he had an idea.

"Randy Baker made bail," he said. He decided to simply throw out the dreaded news right away and wait for his reaction. After he cooled down, he might have a chance.

"Son of a bitch," he answered. "What the hell are you doing out there? How could you let this thing happen?"

He let him gripe and swear and criticize and utter all of the profanities that he was known for and finally he slowed down. That's when Paul grabbed the reins.

"Look, my maneuver didn't work and Randy would

have made bail sooner or later anyway because Ron was brilliant in his argument. That's not my main concern."

"What the hell is your main concern?"

"He kicked me off the legal team. He doesn't like the way I work."

"Shit, I have to agree with him. I don't like the way you work either."

"But I have a plan, Mr. Donovan. This may all work out for the best."

"How? You're not even privy now to inside information anymore. What good can Wayne possibly accomplish if you can't be there to pass him information?"

"But I plan to be in court anyway. I don't think Ron will even be surprised. He'll think I'm sorry for what I did and may at least talk to me. If not, I can sort of edit the proceedings like reporters do and I'll still find out enough to help."

"I don't know. I don't know. We needed someone on Donovan's team. And we don't have anyone else."

"I think he'll work with just Steve and not get a third attorney. Which means that they'll be more vulnerable?"

"Why?"

"Because they'll be more distracted with all their paperwork split two ways instead of three. I think it can work to our advantage. And I have a right to sit in the courtroom and I'll pick up all that I can."

"I don't know. I'm most disappointed in you. And I don't like Randy being out on bail."

"You knew it was going to happen sooner or later."

"I suppose you're right. Well, work it out your own way. I'm sad to say that you're the best I've got and you're not that great. So surprise me."

Then Matthew hung up. Paul was surprised to realize that his proposal went better than he could have imagined. He would have to make things up as he went along, but it looked like he might have a chance to win favor back after all.

* * *

Amilio had to do a lot of digging to find out about Tammy Sinclair. He was able to find something in a closed file. Perhaps a closed classification was not a fair assessment, but no one had been actively working on the case for a long time. Her profile actually had a little information. She was twenty-eight, worked at a brokerage firm and was an utterly above-board professional and not the type you'd think of as getting caught up in any underhanded activities. Friends and family were interviewed and had given out plenty of details about her life that seemed solid and clean. He liked the added information, but realized that the personal comments and insights of the investigators were missing. This one would have to be looked into again. This case had considerably more information than the one on Tina O'Leary, so he felt happy about that.

He conferred with Dave the next day. "I'd like to get another set of eyes on this one. I want to get out to the crime scene. You got any time?"

"No, I don't. The Baker case needs some help and I'm first line on that. Sammi might be able to go."

"Okay with you if I ask her?"

"Sure, she's involved anyway and I think she'd like to be more active."

"Okay, what are you guys doing right now?"

"We're working with Ron Donovan, the lead attorney. He has all sorts of details that he's looking for and is using us as investigators. Plus, Randy just got out of jail and we want to interview and work with him a lot at home. He's tethered, but he has tons of information we need."

"Yeah, he knows a lot about that ASAC group, right?"

"Absolutely. We want to catch the real killer of Beth, but we believe it's tied in with that ASAC group, so hopefully we can get them both."

"Alright and I'm working these other murders and I wouldn't be surprised if they were all tied in."

"I'm counting on it," said Dave as he left to join Jim and Tom on another mission.

* * *

Later that night, Dave walked into his home, tired, disgusted and confused. The three referees had been sniffing out details at the crime scene again and didn't come up with anything new. Dave believed something had been left behind and hadn't been found yet. His disappointment showed.

"Hi, honey, you hungry?"

"I guess. Excuse my mood; I'm a bugger right now."

"What's the matter?"

"We spent four hours at that crime scene again. And we got to see the pictures that Randy took and everything checks out. I was hoping for a discrepancy. There's always something, but we haven't found it."

He was still stomping around the room in confusion.

"Sorry, I'm probably driving you nuts," he said. "But when I'm in that house, it's like the damn building is trying to tell me something and I'm not getting it. I can feel it. Something else is there, but none of us can find it."

"Could be you're looking too hard. You've got to relax and let your inner thoughts come forward."

"I know. And I know when I try too hard everything seems to shut off. But that's hard to do. We haven't come up with much, although Ron seems to think that he'll be using a lot of innuendos at the trial. But I'm sure he'd like to have more solid facts."

"And with any luck he'll have more by that time. We've got a while yet, right?" she asked.

"That's true. And Randy's going to be getting some copies of those papers that he made and give us and Ron a set. There's a lot there that could be used. Anyway, it's not a secret anymore; the prosecution has been talking about it so we may as well bring it to the surface."

Sammi thought about that for a moment. "But wouldn't that prove that Randy did steal information and make it worse for him."

"Apparently not. The data that Randy made copies of is known by most of the employees. So stealing it is not exactly a valid argument. It's not something they talk about, not if they want to keep their jobs, but it is known. But Randy wanted tangible proof to show people and that's why he made copies."

"Really? I guess I'm surprised."

"Well, let me put it this way. A lot of people aren't positive about what they've heard, but they're suspicious and keep to themselves about it."

"Sounds to me that they have a lot of nervous employees working out there."

"That's what I thought, but Randy said that people seemed to know what to pretend they didn't know. Does that sound right? Know what I mean?"

Sammi laughed, "Yes, I get it."

"But the company's been solid for years, good benefits and perks, so people stay on. Most think the other activity is none of their business and doesn't affect them."

Sammi nodded and understood. People looked the other way to keep a decent job. She wondered what would happen when a lot of this information came out in court. How would they feel about their company then?

"I've got something new for you," said Sammi.

He turned and looked at her, hoping for once today that the news would be good.

"What's that?"

"I found out what that flower was in Tina's hand?"

Dave looked interested.

"It's called a 'forget-me-not.' It's not that unusual and I guess they use it in special bouquets and stuff."

"Intriguing name. The connotation could be interesting," he said.

"That's what I thought."

"How'd you find out?"

"I stopped at a florist shop on the way home. I had the picture with me, the enlargement of her hand, and it showed the flower quite well."

Dave smiled. She always thought of something.

"I wonder if that name will end up being important."

"You never know. It could be an ego trip for her ex-husband. Who knows? But it will be interesting to find out how it ties in."

Dave nodded, took a deep breath and put his head against the back of the couch. A deep exhaustion had settled upon him that came from working hard on something without many tangible results. He was waiting for sudden revelations when facts began to gel together. He was trying to hold on to that positive thought.

"Amilio and I will be going out starting tomorrow on the case of Tammy Sinclair. We want to see the murder scene and also talk to some of her family and friends."

"He wanted some extra eyes working with him. I think the two of you'll make a good team."

"I do, too. Amilio is quite perceptive in his own way. I'm not sure exactly how his mind works at this time, but I'll find out. I find him very insightful."

* * *

The next day found Sammi and Amilio on the way to the crime scene. Neither one had had time to delve into the information that was available, but then being at the scene and interviewing people would enable them to write their own updated file.

Sammi said, "I've heard there were crime scene photos. Have you seen them yet?"

"No, but I've requested them to be forwarded to me as soon as they can be found in that dead file. This case happened well over a year ago and the files are buried somewhere."

"How far away from home was she murdered?" asked Sammi.

"About fifteen miles, I think. She commuted to Wilkes-Barre from her apartment in Plymouth. Her body was found about five miles from her office."

"Where did she work?"

"You know, I'm not sure. I can't remember the

name of the company, but I think it was a brokerage firm."

"I see. Was this a weekend night?"

"Yes, actually it was, a Friday night. She'd been downtown with a few friends, kind of dinner and a show or movie or something and then they all left for home. Tammy didn't make it."

"She lived alone, right?"

"Yes, and it was in a nice area of town. We can take time later today and go through this file step by step, if you like."

"That would be good. I'd like to be prepared when we start interviewing these people."

Amilio looked over at her with respect. He knew she was gathering the scenario in her mind.

"You like to get a feel for things, don't you?" he asked.

"Yes, I do. I need to feel comfortable with the circumstances before I can begin to evaluate the situation."

"You're somewhat methodical; I didn't realize that about you. And you notice all the little details, but that's good. That's why you can find out things."

"I think I drive Dave crazy at times, but that's how I am; you're right."

"He admires how conscientious you are about details. And I do, too. Because the more I think about it, that's where the answers are, amiga."

* * *

Then they turned the corner and Amilio slowed down. They approached a vacant lot and he stopped the car.

"This is it. We need to get out there. She was found right near that light pole in the center of this field."

"Another one dropped off in a vacant field?" said Sammi.

Amilio simply nodded.

Sammi read from the somewhat detailed report that Amilio had been able to find. Another one found in a vacant field. Her right shoe was missing, same as Tina, and she was raped and murdered by strangulation. She understood why some people might think the murders were connected. There were some similar features, but many killers used copycat techniques to throw off the police. Tammy's blouse was not torn, her keys were not taken and she had worn a career-type jacket that had been found several feet away, tossed into a dumpster, which seemed out of place in this field. Also, her suffocation has been caused by some type of rope or cord and not by a person's hands. To Sammi, hand choking was much more personal and passionate. Tammy's death seemed to be more the work of a man who'd gotten his rape, and was through with this woman and wanted her dead more out of fear and not out of passion or rage.

"Anything else?" asked Amilio. "You want a copy of this file?" He was quite sure that she would.

She nodded. "I feel that I'm missing something. Don't you hate that? I feel that there's something right here in front of me and I'm still not getting it."

She looked around the vacant lot. She knew it had been too long since the murder had occurred to find any physical evidence. Another winter, spring, summer and fall had taken place in this field since that dreadful night. The evidence would have evaporated like the seasons.

"You get very intense, don't you?"

"I don't mean to drive you nuts..."

"No, no, I didn't mean it like that."

"But I've got this feeling that something is just under the surface and won't seem to come up to me yet. I know it will in time if I keep fighting for it."

"I understand. I've felt that way myself on occasion."

She looked over at him and smiled, as she said, "Yes, I'll bet you have."

He understood. "I'd like to talk to the parents tomorrow. Can you make it? They're still quite emotional even after all this time, I hear. This daughter apparently was responsible, smart, and great in college, even did some charity work. Everything about her was above board. So the wounds will still be raw when we talk to them."

"What's your take on this murder? You've never said," Sammi asked.

"Wrong place, wrong time. She wasn't one to take chances and apparently didn't do stupid things. She had landed a good job at that brokerage firm, had a good chance for promotion and was working hard to etch out a decent career."

"Any boyfriends? None are mentioned here."

"Don't know anything about her dating anyone. Those can be questions for her sister and her other friends. I'm setting everything up as soon as we can. We need to get a fresh look at this case."

"Sounds good."

* * *

By the next day Sammi and Amilio were at the Sinclair home. Mrs. Sinclair answered the door and invited them into the living room. They had coffee waiting and seemed quite apprehensive. In order to relax them Amilio introduced himself and Sammi and began by letting Sammi take the lead.

"We're sorry about your daughter. I know it's hard to answer the same questions over and over again, but I'm new on this case and we want to cover everything we can that might help."

"Oh, we don't mind; anything that might help catch her killer," answered Ellen Sinclair. She was petite and gave a rather timid appearance, but showed an inner strength as she spoke. "But we can't help being anxious either. It's never left us from the moment we found out."

Dan Sinclair nodded. Although he seemed more relaxed, his demeanor as well as his words belied his inner feelings. "Don't let our behavior bother you in any way. Some days are better than others, but it never goes away, even after a year."

Amilio began. "When was the last time you saw your

daughter?"

"She stopped by for dinner on the Wednesday before she got killed," answered Dan.

"But she called me on Friday afternoon," said Ellen. "She wanted to know my schedule for Sunday. Sometimes we went shopping together."

Sammi puckered her lips as she continued. "Did she have any boyfriends that she talked about, or even any guys she may have mentioned?"

The Sinclairs looked at each other. "No," said Dan. "She'd had a relationship with someone in the prior year that went sour. He'd met someone else and Tammy was quite hurt. So she stayed shy of guys for quite a while. But I think she did date some, didn't she honey?"

Ellen nodded. "She had talked about someone a few months before. I know they went to a play or something. Not sure if he was a boyfriend or just a friend though."

"Do you know his name?" asked Sammi.

She hesitated, "No, I don't remember."

Sammi turned to look at Amilio, but didn't say anything. Her look gave him a clue that something wasn't right. However, they moved on to other things.

"Did she ever mention any concerns about anyone, man or woman?"

Again a suspicious look crossed Ellen's face, but she said nothing. This time it was obvious even to Amilio.

They both answered negatively to that question.

"Okay," said Sammi as she continued. "Who did she go out with that last Friday night? We heard she went to dinner and then somewhere else. Do you know where and with whom?"

Dan answered that one. "Yes, she had called Friday like Ellen said and she went to dinner and then to some dance club with Mitzi Larner and Gail Mathers. Those are two friends she's had for many years. Her sister might have joined them, too. She talked about it."

Sammi asked, "Now her friends, you said they'd known each other a long time. Did they go to school together?"

"Yes, both high school and college. They were pretty much each other's shadows for most of their lives."

Dan and Ellen smiled remembering and she added, "Both of them used to spend a lot of time here."

"We're going to be talking to them again."

Dan jumped on this point and said, "I don't think anyone's talked to Gail and only briefly to Mitzi. They all left the club at the same time, got into their cars and went their separate ways. They get extremely upset about Tammy to this day."

"Did either one of them see or hear anything?"

"No, I don't think so. They've never said anything to us."

Sammi looked a little troubled, but didn't say anything. She finally asked, "Do you know how we can get in touch with them?"

Ellen went and got them the information. Other aspects were discussed, but they left saying that they'd possibly want to talk to them again in the future.

* * *

Sammi sensed that Amilio was looking at her questioningly when they got back to the car.

"What gives, Sammi? Something went on in there. You looked pale and quite taken aback at one point. I don't think they noticed it, but I did."

Sammi glanced over with a knowing smile. "I think you're getting to know me too well."

He smiled, but was happy to be in her confidence.

"Okay, you said that you noticed something in there, too. And you did. Mrs. Sinclair is holding something back. I know what it is, but I don't know why."

"Really? I can't understand that," he said. "We're trying to find her daughter's killer."

"I know, but when we asked her for the name of the friend that accompanied her daughter to that play, she said she didn't remember, and she was lying. She did remember, but she didn't want to say. I wonder why."

And Sammi had the name, but didn't want to tell Amilio. He was suspicious of her enough already. There were other ways for him to find out, like when they talked to Tammy's friends.

"I noticed she looked kind of funny when she said that," he remarked.

"She's hiding something else, but I couldn't pick that up. Also she said that none of the gals heard or saw anything. That's not true either. Well ... maybe it's true, but she thinks it's not. She believes one or both of them have information that they've kept hidden."

"Are you sure you're not psychic?"

"No, I'm not, but I picked up a lot in her body language when she answered that question. She's definitely hiding a few things and it doesn't make sense to me."

"Me neither. Why would she do that?"

Sammi smiled and got thoughtful. Mrs. Sinclair was a bit of a mystery to her. She loved her daughter and wanted her killer found, that was obvious, but she wasn't willing yet to cooperate about her daughter's latest friend, Robert Anderson.

* * *

The referees went to Tom's place the first few afternoons that Randy was home from jail. They had much that they needed to discuss with him privately and he had given each of them a copy of his stashed information.

"Wait a minute," said Tom. "This document and the emails prove that ASAC was going to give China information that was supposed to be top secret regarding some technology on U.S. computers."

"And that's but a small part of it," replied Randy. "What worried me even more was that they deal in sophisticated technology regarding government projects. And they were trying to make use of some of it for upcoming negotiations ... I don't know all about it, but it had something to do with our future submarine projects."

"Holy shit," said Jim, "that's subversive activity. They were charged for similar activities before, but they beat the rap. And they're at it again?"

"This is more of the hidden secrets that I was able to copy," said Randy. "This one is not so well-known by other employees, but there are still a lot of suspicions about their international dealings. They want to become a monopoly on their products in the United States and worldwide, if possible. And these companies they deal with are no competition to them, but will aid them in damaging their competitors in the U.S."

"How long have you known about this?" asked Dave.

"This particular deal ... not very long. It came about at the same time that Beth started to get surprising notes from Matthew whenever she went to lecture. We started to realize how deep into things they were and that's when we started talking about getting in contact with you, Tom. We knew we had to do something, but had no idea how to go about it. You can't simply walk into a police department or the FBI with stuff like this and have them believe you. They'd want to investigate us first and that would have put all of us in danger. We talked about getting you involved less than two weeks before Beth was killed."

They were all quiet for more than a few moments. If only Randy had called Tom, if only they'd had a chance to get involved ... if only, if only. There was no reason on this earth to make Randy feel worse than he already did. It was time to move on and see what good they could do with this information.

"Okay," said Tom. "If they come at you for stealing information from their company, then Ron can bring up what this information is. That would be playing into his hands. And now since Paul Ryan isn't there, he should be able to keep his strategy a secret."

"Yeah," Dave said. "This stuff would have to be kept secret and then Ron could whip it out at the right moment and surprise the hell out of the prosecution. He's got to start getting them off their stride."

Randy said, "The thing to remember is that I didn't do this. There's a murderer out there and he must have left some clues. We've got to nail him."

"But as many times as that house of yours has been gone over, nothing was found, or at least very little," said Jim.

They all turned to look at him.

"Well, I was referring to those ... what shall I call them ... not even partial fingerprints we found on one of the dresser drawers. I wish we had something else to compare it to, but we don't."

"It was obvious they all wore gloves, but one glove must have developed a hole in one of the fingers, we think," said Tom. "So we have just a little of the tiny ridges and whorls and valley patterns that we find in fingerprints. It's not enough to use on its own, but could be an additional clue if we knew who did this. If we could match this to a complete fingerprint, it could be huge. After all, fingerprints have a one in 64 billion chance of matching up with someone else."

"What are we supposed to concentrate on right now?" asked Randy.

"Ron says he needs any leads we can get, be it about the subversive or immoral activity. He'll find a way to get it in. He thinks it could give him another motive as to why they'd want Beth killed and you blamed for it."

"Remember, I heard that one of the neighbors did see three men walk up to the house that day about 3:45 in the afternoon. That should show that someone else besides me could have done this."

"It's a start," said Tom, "but didn't anyone else see or hear anything? Denver said there was a lot of yelling at first when these guys entered your house."

They shook their heads.

"That's crazy," said Jim. "Someone must be scared. There's always something. We simply have to find it."

They went back to studying and scrutinizing the material that Randy had provided. This was scary stuff and it was proof against ASAC that had to be kept secret for now. Dave wondered what this company was all about. They had been profitable for many years and yet they chose to get involved in these rebellious activities. Why? He couldn't figure it out. They had checked out all the owners and none were from a foreign country who might want to retaliate against the United States. He had an idea.

"Has anyone looked back into the family tree of these people on the committee? Do any of the extended family members have a reason to want to cause trouble against us?"

They shook their heads.

"We haven't been able to find anything," said Jim. "Maybe it's all for power and profit."

"Yeah," said Tom. "That could very well be true. I've heard these guys have some pretty big egos that they flaunted around. It's quite possible it's all for power."

Randy had to agree. "You didn't ever step on Matthew's toes or even disagree with him in front of anyone. Once, when there was a hint of disagreement, it was immediately taken behind closed doors with only the main committee there. Prestige and self-importance was always high on their list."

Dave said, "With that kind of personality and the need to feel above the crowd at all times, well ..." and he didn't finish. His thoughts were muddled.

"Go ahead and finish," said Randy. "What's on your mind?"

"Well, it does seem kind of far-fetched to me, but all I've been hearing about this Matthew and a few of the others at the top, is that they have such big egos and must appear to be top notch at all times. Well, what if something was upsetting their self-image in a big way? I know they've wanted to get this monopoly for their products for a long time, because that was important to them. But what about the personal side? It could be that we've been looking in the wrong direction."

"What do you mean?" asked Jim.

"Well, this murder and the fact that they made it look like they were trying to find stolen information could have been the real cover up. The missing data was probably legit, but what if this murder was more personal and the main reason for these games. Randy, you said that Matthew had fits because Beth didn't play his game. After that she refused to go back there, but he still pursued her. Could be this entire thing was more about that. It could have made him furious because she wouldn't play the game; after all, men at the top are used to having their pick of women, right?"

They all nodded. And Randy offered, "He pursued her with phone calls and little notes and a few presents, but she sent them back. And that was more than a year after she quit. We both thought that was bizarre because she had never dated him, never succumbed in any way. But I see what you mean, Dave. He certainly was one guy who couldn't take no for an answer. I'm sure it really bugged him."

Tom said, "His ego probably couldn't handle it, and he had to find a way to retaliate."

New thoughts and ideas were now facing the group. They could have been looking in the wrong direction. The answer was possibly more in plain sight; Beth was killed because she'd refused to play Mathew's promiscuous game.

"But that does seem bizarre, doesn't it? No one does stuff like that. Kill a woman because of a rebuff?" asked Randy.

"But these people don't think like we do. I realize that not all men at the top are as strange as this group, but we are playing with a weird group of people here," said Dave. "Sammi was able to find out that Matthew's dealings at the bank were different, too. And the main reason they got one loan was because Smiley Sturges was in on it. The bank would have never given the loan to Matthew. But this info is rather confidential, okay?"

They nodded.

"So you think Beth could have been killed mainly because she wouldn't indulge in Matthew's favorite pastime?"

Dave said, "I mean that could be a big part of it. It could be the main part and we've been concentrating on the other side of this picture."

"Well, it wouldn't hurt to look deeper into this side," said Jim. "God knows we aren't finding out that much about China or Russia. This may all come together later on."

"I feel that we can't ignore anything," said Dave. "We know these guys are different, in that power and being the leaders in their industry would be important, but it may not be all there is. Let's keep an open mind going forward. We don't have that main lead we need yet, so let's broaden our scope."

They all agreed that was a good idea. In fact, most came out of this meeting with a little more enthusiasm. They'd been hitting dead ends all over the place. Would the conquest of women for these guys give them some of the clues they were lacking?

CHAPTER TWELVE

"Did you get the pictures of Tammy Sinclair's crime scene yet?" asked Sammi.

"I should have them later today." Amilio was thoughtful for a moment, then added, "I wanted to get out there and talk to some of her friends. You want to come?"

"Yes, I would. I feel that I'm in this one now. I hope you don't mind partnering up with me."

"You kidding? It's a pleasure. You're teaching me to notice a lot more of the little things."

Sammi laughed. "Well, you have your ways, too. When do you want to get out and see her friends, and there's her sister, too?"

"I have to call them yet and set something up. I'll let you know."

Sammi was happy to be in on this one. Everyone else was involved. Julie was working on the computer side, Jill was caring for Denver and the three referees were busy trying to solve Beth's murder and to find out more about the rebellious side of this company. She was happy to have a part in this, too.

"Okay," she said.

"You available any time this week?"

"I'm sure I could work it out. Just let me know."

That night at home Sammi found out that the trial was moved up on the docket and would start within a week.

"That means they'll be in court for the preliminaries and then they have to pick the jurors -- it should take a couple of weeks anyway."

"But it seems a sudden move, doesn't it?"

"Apparently not. Ron seems fine with it and didn't feel it was at all unexpected. The prosecution was pushing for it to be tried as soon as possible and Ron didn't have any objections."

Sammi said, "But that Werner guy is still on the prosecutor's side of the table and that could mean trouble."

"That's true, but he doesn't have his partner on the other side anymore. Although I hear Ron is relaxed a little, Werner still makes him nervous."

"I can understand that."

"Me, too."

"So does he have a plan or not? I hear he's still in the dark on this one."

"He is. But he has plenty of stuff to present for reasonable doubt and he feels good about that. Yet, he could use more. He's mentioned that."

Then Dave told Sammi about the latest discussion about the direction on this case.

"That's a thought," said Sammi. "Could be there's a connection and Beth's murder might be the main part of it." She thought for a moment then said, "Not too unbelievable."

"We've got to keep an open mind on this. Anything could be important."

"I'm going with Amilio later this week to talk to Tammy Sinclair's sister and friends."

Dave raised an eyebrow. "He's going to get used to you," he teased.

"This is a tough one and he could use extra help. Besides, I like being involved like the rest of you."

"I wanted to hire you years ago, remember?" Dave smiled and added, "You're working with us anyway."

"Yes, I guess I am."

* * *

The interview with Tammy Sinclair's sister was the first one to be set up. Both were extremely excited to see what would develop. And Amilio had something else to offer Sammi.

"See that manila envelope on the back seat," he said.

She nodded.

"That's the pictures from Tammy Sinclair's crime scene. That's an extra set for you."

"Good. I'll study them tonight and it'll give me a chance to understand the scene better before we interview her friends. Parents and sisters are great, but usually it's the friends who really know what's going on in your private life."

Amilio agreed. "There's a lot of things you don't tell your family."

"Right," was all she answered.

"You know that anonymous call said that we should look into this killing because it had something to do with ASAC. My mind keeps whirling around about that. Do you think this killing could be connected to Tina O'Leary? Wouldn't that be something?"

"You never know," said Sammi.

"But," said Amilio, "I hear a 'but' in your voice."

"It's just that the facts about Tina point to her ex-husband. It doesn't seem likely that he would be connected to Tammy Sinclair. But then, we must keep an open mind."

"But he works for ASAC too, right? Not in this state, but the same company."

"That's true; there could be a connection."

Then Amilio parked the car. They had arrived.

* * *

Debbie Sinclair answered the door to her apartment and invited them in. After her sister had been killed she'd gotten a roommate, who was presently at work. To Sammi, she had a slight resemblance to her sister, at least to her photos.

"I'm glad to see you're still working on my sister's case. Mom and Dad told me you talked to them. But it's been such a long time and we haven't heard anything. I sort of thought she was forgotten."

"She wasn't. But sometimes the clues and tips are slow to come in and we're going over old stuff again to see if anyone remembers anything new. We want to find her killer." Amilio showed strength in his face and Debbie felt more at ease.

Sammi realized they were confronting a fairly confident and attractive twenty-five year old whose eye contact with her ensured she would do everything in her power to help solve this crime.

Sammi continued. "And we know it's hard to keep bringing up all of these hurtful memories, but we keep digging for more clues."

"Actually, they never go away anyway. It's been over a year and I thought it would have gotten a little easier by now, and it has in one way, but not much. It's still so hard...."

She couldn't continue, was choked up and had to pause for a moment.

"It shouldn't have happened especially to her. Of everyone I knew she was one of the best people ever. And not because she's my sister, but she had a good heart."

Then she offered everyone coffee and they got down to business.

Sammi began. "I know you were interviewed a while back and I know it's been a while now. But..."

"Ask anything you want. I wish I knew more, but ask me anything."

"Okay," she said. "You weren't with your sister the night that she got killed, right?"

"I was there for dinner, but I had other plans so I left after we ate. It was about 7:00 PM when I took off."

"Oh and where did you eat dinner?"

"We had gone to Hubner's Café on Third Avenue. That place has been special to us for a long time and we'd go there at least once a month."

"Okay," said Amilio. "So there were you, your sister, Mitzie Larner and Gail Mathers, right?"

"Yep, that's right."

"And what time were you there?"

"I got there a little before 6:00 PM, but the others, including my sister got there by about 5:30 PM, I think. Our reservation was for that time."

"Oh, you had a reservation?" asked Sammi.

"Yes, my sister made it. She was always exact about everything."

"Then it would have been made in her name?"

"Probably."

Amilio nodded. "Okay, did any of you see anyone you knew in the restaurant?"

Debbie paused and had to think. "Sorry, I don't think anyone asked me that before, let me think. Oh yeah, this one guy came up to the table ... I think he worked with my sister. Yeah, yeah, that's right. It was obvious he liked her; that's what Mitzi thought."

"How did your sister react?"

"She didn't say much to him at all, but I know she was glad when he left. And I remember she said she worked with him, but found him a little strange."

"Do you remember his name?"

"No, I don't, but I kind of remember what he looked like. Actually he was kind of good looking."

"So if you saw a picture of him, could you recognize him?"

"Yep, I'm pretty sure I could."

Sammi asked, "Can you describe him?"

"He seemed a little older, maybe thirty-five, dark hair and was wearing a suit, probably came from work, too."

"Was he alone or with friends?"

"I don't know for sure, but I think he was alone because I saw him sitting alone at the bar for a few minutes. He was just looking around the place."

"Anything else you remember?"

She paused, thinking. "No, I don't think so."

Then she became aware of something and said,

"Yes, there was something else. When this guy got up and left, which was before me, he yelled to Tammy from the door, "Don't forget.""

"Don't forget what?" asked Amilio.

"He didn't say, but my sister wrinkled her nose and was glad when he was gone."

Amilio found it interesting that there was nothing about this in the notes. A chance question had brought up a lot of information.

They went over some other older information and concluded within the hour. They had a few fresh ideas and thanked Debbie, letting her know if they needed to talk to her again, they'd be in touch. She had no problem with that. She was hoping she'd helped them.

* * *

"I wonder who that guy was," said Amilio. "It would be hard to find him with what we've got."

"But Debbie said that she remembered what he looked like. She thought he was good-looking."

"Then again, we'd have to pull pictures of all the guys working there within a certain age on a hunch. Not sure that's a good idea right now."

"Right. I don't think Dave and the others want to create waves right now. Later might be better."

"I was able to make an appointment with her friend Mitzi Larner tomorrow morning and I'm trying for the other one by the afternoon. We've got to get all this information together and see what we've got."

Amilio dropped Sammi off at home and she took the envelope with pictures hoping to see something in them.

Dave hadn't arrived home yet so she poured a cup of coffee and went to sit in the living room. She opened the envelope and started looking at the pictures. Something was bugging her, but she couldn't focus on it. She'd heard something today that had jogged something in her memory. Oh well, soon it would come forward.

The pictures pretty much confirmed the report as to

the position of the body and the wounds described as well as the missing jacket found nearby. Everything seemed to fit together and nothing was out of place conjuring up any new ideas until she came to the last picture. It was a close up of the head, neck and upper torso area. Sammi sat spellbound for a moment. She must be seeing things. She ran for a magnifying glass to be sure she wasn't imagining things. No, she wasn't. There it was, in her right hand; the same flower that was found in Tina O'Leary's hand. Tammy Sinclair's hand held a forget-me-not flower. Then she remembered another thing. The guy that had come up to the girls' table in that restaurant and taunted Tammy had spoken before he left. He had said, "Don't forget." Coincidence or just an off-the-cuff statement remained to be seen. But she thought not.

She sat still for a while giving her mind a chance to recall memories and refocus on her abilities. Was her imagination running away with her? Her thoughts were rather bizarre she thought. This would be too crazy to be true. *I must be mistaken*, she thought. *But I'm beginning to feel that these killers are telling their victims in a rather macabre way, not to forget them.* They were the conquerors and not to be forgotten. Her body was covered with chills as Dave walked in the back door.

She ran up to him and gave him a long and needy hug. He immediately felt her tenseness and held her until she relaxed a little.

"What's going on with you?"

"I need to take a deep breath, relax, have dinner with you and prepare for a discussion later on," she said.

Dave looked intrigued.

"Okay, I'm starved," he said. "Let's eat first."

Conversation was stop and start during most of the meal. Sammi was quite thoughtful and Dave interrupted her thoughts shocking her a few times. When dinner was over Dave was happy to get some wine and start on something that was extremely heavy on Sammi's concentration.

She first told him everything that had happened today. Then she showed him the pictures. At first, he didn't see it, but then she pointed out the flower in Tammy's hand. Even Dave was startled. The thoughts going through his mind were similar to hers. This couldn't be a coincidence. But it was too bizarre, too fantastic to have any connection to reality.

"Sammi, you think this is connected to ASAC, don't you?"

She started out slowly. "Yes, I do. I'm beginning to think it's all connected to ASAC, Beth's murder, Tina's murder and now Tammy's murder. How we'll ever prove it, I have no idea, but it's a gut feeling, Dave. This isn't a serial killer in the usual sense, but something is going on over there. What could it be?"

"Damned if I know. But we've got some weird people at the top who feel they're entitled, remember? They target certain women and if they don't come across they kill them or have them killed and plant this flower as their sign of victory or something. Damn, I don't know, but I've got a sick feeling, too."

"Yet, Tina doesn't fit the usual profile and Beth didn't have a flower," she said.

"But Tina's ex- worked for the company, so he could have had help killing her and I keep thinking that Beth wasn't supposed to be killed so that's why they didn't have a flower with them."

"I don't know, Dave, there are a lot of maybes here."

"I know, but remember we're only beginning ..."

The telephone rang. It was Sergeant Brady.

"Get Sammi on the phone, too."

"They were doing some early preliminary work in court on the trial today. And Paul Ryan was in the audience. Ron was somewhat unnerved by that. Paul even came over to say hello to him and stated he wished to witness the proceedings anyway. He still wanted to learn from Ron. Now Ron felt that he didn't want to bar him from the courtroom, although he could have; he thought that might play right into ASAC's hands. The situation has him worried."

"God, I can understand that. You've got to wonder what they're up to now."

"It's kind of scary. He wants Sammi in court starting next week when everything official takes place."

"How does he plan to do that without arousing suspicion?"

"Here's what we've decided to do. We're allowed to have a department representative at this trial everyday because Tom is a personal friend of Randy. That will be Amilio. He'll sit in the usual spot for our reps so there won't be any questions as to why he's there every day. He picks up a lot of things, too and Ron's planning to use Sammi in some way. He's going to have her sit about two rows behind their table and occasionally, he'll confer with her or have her go and get something they need, so it will look like she's part of their team. He's a person short right now, so that should work. But he wants her there to see what she can pick up. He wants both of them to keep an eye on Paul Ryan and hopefully pick up some damaging evidence that they can use. Any problem with that?"

"No problem here," said Sammi. "I can do that."

"And with Amilio around, I'll feel better," said Dave.

"I thought about that," said Sergeant Brady. "And he'll be valuable because he picks up things, too. Personally, I'm kind of glad this came about. We should be able to gather some information since Paul's not being planted there for nothing."

"Unless," said Sammi, "they thought that Ron would have him barred and that would show prejudice against ASAC from the beginning."

"But what good would that do?" asked the sarge. "Can't figure that one out either way."

"That's true; they can be tricky," said Dave. "Okay, then, next week, right?"

"I think Tuesday, but I'll let you know, Sammi. And thanks."

"Sure, I'll be ready."

* * *

Later that night Dave turned to Sammi and said, "Jim and I will be following up a few leads in the neighborhood. I'd personally love to stop by that courtroom myself, but I don't think Sergeant Brady wants me there. It looks like it will be you and Amilio."

"What are you so worried about?"

"These people are playing for keeps. And nobody knows what they have in mind."

"But I'll be working on Ron's team. They won't pay much attention to me."

"But you were introduced to Paul before remember, that day when we went to court? I hope he won't wonder about you."

"No, I don't think so. He was kicked off the team and he'll believe that Ron needs a little more help, kind of like a gofer, I think."

"You're probably right. And you'll be right in the middle of everything. You can even clue Ron into what the prosecution has in mind. I kind of like the idea of turning the tables on them, don't you?"

"I do," Sammi said, smiling. "It's like playing their game against them."

"It is at that," Dave said.

"And now the game will get very interesting," Sammi said, rather tongue-in-cheek. "So what's going on in the neighborhood?"

"Not sure yet, but we have to check out a few of the neighbors. Apparently one saw the three men walk up to the door. We already knew about that. But another came forward, as well as a third to admit that they heard some very loud noises, like an argument about the same time. Doesn't sound like much, but we have to look into it."

"And, of course, you never know. What about the guy that Denver stayed with until the police came. Did he hear or see anything?"

Dave turned to look at Sammi searchingly. "I never heard anything about that. I'll have to make a note and see if he's one of the new witnesses. If not, I'd like to know about him myself. Thanks, Sammi."

She smiled. They certainly had more work cut out for them. They were only making a little progress for all of the hours put into this case. She hoped that in the near future everything would open up.

* * *

Early the next morning she got a call from Amilio about meeting with Mitzi. She was ready when he got there and they were on their way to meet with one of Tammy's friends who'd been with her the last few minutes of her life.

"This should give us the information we need," said Amilio. "They can tell us what her attitude was with this guy."

"That would help. I wonder what kind of relationship she had with him. Apparently she wasn't crazy about him, but was he just a nuisance or did he worry her?"

"That's right, Sammi. Some guys are more like pests, that's true, but others can scare some of the girls. I'd like to know about that, too."

They were waiting outside Mitzi Larner's place when she arrived. Apparently she had gone to work for a short time, but made it back in time for their 10:30 A.M. appointment.

"Mitzi had barely opened the door to her apartment when they approached her.

"Whoa, you're already here. Well, come in," she said and they followed her into her place. "Give me a moment okay. It was a fast ride home."

She disappeared, but was back within a few minutes dressed casually and ready. "I'm going to need some coffee. Let me put on the pot for everyone."

She had a small one-bedroom apartment in a pleasant area of town. It was decorated with care and taste and with the theme of a twenty-seven year old mentality. But she told them she felt safe here. She held a nice position at a bank, but was still on the lower rung of the ladder.

But she liked it and hoped to move up in time and also improve her home.

Amilio got to business quickly.

"Okay, we need to go over that last night you spent with Tammy. We understand you ate dinner at Hubner's Café with Tammy, Gail and her sister Debbie."

"That's right. Tammy, Gail and I got there in time for our reservation at five thirty, but Debbie came by about six o'clock."

Amilio was taking notes now. "Did you see anyone you knew in the restaurant?"

"No, most of our friends don't frequent that place, but we all like it and go there often. But there wasn't anyone ... wait a minute. There was this guy ... I think he worked with Tammy." Mitzi took time for a sip of coffee as she sat cross-legged on the couch. "I'm pretty sure she worked with him, but he gave her the creeps, she said. He was always around her desk somehow and he had nothing to do with her department. She had mentioned him before and when he approached the table Tammy said, "That's that guy I told you about, the one that's always around."

Sammi asked, "Do you know his name?"

Mitzi thought for a moment and said, "I'm pretty sure she said, 'Hi, Danny,' but I'm not absolutely positive. Wait a minute. Yes it was Danny because I thought to myself, "Oh yeah, Danny Boy -- just like in the song." His first name was Danny, but I wouldn't know his last name."

"Okay," said Sammi. She looked at Amilio and caught his eye, but he seemed to be simply following along. Sammi knew there was more here. She had heard Mitzi's thoughts and she knew this guy, too. She thought he had tried to pick her up at a bar one time or other, but she declined.

Then suddenly Amilio asked, "But you had never seen him before?"

Sammi wanted to smile, but couldn't. He was picking up clues very well. She knew that was not a searching question, he'd felt something. He was good.

However, Mitzi reacted. You could tell that she was feeling caught in something. She answered in a slightly embarrassed manner.

"One time about three months before, I was out with some friends at a bar. This Danny tried to pick me up. We all thought he was acting strange that night and it kind of unnerved me."

"Strange in what way?" Sammi asked.

"Well, bar life can be different sometimes. Although some guys can be pushy, most follow certain rules of behavior. He didn't. He was grabby with me when he first walked up. Initially I thought he must be drunk, but he really wasn't. Then he acted like it was a foregone conclusion that he would make it with me that night. I know drunks do that or guys on the make will make suggestions, but that's not what he was doing. He would fend off anyone who tried to come near me and say that I was taken and ... I don't know, other weird stuff, but his mannerism was bizarre like he was simply out of it. We all thought he must be high on something. We left as soon as we could and asked the bouncer to make sure he didn't leave until we got into our cars and were out of sight. The bouncer is someone we know so he cooperated. I was totally embarrassed about the incident, that's all."

"But you didn't do anything wrong," said Amilio.

"No, but my mom doesn't like it when I go to the bars and I didn't for a while after that. Anyway, when Danny came over to our table, I could tell he didn't recognize me at all and kind of was after Tammy. But she turned him off."

"Did it make him mad?"

"It didn't seem to. He joked around quite a bit, but teased her about remembering something. Then he left our table."

Amilio looked over at Sammi eagerly as he asked. "Did he say anything else?"

Mitzi thought for a moment, wrinkled her nose and said, "Well, later, it was kind of weird. At the door before he left he turned to Tammy and said "Don't forget."

"How did Tammy react?"

"She didn't even react, but was glad he left and said, "That guy is utterly weird."

* * *

Mitzi got everyone a refill of coffee before they continued. She was surprised that this interview was taking all of this time.

"After dinner where did you gals go?"

"We went over to Vladimirs. It's considered a nice place and they have a good band there. Friday nights usually pulls in a nice crowd."

"Anything unusual happen there? Anything at all. "

This time Mitzi took a few minutes to think about it. "It's been a while now, but I don't think so."

"You didn't see this Danny guy there, did you?" asked Sammi.

Without hesitation she said, "Oh no, both Tammy and I would have reacted to that one. I didn't see him. I mean, it doesn't prove he wasn't there. It's a rather large place and pulls in a lot of people. But I didn't see him."

"What time did you leave?"

"We all left together around 12:30 AM. I had to work the next day and the others had had enough by then. It can get rather noisy, even for me."

"So, nothing unusual happened?"

She shook her head seriously. "Nope, just like other times. We usually park close together and wait until we're all in our cars and pull out at the same time. We did that night, too."

"Okay," said Sammi.

"Honestly, I wish I knew more, but I don't. Gail and I both realize that it could've been us. We want you to get this guy and find out what happened to Tammy that night."

"Okay, we appreciate your help."

"Do you know of any friends that Tammy had from work?" asked Sammi. "Did she pal around with anyone?"

"Well, she had this one friend Robert Andersen, simply a buddy, I think. He used to go to lunch with her. They were both working toward becoming brokers themselves so they discussed a lot of business. And I know she sometimes mentioned that she'd been to lunch with a few girls, but I have no idea who they would be."

"So she didn't get together much outside of work with these people."

"I honestly don't think so."

"Okay, thanks again. I think this will be it for today, but we may be in touch again."

"Sure, anything I can do to help."

* * *

Amilio looked over his notes. "We have a confirmation for that Danny Boy, and have a new name Robert Andersen."

And, in Sammi's mind the name Mitzi had thrown out so casually was the name she had heard on Tammy's mother's mind. But she still wondered why her mother chose not to share it. They were simply friends from what she could determine.

"I wish we could find a way to find this Danny; maybe later."

"True, but I'd sure like to know where our Danny Boy went after he left that restaurant. I'd love to hear if he has a good alibi or not. There's something going on there, Sammi."

"And considering his strange behavior a few months back with Mitzi, he's got to be someone to be concerned about. Too bad we don't know his last name."

"We'll hold on to this one right now. We've still got that interview with Gail this afternoon and then we can take time to study this stuff more."

"Wonder how Dave's doing interviewing those neighbors? They were hoping to get more insight into this."

"It does seem strange to me that nobody saw or heard much in the middle of the day."

"Maybe they'll have more tonight."

"I sure hope so."

* * *

Amilio was musing as he said, "It'll be interesting to see if both of these girls felt the same way about the evening."

"Everyone has a different take on things," said Sammi. "We've already talked to the parents, and then her sister and now one of the friends who were there that night."

"Right and I got a call from MKG Financial ...." He stopped abruptly as he saw the look on Sammi's face. "Well I have a buddy that owes me a favor so I asked him about getting a list of names of people who work at that firm.

"That's the brokerage firm where Tammy worked?"

He nodded. "They said we'll be receiving a list of all personnel with pictures by tomorrow. And that means that we can scan for anyone named Danny, but we'll still have to confirm with the three girls again."

They had stopped for a quick lunch and were able to relax for a few minutes. It helped to get their thoughts in sync.

"That's a good move," said Sammi. "We can't get close to ASAC right now, but this Danny guy might give us something to point us in the right direction."

"And sometimes that's all you need." Amilio was focused now and getting anxious.

"You ready to go," he asked. "It should take about forty minutes to get to Gail's place and we should just make it in time."

* * *

All the way to Gail's house, they talked about the case, and how they would approach this next interview. It could be tricky, but they needed to make sure that they would make the best use of this opportunity.

"Okay, here we are," he said. "Any thoughts before we go."

She shook her head.

"Okay then."

Gail's apartment was somewhat larger than Mitzi's place, but then it was understood that her family had some money and helped her out. Gail had graduated from Willamette University in Salem, studying art. She was quite talented in both painting and sketching. She had made a variety of career moves already, and was offered more because of her varied abilities and recognized talent. Yet, she was still looking for her niche.

As they settled in an updated living room, Gail offered, "I'll tell you all I can. I've told everyone who asked what I knew before, that we all left together, all three of us as we usually did. We got into our cars and drove out the exit together. We always did that to make sure we were all on our way."

She looked down nervously. They gave her a moment.

"We'd like to backtrack to the dinner you had at Hubner's Café."

She looked somewhat surprised, but said, "Okay."

"We understand you were there about six o'clock and left a little after eight thirty," asked Amilio.

"Actually Mitzi, Tammy and I got there around five thirty. That's the time Tammy made the reservation for and Debbie got there around six."

That certainly checked out. They wanted to be sure because you never knew when time could be important.

"Okay," said Sammi. "Did you see anyone you knew? Did anyone come up and talk with you?"

Gail didn't hesitate to mention Danny. "There was this guy from where Tammy worked. Apparently, he made her uneasy. She'd mentioned him to us before, but not by name. She used to talk about this guy at work that always came around her desk and didn't have any business being there. Anyway, she thought he was weird.

Well, he was at Hubner's that night and came over to the table for a few minutes."

"And you didn't remember ever seeing him before?"

"No, I didn't, but Mitzi did. He didn't remember her so she didn't say anything at the time, but later told us that she was at some bar one night and he was smashed or something. Anyway, her and her friends left early because he was so annoying."

They continued to take notes.

"Do you know his name?"

"I think she called him Danny and I know he worked at the same brokerage firm, but honestly, that's all I know about him."

"Would you recognize him again?"

"Oh yeah, he was quite nice-looking. I was surprised that both Mitzi and Tammy thought he was annoying because usually good-looking guys get their share of girls."

"Anything else you can remember?"

"Well, he did yell something to Tammy from the doorway as he left, but I don't remember what he said. Tammy kind of wrinkled her nose and said something again about him being kind of weird."

"Okay and then later you went where?"

"We went over to Vladimirs. They have a good band there. We've gone plenty of times, especially on Friday night."

Again Sammi asked, "anything unusual happen that you remember?"

She puckered her lips and shook her head slightly as she answered, "No, nothing out of the ordinary. We all danced, had a good time, and left a little after twelve. Mitzi had to work the next day."

"Did Debbie leave at the same time?"

"Oh, she didn't come. She had other plans."

So far, everything was checking out and that was good, but also frustrating. Sammi looked over at Amilio who had a clear and calm expression. He wasn't picking up anything and neither was she. The colors around Gail were honest and she could believe her story as her thoughts confirmed everything she said.

"One more thing," asked Sammi, "when you left the parking lot, was it just the three of you or did you notice any other cars getting ready to leave?"

Now that stopped her for a moment. She seriously thought about that question.

"There's nothing I can be definite about, because around twelve o'clock at night people are still coming in and others are leaving, but when we left we were the only ones in the parking lot walking out that I remember. That's one of the reasons we all leave together; it can be kind of eerie at that time of night. But I do remember seeing a type of flash coming from a car; it was like someone using their lighter. It was real brief and I'm not absolutely sure."

"But you think you saw a flash of light?" asked Amilio.

"Well, yeah and I remember thinking that someone must be waiting for someone. But I'm not sure. I was moving fast to get to my car."

"Well, okay," said Sammi. "I think that's all we need for now. We'll be calling you and Mitzi and Debbie down to the police station in the next few days. We'll have some pictures from the brokerage firm and want to know if you could identify this Danny person."

"Okay," she answered. "I think I should be able to pick him out." Then she paused and said, "Do you think he had anything to do with this?"

"We don't know. We're just following leads right now."

She nodded her head as she said, "I sure hope you get this guy. Mitzi and I keep racking our brains trying to figure out if there was anything we could have done. If he gets caught and we know what happened, I hope that will alleviate my guilt."

"You've got nothing to be guilty about...."

"I know, I know, but it could have been any of us.

We know that. But he picked on Tammy and we'd really like to know why. She was such a good person."

Gail was rather chocked up at this point, but managed to maintain her composure in an uneasy way.

"Talking about Tammy brings everything back. She was my best friend since Grade 9. She knew everything about me and I knew everything about her."

As a quick thought Amilio asked, "Did you know about Robert Andersen?"

"Oh sure, he was a friend of hers from work. They occasionally went to lunch and stuff; they were both hoping to become brokers and helped each other out."

"Was there anything between them?"

"Oh no," said Gail emphatically. "He's gay. But Tammy thought he was a great person and didn't care about his preferences. She always said that we shouldn't judge others. But they helped each other at the firm and she thought of him as a good friend. I know he was devastated by her death."

Sammi raised an eyebrow.

Gail noticed and answered. "I talked to him for a moment at the funeral."

"Well, okay then, if you think of anything at all, let us know. We're backtracking over everything."

"Any new leads, yet?" she asked.

"Sammi here has been recently added to our unit and we've got others working with us, too. We all want to get this guy."

* * *

Sammi was the first one to jump on the latest information.

"I think I understand why Mrs. Sinclair hesitated to talk much about this Bob Andersen. I think she had a problem with the gay part."

"A lot of that generation isn't so open about letting people be who they are. She was probably embarrassed," Amilio said.

"I could feel something when this guy was mentioned and she wouldn't even give his name. I don't think of him as a suspect, but I'd still like to talk to him."

"That might be a good idea," he said. "He works there and might have some ideas of some of the guys around, especially that Danny guy. In fact, that might be the best way to set it up."

"Let's see what he knows."

"We'd better do it on Monday. Looks like we're going to be in court by Tuesday of next week."

Sammi was anxious. "Have you heard definitely the trial will start on Tuesday?"

"No, no, I haven't. But that's what they're aiming for. I know some of our days will be boring; all trials have their boring parts. But I think and hope we may have some surprises for the prosecution before this is over."

Sammi had to agree with that. Although this case was slower than some, so much in the background was coming forward inch by inch. Even Dave who'd been quite worried at the beginning was noticing a pattern emerging. No one yet knew where all this would lead them, but some enthusiasm was beginning to emerge and a new strength and dedication was helping them out daily.

CHAPTER THIRTEEN

Amilio went alone on Monday to the MKG Financial Group to talk with Bob Andersen. He preferred Sammi to be with him, but she was needed at the bank and they felt either of them could have performed this interview. Amilio had time to wander around the place, get a feel of the pulse and atmosphere of the environment and decide whether there would be any information there. And there wasn't; at least not yet. Mr. Andersen was polite, personable and as helpful as he could be, but he didn't really know that much. He knew Danny and was able to tell him that several girls were annoyed with him and some a little tense when he was around. But he hadn't done anything wrong and no official complaint had been issued against him. But Amilio planned to keep him in mind and follow up further at the appropriate time.

* * *

Taking her seat in the courtroom on Tuesday, Sammi felt surreal about the circumstances that had gotten her into this position. She shifted slightly in her seat a few times as she waited for the drama to begin. Amilio wasn't there yet and even the defense team came in about ten minutes after she had sat down. She looked around to find that only a few people were there, but more began entering each moment. She thought back on her life, especially with her grandpa. She felt him around her and asked for his help. After all, he was the sole other person in her childhood who could also hear other people's thoughts. She wished he was around and they could be working this case together. But then she remembered, in a special way, he was always around.

"Sammi, I need you to move to this other seat."

Ron Donovan had taken his place at the defense table and realized that he needed Sammi in a strategic place where he could confer with her with the least amount of effort on his part. She hadn't noticed Paul Ryan yet, but Ron seemed to know her question.

"He was sitting over there," he said pointing to a chair just two seats over from hers. "I don't want to take a chance that he could overhear anything we say, unless, of course, I want him to hear. So I'm moving you over here and I'll have this seat designated for you, as an aide to my team. Any problem with that?"

"No, not at all. I'll help out any way I can, but I guess I'm not sure what you want me to do."

"I've heard you're good at picking up information. So do what you do best. Use your expertise to find out what's going on around here. I mean, Paul's here for a reason and the prosecution's had unfair advantage for a while. I need to even up the playing field."

"Okay, and if I hear anything detrimental that I need to tell you immediately, what do you want me to do?"

"That's right; I guess we need a signal. I don't imagine that will happen too often because most things you'll hear can wait until the end of the day, I would think. But, if you happen to hear something, then get up and come down to the table with some type of paper in your hand, and give it to me. Then I'll ask for a break."

"Okay."

"But that's only if it can't wait. Otherwise update me at the end of the day if you have anything I should know about."

"Understood."

At that moment Amilio showed up and joined them. His job was a little simpler. He was to be the eyes and ears for the police department. Still, he, too, was intuitive and was given the same privilege as Sammi.

"Okay," he said, "the day has arrived; lots of activity going on here. I don't think I appreciated that before."

"Courts can be quite intimidating to the outsider who

doesn't understand all of the procedures. But a lot of this is preparation and protocol. The real stuff doesn't begin until we start examining the witnesses. We've got a long road to go."

Then attention was called as Judge Milan Grogen came into the room. No one seemed surprised. Apparently Ron expected that judge. He looked around and was surprised that Randy Baker wasn't at the defendant's table yet.

"Where's your client?"

"I was told he'd be here by now."

The judge turned to the bailiff and said, "Find out what's going on."

At that moment the doors opened and in walked Randy with two official escorts who apologized, but mentioned a serious wreck on Highway 81 that brought traffic to a standstill in all directions. Even the judge had heard about it and had them sit down immediately to get things started. No one was admonished.

"Now, I realize this means that you haven't had any time to confer with your client this morning," said the judge as he looked at Ron. "I plan the usual, reading of the charges, and some of the procedures that I insist on in my courtroom. After that, I'll take a twenty minute break and that should give you plenty of time to prepare."

"Thank you, Your Honor," said Mr. Donovan. He seemed pleased with this judge who had a reputation of fairness, wasn't overly sensitive about others taking control of his court and was considered laid back, yet quite shrewd and calculating. They couldn't have hoped for anything more.

Amilio was situated four seats behind Sammi but to the far right of the court. She couldn't turn to look at him without being obvious, which was probably good. She was nervous and fidgeted a little; she couldn't help it. Who'd ever believe she'd be in this situation?

She began by concentrating on the prosecution side of the table. James McLean, the lead attorney was all business, moving his notes around and connoting a type of nervous excitement as the trial was finally beginning. His thoughts were dire and he believed Randy Baker was guilty and he intended to prove it, but that was his job. And the other member of his team, Gary Duncan, was in the same frame of mind in an honest fashion. That was okay. Sammi didn't see anything wrong there. They had a job to do and they wanted to win.

But Werner Berman's thoughts were all over the place. He was mainly trying to keep an ear on the defense table. Sammi didn't think he could do it. He was too far away, but he had thoughts of bugging the defense table, yet she wasn't sure he would do it. He hadn't done it yet and it seemed like more of a fantasy to him. It was too big of a chance to take. However, his concentration would be mainly on the defense table with the trial a secondary consideration.

Sammi then concentrated on the defense table. She had checked out Ron several times and he was legit. His life was dedicated to the FBI and he was extremely con- scientious. He had great talent as a defense attorney and Sammi felt Randy should be happy to have gotten him. Stephen Harrison checked out also. His dedication was to win this case and prove the innocence of his client, Randy Baker. If he had any other thought on his mind it would be to find the real killer or killers of Beth Baker.

So Sammi relaxed and listened to the proceedings. The judge seemed to have no ulterior motives and as some of the legal lingo was a little above her, she let her concentration move around the room. Amilio was trying hard to take in everything that he could. He had great powers of the mind when he wanted, and picked up a lot of data because he was totally aware of the moment. In fact, of everyone she'd known so far in her life, he was closest to her and her Grandpa. Although she knew he couldn't hear thoughts like they could, she thought he could have been a candidate if he wanted.

Then she canvassed the audience and landed on

Paul Ryan whose thoughts were constantly panicked. He needed to get back into the good graces at ASAC and so he was casing everyone persistently. His thoughts were mostly irrational and distressed. He needed to be valuable and would invent something if he had to.

Then, for some reason Sammi broadened her scope and was shocked at something she heard. My God, she had to get to Ron right away. But the judge said they'd be taking a break real soon. She was getting nervous; she couldn't wait. She had learned one important lesson in this trial already. Don't underestimate ASAC. Keep trying to pick up everything you can, even from the most unsuspecting people.

At last the judge declared a break and Sammi was at Ron's side immediately. She needed to talk to him privately. He showed surprise, but followed her quickly to a private room.

"What's gives?" he said.

"The bailiff," she answered. "He works for ASAC."

"No shit."

Ron was quite angered, but worried. The look on his face was astonishment. Wasn't there anyone they could trust?

"And you know this for a fact?" he asked.

"No doubt," she said. "I've checked out the court reporter, too, and he seems to be okay. But I've got a feeling, and it's just a feeling, but if you replace the bailiff, they'll insist on another court reporter, one of their own."

"My God, what the hell's going on here?"

"I don't know, but I'm telling what I've found out."

"Oh, I don't doubt you, Sammi. Ben Collier said you were the best and I trust him. But it seems that ASAC must have some big stakes in this murder, probably a lot more than we thought. I'd been leery of them before, but obviously not as suspicious as I could have been. Okay, I've got to get to the judge to replace the bailiff and not change the court reporter unless I agree. Anything else?"

"That's all I know right now, but if I discover anything else I'll let you know."

"Thanks, Sammi. You're amazing. I'm always going to be looking over my shoulder now and I've got to be able to concentrate on Randy's defense."

"That's what you've got me for. And the first few rows of people are okay. They are friends and some spectators who check out. I don't want anyone around you to hear your strategy, okay? That's what I figure my job is right now. You agree?"

"Absolutely."

By this time, Amilio had entered the room and was listening with a knowing sneer.

"If anything's going on, Sammi will pick it up. She's amazing, isn't she? I'm not hearing anything around me. We want you to be able to do your job, Ron, and not worry about anything else. That's our job. You just get Randy off and help us find the real killers."

"And with you and Sammi around, I can do that. Okay, the break is over and now I have to get to the judge. That's my first order of business."

When the judge came out of the meeting with Ron Donovan, he adjourned the court until Wednesday morning. He looked somber and thoughtful although it was clear that he was definitely irked. Any innuendos, although not always proven were taken quite seriously. They would have a new bailiff and the same court reporter on Wednesday. Sammi realized that Paul Ryan had one more thing to be upset about.

* * *

That evening Dave had to ask Sammi how she knew about the bailiff. After all, he was situated about twenty feet away from her and although distance didn't matter to her usually when she concentrated on other people's thoughts, he felt the noise of the courtroom would be totally distracting for her.

"That was more of a challenge for me; you're right, but I had streams of worrisome colors that lead me right to him. So I put all of my efforts together, and I didn't have to concentrate on that bailiff very long. You see, Paul is sitting about two rows behind me and he's one nervous guy about now. He kept thinking of the bailiff and hoping he could pick up something. Honestly, Dave, I'm lucky Paul is sitting so close to me. He's telling me a lot."

Dave laughed; he couldn't help it.

"How about you? Anything new with the neighbors?"

"Actually we do. One other neighbor heard some loud and angry voices coming from Randy's house. It was a woman living on the west side of them. She knew Beth's voice when she heard it, but she said she heard two other men and neither voice belonged to Randy. She knows him too well. So that was good. And Michael Gater is the neighbor who took care of Denver. He said he heard some commotion, but the strange part is that no one heard the shots."

"But they were all in the house by then; maybe that's why. The argument no doubt took place when the guys arrived and were still on the porch."

"True, yet a shot is quite loud. But, who knows?"

"Was there only one shot? Did anyone ask Denver?"

Dave turned to her with his face in thoughtful mode. "No, there were two shots. I remember hearing that Beth got off a warning shot and that must be when they got the gun away from her. Then, of course, they took her gun and shot her with it. And two bullets were missing from the gun, so that checks out. But I'm not sure if they ever retrieved that first bullet."

Sammi was somewhat anxious. "This trial is going to be a challenge for me. I could hear something important from any area of that courtroom. I'll have to be continuously aware of everyone around me, more so than usual."

"Well, don't forget to relax. You told me that you always do better that way."

She nodded.

Dave said, "I might be late tomorrow night. Jim and I want to check out a few more things later in the day. I'll call you."

Sammi looked disappointed, which prompted Dave to ask. "Why? What's wrong?"

"Jill had asked us to go over for dinner tomorrow night and I was hoping you could make it. I did want to touch base with Denver again; I need to keep hearing what's on his mind."

"And you've been worried that he's been keeping something hidden, haven't you?"

"Yes, he is. And it's quite important to him. What I mean is I don't think it was the terror of the situation, which, of course, would be understandable. This almost hits me as a private matter. I can't get a real feeling about it yet. I'm hoping it'll surface soon. It may be something we could use in court."

"True, and that little one's been through so much, yet he seems to be holding up pretty good. Who knows about later?"

"Children can be quite resilient and hopefully he'll have his dad around. They can mourn and work out things together. That should help them both."

Silence overcame them both. There was so much involved in this case. Where would it lead?

* * *

When Sammi walked into Tom and Jill's home the next night, she felt a tension permeating the air. Randy was there and everyone seemed relaxed outwardly, but she knew. Randy's thoughts were all over the place from rehashing his first day in court to thoughts about his dead wife to worry about his young son, Denver. Tom and Jill were worried as well. But there was an added tension that she hadn't yet been able to understand.

"Where's Denver?" she asked.

"He's not feeling well today," said Randy. "Honestly, it's starting to happen a lot lately. I don't think he's physically sick, but I guess all of this tension and worry is getting to him."

"I'd be surprised if it didn't," Sammi said.

Tom came in with his own observation. "But we have a long way to go. If he's already feeling the brunt of it, we're trying to decide if we should have him see somebody or not. What do you think?"

"I'd like to talk to him for a few minutes before dinner. Would that be okay?"

"Sure," they all said.

Randy added. "Anyone that can get me some insight into his thinking right now would be great. He's a little guy who keeps so much inside. And he always says that you're a lot like his mother. He may open up to you."

Sammi tapped lightly on Denver's bedroom door. He invited her in.

"I hear you're not feeling well. I'm sorry."

He looked at her and smiled. "You know better, don't you? I'm aware that you know about me, but I don't know how. You're a lot like my mom."

And with those words he shed some tears, something Sammi hadn't seen from him since the first few days that it happened.

"I can't get her out of my mind. I keep trying to remember what she looked like and sometimes I can't. I can't even remember what my mom looks like. I try to keep it to myself because I don't want to upset my dad. I know he misses her, too. He's got enough on his mind."

Then he became quiet. He looked at Sammi who'd moved up to his bed and sat down in a nearby chair. She smiled slightly.

"I think your dad is worried a little about you."

Before she had time to continue, Denver jumped on that statement.

"Oh no, he doesn't have to. I don't want him to worry about me."

"But you spend more time in your room saying you don't feel well."

Denver sat up at this point, wiped away his tears and said, "I do that so he won't worry about me. I feel so unhappy sometimes, but I don't want him to see it. He's got enough to think about."

"But you're his biggest concern. I think it would be okay to let him know what you feel."

He stopped, looked at her in a knowing way and said, "You know how I feel, don't you?"

"I know you're sad about your mom, and you're worried about your dad. You know he's innocent, but innocent people sometimes go to jail. And you wonder what will happen to you, if he's convicted."

Denver took a deep breath and confirmed her statements. He was worried about himself and thought that was selfish of him.

Sammi knew he felt guilty, she'd heard his thoughts. "It's okay to be worried about yourself. We all worry about ourselves, but your dad will make sure that you're taken care of, you know that, right?"

He nodded. Other thoughts were beginning to creep into his consciousness. One was the last few minutes with his mother, when Sammi helped him realize how she protected him right until the end.

Sammi said, "Yes, she made sure you'd be okay, didn't she?"

Denver looked over at her, but wasn't even surprised anymore. She always knew, just like his mom.

"Yeah, and it killed her."

"But those men were bad people. If they had known about you, they'd have killed you, too."

"I know that and I can't understand why. That's what bugs me a lot."

Sammi said, "Maybe it would be a good idea to get your dad up here with us. He's very worried about you. And what you're so anxious about is normal. He's more concerned about you right now because you won't talk to him."

Denver looked surprised. He didn't realize. He

thought he was doing a good job of hiding his fears.

He nodded okay and Sammi called Randy to the room. She was about to leave when Denver called her back.

"I'd like you to stay, too. Okay?"

The three of them went over most of Denver's fears for his dad and himself. His dad had to remind him that he was the adult here and he would do the worrying. He told Denver his job was still to be a ten-year-old kid, a sad one at times who'd lost his mom in a terrible accident, but one who had a dad who loved him and would always make sure that he'd be okay. It was an emotional scene for Sammi to witness.

As he relaxed, Sammi heard other thoughts on Denver's mind. Finally, some of his biggest fears were starting to surface, but he wasn't yet ready to tell anyone, not even his dad. And his thoughts weren't yet high enough in his consciousness for her to totally understand or hear them, but it was a move in the right direction.

On her way home, she marveled at the human mind, even at the level of this young ten year old gifted child. He had the same fears and feelings of isolation as any other child and yet needed to be included as everyone else. He was so protective of his father. Even with their enlightening discussion tonight, when he realized his father could handle all that he needed of him, Denver still wasn't ready to let out his secret. Something was quite traumatic for him and hadn't yet settled enough in his psyche for him to divulge it. But the time was getting closer and as he got stronger and more self-assured he'd spill what was on his mind. And Sammi had the distinct feeling that she was the one he'd tell when the time was right.

* * *

At home that night Dave shared that only one bullet had been retrieved, the one that got Beth Baker in the back of the head. It seemed they had discovered other scuffles in the blood around her body. There was nothing significant to work on, but Randy's footprint had been clean and distinctive, but something else was messed up on the same side and a few slight hesitations on the other side. It was most confusing.

"What does all this mean?" she asked.

"It could mean anything. One of the killers may have gone up to her body to make sure she was dead. That's about all we can think of."

"Probably not worth getting upset about, especially if there's nothing clear that could be used. You found one clear footprint from Randy, but other footprints had to be his walking up to the body. And the others, who knows? There's nothing clear about this murder scene anyway."

Dave said, "We've decided it wouldn't be worth putting Denver on the witness stand. Everything available is already known either in pictures or from the crime scene itself. He couldn't add anything more, so we decided to let it go. Ron Donovan agreed with that."

"I'm glad to hear that. That would be so hard on him."

"Ron said that something else a lot stronger would have to come up and it hasn't happened yet."

Sammi didn't say anything. It wasn't her place. But she thought that if Denver's hidden thoughts were ever to surface, he might have something important to tell.

"Are you feeling better about the case now?" asked Sammi.

"Well, Ron seems to think that there are so many loopholes in the prosecution's case that reasonable doubt will be all over the place."

"That's right," she said. "Everything has to be proven beyond a reasonable doubt."

"And his fingerprints are not on the gun. Beth's prints were the only ones found which means the killer had gloves on. And since the house was ransacked extensively and no fingerprints were found anywhere, except that partial I told you about, that should point away from him."

"Okay, but Randy's prints would be all over the

house; I mean he lived there. They could say he tossed things around to make it look like a robbery gone wrong."

"True, but Ron's answer to that, at this time, is that people usually toss around a few things here and there, but this house had everything tossed around and turned inside out. It would have taken a lot of time for him to do that alone. And we now have proof that Denver was there so ..."

"So what?"

"I don't know, the more we talk about it, the more confused I get about how the jury will perceive it. I guess that's up to Ron to make it look good for Randy. But I wish we'd get more evidence about these other killers. If they were from ASAC and the motive is muddled, well, I don't know."

"I was thinking ..."

And then the telephone rang. It was past ten o'clock. They looked at each other and wondered who that could possibly be. A late night call was usually not good news. Dave answered; he was closer.

"Sure, she's here; wait a minute."

He shrugged his shoulders and puckered his lips. He didn't recognize the voice, but it seemed nervous.

"Oh, hi, Charmaine, what's up?"

"Just listen, okay, I have a moment, that's all. I've overheard a few things you need to know about. You have to check out a gal by the name of Patsy Elmore. I think she now lives in Allentown. She moved there about three or four years ago and lives with her brother and his family. And she's scared, so she might not talk to you."

"Scared about what?"

"Here's what I've heard. She was attacked back then by some guy who works for ASAC, but she got away. There's a scheme over there and it's real scary. Be sure to ask her about the Gentlemen's Group. I have to go. Don't contact me for a while. I could get in a lot of trouble telling you this."

"Do you think you'll need protection?"

"No, but I'll need privacy; don't contact me right now. Later, when this is over, we'll talk again. Bye."

And Charmaine hung up abruptly. Her voice was nervous and halting throughout the call. She barely talked above a whisper and Sammi had the feeling she was looking around her at all times to see who might be listening. Her thoughts were in a panic and wondered if she'd get away with saying anything, but she felt she had to. Sammi would have loved to see her get protection, but had to respect her wishes.

After Sammi told Dave, he looked quite confused.

"What the hell's this about? Another girl attacked and it's connected to ASAC?"

He shook his head.

Sammi said, "I can wait until tomorrow, but I'll have to call Amilio and get out there with him. Do you want to come?"

"I'll see what's going on? It might be better if the two of you go. I wonder what Charmaine's trying to tell us."

"And," she said, "I wonder if this is new information or if she finally had the nerve to say something. Her thoughts led me to believe that she's known about this for a little while."

"At least it's another lead and another possible connection."

"I hope this one goes somewhere."

* * *

Sammi put through a call to Amilio first thing the next morning and updated him on Charmaine's call.

"God, Sammi, I've heard that term 'Gentlemen's Club' a few times in connection with this company, but damned if I can remember where. I figured it was just a term they used to refer to the higher echelon of the company. I'm going to check with my friend and see about Patsy's history with ASAC and her leaving. If she's living with her brother, maybe the last names are not the same ... if she was ever married, that is, but we could check her out through her Social Security number. She's obviously working again, somewhere."

Amilio couldn't seem to settle down. The juices were flowing and he was really hoping they were onto something.

"What else is going on at that company? What is this Gentlemen's Club? I've heard that term a few times myself."

"I'm gonna put a rush on this stuff and see if we can find her fast. She might be one of the keys to this entire murder stuff. Now, we still have to be in court and Ron's told me you've given him some good information so far. We're gonna have to get to this Patsy on the weekend."

"The sooner the better."

"Okay, let me see what I can find out about where and when and I'll get back with you."

"Okay."

* * *

Sammi realized some strange issues on her mind as she put down the phone. She hadn't talked to anyone about the few times that she heard Paul Ryan mention this Gentlemen's Club. One of his aims was to get back in good standing with ASAC so he'd have a chance to join it. But it was never clear to her exactly what it was about, but her suspicions ran all over the place. Was this a social part of the company or was it a higher rung on the ladder of accomplishments that workers wanted to achieve? The secrets of this company ran deeper and more secretive as they delved more into this case. What was this company all about?

Thinking back on her time in the courtroom made her wonder if anything would ever be solved. They needed a suspect other than Randy; they needed someone else who'd have a good reason to kill Beth and so far nothing was happening. They had all kind of subtle information and irritating innuendos about what was going on both in that company and its relation to Beth's murder, but when would that special clue burst forth and give them that aha moment. It had to be getting close, but she realized that she wasn't associating with the right people. She wasn't hearing anything that was pointing in the direction of the true killer.

Sammi and Amilio didn't associate together inside the courtroom. Although everyone knew both of their purposes, at least in general, they tried to keep their positions separate and let others guess about them. She'd gotten enough looks and gazes from Wayne Berman from the prosecution team. He eyed her quite often the first week or so, but finally seemed to accept her presence as an aide to Ron Donovan, who did seem to need an extra person on his team.

The prosecution's case was moving along slowly. And that was good at this time, because all of the research and investigation was taking a lot of time. Although the witness logs were presented at the beginning of the trial, Ron had allotted himself the privilege of adding one or two more on short notice for discretionary reasons and the judge allotted him the ability to do that. And the prosecution wanted the same privilege and it was granted. Ron had said he didn't mind at all. He was clearly thrilled the judge gave him more room for improvement.

* * *

Amilio moved fast and had the information by Thursday. He knew where Patsy Elmore lived and where she worked. But he had a few questions for Sammi.

"What's the best approach? I can't just call and try to make an appointment with her. She doesn't know us and that could scare the hell out of her. She could even run. I guess we should take a chance and show up in person, right? It'll be a little easier with you being there. Could be another female will make it more comfortable for her to talk with us."

"I think you're right. There's no easy way to do this. We don't know anybody who knows her and we don't actually know what happened to her. Your details are kind of skimpy."

"You're right there. She had worked for the company for seven years, had a good position. Now I'm not sure what she did, but she had two promotions, so she must have been doing well. And then she abruptly leaves with no notice or anything. That's strange on its own. I've looked through all of our police files and there's no report of any attempted rape or beating or anything about that time. So she didn't report it. It looks like she wanted to get herself the hell out of there. She must have been pretty scared."

"And to me that means she knows something, or she heard of something and thought it would be safer to simply leave."

"Really, Sammi, what the hell's going on over there?"

"I wish I knew, but I think we're going to find out soon. Look, Amilio I believe you're quite intuitive. You notice a lot of little things, just like me. Between the two of us, if we can get to talk to her I'm sure we'll come away with some information with her cooperation or not."

"Now this might get us closer to solving these other two murders, but what this has got to do with Beth Baker and getting Randy off, I don't know."

"Me neither, but I've always felt all this stuff was connected in some way. The bottom denominator is ASAC. It's no coincidence that everyone worked there or had a strong connection to this company."

Amilio laughed. "And Dave tells me you don't believe in coincidences."

"That's right; I don't. So we need to find this connection."

"Okay, you can make it Saturday, right?"

"Sure, I'll be ready."

* * *

Sammi would have liked Dave to be with them, but he didn't think it was the best idea.

"I think the two of you would do better alone, besides I have to get over to interview a few more people with Jim. We may have another neighbor who's willing to come forward now."

"After all this time?"

"It seems that more people are getting their nerve together, especially since others have come forward. And the more people we get who'll admit seeing three men walk up to their front door about the time of the murder, the more reasonable doubt that would create in the jury's mind."

Sammi nodded, but she sat there in disappointment. There was no doubt that she would have liked him with her.

"Okay, give. What's bothering you?"

"I like it when we work as a team. Amilio is okay, but I work best with you and then I don't have to worry about what I say. It's easier working with you."

"But we can discuss everything later like we always do."

"I know, but then I can't always take advantage of the moment. If Patsy's thoughts take me in an unusual direction, how can I explain that to Amilio?"

"Sammi, you don't have to explain anything, or you could say you had a feeling. He knows you're sharp at what you do. He'll no doubt think you're psychic, but that's okay. I wouldn't worry about that."

Sammi thought about that comment and said, "I guess you're right. I just like working with you; I'm used to you."

"I'm happy about that, but you'll get used to Amilio. He'll give you space for whatever you do and not ask any questions. He might tease you a bit, but that's all. You can trust him, too."

"I know you're right. I guess I'll have to get used to him."

Dave looked over and smiled as he said, "But don't get too used to him, okay?"

CHAPTER FOURTEEN

Amilio and Sammi grabbed an early breakfast and headed out to Allentown. Patsy's brother had lived there for the last fifteen years, with his wife and two boys. Amilio was hoping that the atmosphere of a family-type home would be conducive to getting her to talk more comfortably in her own environment. At least he hoped it would.

"That's if she invites us in ... and if she's even home. I hope so because we need a break and I think she could give it to us. At least she must know something," said Sammi. "She'd worked there for seven years."

"Yeah and with those promotions, she must have gotten privy to a few things. Don't you hate cases like this? We wrack our brains and spend hours and get hardly anything."

"I think Charmaine has given us a lot."

"Well, yes, she has, but ... it's like we've got all these pieces of a puzzle starting to fit in, but they're all on the outer border and we can see a little bit of the scenery, but we can't yet get a real hint of the real picture." Amilio's frustration was taking center stage.

"And Dave and the others keep following up on all these leads with very few definite results. That crime scene left more questions than answers. There were scuff marks around Beth's body that weren't made by Randy and not identified even yet."

"Possibly one of the guys wanted to make sure she was dead? That thought keeps crossing my mind, but somehow it doesn't feel right. I don't know. Oh hey, here we are 27864 Manchester; not a bad neighborhood, not rich, but not bad. Kind of nice, don't you think?"

"Yeah, homey in a way. Kids around playing outside ... rather comfortable."

"Are you ready?"

Sammi nodded. "I sure hope she's home. I hated doing it this way but we don't have a choice. I know this will be a delicate situation, but I think a surprise visit was the best option."

Amilio said, "She could deny everything or say we've got the wrong person and then what?"

"I think she'll be shocked for one thing, so her reaction will give her away. Anyway, I guess we have to play this one by ear. Let's see how it goes."

Sammi knew she'd pick up what she wanted to know quickly from Patsy's thoughts. At least then she'd be sure if they were on to something or not.

They got out of the car and walked up to the door and rang the bell. It was 11:00 AM on Saturday and a good time to catch her home. They both were quite sure there were answers somewhere behind these doors, answers they needed badly.

* * *

A middle-aged man, casually dressed, with a slight build and fuzzy brown hair answered the door in a friendly manner. He seemed to be congenial and welcoming, but at the same time he was cautious and guarded as you'd expect with strangers.

"What can I do for you?"

"I'm Detective Amilio Hernandez and this is Sammi Patterson from the Scranton Police Department. We'd like to talk to your sister, Patsy."

There was no doubt that his face showed shock and apprehension.

"What's this about?" he asked trying to get a feeling about this sudden and unexpected visit.

"We need to speak with her about some past issues. Is she home?"

He nodded, as he said, "I'm her brother, Ray. I'll go get her."

He paused another moment, then obviously decided to let them in. He was gracious as he showed them to the living room.

"Please wait here," he said as he turned rather methodically and left the room quickly.

It took quite a few minutes before he returned with a girl of about thirty plus who seemed rather confused, shy and definitely nervous. She was quite attractive with her brown hair equally matching her striking brown eyes that seemed to be moving rapidly from one intruder to the other. You could tell she expected the worst or at the very least some bad news as the seconds passed slowly. She was about to speak when a boy of about eight years old showed up investigating the new guests, but was told to go to his room and let the adults have privacy.

"I'm Patsy Elmore," she finally said as she ventured to get the business started. "I haven't done anything wrong. What do you want of me?"

Amilio immediately jumped on that opening statement. "We know you haven't done anything wrong and we're not here to accuse you of anything. We were hoping that you might be able to help us."

Patsy's face showed a look of cautious relief as she took a seat across from them. Her brother asked her if she wanted him to stay. She nodded.

"Okay," said Sammi. They had decided ahead of time that Sammi would get things started and possibly be able to begin a meaningful conversation that would relax her and edge her toward wanting to help them. But Sammi had other reasons, too. The first thoughts on Pasty's mind were of her attack and she hoped these police didn't know about that. So Sammi had to find a tactful way to nudge her into areas that Patsy's mind tried to hide and didn't want to discuss.

"We'd like to ask you about the time you worked at ASAC. I understand you worked there for over seven years."

Now her thoughts went to nervousness and agitation.

Why do they want to talk to me about ASAC for? I didn't report any of the problems I had. I just ran away. I wanted everything kept quiet. It was safer for me that way.

But she spoke with style and calmness. "Yes, I worked in the accounting department for a while."

"Did you enjoy your position there? Did you think it was a good company to work for?"

Even Amilio noticed the look on her face, but even more telling was the look on her brother's face. He was worried for his sister. It was as if he decided that the time had come and there was almost a relief in his shoulders and body language. His thoughts told Sammi that he hoped she wouldn't lose it again.

"I liked it while I was there ... the work was good and I did rather well. I got a couple of promotions."

Amilio asked the question that got everything moving in the right direction. He leaned forward, showed concern on his serious and thoughtful face as he asked, "And why did you leave?"

Patsy couldn't hide it. She made a valiant attempt, but her eyes clouded up despite her efforts to resist.

"Sorry, I'm a little emotional today," she said trying to hide her feelings.

Now Sammi took over and played her cards well. She decided honesty was the way to go and knew from her thoughts of desperation that she didn't want to lose any time bringing up the painful subject. "Look Patsy, although there was no report on file, we have heard that you were attacked by someone at that company and that's why you left in such a hurry and never even gave notice. We heard it was a vicious attack that would have frightened anyone. We have reason to believe that there are problems inside that corporation and we're trying to find out what's going on. Can you help us?"

Then Sammi sat back as did Amilio and waited. Her brother Ray was anxiously waiting to hear what his sister was going to say. *It's about time you tell them, Patsy,* he thought. *Come on, honey, find your nerve; tell them what happened to you.* He was waiting for a chance to be openly supportive of his sister.

Hearing Ray's thoughts allowed Sammi the ammunition she needed to continue. Patsy was still swerving back and forth, trying to decide what to say. Sammi wanted to make it a little easier for her.

"Look Patsy, we think something's going on inside that company that has been kept quiet for a long time. We need some information to help us out, that's all. We won't even tell anyone where the information came from if you don't want us to. But we know you must have found out a few things and that's why you were attacked. You could help us out a lot and some of the other women ..." Sammi knew that Patsy was not aware of any other women being hurt, which is why she used her trump card. Her thoughts said that she thought she was the only one, although she did have other suspicions of other girls at the company who were afraid.

"Other women?"

"Oh yes, there have been other women attacked and some haven't been as lucky as you were. Some were killed."

Patsy looked down for a few minutes as more tears began to fall. She said, "I did hear about Beth Baker being killed, but I thought I heard her husband did it."

Amilio piped in with, "There's no way her husband did it. He loved his wife and they had a ten-year old son. They were a happy family. He's being framed and that's another thing we're trying to prove."

Patsy was quiet and obviously thoughtful. Sammi heard some amazing thoughts crossing her mind. She looked over at her brother who had obvious sympathetic support for her. In fact it was his look of confirmation that helped Patsy make up her mind. But not before Sammi had heard, *God, it's been over three years and I'm just as petrified today as I was back then. I know they've found me and know where I'm at, but I've kept quiet and I thought I'd be safe. So far, they've left me alone. But there is no safe place for me. There's no peace for me, until I clear my conscience.*

Patsy put up her hand signifying that she needed a few minutes more. She was trying to make a decision. They waited and decided to take a break.

* * *

Sammi and Amilio got up for a few minutes and walked around the room. They needed to take a breather, too. This was quite emotional and they knew they were on the verge of a breakthrough. Would she have the courage? Would she finally be able to get it together and make that critical decision?

She seemed ready to talk. "I have to tell someone so I guess the time has come. But I want to see your badges first. I want to be sure who you are."

And with that Amilio showed his identification and Sammi's position was explained. She seemed to accept the evidence, but had her brother look at the proof as well.

"I don't know if I'll ever be safe anywhere, but I haven't felt safe for years. That company ruined my life in more ways than one. And I can't stand living with this anymore."

Ray said, "Patsy, you have to do it. You'll never get over this until you do. You've been walking on egg shells all of these years not really living anyway."

He looked over at Amilio and Sammi. "She's been petrified for years now and it never goes away. Some people over there are crazy and should be put away as far as I'm concerned. But it seems to me it's too late now, right? I mean it's been over three years since her attack."

"We believe everything ties in together. We need to know what happened to your sister and hopefully that will help us shut down whatever they're doing over there. Others are involved, too."

They all looked at Patsy and waited. She had tears coming down her face, but was trying to stay in control.

"Isn't this stupid?" she said. "After all these years

and I'm still so scared. I did get some help, but it never did any good. Give me a minute, okay?"

She looked over at her brother. "Raymond ..." She didn't finish. He knew.

He nodded, looked over at her as he puckered his lips. The atmosphere of the room was hushed with quiet expectancy. This was Patsy's moment, her time of cleansing and the body language, demeanor and the thoughts Sammi could hear told her she had indeed reached her moment of truth.

"Okay, well, you're right. There is something unbelievable going on over there. But I need to start at the beginning. I got a job in the accounting department right out of college. I was twenty-three years old and excited about working for this company. I thought getting this position was the luckiest thing that happened to me. I had areas to grow in and learn a lot and because I wanted a good career, I worked hard. After I'd been there about three years, I got promoted to a lead accountant position in the production department and that's where my problems started. They involved some of the upper echelon of the company. Jonathon Morley noticed me in a meeting one day and from then on wouldn't leave me alone. He was a married man and I told him, politely, that I wouldn't go out with him. But he pursued me and sometimes I'd find him at the same places when I'd go out at night with my friends. He'd ask me to dance and be angry if I refused."

She stopped for a few minutes and took a breather. Her brother went out, got coffee for everyone and gave Patsy time to relax and get herself settled down for the tougher part of her story that was to come. Sammi could hear some incredible thoughts flash through her mind swiftly, but waited patiently for her words to confirm the inferences.

"Well, this Jonathon kept reminding me that he could do me a lot of good in the company and also a lot of harm. At first I took it as someone who was a bad sport at being rejected and giving me a hard time, but then things started to go bad. I'd find notes on my car, nasty ones. Twice one of my tires was slashed in the parking lot and once my front windshield got cracked. And usually when I'd get near my car and notice the damage, he'd be close by smirking. Other times in meetings, he would be flirty with me again and he never left me alone. He told me that he was entitled ... that's the word he used. I was always a nervous wreck. And he also said, that he'd make sure I'd never forget him; he said that a couple of times. I didn't know at that time what that meant."

Patsy stopped for a few moments and drank some coffee. She needed to sit for a time and collect her thoughts. The difficult part was approaching.

Sammi and Amilio looked at each other trying to guess what was coming. Sammi knew. She'd heard her thoughts and it wasn't pretty. It sounded too incredible, too bizarre.

"Most of us girls had heard rumors about a group called the Gentlemen's Club."

Now this perked up Amilio's interest; he was interested in the Gentlemen's Club. "This had nothing to do with the work environment. It meant that there was a group of men, starting with the top men in the company and trickling down to other favored members who weren't that high up yet. They all seemed to believe that they were entitled to have any woman they wanted, no matter who or what circumstances. And if they were refused, there were consequences to pay."

She paused and stopped for a shaky moment. Ray took over as he had a few statements he wanted to say.

"This is all true. Patsy used to tell me about this stuff. It was unbelievable to me. These guys think they're privileged and have the right to anything they want and in this particular club, it's women."

Ray shook his head in disgust as Patsy signaled to continue.

"What he's saying is true. I couldn't believe it and asked Ray if he'd ever heard of such a thing. And, of course, he hadn't. Some rich people think they own you, if you work for them, but these men were way over the edge on it. I worked with one girl who told me that one of them had tried to rape her. And he told her never to tell anyone or she'd be wiped out. She kept quiet, but quit soon after."

"So you mean there's an actual club type group of guys who go out and use women and think this is their legal right?" asked Amilio.

"Yes, that's it exactly. It's hard to talk about because it seems like something from a Frankenstein movie. But it's true, all of it. I wanted Ray to stay in this discussion because I didn't think you'd believe me on my own."

Sammi jumped in on that one. "Actually, we do believe you. Other stories we've heard were pointing in that direction so we were trying to find out more."

"Would you excuse me for a few minutes?"

And she left the room immediately. She seemed in control of herself and rather peaceful as her story was finally being told. Her brother took this opportunity to add a few of his own comments.

* * *

He fidgeted himself trying to control his nervousness but it was obvious that he'd been concerned about his sister for a long time. And, of course, he knew that it might be dangerous for them to cross this group.

"My sister's been a basket case for three years now and she was a gutsy kid before then. She worked hard at college and spent long hours working overtime to make something of herself. But when this happened, she changed. She was petrified so I had her stay with us. Our parents died several years back, so I didn't want her to be alone. She's a changed gal."

"How much do you know about the attack?" asked Amilio.

"I'd rather her tell you about it. After that, I'll answer any questions you have."

Amilio nodded and agreed. Sammi had been in

deep thought and Amilio couldn't figure out what was happening with her. But he knew she was onto something.

Sammi waited with her thoughts racing around in her head. She'd never heard of anything this crazy before. She couldn't wait to discuss certain points with Dave. Amilio would have trouble realizing how she knew, but Dave would be home tonight and that would help. She hoped that Patsy would tell them the entire story, or at least most of it. This would open everything up.

Patsy returned with something in her hand. Sammi was thrilled. She knew that she was prepared to talk about the most important part.

"Okay, well, the last day I worked there I had left to meet a few friends for dinner. And Jonathon followed me as he'd been doing for a while. His ego couldn't take no for an answer. I knew for a fact, at least I'd heard, that the group always conferred with each other about girls who were 'difficult' as I was called. They had to deal with me because if they lost their grip on any of us, they were heading down, and not up. And that couldn't be allowed."

Patsy took a deep breath before she continued. "This particular night, two of my friends walked me to my car because I was scared. And I left the restaurant without seeing him, but he was tailing me. I had been his failure and that wasn't permitted. He forced me off the road on a quiet part of the highway. He didn't try to rape me, because he was too furious for that. He told me I was dead and I might as well know it. He started to attack me and punched me hard in the stomach and I went down. Then he kicked me in the head and beat my face. All during this time he was laughing and said, "You'll never forget me now." Then he took a rope and started to choke me. That's all I remember, but I think I saw car headlights in the distance and that must be what scared him off. I'm sure he thought I was dead. I must have lain there for hours, because when I started to come around it was getting light. As I moved slightly I realized how badly hurt I was. I barely made it back to the car by crawling at a snail's pace and I called my brother from my cell phone."

This was when Ray took over. "There wasn't one part of her body that wasn't bruised or bloody in one way or another. It was the most God-awful sight I've ever seen. I don't know how she lived through that. I wanted to take her to the hospital immediately, but she screamed for me to take her home and so I did. My wife was with me and she drove my car home."

"That was smart," said Amilio.

"Well I didn't want my Carole to be caught in her car, just in case ..." he never finished his sentence. All knew his primary fear.

"So I cleaned her up as best I could and gave her some pain pills and she slept for almost twenty-four hours. When she woke, she was hurting a lot, but it didn't seem that any bones were broken, although one tooth had been knocked out."

Sammi had tears listening to her story and Patsy saw them. Although most women would take an emotional side to this story, so did Amilio and her brother.

"I never went back. I never called or anything. I stayed away. I had others close my apartment and I moved back here with my brother. It took a while to heal physically, but I've never healed emotionally. I'm always scared."

She started to cry again. Sammi went over to put her arm around her. "You've been through hell and made it back. I'm proud of you."

"Thanks. But I'm not very brave these days. I go for a while and do quite well and then I'm down again. It never ends."

Now Amilio took the time to talk to them about Beth Baker's murder. He told them all he could and it was obvious their suspicions were on target. He was sure this ASAC group committed Beth's murder, but they were still lacking solid evidence.

"It's like they have this empire and they're the kings

and if a female subject doesn't act the way they want, she's eliminated," Patsy said. "I'm supposed to be dead. I'm sure they know I'm not, but since I ran away they feel I'll never surface again. At least, I hope that's what they believe. I haven't heard from them since I left."

Ray said, "This is the most bizarre thing I've ever heard of. I don't have a clue to the mentality of these guys, but obviously they're insane and must be stopped."

Patsy obviously had a tough question on her mind that she was trying to get out. Sammi helped her along.

"I know you want to ask something, go ahead."

All eyes turned to Sammi and she realized that she'd been too obvious. She simply kept an even expression on her face and didn't falter. God, she wished Dave was here. He made her part of the job so much easier.

"Yes, I do," she said and paused. "Will I have to testify or anything like that? I'd rather not, but if it comes to that, I'll see if I can mange it. I'd like to have some hand in getting them shut down. I'm one girl and I've already told you about one other female. But there were many others who worked scared all day long."

Amilio shook his head. "This is the strangest group I've ever heard of, the weirdest. Do you have any idea how many guys are in this group?"

"Everyone at the top, except maybe Smiley Sturges. He's pretty straight and probably has no idea what's going on. He was the gentlemen. I've always believed that Matthew Carnigan was the leader and it was his idea in the beginning. But there were a lot of others; I'm not sure how many. There were a lot of lowlifes working there and they all wanted to join that club, because then they would be protected if something didn't go down well. I heard others that didn't even work for the company were involved."

On a spur thought Sammi asked, "Have you ever heard of Bobbie Armore?"

She shook her head, "No, I don't think so."

"Okay, just a thought," said Sammi. "Well, I think

we have a lot of information here, Patsy. And some of this is what we were looking for. There are connections all over the place to other murders and attacks. We may want to talk to you again, but we'll be very discreet, okay?"

"Okay. I feel better now. I hope we can halt this craziness and stop these guys from doing anything more."

As they got up to leave, Patsy remembered something else. "Oh, this is what I left to go get. Ray said this was in my hand when he found me."

Sammi had chills up and down her body and Amilio reacted the same way. Patsy was showing them a forget-me-not flower, which was usually put on dead victims. They mentioned the other victims who had a flower. But she had one more piece of the puzzle for them.

"When they were tired of a girl, they would break it off and that girl would be left alone as long as she accepted the situation and kept quiet. Then they usually sent her a bouquet of these flowers as a condolence. Most girls who got these bouquets were thrilled, because it was over for them."

"Hold on to that flower, will you? We might need it in the future. Keep it in a safe place and in that plastic folder you have it in. It might be good evidence that we could use later on."

* * *

When they left Patsy's home, they both sat quietly in the car for a few minutes; Amilio didn't even turn on the engine. They were both exhausted and it was mostly from the information that was beginning to gel.

"What the hell are we dealing with here? We've got a bunch of neurotic people in this company who want to play by their own rules, which includes fraud, subversive activity, assaults on women, murder if they don't comply and the most bizarre activities I've ever heard of. Honestly, Sammi, I could never have imagined this, could you?"

"No, but Dave and I both felt it was all connected. Yet I never realized the games being played. This is almost like a sect with these guys and it seems to be against women. I think we're getting closer to finding the connection to Beth."

"You still think that it's connected? I guess I still thought that one was a separate case," said Amilio.

"Oh yes, it's connected, and now I believe more than ever that Bobby Armore killed his wife. He left a tell-tale sign that I'm sure in the future he's going to wish he hadn't."

"We've got a lot of stuff to process here and we need a meeting with the sarge, the three referees and you quickly."

"I think the sarge will want to clue Ron in on the latest, too. He's getting further into that case without much ammunition."

"Maybe he can use what we found. It might be tricky, but he has to get the activities of this ASAC group into these proceedings. The prosecution has already thrown in the stealing of documents at ASAC so he sort of opened the door, right?"

Sammi said, "That could be difficult, but I have to agree. This has to get into this trial. It would go a long way to prove Randy's innocence. But the ringer is that we have to connect Beth's murder with someone over there and that's not happening."

Sammi was quiet. She knew these guys were connected to all of these murders, but where was the proof? Patsy's thoughts confirmed her words totally.

"You know we're doing our jobs, Amilio. And Dave and the guys are doing their jobs. I think we have to get this newest stuff to Ron and he'll find a way to use it."

Amilio nodded as he started the engine. There was more than one murder to solve and more than one element to this case.

* * *

Dave was thrilled at the latest news. "This proves we're on the right road. It's that group at ASAC. What is with those guys? They act as if they run the world or they want to. What makes them feel so entitled anyway? I mean a lot of people have money, but don't act like this."

"That's true, but the leader seems to be that Matthew Carnigan. Did you hear about his background at all?"

"No, I don't think so. Why?"

"His father died when he was six years old, and of course, his mother inherited the money. Immediately afterward she started with a parade of other guys, I've heard. That little boy could have felt abandoned by his father and by his mother, even though she was still living with him. He probably felt that she had no time for him. And what does that remind you of?"

Dave slowly turned to look over at Sammi from his lounge chair. His mind showed recognition of a memory they had both shared. "Reminds me of that case we worked on in Philadelphia with those abandoned kids. The anger and hate they felt was unimaginable. I'll bet this Matthew has no conscience either. He doesn't think one thing about having these girls killed. If they pose a threat, they're gone. Gees, though, this is a grown man acting like a kid with a temper tantrum."

"But in the mind and feeling part of his being, time has not passed and he's angry with his mother just like when he was six years old. He's never grown past that time in his life. I'm not sure how this entire group works, but I know that Matthew is considered the leader, so to speak. But does everyone bow to him and is he the one that gives the okay to kill these girls that don't cooperate. They have rules in this club like any other. It might be real interesting to find out what they are."

"This is getting too bizarre."

Sammi said, "I feel like I've been watching a horror movie. This seems so unreal. What do we do next?"

"First thing tomorrow, we have to meet with the sarge. I'm sure that he'll call a meeting with everyone, including you and Ben Collier. We need to brainstorm this entire scene. I'm curious what Ron will want to do.

This is great stuff, but how much proof do we actually have? And even Patsy, who sounds like she'd be willing to testify, is one person whose testimony could be considered hearsay and sour grapes. We still need to find out who murdered Beth Baker. To me, that's the common denominator. If we could find that out, then all else would fall into place."

Sammi didn't answer for a bit, but she felt all along that was the road to follow. But the leads simply weren't there.

"Did anybody in the neighborhood see or hear anything significant. All I've heard is that a few of them heard loud voices after they saw three men walk up to the door."

"That seems to be about it. Damn, we're missing something. Something else has got to be there. No one commits a perfect murder."

"It's good that Randy made copies of some of that stuff, but I don't see where that helps a lot, do you?"

"No, but it could lead to get some subpoenas later on to get more documents. But it all has to be admitted first ..." Dave never finished; he was exhausted and couldn't think anymore.

Sammi said, "I'm finished for tonight. I simply can't think anymore. Let's wait to see what Sergeant Brady says tomorrow."

* * *

Sergeant Brady's office was one hot scene the next day. Everyone was there except of course, Sammi, Ron and Ben Collier; they'd have another meeting with them soon. The three referees and Amilio were trying to make sense out of everything, which was impossible, but they wanted at least to have a plan of action together before they met with the others.

"Is everyone as confused as I am?" asked the sarge.

"Hell, yes," said Jim. "But I think we should let Ben decide what he wants us to do next. After all, he deals with this stuff all the time."

"Getting a meeting with everyone might be too complicated and we don't want anyone getting suspicious. We're getting some important information here that we need to keep to ourselves. It's like we've got a serial ring to deal with. This is touchy stuff."

They sat there mostly shaking their heads in disbelief. None of these officers had ever seen anything like this in their entire careers. This was a game breaker.

"Let me call Ben Collier first. He'll deal with Ron and let's see what they think we should do. We'll meet again later."

* * *

Amilio was the only one that wasn't sitting around Dave's desk. He was too wired for that. He was almost doing a pacing or dancing step as he strolled around everyone.

"Well, I've got one thing I want to do," he said. "I want to find that Bobbie Armore. We have enough to bring him in on suspicion of something so we can interrogate him. He might have more information to give out than we figured. Sammi is convinced that he's the one who killed his ex-wife. And who knows what she'd find out in an interview."

"That's an idea," said Dave. "We've all been sitting back here and concentrating on this company's fraud and subversive activities, but now we need to find out about their more personal actions. We could find out a lot from that area of their lives."

Jim added. "What about that Danny boy that was hinted at in that other killing? God, I think it's time we followed up on those leads. I'm getting kind of antsy now because I've got a feeling we've been going down the wrong roads."

"Look guys," said Dave. "I agree with you. Damn, it looks now like we've been so focused on the hidden information that Randy had, we've ignored this other stuff. We all thought it was too bizarre to be true, but let's wait to see what the sarge finds out from Ben. We need to investigate what Ron wants us to do to help clear Randy, and then I think all hell will break loose anyway."

They all nodded. There were too many directions given out from this company. And the fact that they had two attorneys planted on either side of the aisle led one to believe that it was the company's welfare that they were trying to protect. They had purposely put out the wrong signal and led everyone down the wrong path. Until now everyone had bought their deceptive trick, but they felt things were turning around.

Tom said, "I think they've fooled everyone for a while. They wanted us to believe that they were doing something subversive or whatever, and maybe they are. Apparently those types of charges had been easy for them to overcome in the past and they felt that they could do the same in the future. And we fell for it."

"They fooled us all," said Amilio. "It did seem that was the area they were trying to hide. And seriously guys, who would have guessed they were trying to hide this Gentlemen's Club thing? Who would believe it? Hell, I'm still having trouble believing it right now. They're all crazy over there."

"We're dealing with people who have a dreadfully different grasp of reality. And for that reason alone, we can't let them know that we have even the slightest idea of what they do." Dave was adamant about this. "Now I'm not sure if we're dealing with totally insane people by the usual definition of the word, but if they're doing what we think they're doing, we can't take any chances. Patsy is still alive and they know it, and Sammi's involved a little, too. I'm worried that there might be others we haven't discovered yet. So let's take everything with more caution than we've done ever before. This is really scary business."

They all agreed. They were dealing with a different caliber of person here. No chances were to be taken and they had to await direction from their sarge. It was the waiting game again. But this time, when they moved for-

ward, it would be together with one solid goal in mind ---
Bring Them Down.

CHAPTER FIFTEEN

Matthew had called a meeting of his special group for many reasons and none of them were good. He'd gotten a call from Smiley Sturges who was upset at the news of the Beth Baker murder trial. For some reason, he'd been so involved in his work that he hadn't heard much about it. He didn't suspect any involvement from the company, so that was good, but he was asking curious questions, which unnerved Matthew. He wanted to find a reason to get him off to Russia within the next day or two. That was one hot item on his mind. Secondly, he was worried about the trial. Nothing was going the way he'd hoped and he was beginning to sweat. *No one could tie that murder back to the company,* he thought. *No, they always covered their tracks.* But they were blindsided in this trial as never before and he didn't like that. And he wasn't happy with Paul Ryan either, but they didn't have anyone else. What to do? What to do?

The phone rang. Matthew didn't answer it immediately. Sometimes he didn't like to let in the outside world – it confused him. He didn't like to get his thoughts mixed up. He liked to be inside himself where everything went his way and his goals were met every time.

There was a light tap on his door. It was Miriam, his secretary. He buzzed her into the room.

"That phone call was from Jonathon," she said timidly. "He's very anxious to talk with you."

"Wait a few minutes and then call him back for me," he said talking right past her. He never gave Miriam the courtesy of looking directly at her – that would make her feel like a real person, an equal. And he didn't feel that any woman was equal to him or any other man for that matter.

She half curtsied and left; that made him snicker. He loved irritating her and he got a chance to do it everyday.

Miriam walked back to her desk and decided to wait about five minutes before she placed the call. Her job was tiresome and quite nerve wracking, but she needed the money. It was quite difficult for her to act like a timid, shy and submissive female that he insisted upon having in his employ. She knew his priorities when she took the job, but felt she could handle the situation. But she thought her boss was pathetic. Him and his little group of retards who thought they were above everyone else. She almost pitied him in one way. She laughed about the buzzer system. He had installed a ridiculous buzzer that made him feel important. He had a glass window to his office anyway, and people could see that he was there, but he insisted on having to buzz them in which made him feel that they had his permission to be in his company.

Actually, Miriam felt that she had learned a lot working for this strange man, because now she could handle anyone. A lot of his business dealings were shaky at best but he had no idea how much she knew about ASAC. He thought she knew nothing – she was a female. She often wondered why he wanted a female secretary.

Suddenly, she saw him get up and walk toward the door. It was time for her to act submissive again.

"I think it's time for you to place that call," he said smirking.

"Yes, sir. Right away, Mr. Carnigan." And she immediately picked up the phone and dialed Jonathon's number.

He had walked back into his office, which gave her time to breathe again for the moment. He was one piece of work, she thought. If only he knew about her. She had flubbed up her application, because if he knew that she had graduated from college with a 3.5 GPA and then went on to get a PhD in Philosophy, it would shatter his image of her, and cost her this job. Yet she made more money here than she could from teaching at some college, and it was her aim at some future time in her life to fulfill her original dream. Someday when she was financially settled, she would do what her heart wanted.

Miriam knew that Matthew liked the women; in fact, his passion for them was quite strong. She had suspicions about that side of his life, but he had never approached her in that way and neither had any of the others in his group. She knew why. She dressed down as much as possible and looked like the most unappealing person around this planet. But she knew that was what he wanted and she had absolutely no problem with that. It kept her in a safe area in this company and she worried for some of the other girls. She'd heard rumors, and some she had found out weren't rumors at all. But there were a lot of innuendos that couldn't be denied, but she was okay as long as she watched her step.

A few minutes later, all of the men from Matthew's inner circle came for a special meeting. The one missing person was Smiley Sturges, but he was usually conveniently missing. She knew that he didn't think like the way others in this group thought about women and was concerned about certain underhanded dealings, which was why he wasn't invited. *What were they up to this time?* She wondered about that. They had barely edged their way out of the last chapter with the police and the courts, and it seemed like they were at it again. And she wondered about Randy Baker and his wife. That murder had her wondering more than usual. She felt some tiny sensations moving up and down her spine when she let her mind rest on that episode. She'd met Beth Baker a few times several years back. An incredibly bright woman and capable in her field, but she was a straight shooter, happily married and interested solely in the work at hand. And that had angered Matthew who was particularly fixated on her. She had seen her several times come out of his office in an obvious nervous condition. She had walked directly passed her desk and didn't offer any word of civility at all;

she was definitely frightened and wanted to get out of the area quickly. She wasn't sure what it was all about, but she had her suspicions.

"Miriam, I hope you're not daydreaming out there. I need the usual coffee set up, overheads and telephone lines. You haven't forgotten, have you?"

Mr. Carnigan yanked her out of her daydreams.

"Oh, no, Mr. Carnigan, I've ordered them and they'll be here within a few minutes."

"Well, they'd better. I don't pay you to daydream," he said and turned around abruptly and headed back into his little kingdom.

* * *

"I'd better hear some answers I like today," he said as he walked back into his office. "We need everything under our control and I mean now."

"Well," said Jonathon, "Smiley will be heading to Russia tomorrow night. We've pulled ahead some meetings we want him to attend. He'll be gone the better part of a month. So forget about him being a problem."

"I wish we could be rid of him forever. Someday he'll cause us problems, if not this month, then sometime in the future. He's always a worry."

Jonathon continued. "Well, at least for now, we're done with him."

"Okay, now what about this trial? We don't even know what's going on. Paul got kicked off the defense team and we're in real trouble now. We don't know what they're going to do."

"But Paul's in court everyday, picking up what he can," said Andrew Mincetti. He was always the one who had shrewd judgment in court cases. Everyone in this group listened to his opinions as far as legal stuff was concerned. "As the case moves forward, the theories on both sides will become evident. Sometimes you have to wait and see what happens. You never know how a judge is going to rule so you have to wait on certain issues. We'll handle things as they come up.

"What about Randy being out on bail?" he asked.

"What's the problem there?"

"I thought we'd be better off if he remained in jail."

"I'm not worried about him being out on bond. First of all he had trouble making bail and that doesn't look good for him. He's tethered so the court knows what he's doing and has to let both sides of the aisle in on it. I don't think that makes much difference to us."

"You're okay with it, then."

Andrew continued. "The part that bothers me is that I wish James McLean, the lead prosecuting attorney hadn't brought up stealing secrets yet. I think that was a bad move for us. That opened the door for them to look into our company's business."

"What? Why did he do that? I thought he was working for us?"

"No, No," said Andrew, "he works for the state. Wayne Berner is working for us and I hear he tried to get John to leave it out, but he wouldn't. So now that door's open."

"What the hell can we do? We don't want them going through all of our stuff – Holy shit. What can we do?"

"Don't get all upset right now," said George Addison, "there's a chance that it might not even come up again. I wouldn't think that the defense wants it brought up. That would be detrimental to their client."

"But what if they do?" asked Matthew.

"We'll handle it at that time. They'd have to fight to get subpoenas in order to look at any of our files and there's a good chance that they'd lose there. The courts don't give out subpoenas for anything on a whim. So relax for now. We'll handle it. Andrew and I are in touch with Wayne everyday, so we'll know what's going on."

"I liked it better when Paul Ryan was on the defense team."

"Yeah, that was better, but he does know how Ron Donovan thinks and if he's in court every day, he can still clue us in."

Matthew sat back in his chair. He puffed away on his Behike cigar and almost forgot who was in the room for a few minutes. They all waited for him to come back to earth. No one ever disturbed Matthew when he was contemplating on his cigar.

"Okay," he finally said. "And there's no evidence to tie us to Beth Baker's murder, right?"

"No evidence at all was found. We know that from before Paul Ryan left the team. They're all frustrated right now. And this past week, Paul said that Ron showed a lot of frustration. He hasn't even brought in another attorney, just a woman to use as a gofer for extra help. I think we're okay."

"A woman is being used for extra help?"

"That's right and she sits about two rows behind him and waits for him to ask her for something he needs and she goes and gets it and comes back and waits again for further orders."

Matthew laughed. "That's all women are good for anyway ... taking orders."

That got a laugh out of all of them. They knew that Matthew was now in a good mood. He felt comfortable and sat further back in his double sized chair. He took another puff on his Behike cigar and allowed a smug look to cross his face. He felt again that they were in the driver's seat. They had a woman helping on the defense side. That alone gave him especial satisfaction; a woman on the defense side of the aisle. He laughed inside, silently to himself. That seemed to be the mentality of Ron Donovan and he was glad. That was obviously a plus for their side.

* * *

When the word came down from Ben and Ron everyone was ready to move. They had decided that it was time to get this group once and for all. Their fraud and subversive activities would come to the front in time, but the murder of women was a top priority and when that was resolved, they felt all else would open up. Ron had a shaky case of reasonable doubt as it was. No hard evidence had been found one way or another. There were many innuendos, but nothing solid, and that's what he needed. If they could discover anything at all that would point to another person or persons, his case of reasonable doubt would be much stronger and more effective.

Amilio didn't waste any time in getting to work. He tracked down all of the men named Danny who worked at the MKG Financial brokerage firm and found five of them. Of these, it was a simple process of elimination to find the one who'd been hounding a few of the females; Danny Shelden. He was thirty-five years old and had been with the firm for about ten years. He was definitely a ladies' man and quite persistent when he found something he wanted. He was a hard worker, quite bright and considered an asset to the company. But Amilio was interested in his extra curricular activities that weren't listed on his accomplishment list. He decided to pull him in for questioning and wanted Dave and Sammi there with him. It was setup for Thursday at 10:00 AM.

Dave and Sammi were already in the room when Amilio arrived. Sammi always sat on Dave's left side utilizing a note pad. They only had a few minutes to go over their plan when in walked Danny with two attorneys. When the attorneys passed out their cards, Dave almost did a double take. He called a break immediately to confer with Amilio. He knew that Sammi picked up what was on his mind.

"Do you know who this attorney is?" he asked Amilio.

He shot him a blank look. "That's the same guy who wanted to be Randy's attorney at the jail and Randy refused; his name is Michael Bronton. This guy is an attorney for ASAC. So that means they'll know everything going on in here."

"Crap, what do we do now?"

Dave said, "We interview him, but we know he has

connections to ASAC. At least we know that they're still forcing the game for their side. Remember, the evidence is the evidence. But I needed you to know from the get go, and isn't it interesting that an attorney from ASAC is defending Danny Shelden? There's got to be a connection."

"Oh yeah, there's definitely a connection here."

Amilio paused so Dave said, "Just do what you would do anyway and so will I. But be aware; God, who could believe this?"

When they came back to the table, the attorneys seemed irritated to be kept waiting. Amilio and Dave carried on without any apologies. And of course, everyone thought Sammi was the note taker and nothing more.

"Okay, Danny," started Amilio. "We know that you were at the Hubner Café on the last night that Tammy Sinclair was seen alive."

"Tammy who?" he said. He wasn't going to admit to anything. Every detail would have to be pulled out of him.

Sammi clued Dave that he was extremely nervous about this interview. His mind was all over the place and given out clues that she couldn't relate to him right now. But she'd tell him the pertinent facts later. For now, he'd be difficult.

"Tammy Sinclair, remember?" said Amilio, "She's one of the many gals in this world that you had the hots for?"

"I'm not sure who she is," he said.

"Let's see if I can jog your memory. You hounded her at her desk at least three or four times a day the last few months before she died. Several witnesses at work will confirm that you were always flirting with her and she kept turning you down because she didn't want anything to do with you. Does that refresh your memory?"

He looked embarrassed, irritated and didn't say anything. His lawyers learned over and told him to answer truthfully.

"Oh yeah, I remember now, Tammy Sinclair. Yeah,

I knew her."

"Okay, well," said Amilio, "now we can get started."

"And you were at the Hubner Café the same night she died."

Danny began to answer, "I don't remember ..."

"We have witnesses to that as well."

"Okay, maybe I was, so what?"

Danny's lawyers again cautioned him to answer the questions and not adlib.

"The 'so what' is that we want to know what were you doing there ... following her?" asked Amilio.

"No, No," he said. "I go to eat there sometimes."

"Were you alone?"

"I think I was."

Dave took over. "Did you talk to Tammy that night?"

"No, I don't think I did."

"Why not?"

"I don't think I remember her being there."

"Danny," said Dave. "I think you should know that we have witnesses for all these questions we're asking. You've been lying to us from the beginning of this interview and I have to wonder why. Why are you lying?"

Danny began to sweat a little. He shifted in his chair a few times and eventually said, "Because you want to prove I killed her and I didn't."

Dave looked over at Sammi. He was lying. He was involved in her death.

"If you keep lying to us, that's exactly what we're going to believe. So let's try this again. Why did you go to Hubner's Café that night?"

"Okay, okay. I knew she was going and I was hoping that I'd have better luck with her that night. But she was with some other girls and that made it hard."

"What did you do?"

"I walked over to say hi before I left."

"And what happened?"

"Nothing, she wasn't very friendly – as usual and just

brushed me off."

"And that made you mad."

"I didn't like it, but I didn't kill her, either."

Dave looked over at Sammi again. He was lying. He had help from another guy, but he took part in her killing.

"Now one of our witnesses said that you yelled something over to her when you left. What was it?"

Danny looked extremely nervous now and sweat crossed his brow. He conferred with his attorney who told him again to tell the truth. That was his only defense right now.

"Okay, I said, "Don't forget. That's all."

"Don't forget what?"

"Nothing, it's just a saying."

"That seems like a strange saying."

"Well, a few of us use it sometimes."

"Who else uses it?"

Now that statement made Danny recoil and realize that he'd made a dire mistake. He couldn't take it back, but he wouldn't say anymore about it.

"I don't know really – I must have heard it around."

He tried to stay totally casual in his answers after that. But Dave looked over at Sammi and she seemed to be concentrating deeply and didn't even look over at him. He knew this was because she was shocked at some information she had received and was trying to keep herself in control. He didn't push anything more at the moment.

"And where did you go when you left?"

"Why don't you tell me; you've got witnesses for everything."

His lawyers cautioned him about getting smart with his remarks.

Dave said, "We want to hear it from you."

"I went home."

"Is there anyone who can verify that?"

"No, I was alone."

"Anything else?"

He shook his head.

It was obvious to everyone that Danny was having problems controlling himself. He wanted out of there and fast. Dave prolonged the last few questions on purpose.

"Did you ever see Tammy Sinclair alive again?"

"No, she got killed that night right? You're trying to trick me. If I saw her again, you'd say I killed her."

Dave looked at Sammi. She was satisfied. That usually meant that she had all she needed.

"So you never saw her alive again?"

"That's what I said." And Danny turned to his lawyers and said, "This is crap. The same questions over and over again."

This time Michael Bronton piped up and said, "If there isn't anything else, we're done here."

Dave agreed, but said that he'd let them know if they needed to question him further. His lawyers nodded.

* * *

Amilio plopped himself down in one of the chairs. He looked disappointed that they hadn't been able to shake his story more than they had. There was no proof.

"That didn't seem to give us as much as I'd hoped for. What do you think, Sammi?"

She knew she was on the spot a little. She couldn't just plop out the information she'd received and she looked to Dave for help. Too much right now and Amilio would know. She wasn't ready for that.

"Sometimes Sammi wants to type up her notes before she feels right about what she picked up. We'll do that tonight, right?" he said as he turned to her.

"Yes, give me a chance to do that and I'll make a copy for you, too."

"Okay," he said suspiciously. "But you picked up something?"

"A few things, but I think you did, too. Do you want to share now or wait?"

She threw his game right back at him. He laughed slightly. "Okay, okay, you win. I don't think he was at that café alone. His eyes shifted too much when he talked about that. That's almost a sure sign that someone's lying. Is that one thing you picked up?"

"Yes, I was pretty sure about that, too. Do you know who he had with him?"

Amilio looked at Sammi in surprise. "No, do you?"

"Well, I got some hints from other things he said. I'll put it in my report."

"That's right, that's right. You not only notice all of the little details in pictures, but in speech, too. So putting them together you think you might know who it is?"

"I'll let you know tomorrow after I've gone through my notes."

"Okay, good enough," said Amilio. "Some gal you've got there," he said to Dave.

"I have to agree with that," he answered as he looked at her with pride.

"Okay, you two. I thought you both handled the questioning well, so I could pick up what I did."

They both laughed and knew tomorrow would bring new revelations.

* * *

On the way home that afternoon, Sammi seemed quite edgy. She had a lot of information that could blow this case wide open, at least as far as the murders were concerned. She knew who'd killed Beth Baker and she knew who'd killed Tammy Sinclair. It was strange to her that when they got Danny nervous in the questioning that his mind was all over the place. But then that was true of everyone. We may speak but a few words, but our thoughts take in everything we know about a subject. And with his nervous attitude, Danny's thoughts had taken in a lot of territory. She knew Dave was anxious.

She turned to him and said, "I did pick up some amazing stuff, and it'll take a little while tonight to type it up because as usual, Danny's thoughts were all over the place, in the past, present and future, but not always in that order. I need to get my notes in order. The thing that bothers me is that now I ... we'll know a lot of things, but there's no tangible proof yet. And how do we get it?"

"When I hear what you've uncovered, we'll find a way. Now I want you to relax for a while. I know this type of concentrating is hard on you."

"Yes, I'm exhausted."

"I'll cook dinner and you're going to relax with a nice glass of wine. Later you can type up your notes and then we'll figure out what to do."

"I know this time that Amilio is going to wonder how I found out all this stuff."

Dave laughed. "Then we'll have to put him in the same category as all the rest of them, except that he thinks you pick up a lot from tiny little details and he may think that you just put them all together."

"Maybe, but oh well, that's the least of our problems now."

She was about to say more but changed her mind. She sat quietly, looked out the window and thought about the universe and all the people in it. It was at times like these that she truly missed her grandpa; he could hear thoughts, too. She would have loved to have someone else with whom to confer. *Did she pick up the thoughts correctly?* Yes, by now she didn't have to second guess herself. It was simply that the thoughts on Danny's mind were quite frightening, to say the least. She couldn't imagine how they would move forward on this one. This wasn't like anything else they'd ever worked on.

* * *

Amilio knew that Sammy had picked up a lot of information. He simply couldn't imagine how she did it. He was right there in the same room and he had actually done some of the interrogation, and yet, she was way ahead of him. *She must be psychic*, he thought. He knew she didn't like the word, but to him, there was no other explanation. It's true, that some psychics were crackpots and that's probably why she didn't want to be associated with them, but others were legit. The police department sometimes used a few of them and got decent results. But she noticed all of these tiny little details that he usually missed and he had to admit that Sammi fascinated him. And if she was noticing body language and expressions, too, then she could put it all together and come up with an impressive story. Proving it might be another thing, but they'd probably have another way to go.

Just then Jim came up to his desk and sat down waiting for some new information.

"I've been trying to track down that Bobbie Armore. He's supposed to work for this ASAC Company, but out in California somewhere, right?"

Amilio said, "We know he was in California a while back, but by now he might have been moved around. Doesn't that company have a total index of all of their employees no matter where they work?"

"Are we supposed to make waves right now? I thought this was still supposed to be covert," said Jim.

"Not anymore. I don't think so. The defense lawyers and the FBI both said, 'go for it.' I took that to mean to let out all of the stops. Don't you think? I mean that's why Dave and I interviewed that Danny Shelden earlier today."

"Okay, but he doesn't work with that ASAC Group."

"That's true, but he must be connected with them in some way. That's what I need to find out. But let's double check with the sarge. I want to get to that Bobbie Armore and find out what else we've got."

Jim nodded and they both walked into the sarge's office.

* * *

When Sammi finished typing up her notes, she let out a sigh of relief. Dave would be shocked at some of the information she'd picked up, but he was used to her by now. It was simply that this case was totally bizarre, and definitely more worrisome than any she'd ever worked on.

As she walked into the living room she could tell that Dave was anxious to hear anything at all. *Well,* she thought, *he's in for a shock.*

"Okay, this is unbelievable stuff I have here. Even Amilio will have more questions about me, but that can't be helped. Let me start telling you and then" ... she took one deep sigh, "someone will have to figure out what we can do with this."

"Come sit down and relax, and tell me what you've heard. Remember, you're the one that gets the information and passes it on. I'll present it to Ben first, and he can let Ron in on it. Then they can let us know how they want us to proceed. Let's not worry about that part."

"Okay," she said and simply stared at the white pages in front of her that held information that was probably the most unbelievable stuff she'd ever witnessed. "Danny Shelden and Bobbie Armore were two of the three men who killed Beth Baker."

Dave sat up straight in his chair. He knew she'd have information, but didn't know it would be this specific.

"There's a lot more, so you relax this time. I've had time to digest this stuff, you haven't." She decided to proceed at a slower pace, "Bobbie Armore was the one who actually pulled the trigger and it was planned. It wasn't a foiled attempt at a robbery or anything like that. They didn't know for sure if Beth would be there, but their orders were that if she was, kill her. And that order came from Matthew Carnigan. He'd wanted her dead for a while."

"Holy Shit! This group is what we were beginning to think it was – an executioner's group against women who won't cooperate with them."

"That's what it seems to be. And I did pick up a few more thoughts about that Matthew Carnigan. Most of the people who work with him think he's weird. His philosophy and attitude are way off the track. Most never want to get on the wrong side of him – I guess for obvious reasons."

Dave sneered. He couldn't help it. "What are we dealing with here?"

Sammi grimaced as she shook her head. "Now I'm pretty sure that Bobby Armore is the one who killed his ex-wife, Tina O'Leary, but if we can get some proof of either murder, that would help. Anyway, let me continue. Tammy Sinclair is the interesting one to me, right now. Danny Shelden killed her and he wasn't alone, but I'm not sure who was with him. He felt he had given Tammy all the chances she deserved and more, so it was time for her to go."

Dave puckered his eyebrows.

"You have to remember, all these guys feel privileged and entitled. That's part of this Gentlemen's Club creed. Now apparently no one feels as entitled as Matthew does, he's the master at that. But to get into this club, you have to have that frame of mind, and don't necessarily have to work for the company."

"I can't make sense of this."

"I don't think there's anything logical with these guys. To what I can figure out it started with Matthew Carnigan and I'll bet it stems from the treatment he got from his mother. Regardless, he feels privileged and entitled to anything he believes he should have in life and he hates women. We both know why. So he wants to use them as his fantasies, but when they won't cooperate, something inside of him can't take that kind of rejection. I believe he's had quite a few women killed over the years. Anyone who joins this group has to be willing to kill, if needed. They're promised protection by the company."

"My God, Sammi." He didn't say anymore and remained silent for a while.

Sammi finished with, "I have other minor details that might be helpful later on, but for now, this is it."

Dave took a deep breath. Finally, he said, "I've got to call Ben right away. We can't hesitate with this type of information. It might even be hard to convince him, but at least he knows you so that should help. Otherwise, who would believe this stuff?"

Sammi relaxed as Dave made the call. He was on

the phone with Ben for over a half hour and sometimes he listened for long periods of time. Sammi was sure that Ben was having as difficult a time with this craziness as they had. But they were all trying to muddle through.

Dave looked over and said, "Ben wants another meeting with us and Ron as soon as possible. He'll call back later and let us know when and where."

Dave poured them each a glass of wine as they waited. There was no more talk between them; it wasn't necessary. It was hard to delve into the minds of twisted people and it was incredibly unnerving.

It was more than fifteen minutes later when the phone rang. Tomorrow afternoon they would meet at 2:00 PM at the same restaurant as before. Ron would delay the trial; both he and Ben felt it was necessary. It would only be the four of them.

Sammi was happy with the outcome. Someone was taking her reports seriously. Oh, she always felt that Ben and Dave believed her discoveries, but this time it was a real test for them. Would she have trouble convincing them? Dave was convinced and Ben as well, she knew that, but would Ron begin to believe that she was off the wall? He was the one who could put all this together.

CHAPTER SIXTEEN

Walking back into the restaurant seemed to relax Sammi, who'd had enough problems lately staying on even keel. She remembered the last time she had fought hard to keep herself from being too uneasy, but left with a feeling of accomplishment at the end of a somewhat long discussion. She hoped today would be repeat performance.

They were able to get the same hidden away table in the back part of the oversized café. Ben didn't mince any words, but got down to business.

"I haven't told Ron anything yet. It'd be too much for him to digest on the phone. But I'll take a moment now and catch him up and then, hopefully, you'll have more to clear up with us."

And so Ben started slowly and flawlessly to relate to Ron the circumstances and happenings that had been going on in and around ASAC. Ron listened quietly, at first with no expression on his unreadable face, although occasionally he'd give out a hint of amazement at the story that was being told to him. When Ben finished they all sat back and waited. All wanted to hear Ron's assessment of these latest findings.

"Okay," he said finally, "I'm not questioning you on these latest details, Sammi. I know by now that you don't speak until you're sure of the facts. But I need to let you in on something I've been privy to for a while. I believe you're aware that we've had ASAC under surveillance for several years now. We almost got them on subversive activities a few times, but they always manage to weasel out of everything with their league of experienced lawyers. This was not the only side of the picture; more things began to surface about them. During some of these legal proceedings, other strange facts began to emerge. They weren't connected with any of the business that we were concerned about, but it would have been hard not to take notice. Matthew's name came up several times connected in the murder of a few women. Nothing was proven at the time and we were interested in the other side of the coin, but it wasn't forgotten."

Ben asked, "Was he suspected of doing the killing?"

"To what I remember he was connected in some way, but nothing much was ever discovered and I don't believe much of an investigation was conducted."

Ben nodded, "You were all concentrating on illegal business affairs."

"Pretty much the way it was in those days. We stayed on the topics we were given. The point is that this isn't the biggest shock to me. That guy is rather weird. I've met him a few times in the past and I remember thinking he was a different type of person. No one I know ever got close to him, although he always had his own group around him. The depth of things that has happened here is a surprise, but we need to find out what we can. I need more convincing reasonable doubt to get Randy off. I need to target someone else. And this all sounds good and more plausible to me, but I need proof and we don't have it. How can we get it? Any ideas?"

Sammi spoke up. "Amilio has been trying to find this Bobbie Armore. I'm not sure if we'll ever prove he killed his ex-wife, but he did kill Beth Baker and he, like Matthew, enjoys revenge on females. So I'd like him to be found as soon as possible and be in on his questioning. That may give us other clues."

"Okay, what's the problem?" asked Ron.

"He works for ASAC and I thought we had to be careful not to make waves with that company during the trial."

Ron Donovan nodded his head and puckered his lips. "That certainly was true at the beginning of this trial. And if we could have found out what we needed without tipping our hand, that would have been great. But, we don't have what we need and I don't want to say that I'm getting desperate, but as of right now, it'll be a close call if I can get him off on reasonable doubt with the little I've got. The prosecution has so much more. I'm ready to pull out all the stops. Let's get subpoenas if we have to. We've got a couple more weeks and then this trial will be winding down."

"Okay, then," said Ben, "I'll give Sergeant Brady the go ahead first thing in the morning. Anyone else you want to interview?"

Dave said, "If we could find out who that third guy was, I'd like to pull him in, too. But we don't know his identity."

Sammi added, "But interviewing Bobbie Armore might tell us that. And if their stories don't match up, we could learn something from the discrepancies."

"If I could only find one or two solid pieces that would work in favor of Randy, I'd feel a lot better. From the beginning, the evidence in this case has been hidden from us. We need some old-fashioned luck."

No one could disagree with that and they all left with more determination than ever.

* * *

The next morning Amilio and the referees were given the green light to finding Bobbie Armore, and with Amilio's connections he soon had a list of employees for the entire ASAC Company. Bobbie had moved around a lot. He did start out in California as Charmaine had suspected, but he had also spent time in New Jersey, Arkansas, Oklahoma and Maine. It seemed that he had requested some overseas assignments, but none had come through. Presently he was working in New Jersey for the second time in three years. He needed a lot of convincing to come back to Kingston for questioning, but a subpoena and some threats against his beloved ASAC group did the trick.

When Bobbie Armore walked into the Kingston station less than a week later, two lawyers from ASAC were with him, one being the very familiar Michael Bronton. And Sammi had found out by being in court that Matthew Carnigan was horrified and appalled that Bobbie was being brought in at all. He felt first Danny Shelden and then Bobbie Armore meant that this trial was going into an area that worried him enormously. He was thinking of leaving the country, but held his ground for a while longer.

Sammi again sat on the left side of Dave as a note taker, with Jim, Tom and Amilio all ready for their own line of questions.

Amilio began. "Mr. Armore, you presently work for a branch of ASAC Globe Ventures in New Jersey, is that correct?"

"Yes," he answered confidently. He was dressed stylishly, was quite snappy looking, about forty years old and exceedingly confident in his mannerism. He constantly eyed his lawyers as well as everyone else. It was hard to tell if that was a nervous habit or his usual routine to keep up to pace with the business of the room.

"And what is your position there?"

"Presently, I'm manager of the National Telecommunications department."

"How long have you been in this position?"

"About three years."

"And do you have occasion to visit the headquarters in Kingston?"

"Yes, I do." He always conferred with his lawyers before he spoke and never answered in more words than was necessary."

"Do you know Danny Shelden?"

"Yes."

"From where?" Amilio felt this interview was going to take a long time. He threw a knowing glance at Dave who responded acknowledging that Bobbie was playing this interview as safely as possible.

"He did consulting work for our company."

"What type of consulting work?"

"We worked together on a few projects a while back."

Amilio was getting exasperated so Dave took over. "What projects were these?"

"Oh, I don't remember anymore."

"You don't remember projects that you worked on for your company? Aren't you supposed to be known for your excellent memory? Aren't you acknowledged for always being the first one to remember things?"

Bobbie snarled his bottom lip a little. And his dark eyes seemed angry and pointed. "We worked together on some telecommunications projects."

"Good, now that wasn't so hard, was it?"

That comment irritated him and it showed. Sammi mentioned to Dave to ask him about his ex-wife.

Dave nodded. "Where were you working the night that Tina O'Leary was murdered?"

Bobbie almost fell off his chair. He wasn't ready for that line of questioning. His cover of coolness and impeccable behavior vanished in an instant.

"I wasn't in town at all. I was nowhere around here at that time."

"When was that?" asked Dave.

"I don't remember, but I wasn't here."

Dave couldn't help but stare at him for a moment. Bobbie realized quickly what a stupid remark he had made.

He added at once, "I remember hearing about it from a different town."

"Tina O'Leary was a prostitute and her murder wasn't even considered important at the time. There wasn't any publicity about her death, yet you heard about it from a different town?"

He was angry. His lawyers tried to calm him down, but got no success this time. "I heard about it from someone. I got a call from a friend."

"So you had someone watching your ex-wife and

they called you when she was murdered; is that what you're trying to tell me?"

"Yes ... NO. I didn't have anyone watching my ex-wife. I didn't even know where she was."

Sammi cautioned Dave that he was ready to blow. He had killed her and he was sweating it now.

"How did your friend know that she was your ex-wife? Why wouldn't he call you when he had first found her before she was killed?"

"I don't know," was all he offered.

"He waited until she was murdered before he called you. That seems strange to me."

"That's what happened." His lawyers were on his back to simply answer the questions in as few words as possible.

Tom took over now. "Where were you the day that Beth Baker was murdered?"

"Who?" he said. "I don't know her."

That commented irritated Tom. "I guess you want to play games for a while with me, too. Okay, we've got a lot of time and there are a lot of us here to take turns questioning you. So let me try again. Randy Baker works for your company. Are you telling me that you don't know him either?"

His lawyers cautioned him to answer truthfully.

"Yeah, I know him."

"Okay and he had a wife Beth Baker. She used to give lectures at your company. Are you saying that you weren't aware that she was murdered and her husband is being accused of the crime?"

"I'm aware of that."

"Good, then let's move on. Where were you the day Beth Baker was murdered?"

"I don't remember."

"Try again. She was murdered on December 10th and your records prove that you came to the Kingston office to work that entire week."

"I remember now that I did."

"So where were you at 3:00 PM on the day Beth Baker was murdered?"

"Probably at the office working; that's why I came here."

"Company records show that you left the building at 12:15 PM with Danny Shelden and someone else and didn't return at all that day. So again, where were the three of you?"

Sammi now had the name of the third accomplice. It was Rudy Cameron.

"I don't remember."

"Right," said Tom. "Are you sure you and your two buddies didn't go to Beth Baker's house and murder her? Then you ransacked the place trying to find secrets that you thought Randy Baker had stored away? Maybe that's how you spent your afternoon?"

Bobbie jumped all over those accusations. "You can't prove anything."

His lawyers were livid. They bounced up incredibly fast for a conference with their client, but not before Dave got in another question.

"So you're not saying you didn't kill Beth Baker, but just that we can't prove it. Is that it?"

"I have nothing more to say." Finally, his lawyers were pleased with him. They wanted him to cease answering any more questions.

Dave noticed that Sammi had been writing feverously on her note pad. Hopefully she was getting the rest of the information they needed.

"Are we about finished here?" asked Michael Bronton. "If you don't have any kind of proof then you can't detain my client, and I think we're done."

"For today," said Dave. "But we want him around for the rest of the trial."

That put obvious fear into Bobbie that he couldn't hide. And Dave had another subpoena that Ron had given him to make sure he wouldn't leave in case they needed him as a hostile witness. He had to stay around in case he was needed in the trial. The words he used to answer this latest surprise aren't printable.

* * *

Dave conferred with Sammi immediately. She surprised him by saying that most of his thoughts confirmed what Danny Shelden had to say. But she was able to confirm that he did kill his ex-wife and was the shooter of Beth Baker.

"Great," said Dave, "but we still have to prove it. And that hasn't happened yet. There's got to be something out there that we've missed."

"Yeah, I know," she said.

"I was hoping that we could find some probabilities that could point to him or his partners. Well, Ron is good at creating innuendos that get people thinking. Hopefully we've got thinking jurors."

The others who seemed seriously disappointed joined them.

Jim said, "That guy was pretty smug at the beginning, but we got him riled up. He's as guilty as hell, but we don't have the proof."

Tom said, "This is all fine and well, but it doesn't do a lot to help Randy. Ron needs more concrete proof -- I don't think the jury is going to buy this yet. What do we do now?"

Dave said, "We dig some more. We go back to the crime scene and we talk to more neighbors again. There's something out there and we've got to find it."

It was obvious that everyone was disappointed. They all thought that this interview would net more than it had and although Bobbie had slipped up slightly on a few comments, they didn't amount to much at all. He certainly had been coached, and very well.

Although Sammi had picked up his thoughts, they were related closely to those of Danny Shelden. These guys were in the thick of it, but had covered their tracks well.

Later at the Scranton office, Julie Mucci came over.

She was Jim's wife and hired as a computer expert for the last couple of years. Her present duty had been to monitor the executives at ASAC and report back on anything interesting.

"What's up?" asked Dave.

"I've run across something rather curious. I know you've talked to some of the executives and came up with suspicions and nothing else. But did you ever talk to Smiley Sturges?"

"No," answered Jim, "he never seems to be around."

"And he won't be for quite a while. He's being shipped off to work in Russia for the next couple of months. The reason I bring this up now is that he wasn't due to go until next month, but all of a sudden some meetings were pulled up rather shiftily and from my point of view, secretly and in a hurry. It seems to me that someone didn't want him around right now."

"What do we know about him?" asked Dave.

Julie continued. "He's one of the original partners – I think the only one still active, except for Matthew. He's middle to late sixties, widower, and considered quite adept in his area. He's been the liaison to Russia most of his career and his work ethics have never been questioned by anyone, not even the FBI. He's considered totally above board. The other interesting thing is that they usually keep him at arm's length. He's never told or invited to secret meetings and constantly sent to Russia for long assignments."

"Something's fishy here," said Jim. "Doesn't it sound that they want him out of the way? He might not even be aware of what they do in their subversive activities. And I'll bet he doesn't know anything about this Gentlemen's Group."

Dave said, "I think he's someone I'd like to talk to. He might not be as out of it as much as people think. Maybe he keeps a low profile by choice."

"Julie, any idea how Smiley related to the original partners?"

"I think much better. There were pictures of him at parties with the original John Ascott and his presence was expected at important meetings during the beginning years. It seems that his noticeable absence started about the time that Matthew Carnigan took over. The hints are that he didn't like the way Matthew ran the firm. He thought he took too many chances."

"So you say that he's not due to come back for a while, right?"

"Yeah, as far as I can tell he's not due back for a few months, or until this latest deal is totally confirmed."

"Is there any way we can get to him?" asked Jim.

Dave said, "That's a big risk. I doubt that he knows that much and then ASAC would be all over us and know what we're digging into."

"This has got to be up to Ben and Ron. I think he'd be an asset even with unproved suspicions. You can't tell me that he hasn't noticed something in all of these years." Tom was ready to go with it.

"Let's wait and talk to the sarge. He won't be back until tomorrow, but I think we should all think about this overnight. The FBI might call him back here or Ron might send one of his people over there. Either way, it's not our game. We find out stuff and let the FBI decide."

They all nodded and broke up for the rest of the day. There was a lot to think about tonight. It was time to search inside and decide what the best course of action was. But it wasn't their decision anyway and that was the most frustrating part of the entire scenario. Tom wanted to hop on a plane, go talk face to face with Smiley Sturges and see if he had anything to say that would help clear his friend. But he couldn't do it and he probably wouldn't be the one asked to go anyway. They knew who had committed the murders, but lacked the evidence. An innocent man was charged for the murder of his wife and there was a strong possibility that the real criminals would get off free. They personally knew of three murders and one attempted murder. Patsy was willing to come forward, if needed, but Ron thought her case should be tried separately. They could probably prove that Jonathon and someone else had tried to kill her, but that fact wouldn't do anything to free Randy Baker of the murder of his wife. Wherever they looked, they faced a concrete wall. But all walls had a weak spot and their job was to find it.

* * *

That night Sammi and Dave were in a quiet mood. Everything had pretty much been said and they were both exhausted. They needed one night without any nerve-wracking frustration to unwind and realize that there was another part to this life but these hideous crimes. And so they sat quietly and tried to relax.

"Let's see what's on TV; maybe there'll be a good movie."

"Okay," said Sammi, "and I'll make the popcorn."

She left the room and went into the kitchen just in time to answer the phone.

"Yes, Ben, we're both here ... just a minute." She yelled to Dave. "Get on the extension, it's Ben."

"Yeah, Ben, what's up?"

"Ron and I were both wondering if you'd had that meeting yet with Bobbie Armore."

"We did that today and planned to get with you tomorrow. But here it is. He had been well coached and that same lawyer, Michael Bronton from ASAC is representing him, too. We did get him riled up part way through, but his lawyers shut him up fast. Sammi picked up the same confirmations that we did with Danny Shelden. So now we know who the murderers are and we know that this ASAC Gentlemen's Group do murder for convenience, but there's little proof."

"We were hoping for more; I know Ron was."

"We were, too." Then he told Ben what Julie had noticed on the computers regarding Smiley Sturges.

"You're right. That's one guy that we haven't been able to get in touch with. He's always out of town. Now it seems that that was a matter of convenience. Where did you say he went?"

"Back to Russia, for a couple of months at least. I don't believe that he's all that naïve about what's going on in this company. He has to know something or at least have doubts about things. That could help us out. I wonder if you or Ron would consider sending someone out there to talk with him."

"That'll be Ron's call, but I think it's a good idea. Can't hurt and we still need that one tangible point that will incriminate someone else. It'll be interesting to know whether or not he knows what's been going on inside his own company."

"Okay, we're all planning on getting back to the murder scene tomorrow. I've got to tell you, Ben, there's something there and we haven't found it. But there's got to be something there."

"I hear you. They've kept this case closed up for so long. I know Ron is frustrated, but he has a lot of circumstantial evidence that he says he can use to confuse the jury. Yet, this case is still a guessing game and we need more than that."

* * *

"They sound as discouraged as we are," said Dave. "With all of us working so hard on this, well, we've got to find something." He ran his fingers through his hair, messed it up completely, and yet it fell back into place. Sammi always smiled when that happened.

"You know, Dave, I've been meaning to get back and talk to Denver. He still has something on his mind that he's not told anyone yet. Could be he'll be ready now. I mean, his father is back at home with him and he's feeling more confident and self-assured about his life. I've heard from Jill that his school work is progressing well so this might be a good time for me to have another talk with him."

"Do you have any idea what he has on his mind?"

Sammi looked down for a moment before she decided to answer that question. Then she used her words carefully. "He's kept a secret since that first day when his mom was murdered, so I'd have to believe that it has something to do with that. But whether it's only feelings or impressions, I'm not sure. I do know that it's something that still bothers him. I picked it up last time we were there. He won't let go of it, or at least he hasn't until now. I need to find out what it is."

"Do you think it's wise to push it with him?"

"If it's got to do with the memory of his mom or something like that, that's one thing, but if he realizes that his secret could help his dad be vindicated, I think he'd want to help. That's what I plan to explain to him when I find out what it is. I have to be careful with him, Dave. I can't upset him in any way, so I'll take my cue from him."

Dave nodded in agreement. He wondered if this little boy could hold the key to this murder. Wouldn't that be something? Everyone out here was working overtime and tackling anything that came their way in order to expose the murderer, and little Denver might hold the key.

"I think I'll stop over tomorrow. That's something that I should have pushed a little earlier, but I didn't think he was ready."

"His mental state is still quite delicate. It's good that he's doing well, but anything could upset the cart and we don't want to do that. So you be very careful ... I know you will, honey. I'm just worried."

"I know; I understand. I'm worried, too."

* * *

The next day Sammi went over to Jill's house. She was ready for her when she arrived. Denver's father was in court and hadn't returned yet. And Denver reported having a good day at school, so that helped.

"Hi, Ms. Sammi; it's good to see you again."

"It's always good to see you, Denver. How's school going these days?"

"I like it pretty well. They put me in Grade 7 and I think that's a better fit for me. Of course I still do 8th Grade math and science and those students are accepting me more nowadays. It took them a little time to get used to me."

Then Jill cleverly left to begin dinner and that gave them some time alone, but Denver wasn't fooled.

"I think Ms. Jill knew that I wanted to talk to you."

"You did, did you?" She smiled at him as she said, "you know that you can call me anytime and I'll come over to talk with you, if you want."

Denver smiled and said, "I know that, but I was just now getting the nerve up to talk about something private."

Sammi was astonished. It was the first time that she had heard what was on Denver's mind ... his thoughts had finally divulged his secret, but was he ready?

"How do you think my dad is doing in the trial?" he asked.

"Well, I know everyone is trying real hard to prove his innocence, because we all know that he didn't do it. He loved your mom, and she was only second in importance to you."

Denver half-smiled as he nodded. "I know that. My dad loved us both, and still does. We were so happy and someone had to come along and ruin everything. It still makes me mad."

"I know it does. It would make me mad, too."

"But I remember how happy my mom was and she wouldn't want us to be miserable now. That's just the way she was. I told you that she had a great philosophy and would be telling me her favorite right now: 'keep your thoughts strong." And I'm trying. It's a little easier right now than it was at the beginning, but it's still hard. I guess it'll always be hard, right?"

"I'm afraid so. When someone you love dies, especially in such a nasty way, it does make it harder."

"I know you understand things like my mom used to, and that's why I like to talk to you. Others try to protect me all the time, and that's nice, but I need to face things. I can, you know; I still have my dad. And Ms. Sammi, I've got you. And I like to talk to you, too."

"I'm glad to hear that," she said. Sammi knew that Denver had his secret on his mind and didn't know how to start talking about it. In fact, she was quite sure that he didn't know if he was ready, but he was moving in that direction.

She decided to take a chance. "What's on your mind, Denver? I think something is bothering you."

He looked over and smiled at her. "You always know, don't you? Mom was like that, too. She always knew when I had something on my mind."

She smiled. "From what you've told me, I'm sure I would have liked her. I'm sorry I didn't get a chance to meet her."

"Oh yeah," he said, smiling at the thought, "she would have liked you, too, and you would have had a lot in common with her."

Then he was quiet for a moment. He asked again. "But how do you think my dad is doing in his trial?"

This time he stared into her eyes and didn't even blink. He wanted to pick up everything he could from her. "Honestly, I don't know for sure. There's a lot of evidence against him, but his lawyer Ron Donovan is working hard. He's still hoping to find more proof. If he had something that would point the prosecutors in another direction away from your father, it would help a lot."

Denver held the stare for a moment longer after she had finished speaking. Then he simply said, "You know, don't you?"

Sammi nodded. "But it's your secret. I'd never tell."

"But I think what I did was wrong and my dad will be angry with me."

"No, he won't. I think your father will understand completely."

"Really?" he said and paused for a moment as he thought about that statement. "You're probably right. I'm not sure yet what I should do. I wanted to keep it a secret."

"But I think it could help your dad go free."

There Sammi had said it. She didn't want to put any burden of guilt or responsibility on Denver, but he was a bright child. He realized it already and that's why he was bringing up the subject now. She simply waited. He had to take the time and mull things over in his mind.

Denver was completely serious when he continued. "I'd like to think about this for another day or two. Then if I decide to tell my dad, I'd like you to be here with me. Would you?"

"Of course I would. Your father will respect you no matter what you say. But when he realizes your secret, I know he'll understand."

"I think you're right, but I'd still like to think about it for another day." Then he looked at her questioningly.

Sammi knew what was on his mind and answered his thoughts. "No, I won't tell, Denver. This is your secret."

He smiled, nodded and changed the subject completely.

* * *

On her drive home, Sammi felt pressured. She knew she had made a promise to Denver and it would be unthinkable for her to go back on her word. She hoped by tomorrow he'd want to talk to his dad and empty his heart and mind, which had both been burdened for some time. *Such a little guy,* she thought, *and such dire circumstances in his life.* It caused part of his mind to shut down for a while, but now it was inching along to its former position. Yet, this still could take a long time, and Randy had less than a few short weeks before his trial went to jury. She hoped Denver could make a decision soon.

Walking in the door, she put up her hand to Dave, "I can't say anything right now. You're aware that there are certain lines I can't cross, no matter what." And then she burst into tears.

Dave took her into his arms and caressed her. "This must be so hard for you. Take it easy. There's more than one way to solve this case and Ron might have enough proof for reasonable doubt anyway. I'm sorry, honey;

you're in such a tough spot."

"Well, it may be resolved in a day or two anyway. That's what I'm hoping for. Actually that's what I'm begging the universe for."

They sat relaxing in the living room with their glasses of wine. Sometimes that was all there was to take the edge off a totally disturbing day.

CHAPTER SEVENTEEN

Ben Collier put through a conference call to Smiley Sturges in Russia. It was decided that was the best way to get things started and see if he was aware of anything and if his attitude would be one of cooperation or if he'd try to hinder the investigation further. Ron was hoping that he'd be as straightforward as his file determined and that they'd finally get one person from the ASAC group on their side. To their surprise he was one astonished man who been kept out of the loop for quite a while. Still, he'd had his suspicions from several of the last court cases and would be willing to tell them what he could. He planned to take the next plane back to Kingston and wanted to be around for the proceedings. However, strange as it may seem, he had never heard of the Gentlemen's Group.

In the meantime, Amilio and Sammi went back to court to see if there was anything else they could do. Paul Ryan was there and seemed surprised to see them since they had been missing for a few days.

The first thing on Paul's mind was *I'll have to let Matthew know they're back.* He thought their part in the proceedings was over, but they'd showed up again. And this would make Matthew nervous again. Paul seemed to believe that the case was leaning in the direction of guilty and felt rather smug as he gave his daily report to his boss. Sammi didn't pick up anything unusual, except that Wayne Bermen was eyeing Paul a lot. He wanted him to watch her, but Wayne was really in left field. He didn't have anyone on the defense team to pass him information, so in a way, he was useless.

Some of the neighbors had been called to testify that they'd seen three men approach the Baker home after

3:00 PM in the afternoon on the day of the murder. After that there were loud noises heard as people argued and that type of information pointed to other people being at the home just before the crime. But was it enough? No one had yet proven that these men were from ASAC and part of that Gentlemen's Group that they were trying hard to demolish. Sammi worried if it would be enough. Denver's secret would go a long way to help his father. But she'd never yet crossed the line and told people's secret thoughts before they were ready. She hoped with all her heart that she wouldn't have to do it in this case.

* * *

That evening was particularly tense for Sammi. She kept waiting for a phone call. She would almost force herself to hear that telephone ring, but it didn't seem to help. It remained silent.

Dave noticed her agitation but decided not to intrude on her. He knew she was in a delicate situation and sooner or later the situation would resolve itself, hopefully in time to do Randy some good.

By the next morning, it was obvious that Sammi had passed a sleepless night. He half-remembered her tossing and turning a lot, but kept falling into a deeper sleep as exhaustion of the last few weeks caught up with him.

"You didn't sleep that well, did you?" he asked.

"No, too much on my mind. I hope it gets resolved today."

"You think it might?"

"Yeah, I do. I think today just might be the day."

Dave was happy to hear that. It sounded like Sammi was getting her positive thinking back on track. She didn't usually veer off for too long, but occasionally she broke her own rules.

"If not, I think we should go out to dinner tonight and take it easy. What do you say?"

"Sounds, good, but I think I'd rather wait a bit. When is this trial going to the jury, do you know?"

"By early next week, I hear. But they could take a

long time to deliberate with this type of evidence."

Sammi nodded. "Still, I think I'd like to wait and celebrate after that. At least it will be over, no matter which way it goes. And, of course, we all hope he gets acquitted. But what if he doesn't?"

"Then Ron will start with appeals. And they could go on for a long time, too."

"That's right, but Randy will be in jail in the meantime. I can't imagine what it would be like to go to prison for something you didn't do."

Dave shook his head, "but it does happen more often than we care to admit. Are you and Amilio going to court today?"

"We thought we would. I might pick up something and there's no other place I'm needed right now. What are you doing?" she asked.

"Believe it or not, Jim and Tom and I are once again going over all of the testimony and the clues we have to see if something doesn't pop up at us as strange and telling. I know it seems fruitless, but we don't have any other leads and you never know."

"That's true; you never know when life will throw something positive at you when you're still putting out the effort."

Dave smiled. He liked how she always put out some type of universal message among the daily efforts of life.

For both of them, this day seemed to be one to observe and record in your mind for future reference. Nothing new came up in court and nothing new came up with the sifting through the piles of evidence and court reports that were growing higher everyday.

But that night was when the phone call finally came. It was from Randy Baker.

"Sammi, Denver's on the extension and he wants me to listen in to your conversation, okay?"

"Absolutely. Hi, Denver, how's it going?"

"Good, thank you. I've made my decision. I need to tell my dad something, but I want you to be here when I do, just like we talked about."

"Sure, when do you want me there?"

Randy said, "Jill said she'd like you and Dave to come over for dinner tomorrow night and then maybe all of us could talk about a possible new lead."

"Sure Dave and I can make it."

But Denver was most definite about one thing. "But when I first tell, I want only you and my dad around. Later we can tell the others, okay?"

"Sure, Denver. As I told you, it's your secret to tell. You should be able to tell it any way that you want."

He laughed as his dad said, "Honestly, Sammi that sounds like something my Beth would have said."

Then Denver added, "I told you that she's so much like Mom. And she knows things, Dad. She does, just like Mom did."

"He's quite smitten with you," said Randy.

"And I feel the same way about him. You're a great person, Denver."

That made him laugh and they adjourned until the next evening.

* * *

Dave had heard the conversation and could see the relief on Sammi's face as she put the phone down. The time had finally come.

"This will make a big difference, Dave. I think it'll be enough to tip the scales in Randy's direction."

Dave whistled somewhat under his breath. "You think it's that important."

"Yeah, I think so."

"And how long have you known?"

"Not very long. Denver was so upset and fierce about this secret at the beginning that he kept it hidden way down in his subconscious and when that happens, I can't hear anything. Thoughts have to be near the surface for me to hear them. Also, this was something ... I better not say anymore. I might slip up and I don't want to do that. I'll discuss more after tomorrow night."

"I think it'll be a long night."

Sammi said, "So do I."

* * *

Shortly after lunch, Smiley Sturges walked into the Scranton Police Station. Sergeant Brady was shocked to see him there, but apparently, Ben Collier had decided that was where he should go and possibly be more unnoticed than if he walked into the Kingston Station, which was being watched closely by the ASAC group. The sarge immediately called his referees into a private conference room and asked Amilio to join them.

They filled him in on all that was happening and realized that here was a grown man in his sixties that was close to tears. He had never heard of anything like the Gentlemen's Group, but had heard innuendos several years back. Nothing ever came of it and so he dismissed it. But he stated it was shortly after that time they seemed to find ways to keep him out of town a lot. So Smiley started his story at the beginning, as he knew it, when ASAC was a good company, honest, law abiding and one to be proud of.

"A lot of things happened after John Ascott died. He was the strong force in this operation and he's truly the one who got this company going in the first place. He'd married Matthew's mother and did his best to help out her boy, but he was trouble and problems from the beginning. He thought differently than a lot of people. He felt he was entitled to the best job in the company from the beginning and didn't want to start toward the bottom to learn the business. And so, he never learned anything about the company, except how to flirt with the ladies. He felt entitled to anything he wanted, and it didn't matter if they belonged to someone else. Honestly, I could go on and on about him, but I think that's enough. You get the idea."

Amilio asked. "But did he ever get into trouble because of women?"

"Yes, he did, on several occasions. He could be nasty if they didn't comply with what he wanted. Most of his problems were settled out of court. I heard about a couple of them, but I know there were more. Anyway, for a while his behavior seemed to have improved, but then he was moved out to other areas of the country, so you never know. The company seemed to change when the other brother, Benjamin Ascott died. His son, who was also on the board had rough time with his father's death and took a long leave of absence. He could never get it together after that and never returned. We always kept his name in the title out of respect for both of them. I accepted a smaller capacity because I didn't like what Matthew was doing. He had no respect for his employees, and he was out for himself alone. He and I are the only two left from the original group. He was quite young when he first came aboard, but that was because of his stepfather. He wasn't ready then to lead a company and I don't think he is now."

Dave asked, "But what do you know about some of the dealings of this company? Why were they brought up on fraud and subversive charges?"

"Well, I was told that it was because a couple of employees were stealing information and they were fired immediately. Honestly, I had my doubts back then and I certainly do now. I must admit that I liked it when they wanted me to be out of the country a lot of the time. I didn't have to be in the fray of things. It was my escape, I'm ashamed to say. But all of my dealings were totally honest. Benjamin and I ran a good, honest company."

Smiley stumbled for a few moments. "I don't know how much help I can be. I do believe in the last two court cases that there was more to it than I knew. But I was happy to stay out of it. Kind of cowardly of me, but my background was inventing and I was good at going to Russia and other places to explain how things were made and why we were the best."

Jim asked, "What do you think of the group around Matthew now?"

Smiley looked disgusted as he began. "There's no one I really like. Jonathon Morley to me is a lowlife ladies' man and has no qualifications for being where he is. George Addison and Andrew Mincetti are the same type, but they actually have some brains for running a company. I don't associate with any of them even when I'm in town. I don't care for them and I don't trust them. Matthew would kick me out in second if he could, but my contract won't permit it. But I don't get invited to a lot of meetings so I never know for sure what's going on."

It was obvious that Smiley Sturges didn't know much that would help them. He did know about some troublesome events that had happened a while back, but that would be but a little blip on any radar screen. They mentioned the Gentlemen's Club again and gave him but a small hint of what they thought it was about.

"My God, they couldn't have gone that wrong, could they? I mean I know these guys think they're better than anyone else, but this is almost criminally insane. I hope it isn't true and if I had suspected anything like this, I'd have reported them, business partners or not."

The meeting ended with some satisfaction as to the fact that Smiley could get his hands on any documents they wanted and they wouldn't need a subpoena. That could be very helpful as they moved forward.

* * *

There was no doubt that Sammi was nervous about going over to Jill's house. Seeing Denver and having that important meeting would be a traumatizing event for him, no matter what the outcome. The good part was that he had said he was ready to tell his secret, but she knew there would be many surprised people in the future and some would be from ASAC.

Denver wanted to have the meeting in his bedroom; Sammi knew why and that put a positive tone on the event.

He took a deep breath and looked back and forth from his father to Sammi several times before he had the courage to begin.

"Okay, I've got to tell you something, Dad. I've kept something from you and from everyone else and I don't think that was a good thing to do. I think Ms. Sammi may have guessed what my secret is, but she kept her word and didn't say anything to anybody. You're the first person I wanted to tell, Dad, but I wanted Ms. Sammi here, too. I hope that's okay with you."

Randy was touched by the emotions that were coming out of his son. He presented so much maturity for such a little lad who'd been through a harrowing experience.

"You've been a brave boy throughout everything, Denver. I'm so proud of you."

"But I don't want you to be mad at me, Dad. I think I did a bad thing. I just wanted to have a special remembrance of mom, all to myself."

Randy nodded and then Denver knew that his father understood.

He started his story in earnest after that. "Okay, Mom had me hide in the closet and she put a blanket over me so they wouldn't find me. And they didn't. I heard her running toward the far end of the living room and then I heard the gun shot. I knew, dad. I knew they had shot her and she was dead. I never heard her voice again, so I knew. Then these guys spent a long time looking all over the house for something. They made a lot of noise opening drawers and dropping them on the floor. I know now what they were looking for, but I didn't know then. So I kept as still as I could. One of the guys even opened the closet door, but he shut it right away. I guess he thought nothing would be in there."

Denver stopped for a moment. He was getting to the hard part for him. He looked down and his emotions were pouring out of his little body. Then he continued and then he was finally able to say it. "After a long time, they left. I heard them go out the front door, but then one of them said, "God, I forgot something; Matthew would have a fit." Then he came back into the room and walked over around Mom, I think, and then he left for good."

Randy sat there waiting for the punch line. He had heard all of this before so he knew more was coming. What could it possibly be? He looked over at Sammi in time to see a half-smile. He had a feeling she already knew.

Denver had tears streaming down his face as he continued. "I peeked out of the slats from the closet and I couldn't see anyone. And I couldn't hear anything at all. So I knew they must be gone. I waited a few more minutes and then I opened the closet door slowly and looked around. No one was there. I looked over at mom." The tears were coming fast now. "I knew she was dead, but then I'd known that for a few minutes. I walked up beside her and she didn't look like herself anymore, but I noticed something in her hand. I know that guy must have put it there when he said, '*This is for Matthew*'. She had a flower stuck in her hand and I wanted it. So I took the flower and went to the kitchen and got a sandwich bag and put the flower in it. It was the last thing that my mom touched and I wanted to keep it forever."

Randy's eyes got very big. Denver began to cry hysterically. "You're mad at me, aren't you?"

Randy grabbed his son and told him he loved him and understood. It was okay that he did that. He understood why he wanted to keep this last token of his mother. Then he asked.

"Do you still have the flower?"

He said, "Yes and I kept it in the same sandwich bag so that it would stay nice. I think some of Mom's blood is on it."

Then he got up, went to his dresser drawer and pulled out this sandwich bag with the memento of his mother. Randy showed it to Sammi. She was not surprised that the flower was a 'forget-me-not.'

Randy said, "Can I have this for a little while? You may have really helped your father here; are you aware of that?"

Denver smiled in surprise as he said, "You can have it, Dad, but I hope you're not mad at me."

Randy picked Denver up in his arms and said, "I'm so happy with you right now. You're a great son, do you know that?"

It was a touching scene for Sammi to witness; one she would never forget.

"This is good evidence, Denver. It might help other people know that your dad didn't kill your mother. But we have to give it to the police so they can test it. Maybe you'll get it back in one piece, but I can't promise. What do you want to do?"

He thought for a moment then said, "Mom would want you to be acquitted and go free to come back and take care of me. It's okay; if I get it back, that's great. But if it helps to free you, I'd be glad."

Then they walked out of Denver's bedroom into the living room and told the story to Jill, Dave and Tom. There were two fully shocked police officers who'd spent months looking for some clue, some solid evidence that could help their friend Randy, and here it was, right in front of them, because of the love a little boy had for his mother. And it had been kept uncontaminated in this little sandwich bag, as perfect as the day he'd taken it out of his mother's hand. Dave was so excited he could hardly think. He looked over at Sammi and realized what she had told him earlier. This would break this case wide open, possibly in more ways than one.

Dave said, "I need to call Ben Collier right away. He'll be thrilled and then we'll get with Ron Donovan, your favorite lawyer and mine. But I know we've got to keep this quiet until they move with it. This will be added evidence and I don't know how they go about getting it admitted at this late date, but Ron will find a way."

Dave put in the call to Ben and talked for quite a while with him. Ben said he'd be calling back shortly, and he did. Ron would meet with them first thing in the morning. He'd have the trial postponed, if possible. And he said when the judge realized how and why this evidence had been kept quiet he didn't think he'd have any problem admitting it. The rest of the story would be told tomorrow when they all got together.

Randy sat in the corner crying for a few minutes. His effort in all these months of keeping his worry and frustration away from his son had to be cried out. And Denver went over and sat next to his dad with his arm on his back telling him, "Everything will be okay, Dad. I don't want you to worry." It was a scene no one would ever forget.

* * *

The next day Ron Donovan immediately got a postponement until the end of the week. The prosecution wasn't too happy, but he had asked for a private meeting in the judge's chambers and when he explained the circumstances, it was accepted. Even the prosecution found it hard to refuse. But they wanted to put Denver on the stand and that was still a possibility. That would be discussed later.

When Ron saw the evidence he was amazed. He agreed that it had to go out for testing immediately. He felt he had to notify the judge and ask for a postponement until the evidence came back. They were to test for DNA, blood samples and some sweat beads that were amazingly still in place on the stem of the flower. Apparently, whoever put it there was the same person who had a hole in the right index finger of his glove and had left partial fingerprints around the house. After all the physical activity that he had exerted, sweat had covered his hands. So when the flower was placed in Beth's hand as a sick omen, the sweat, possibly the murderer's blood and DNA were also present. If simply one of these three possibilities came through, Randy would be vindicated. The biggest rush available was put on these tests.

Now the waiting began. Ron was able to put a big rush on testing the evidence. The judge backed up this decision and wanted this trial to resume as quickly as possible. So they were hoping for the DNA tests to be back within twenty-four hours. With that in mind, the trial was tentatively set to resume on Friday morning at 10:00 AM. And, if by chance, the samples weren't finished yet, it would be postponed again. But everyone had to be ready on Friday. The prosecution again positioned itself strongly and insisted on a chance to question the ten-year-old son. This was a condition insisted upon to be fair and above-board. The defense team begrudgingly agreed. They had no choice.

* * *

The waiting was excruciating for all involved. Randy and his son and his entire team of lawyers and friends found it painful to say the least. The result of this DNA test was crucial and all parties involved exhibited many deep breaths and sighs throughout the following days. The prosecution was waiting to see if their case would fall apart or not.

Randy had talked to his son about the possibility that he'd have to testify. He wondered how he felt about it.

"Well, I do have some trepidation inside, but I think I'd like to visit the court room beforehand and that should help a lot. Then I'd be used to the surroundings. After all, you've had to be there almost every day for a while now. I'll be okay, Dad."

Randy had to smile to himself. *Where did this child get these words to speak and where did he get this mature outlook to pressing problems.* He knew, but it still amazed him.

Denver smiled when he saw the look on his father's face. "What, Dad? The way I speak? It drives some of my teachers crazy, too." And that seemed to break the ice and relieve the tension a little.

Denver had to ask, "That DNA should tell the judge a lot, right?"

"We're hoping it will prove that someone else put that flower in your mother's hand and then everyone will know that someone else killed her. But it sure is taking a long time."

Denver said, "But everyone knows that it takes a while to test DNA evidence and they have to be very careful and not ruin it."

"That's true, son," he said. "We want them to do the best job possible."

The phone rang. It was Sammi inquiring how everyone was holding out.

"We're doing okay," said Randy. "But this waiting can sure get to you, but it shouldn't be much longer."

Sammi said, "I was hoping we'd hear something tonight, but nothing so far."

"You mean they might call us at home?" asked Randy.

"They'll let Ron know the minute they get the results and I'm sure he'll call you right away."

"Of course, I should have guessed that."

"How's Denver?"

"Better than me, but then he usually is. He's got such a great attitude."

"It's you and your wife that did that."

"Thanks. I'm so proud of him."

"I am, too."

Later that evening Ron called with spectacular news. It was even more than they hoped for. The blood testing proved that both Beth Baker and Bobbie Armore's blood was on the stem of the flower. And the DNA from the sweat bands also pointed to Bobbie Armore. It seemed that the little hole in the right index finger of Bobbie's glove, the one he thought wouldn't make a difference, was his downfall.

Everyone was to be in court on Friday at 10:00 AM and the prosecution was screaming for Denver Baker to be there. They insisted on a chance to question him. Most of the adults seemed nervous, but Denver was okay. He said he would tell the truth and that should do it.

* * *

Dave and Sammi handled the news with celebration.

There was a good possibility that more than simply Randy's acquittal would come out of this, at least, that's what they hoped for.

"Since all this evidence is being admitted, especially the flower, it seems to me that all of this should lead back to ASAC, don't you think?" asked Dave.

"It does sound like a logical step. Even though Bobbie Armore is only linked to the murder of Beth Baker, this flower should link more stuff together."

"And remember that Patsy wasn't able to testify before because nothing was lined up together, but now, I think Ron will push for that so the judge will have some grounds to consider further charges. This came out better than we could have hoped for."

Sammi smiled. She had to agree with that.

"When did you know that Denver had this kind of dynamic evidence?"

"I've known for a while. At first I guessed that he had some kind of secret deeply buried and I couldn't tell what it was. But about last month it came to the surface a few times, briefly, but long enough for me to know the importance of his token secret. I doubt he ever realized how vital his souvenir was, but wasn't he excited when he knew that it could help his dad?"

"Yeah, he's a great little kid. Sometimes I'm amazed what comes out of his mouth and I have to adjust, but he's such a charmer."

"He is that."

"And you're a charmer, too, my dear. This was a hot piece of information that you had to keep to yourself. What would you have done if he hadn't come forward?"

"I'm not sure. I've never yet had to break my rule, but this time ..." She didn't finish.

"We couldn't let Randy go to jail," said Dave. "I'm not sure what I would have done either."

"I felt I might have to have another talk with Denver. He's so bright anyway that I thought I'd have to let him know the importance of what he had and that would probably have done it anyway. He wanted his dad out of jail and home with him."

"And Matthew Carnigan must be one nervous and unhappy man right now."

"Does he know about this evidence? I would think his people would have kept this from him for now."

Dave thought about that one. "You could be right, but sooner or later all hell will break loose on that guy and his company."

CHAPTER EIGHTEEN

Everyone was in the courtroom on Friday by the time the clock struck 10:00 o'clock. All of the newspaper reporters had gotten wind that something crucial was about to happen and they were poised in position. The lawyers had taken their seats and Bobbie Armore and Danny Shelden had received their subpoenas and were present. Of course, all of Randy's friends and supporters were there and Denver sat directly behind his father as he waited to testify. But back in one of the last seats in the court room in an inconspicuous area was Patsy Elmore and her brother Ray. She was ready and willing, if needed today and ready and willing if needed later on.

When the judge called order in his courtroom, a hush fell on the capacity crowd that wasn't there a moment before. No one wanted to take the chance of offending His Honor and being forced to leave, so all followed the rules exactly. The judge gave the floor to Ron first, who repeated his evidence that had been found and asked that it be admitted. The results of the DNA tests were entered into evidence.

An ashen-looking Bobbie Armore was the first on the stand who refuted everything that Ron intimated with him and gave an alibi that was iron clad. He would admit to nothing and stuck to his story, but his voice was increasingly weak and shaky. The evidence spoke for itself and he was remanded into custody, held without bond at present. The same fate awaited Danny Shelden as well as their third accomplice. The District Attorney could do nothing to soften the blow and his expressions showed he wasn't too disappointed. After all, he wanted justice and while at first he believed Randy Baker was definitely guilty, his mind had softened in that regard. But he needed to question Denver Baker. And today was mostly about his testimony. Was it reliable? Was everything as it seemed? Today would be the day everyone would find out.

Ron Donovan questioned him first, carefully, and tactfully as was fit for a child of his age, including all of the details that he knew the prosecutor would try to tear apart. He held his ground and told his story without much tension. Then it was the prosecution's turn.

"Okay, Denver Baker, I hope you're relaxed and comfortable because I need to ask you a few questions."

Denver nodded.

"I know that you realize that there are two sides to every story and I have to get my turn to ask you questions, too. Do you understand?"

"Yes, I do understand, Mr. McLean."

"I want to ask you if you know the difference be- tween the truth and a lie."

Denver didn't make any kind of grimace but simply answered the question. "Yes, I do, sir."

"And you are planning to answer truthfully to the questions I ask. Is that correct?"

"Yes, sir, I will."

"Okay, then. First, I'd like to know if you got any special instructions from your father or Mr. Donovan re- garding what you would say."

"Yes, I did," was all he said.

"Oh," he said with some lilt in his voice. "And what were these special instructions?"

"They both told me to tell the truth," he answered.

"Oh, okay. That's good. You should tell the truth. But you do realize that your father is on trial for murder, right? And that's a serious crime."

"Yes, I know that, sir."

"He is accused of killing your mother; you know that, right?"

At this point, the courtroom mumbled a little, but

enough to cause Judge Grogen to call order in his court-room.

"Your Honor," said Mr. McLean "I've got to be able to know where this child's mind is at. He's professed to be a bright young boy. I must be given some leeway for my questions."

"I agree and as long as you stay within the limits we talked about, you'll be fine. But I urge you to be careful, this is a delicate situation."

Mr. McLean nodded and walked around a little. "Okay then," he said turning back to Denver. "Do you want me to repeat the question?"

"No," Denver said, "I remember it. I know my dad's in a lot of trouble here, but he didn't kill my mother."

"I'm sure any good son would say that."

Denver smiled.

"But you do realize that your answers are very important?"

Denver nodded.

"Now, did your mom and dad argue a lot? Most parents do, so that would be normal, but I need to know if your mom and dad yelled at each other or argued a lot."

"Occasionally my mom and dad sort of argued, I guess. My mom used to tell me that they were having a hot intellectual discussion."

There were snickers throughout the courtroom but they settled down fast as Judge Grogen eyed his entire courtroom.

"Did they have these hot intellectual discussions often?"

"No, not very often."

"Did they have any arguments shortly before your mother was killed?"

Denver thought for a moment and then answered. "No, we were all excited about Christmas and talking about presents and parties. No one argued during that time."

The lawyer decided to cross over to another topic.

"Now you hid in the closet when the killer was there, is that right?"

"My mom put me in the closet and covered me up with a blanket so no one would find me. She did that when she saw them walking up the sidewalk to our house. And there were three men that came into our house and hurt my mom."

"But if you were in the closet, how did you know there were three men?"

"I heard three different voices and they scared me; I remember them."

"Could you identify these voices if you heard them again?"

"I'm not sure; I don't think so.

"Okay so tell me what you did after these men left."

"Well, they all left, but then one of them came back again. His footsteps sounded like he walked to where my mom was on the floor. Then he said, "This is for Matthew" and left. After that I didn't hear anyone for a few minutes so I slowly got out of the closet and walked over to my mom. She didn't look the same to me anymore. Then I saw a flower in her hand and I wanted it as the last thing from her. I took it and then went into the kitchen and got a sandwich bag and put it in so I'd have something of my mom to keep."

"Did you ever open that bag again?"

"No, I never did. I was going to keep it like that forever."

"So what did you do with the bag?"

"I kept it in my dresser drawer until I told my dad and Ms. Sammi about it and then my dad gave it to the police."

"But you didn't see your dad give it to the police, did you?"

"Yes, I did. They were in the living room of Mr. Tom's house ... that's where we're staying right now. My dad gave it directly to Detective Dave Patterson."

And on and on the questioning went until finally the prosecution realized that nothing was scoring points for his side. He realized this was a dead issue. When the prosecution ended, Ron immediately asked for a dismissal of all charges against Randy Baker and the prosecution concurred.

* * *

Ben Collier had walked into the courtroom unnoticed. When all was over, he approached the referees and said he wanted an immediate meeting with them and Sergeant Brady. Ron was invited as well to get the legal aspects pinned down.

"We've got to get to Matthew Carnigan immediately or he'll skip town and we'll never find him. All evidence is pointing to him to be the head of this Gentlemen's Group and honestly, the evidence seems to be piling up," said Ben. "We've got them all wanting to run and we can't let that happen."

Ron said, "We've got enough to grab them and hold them for some time as we gather all the proof. We should get warrants right now."

"That's what I want," said Ben. "Everything is being tied together. We've got Patsy Elmore waiting to testify and she had that flower, too. Besides, she can identify Jonathon Morley as her main attacker. And all of those other murdered women had that same 'forget-me-not' flower. Hell, I've heard that Matthew Carnigan always has a bouquet of them in his office. I guess he needed to be prepared. This is a nasty murderous group and I want to get as many of them as we can."

"Understood," said Ron. "Looks like we'll have a lot more work in the near future. Who'll you be going after?"

"Every one of those guys that are in his group at the top. I don't think we'll have a problem. I heard on the way over here that Bobbie Armore and Danny Shelden are already starting to try and plea deal and they're spilling their guts about everything they know. I think they'll give us a lot of ammunition," said Ben.

Other than the three referees, Amilio and Sammi were also in this meeting and sat there amazed at how quickly everything was occurring. At the beginning of this case it was hurry up and wait, hurry up and wait. But now the waiting was over and the real killers were being brought in. The time had come to end a nasty murdering group.

"We'll meet back here in about two hours and then I want to get that Matthew Carnigan arrested immediately. Anyone know where he's at?"

"Julie keeps track of these guys," said Jim. "She'll know."

"Okay, that's all for now," said the sarge.

Dave turned to Sammi. "You want to come when we pick him up?"

"I think I'd rather miss this one. You can tell me about it, okay?"

"Fine by me," said Dave. "You go home and I'll see ya later."

* * *

Sammi was happy to be on her way home and have this messy case behind her. She loved seeing Randy and Denver walk out of the courtroom together to start a new promising beginning to their recently traumatized lives. And she had enjoyed talking to Smiley Sturges who had come to court. He had heard rumors for years about his company, but was still shocked at the involvement that his colleagues had gotten themselves into. He actually apologized for happenings that were not his fault, vowed from now on that he would be running a moral and honest company and be aware of what was going on around him. He'd be holding the reins with a steady hand, but then everyone else would probably be in prison.

Her cell phone rang. It was Dave. "We're on our way to ASAC in Kingston. It appears that Matthew is giving a presentation for his employees on how to retain the trust of their clients."

"That's too funny," she snickered. "But you be careful and stay safe."

"I will. I love you, Sammi," he said.

"And I love you, Dave Patterson."

* * *

Upon entering the auditorium, they found Matthew at the podium giving a strong pep talk to some of his salesmen. When he saw them enter, he faltered somewhat, but it was obvious that he had no knowledge what had happened today in court.

"What do you want? I'm in the middle of giving a speech here."

"I think you're speech is over," said Ben Collier. He had his associate Jeffrey Slade with him and together, along with several other FBI agents, approached the podium. This caused Matthew to falter back in his steps.

He didn't even try to run but asked again what this was all about.

Ben Collier was happy to oblige. "You're under arrest for ordering the murder of Beth Baker, Tina O'Leary, Tammy Sinclair and the attempted murder of Patsy Elmore."

His face took on a totally different appearance as fear, disbelief and anger clouded in on him all at once. When he spoke his voice took on an odd tonality and his shakiness merged into other realms.

"You're all wrong," he said. "You're making a terrible mistake." Then he turned to another colleague on stage and said, "Tell them, will you? They don't know I'm entitled and I've earned my right to do as I wish. When I get this all straightened out you guys will be in a lot of trouble. I'm Matthew Carnigan and I can do what I wish. I'm entitled, don't you know that?"

Dave was at the back of the auditorium and listening to the ravings of a crazy person. *Did he really believe what he was saying? He sounded like a lunatic.* He looked over toward Jim and Tom and they, too, were surprised at the speech that didn't have any semblance to reality at all. Sadly they all realized he was living in another world.

Why hadn't anyone noticed?

"You're all gonna be sorry about this. I'm entitled, don't you know that? I can tell you what to do, but you can't tell me. I've known that since I was a little child. How come you don't know it?"

Dave thought it was a sad scene. And as Matthew passed by close to him with his hands in cuffs followed by three FBI agents, he looked over at him and said, "You there, you'd better help me. These people are crazy. Don't you know I'm entitled, either? What's wrong with all of you? Ask my mother. She'll tell all of you about me. There are only a few special ones left in the world. You can't do this to me. I tell you that you can't do this to me. I'm a special one."

"Quiet down, Mr. Carnigan, quiet down," said one of the agents.

"But you don't understand. You're ruining my dreams. I have a right to my dreams and my life. You're not following my agenda at all."

And Dave had to listen to the ramblings of a dangerous yet miserable fool whose mind had obviously left the sane level a long time ago. He was almost happy when Matthew was out of his hearing area and he didn't have to listen to his voice anymore. It had an unusual pitch and eerie scratchiness to it. He shook his head as he turned to leave. None of the referees even talked to each other. They wanted to get home and away from this situation. No one got any pleasure over what they'd seen. The only words Dave had on his mind were pathetic and pitiable.

* * *

At home, Sammi was ready with a hug, dinner and a celebratory glass of wine. She'd seen the look on his face and the drooping of his shoulders as he walked in the door. They sat together on the couch not saying a word.

Finally Sammi said, "at long last this case is over."

"That's true," said Dave as he put his hand on her knee. "We've finally got this one behind us."

"He's a good example of the power of your own

thoughts. It seems to me that he could have used some professional help when he was little because all those separations in his early life caused some warping in his thought world. I'm sure he's been unhappy most of his life."

"Did he ever marry?" asked Dave. "I don't remember hearing anything about that. I mean he's single now, but was he ever married?"

"I don't know, but it might be interesting to find out."

"The lawyers have a lot of work ahead of them, but luckily the evidence is pretty much present and accounted for. And then ...

The telephone rang; Sammi answered. It was Charmaine Bolder.

"I just heard that they arrested Bobbie Armore for the murder of Beth Baker. I'm thrilled."

"It's too bad that we couldn't get him on Tina's murder, too, but we haven't found a good enough link. Maybe we'll get him for that one in the future. "

"Honestly, Sammi, I don't think Tina would mind all that much. At least we've got him on one murder and he'll be off the streets."

"That's true. I'm glad about that. What are you doing these days?"

"I'd been made guardian by Tina for her little boy before she died; his name is Jogan. He's about six years old now. But I was afraid to do anything in case Bobbie would find me. She had placed him in an orphanage run by nuns in New Jersey, but he was never to be adopted. The nuns agreed with her after she told them her story. So I'm planning on finding myself a good job, saving some money and by next year, I'll bring him to live with me. Who knows? I may even meet someone nice and make us all a good family. Wouldn't that be something?"

"It would and I know you can do it. You've got your college degree and could probably find several decent jobs."

"Yeah, that's what I want to do. I've already left the profession. I'll always carry the memory of Tina with me anyway and I have her cat, Maybe, so now maybe" ... she laughed, "I can create a life for me and her son. I hope so."

"Look, Charmaine, if you ever need any help to get started or later on, let me know. I'll always be there for you."

"Thanks, Sammi."

"Please keep in touch."

"I will. I'll always want to keep in touch with you. Bye."

Dave had heard most of the conversation and Sammi told him the rest.

Dave said, "I think she's got a good chance to make it."

"I liked her from the beginning. I'm so excited for her."

Dave smiled and relaxed his head back on the couch. He put his arm around Sammi and enjoyed the first moments of total relaxation he'd had in quite a while.

"This is nice and relaxing," he said. "I'm glad we've got time for us now."

"Well, don't get too relaxed," she said.

He turned to her and said, "Why not? What's on our agenda now?"

"Our honeymoon. We've got to get ourselves to Aruba."

He laughed and nodded. "Now that I can agree with. And this time we're going to make it for at least a week."

And so it was finally over; the murder case of Beth Baker. It had gone in many strange directions, but no one could have guessed at the beginning of this mess, where it would lead. People's thoughts create the experiences in their lives, good thoughts create good endings, and sinister thoughts latch on to any negative activity around. Matthew Carnigan had never gotten the help he needed to get his twisted thoughts straightened out. If he had, at least three women would still be alive, possibly more. If only people realized that thoughts are the creators of their destiny. Everyone should guard their thoughts very carefully since they do create your future.

Made in the USA
Lexington, KY
27 January 2011